CLAIMED
BY THE
HORDE KING

ALSO BY ZOEY DRAVEN

Warriors of Luxiria

The Alien's Prize

The Alien's Mate

The Alien's Lover

The Alien's Touch

The Alien's Dream

The Alien's Obsession

The Alien's Seduction

The Alien's Claim

Horde Kings of Dakkar

Captive of the Horde King

Claimed by the Horde King

Warrior of Rozun

Wicked Captor

Wicked Mate

The Krave of Everton

Kraving Khiva

Prince of Firestones

CLAIMED BY THE HORDE KING

HORDE KINGS OF DAKKAR - BOOK TWO

ZOEY DRAVEN

PROLOGUE

I watched her in the darkness. She was small, sad, focused, and completely unaware of the danger she was in.

Foolish.

A foolish human. Not the first I'd encountered. Not the last either.

A sense of dread pooled in my belly as I watched her load her bow with a worn arrow. The frayed feathers at the end of the shaft were *thissie* feathers, plucked directly from the wings. In the moonlight, I recognized the bright blue shimmer as she leveled her bow, the cord pressing into her cheek, keeping her weapon steady. *Thissie* were rare, delicate, beautiful things.

When I sensed movement to my left, I held my hand out, stilling my *pujerak* from approaching. As of yet, the *vekkiri* female had not committed a crime. We were to wait and watch.

I heard her exhale a small puff of air. I could not peel my gaze away from her as she released her arrow. I heard the whistle of it. Then I heard it squelch into the *rikcrun*, emerging from its burrow for a night of gathering.

Still, I watched her. I thought her dark eyes looked sad and I studied the way her shoulders sagged. That dread returned, tenfold.

To my left, my *pujerak* said quietly, "*Vorakkar*, we must take her now."

Mercy.

The word—the human word, which made me uncomfortable and doubtful—rang through my mind, but as *Vorakkar,* my mind was already steeled. It had to be. *Vekkiri* knew the laws of our world. As of late, they had pressed and challenged those laws. The evidence of it was right in front of me.

Still, I hesitated.

"*Vorakkar*," my *pujerak* urged. "We must—"

I cut him a dark look, tearing my gaze from the *vekkiri* female for the first time since I spied her through the dark trees. My *pujerak*, my second-in-command, immediately locked his tongue behind his teeth. I understood his impatience. He wished to return to the horde encampment, for, in his eyes, small matters like punishing *vekkiri* were beneath him.

"We wait," I said.

My eyes returned to her. As a horde king of Dakkar, I knew what I had to do, what was required of me.

I had to make an example of her, of the small thing that reminded me more of a *thissie* than a law breaker.

Mercy.

It was something I could not grant her.

1

My lantern was dying. The flame flickered and my stomach rumbled.

Eyes returning to the dark burrow in the earth, I pleaded for the thousandth time with the thick, hesitant, smart grounder within.

Please come out, so I can kill you, I begged silently. *Please come out.*

My lantern died with a whisper and for a moment, depleted of the small golden light that had illuminated the space I'd occupied for the last hour, I was plunged into darkness. My eyes adjusted slowly, aided by the crescent moon's light filtering in through the branches overhead. The forest outside our village was called the Dark Forest for a reason. It was a tangle of trees and rapid growth and decay. But the grounders liked to feed on the decay and since the herd of *kinnu* had moved on last week, grounders would be the village's only source of meat for the rapidly approaching cold season.

I didn't like being this deep in the Dark Forest, but I was small and I was good with my bow. I could navigate the forest easily, which couldn't be said for the other hunters in our village.

Shivering, I hunched my neck deeper into the tattered scarf I'd brought with me. Blowing out a short, quick breath, I went through my routine to help pass the time, to help calm my nerves.

One, I started, glancing up overhead, spotting an object shooting across the sky, far beyond Dakkar, probably on its way to a neighboring planet for deliveries. *A merchant vessel.*

Two, I glanced at a tree to my right, *a deep scar in the trunk that looks like a teardrop.*

Three, my eyes dropped to my feet, *a finger-sized hole in my boots.*

Sliding my fingers over my weapon, I started over, but this time I closed my eyes.

One, the raspy cord of my bowstring.

I moved my hand to the earth. *Two, wet, mushy ground.*

Three, I touched a crawling vine to my left, *slick but fuzzy leaves.*

Next, I did sounds.

One, the thumping of my heart. Two, the rhythmic, deep croaks of the chitter bugs. Three, a branch snapping—

Breath hitching, my eyes flew open and I froze, my fingertips coming to my arrow. I stayed perfectly still as I scanned the dark forest in front of me without moving my neck.

I waited for long moments, listening for anything big enough that could snap a branch, but heard nothing. Still, I was uneasy. Glancing back to the quiet burrow, I contemplated leaving for the night, but I knew that if I didn't make my quota, I wouldn't eat. My last meal had been yesterday morning and it had only been a shriveled root my neighbor, Bard, had given me out of pity.

If I snagged one grounder, I could get a bowl of thin soup from the kitchens. Two would get me herb bread, a small chunk of boiled *kinnu* meat, *and* a bowl of broth soup.

Mouth watering, I stayed and waited.

My patience paid off. Even I was surprised when I finally heard the telltale signs of a grounder shuffling its way to the surface with its claws.

Heart pounding, I lifted my bow, effortlessly and silently sliding my arrow into place. The raspy cord of my bowstring pressed into my cheek as I leveled it and steadied it against me.

The grounder appeared, its black head poking through the burrow. The sliver of moonlight gleamed off its three beady, black eyes and I used that reflection to guide my shot. I waited only a moment more, a moment for the grounder to heave its small body out, before I released my arrow.

The shot was clean. It hit. My lips pressed together as I lowered my arm, a dull sense of relief flowing through me.

Unfurling my body to stand, I realized my legs were numb and I winced, aching from the position I'd maintained for the majority of the night. I approached the grounder slowly, snagged my arrow from its head, and hefted it up.

I looked into the burrow and started, my fingers gripping my arrow tighter, my breath quickening.

Three eyes were looking back at me from the darkness. Another grounder. It stared, unmoving from its home, frozen.

I can have meat and bread tonight, I thought, my arrow twitching in my hand.

But I hesitated. I looked at this creature, staring up at me from the ground, and I suddenly wanted to cry. I'd thought that grounders were solitary creatures, creatures like me.

My stomach growled but the noise didn't scare the grounder away. Instead, it was me that looked away. I had one dead grounder. It would get me soup and, knowing from experience, I could survive on that.

I turned away, my footsteps squelching into the wet earth.

Returning to my spot, I picked up my bow, looping it through my arm and around my shoulder, and my dark lantern.

I looked back at the darkened burrow just once. Then I left the forest.

When I returned to my village, I waited for the guard to open the gates and then I veered left, towards Grigg's home. It wasn't far from the entrance of the village, but it was guarded, considering Grigg had the vast majority of the village's supply of credits. I ignored the way the guards looked at the dead grounder hanging from my grip and knocked once on Grigg's door.

When I heard him call out inside, I entered. The older man was seated behind a table, looking over curls of parchment, scribbling notes. I'd often wondered if Grigg had become the village's leader just because he was one of the only villagers that knew how to write our language and read it.

"Nelle," he greeted when I walked inside. It was warm in the house, no cracks in the walls. Grigg's attention returned to his parchment. "You brought me a grounder, I see."

"Yes."

"Only one?" he asked, his lips tight when his gaze returned to me.

"There were no others," I lied. "It took me all night to get this one."

"Kier brought me three," Grigg returned, leaning back in his padded chair. "And Tyon brought four."

My fingers grasped my arrow tighter. The weight of the dead grounder suddenly felt very heavy. I merely hefted it onto the table and said, "My credit."

Grigg glanced down at the grounder disapprovingly and nudged his parchments out of the way so its black, sticky blood wouldn't get on them.

"Very well," Grigg said, reaching into a locked box on his

table. I heard the rustle of credits inside and I felt greed and *want* growing in my chest, though I tried to keep my breathing steady. His hand paused. His eyes ran down my covered body, lingering on my small breasts, and my arrow trembled in my palm. "You want two credits tonight?"

I couldn't judge what other hungry women might do in my village, but I knew one thing for certain: I would never be desperate enough to fuck Grigg for an extra credit.

"One," I said, hating the way my voice shook, hating how my throat closed.

The older man's eyes narrowed and he tossed the credit onto the table, though it skidded and rolled onto the floor. I crouched, my fingers scrambling for it, the metal scraping into my palm.

Then I turned, eager to leave. At the door, he said behind me, "Remember how powerless you really are, girl. I'm being nice, you know."

His unspoken words chilled me. What he meant was that I was a young woman—one of the few in our village—living alone, with no protection but my bow. I had no one. No family, no husband. If he wanted something from me, he could take it.

"Kier tried to take from me once," I said. I remembered that night, remembered the panic, remembered his rough hands. I turned to look at Grigg. Though I was frightened, I couldn't show it. I'd learned that a long time ago. Meeting the older man's eyes, I said, "And he ended up with my arrow in his shoulder. *I* was being nice by not shoving the arrow into another place."

Grigg's mouth thinned.

I held his eyes, then I turned my back and left.

Once I was out of sight from the guards, I brought a shaking hand up and readjusted my bow, tucking the arrow into the band around my waist. I made my way to the kitchens, though nausea now churned in my belly. Because I knew the truth. I really was powerless. I was small and weak and hungry and alone. My only saving grace was that I was good with my bow and Grigg knew that. It was my only leverage.

My gaze tracked up to the sky, remembering the merchant vessel from earlier. I tried to imagine what my life would be like on another planet, but couldn't. Dakkar was all I knew. But sometimes, I just wanted to float away, float into the stars, and *leave*.

I passed Kier on the way to the kitchens. He glared, that simmering rage boiling just beneath his exterior. When I'd first seen him, I'd thought him handsome with his dark hair and his light blue eyes. We'd been children then. Now, he just felt cruel. I could still feel his cruelness, like creeping shadow hands, even from a distance.

That night, only a few moon cycles ago, when he'd tried to take from me, he'd said in my ear, *"You're lucky, Nelle. Be glad I would fuck such an ugly, strange girl."*

I averted my gaze and ignored him, cutting a wide berth around his intended path. When I reached the kitchens, I slipped quickly inside, giving Berta my credit when she saw me hovering by the door. She harrumphed, always put out when she needed to serve food, but nevertheless, she slipped me a little square of bread when she passed me the bowl of soup.

She didn't want a thank you, so I didn't give her one, but I nodded in acknowledgement of her unexpected kindness, knowing she could get in trouble if Grigg found out.

Turning into the corner of the kitchen like a greedy, starved animal, I stuffed the small square into my mouth and chewed the dense, flavorless, powdery thing until it dissolved on my tongue. Then I chugged down the soup, knowing better than to take the food back to my home, unless I wanted to risk having it stolen. I ate fast because I always feared that it would be taken away.

When I was done, I gave the bowl back to Berta, said good-night, and left. The streets were quiet in our village—not the smallest village on Dakkar by far, but certainly not the largest either, or so I'd heard—and I quickened my pace. When I reached home, I bolted the door and pushed the table in front of it.

My feet felt like boulders as I dropped my bow and lantern onto the table. But I kept my arrow close, the only one I had left, tucking it next to me when I dropped down onto the blankets on the floor, stroking the feathers at the end of the shaft. Once, they'd been beautiful. Now, they were dirty with use, sullied. Still, they were precious to me.

As I sunk into sleep that night, for the hundredth time I mused that humans on Dakkar feared the Dakkari the most, feared their massive, battle-bred hordes and the powerful horde kings that led them.

But me?

I feared humans more.

VIOLENT POUNDING on my door woke me the next morning. In an instant, I was pulled from sleep, my hand fumbling for my arrow, which had rolled a short distance away during my thrashing through the night.

I calmed when I realized no one was attempting to break down the door. Groggy but wary, I called out, "Who is it?"

"Edmund," a voice came.

My brow furrowed, but I rose from my bed of blankets and pushed the table that blocked the door away. When I unbolted it and pulled it open, I found Edmund there, one of the gate guards.

"What is it?" I asked, frowning, noticing that it was barely dawn and the chill made me shiver.

"A horde came during the night," he said slowly, watching me closely. "They told Grigg they saw a female hunting last night in the Dark Forest."

My stomach dropped.

I was the only female hunter in the village and hunting was forbidden by the Dakkari. For humans, at least. It was a law agreed upon when humans first began settling on Dakkar as refugees, long ago. To break it was punishable by death. I'd heard the Dakkari had killed humans for much less.

Edmund studied me. I saw pity on his face, the same pity Bard had worn when he'd given me the old root to eat.

"Grigg told them it was me," I guessed, my voice soft.

Edmund inclined his head.

"I'm sorry, Nelle," he said. "They are waiting for you."

2

Jana had told me once that the best thing I could do for myself was to rely on no one. Not even her. That way, I would never be disappointed and if something went wrong, I would only have myself to blame.

She hadn't been my mother, but she'd been the only person like a mother I'd ever known and in my own way, I'd loved her. And I thought of her and her old words as I walked to the crowd of gathering villagers near the entrance, Edmund's heavy footsteps behind me.

Numb.

There I was, very likely walking to my own execution and all I felt was numb. In the back of my mind, I wondered if that was normal...if people often felt numb right before they died.

Then again, was I truly normal? I'd always been called strange. Not only by Kier. By many.

Despite the early hour, word must've already traveled about the Dakkari's arrival. Villagers had gathered, though they were a healthy distance away from the horde that spilled into our walls.

As if I could make them disappear if I didn't acknowledge their presence, I didn't look at the Dakkari, though I sensed them. Their silent, but heavy presence that seemed to suck all the sound from the village, except for Edmund's footsteps behind me and the crunch of his boots over the village roads I'd walked countless times before.

And this is to be my last time, I thought.

Grigg approached, but I didn't look at him either. Instead, I shifted my gaze to the crowd of villagers, searching for familiar faces. Berta was there, but Bard was not. Kier leaned back against a pillar near the kitchens, arms crossed over his wide chest, watching me, one of his friends, Sam, at his side. Marie, an old friend of Jana's, pressed her lips into a grim line when I met her gaze. She'd always been tolerant of me but I didn't like the fact that she was there.

"Nelle," Grigg said quietly. "You know I had no choice."

I looked at Grigg then, meeting his brown eyes that looked *almost* apologetic. Jana had been right. I couldn't even be disappointed that he'd sold me out because *I* had broken the laws of the Dakkari.

"I know."

He looked surprised that was all I said. There was a lot more I *could* say, but I simply didn't want to waste the breath. I didn't want to spend my final moments talking to Grigg of all people.

Then again, there was no one at all I would talk to. Except Jana, if she was still alive. If her hair hadn't turned grey and if she hadn't died in her bed of fever as I'd desperately tried to press cold cloths to her pale skin.

Maybe this is better, I thought quietly. *Maybe this is a blessing. No more hunger, no more fear, no more worry, no more loneliness.*

I stepped away, approaching the presence of the Dakkari horde, Edmund's footsteps no longer behind me.

Clutching that numbness tight around me like a blanket, I finally looked up, giving into my morbid curiosity. My footsteps didn't falter as I took in the scene before me, though a sliver of fear finally pierced my heart.

Over fifty Dakkari horde warriors lined the entrance to our village. Beyond the gate, I spied the creatures they rode across the plains of Dakkar, with their black scales and large talons, gold swirls painted over their wide flanks. The warriors looked like primitive beings from old legends, scarred and strong and unyielding.

Then I saw *him*. The one who I knew I would answer to. The one who I knew would order my execution.

A horde king of Dakkar.

He sat on the back of his black beast, the only one not outside the walls of the village. It stamped its clawed talons into the earth, restless in the silence, billowing up dust, though its master remained as still as the mountains in the distance.

Towering over his horde warriors, towering over *me*, there was no denying the unbridled power that rolled off his body in waves.

His chest was bare, his skin golden from the sun. Lines, swirls, and words in a language I could not understand decorated his flesh in deep golden ink, shimmering in the early light. I traced the line of one, which started at his shoulder blade, ran down the length of his sculpted chest, and disappeared into the loose tanned hide he wore, which covered his genitals.

A long, dark tail jutted behind him. When the black-scaled creature turned slightly, I saw the base of it was decorated in three gold clasps, similar to the cuffs he wore around his wide wrists.

Then, I finally met the horde king's eyes.

They were grey. Unlike human eyes, Dakkari eyes were pitch black with only a ring of color for their irises. Most were gold or red. But his were grey.

That wasn't all that was unusual about him. Dark blond hair

spilled just past his shoulders. blond hair was rare, even among humans, at least in our village. On Dakkari...well, I'd never seen a Dakkari with hair that color.

He was handsome, I noted. It was a fact, like his blond hair or grey eyes. His jaw was sharply sculpted, the bridge of his nose flat, his proud cheekbones high. His eyes were unreadable as I looked into them, though he studied me as I studied him.

His beauty meant nothing. Kier was handsome as well, but he was cruel. This horde king was beautiful, yet he would kill me. I was strange and ugly and I was about to die. It didn't matter. Nothing did.

For the first time, I thought that perhaps I *should* fear the Dakkari more than I feared humans.

A Dakkari male stepped between us, breaking my gaze from the horde king, though he hovered just on the edge of my periphery.

"Drop your weapon, *vekkiri*," the male said, his voice raspy and cold. His eyes were ringed in red, not grey. "Unless you intend to use it."

I blinked, not sure if I was more surprised that he spoke the universal tongue or that I was clutching my last arrow in my palm, unable to remember when I'd grabbed it.

Staring down at it, I looked at the pitiful thing. Grounder blood still decorated the tip and I remembered the second grounder that had looked up at me last night from its burrow. Those three eyes...dark and silent and frozen.

As for the shimmering feathers at the end of the shaft...I ran my fingers over them, feeling their tickling softness, remembering the creature they'd come from. I'd called her Blue. I'd found her with a broken wing in the Dark Forest one summer, long ago. I'd brought her home, fed her pieces of my meals, and she lived with me for many years until I found her dead one morning without warning.

I'd cried for hours. It had been after Jana had died and Blue had made me feel a little less alone. I hadn't cried since.

Before I dropped the arrow at his feet, I plucked Blue's feathers from the end of the shaft and kept them tightly squeezed in my palm.

Then I looked up, tilting my head back to the sky. It would be a beautiful day, just on the cusp of the cold season before everything would turn grey and white and blue. Any day now the winds would come and they would change everything.

"We saw you hunting last night, *vekkiri*. Do you deny this?" the Dakkari male said.

"No," I said, still looking up at the sky. I saw the faded outline of the crescent moon and I traced it with my eyes. "I killed a grounder last night."

The Dakkari male paused, his lips downturned into a scowl when I looked back to him. Perhaps he hadn't expected me to admit it, but it was the truth, wasn't it?

"Do you know why we have come, *vekkiri*?"

I didn't say anything.

"There have been reports that *kinnu* herds have grown low," he continued. "We suspect that your village has been hunting them, though you know our laws."

My brow furrowed. The *kinnu* had moved on.

"You hunt them too," I said to him, which was probably not the wisest thing to say before his horde king ordered my execution. But that was the beauty of it. I had nothing to lose.

But he could make your death slow and painful, I realized belatedly.

"There is a balance to giving and taking," he growled, "but your village has only taken. Now, once the cold season ends, the horde that relied on those *kinnu* will go hungry due to your over-hunting."

Lips parting, my breath whistled from my lungs. "Go hungry?" I whispered, a flicker of disbelief and rage igniting in my chest. "What do you know of hunger?" My gaze locked on the horde king, sitting atop his black beast. "What do *you* know of it?"

Those grey eyes narrowed on me and warning bells went off in my head, but I didn't care. Maybe I was mad, as mad as the villagers whispered.

I froze when the horde king swung his leg off his creature, dismounting with a surprising grace, though the impact of his weight seemed to shake the ground.

Sucking in a breath, I held it as he approached.

Show no fear, or he will know how weak you really are, my mind whispered.

Does it even matter? I wondered next. I was about to die. I could piss my pants in fear and I would be dead before it cooled. It didn't matter.

The horde king came to a halt next to his messenger and my hands shook with that fear.

He was a *wall*, I realized. A wall of muscle and strength and power. I couldn't see anything beyond his broad shoulders and the ridged lines of his chest and abdomen. He was a block in my vision. He was all I saw.

"I know hunger well, *vekkiri*," the horde king said, his voice dark and rich and cold.

Purposefully, I avoided his eyes, keeping my gaze on the ground. Jana had told me a story once, of demons that could take your soul if you looked too closely and for too long.

And this horde king...he was a demon made flesh.

"Identify the other hunters," he rasped, "so you will not be alone in your punishment."

I'd never hunted *kinnu*, for their flesh was too hard to pierce with simple arrows and my level of strength. Kier, Tyon, Sam, and Ronal had hunted the *kinnu*.

Though I owed them nothing—though I *certainly* owed Kier nothing—I kept my mouth shut. Ronal had a young daughter and Tyon had just taken a bride in summer. I liked his bride, Piper, and I didn't want to make a widow out of her.

"*Nik*?" the horde king rasped. "You will not say? I know you did not hunt them alone."

Still, I said nothing.

"Very well, *vekkiri*," he said. My hands began to tremble at my sides, the blanket of numbness beginning to slip. "This is what I must do. These are the laws of the *Dothikkar* and Kakkari demands blood as payment."

He said the words quietly, as though to himself, as though in reminder.

Kakkari? What did their goddess have to do with my execution?

When I looked up, I saw his jaw was hardened, his face cold and unyielding. But he wasn't looking at me. His eyes were unseeing, far away.

"*Bnuru kissari, darukkar*," he called out suddenly, making me flinch. It echoed around the clearing and I heard movement behind him.

"*Kissari, Vorakkar*?" the messenger said beside him, seemingly surprised by whatever the horde king had ordered.

"*Lysi*," the horde king growled, his tone welcoming no more questions.

Another Dakkari male appeared in my vision and the horde king stepped away. A hulking, massive horde warrior, with dark hair and gold eyes, with gold clasps in his hair and a deep scar running down his side, came forward.

In his left hand was a coiled whip.

Realization hit me, along with sickening dread. He would have me whipped *before* he killed me?

"Face your village and kneel, *vekkiri*," the horde king ordered.

This was it.

Clutching Blue's feathers in my damp palm, I turned. I faced my village and I kneeled, though I felt like I wasn't in my own body at all. I wondered who the grounder I'd killed last night would feed.

I closed my eyes for a brief moment.

One, my heartbeat in my ears. Two, the ringing sound of a sword being unsheathed. Three, silence from the village.

Because the silence was as loud as a scream.

Footsteps approached and I opened my eyes. They were the horde king's, but he stopped in front of me, a few paces away, his back to the villagers.

Then the warrior approached, his footfalls vibrating the ground around me, little pebbles digging into my knees. My eyes opened, but I saw nothing as I felt his sword touch the back of my neck.

My numbness left me when I needed it most and I began to tremble.

I don't want to die.

The thought came suddenly, fiercely. Tears pricked my eyes but I looked up at the sky and saw another merchant vessel, as faded as the crescent moon, pass Dakkar. I wondered where it was going, who and what it carried.

If I had another life, I would not be here, I thought.

But I didn't. This was the only life I had, the only one I'd known. I mourned that now. I'd dreamed of other things, things I knew I would never have...like family, a safe home, companionship, *love*.

I wanted to laugh at that foolish dream. Love didn't exist in a place like this. It never could.

With one swift motion, the warrior sliced his sword down my back, but it didn't puncture my skin. Cool air floated over my flesh and I clutched my thick tunic to my chest so it wouldn't fall down my arms and bare my breasts.

With my back exposed, I craned my neck down from the sky and met the horde king's eyes. Demon or not, he would still own my soul.

"Five lashes for your crime, *vekkiri*," he said, his voice hard and guttural, his eyes like flint. "I will only give you one if you name the others."

A weak part of me almost told him. I was only kneeling there now because the Dakkari had seen *me* in the Dark Forest, but they could have easily seen Kier or Tyon.

But I met the horde king's eyes and said nothing. Instead, I hunched down, breathing deeply through my nostrils, looking down at Blue's frayed feathers peeking through my fist. They had once been so beautiful and I'd ruined them with time.

The end of the whip slapped on the ground when it unraveled behind me.

The horde king waited another moment, as if waiting for me to change my mind.

Then his voice came quietly, piercing the air around me, "*Bak.*"

The whistle of the whip through the air—

My body jerked when the first lash landed across my exposed back. The pain didn't register, not at first. But when it did, it was scalding hot and icy cold. I felt it in my fingertips, in my chest, in my legs, in my lips, in the roots of my hair. It was everywhere, all around me.

Through my heaving breaths, I looked past the horde king, at the crowd of my fellow villagers, people I'd grown up knowing yet hardly knew at all. A mixture of faces that blurred with the pain. I didn't recognize anyone.

"*Teffar*," the horde king commanded, his tone hard and merciless.

The second lash hurt more than the first. I went dizzy with it and felt my fingernails pierce into my palms when I squeezed them too tightly. I swayed, on the verge of toppling over onto my side, but kept my knees planted firmly. I thought of the grounder looking up at me from the burrow and I wondered if I'd killed its friend last night, its companion. Did grounders have companions, mates? Why did my life matter more than theirs?

It doesn't, I thought. I took a life and so I was being punished.

He was stripping my numbness away, making me feel too much. I'd never felt closer to death than right then. I'd never felt closer to life either. It was strange. A strange combination that swirled in my brain along with the pain and the realization that if I had a choice, this wasn't the life I wanted.

Through the cloud of pain, I perceived the horde king stepping closer to me. Tears leaked down my cheeks, though it didn't even register that I was crying.

"*Vorakkar*?" the horde warrior behind me called out.

The horde king was so close that I heard his sharp exhale whistle through his slitted nostrils. Was he hesitating? No, surely not.

"*Teffar*," he growled.

I couldn't help the muffled cry of pain that escaped my lips when the warrior landed the third lash. It tore from me, a strangled, desperate sound.

A shadow cast itself over me. When I looked up, through my watery vision, I saw him. A wall that blocked out all light, steeping me in darkness. My back felt cold, but hot with my blood.

Glaring up at him with all the strength I could muster, I showed him my fear, my sadness, my pain, my grief, my rage.

Then a veil of realization, of crystal clarity spread over me, pure and untarnished. I had carried all those dark emotions with me through life, but I did not have to take them with me when I died.

I didn't want to.

That was what Jana had done. She'd left her sins with me and died free.

Letting peace take their place, I made the effort to let them go, one by one, imagining that they were arrows from my bow. I shot them far away, their poison disappearing, as tears dripped down my face.

The horde king's icy expression morphed and changed. His brows drew together, his lips pulling into a grim line. He peered down at me, stilling, and I wondered *what* he was looking for.

Then the grey rings of his irises widened, his jaw clenching.

Perhaps he was a demon who would steal my soul away, but I looked back at him and I looked *close.* I wasn't afraid anymore. And as I looked, as his light grey eyes bore into mine, I felt like he *was* consuming my soul. Jana had been right.

"*Nik,*" he breathed. "*Nik.*"

Hovering in that place between death and life, perhaps a little crazed with pain and loneliness and the sound of silence from my fellow villagers, I whispered through dry lips, "One, two, three. You said five, horde king."

3

Reeling, as disbelief faded into horror, I stared into the dark eyes of this female...and I saw it.

Kakkari's light, her guiding force. It manifested in different ways for different Dakkari, but it was unmistakable and undeniable. I'd experienced it twice before in my lifetime, though not *through* another, and it had led me to this.

To *her*?

For a moment, I was suspended, frozen in place, speared by her dark eyes and the knowing within them.

As a horde king of Dakkar, I'd endured much. I'd killed many. I'd saved more. I'd protected my horde and punished those that threatened it.

And as I stared down at this human female looking back at me, shivering against the pain of the whip—pain I knew well—I felt exposed. I felt as if she'd peeled back my flesh and exposed the monster underneath, when I'd never wanted to be one, when I had sworn in whispers during the night that I would never become one.

"*Vorakkar?*" the horde warrior called out, his bloodied whip poised, waiting for my order.

"*Nik*," I choked out, holding up my hand. "*Pevkell!*"

Enough.

"Will you kill me now?" she whispered, tears tracking down her cheeks. Her face was so dirty that the tears streaked her skin.

She thought me a monster. And I was. No better than the bloodthirsty Ghertun that roamed our lands, killing and pillaging for the sake of it.

"*Nik, kalles,*" I rasped out. *No, female.* "I was never going to kill you."

I heard the truth of that in my own frayed voice, but I *had* always meant to punish her, though I had never harmed a female—Dakkari or *vekkiri*—before in my lifetime.

Her eyes slid shut and I felt like I could breathe again, without the weight of her eyes. Dread rolled in my belly. It was the same dread from last night, when I'd watched her in the darkness. Had I known then? Had I sensed Kakkari's pull in this female even then?

She has the strength of a Vorakkar, I thought, restlessness rising in my chest. She was small, young yet somehow old, with bones as delicate as a *thissie*. She looked half-starved, unwashed, and her clothes were not suitable for the coming cold season. They hung off her in rags. Yet she'd withstood the lashes of the whip. She hadn't looked at her fellow villagers, but rather, she'd looked beyond them. She hadn't told me who was responsible for the *kinnu* herd thinning, though there was obviously a lack of loyalty on their side.

"*Vorakkar,*" my *pujerak,* my second-in-command, called out.

"*Neffar?*" I snarled, my nostrils flaring. I looked up at him and I realized that he was watching me carefully, as were my horde warriors beyond him. He had expected me to execute her. Swiftly, easily, as was my duty when *vekkiri* broke the laws of our *Dothikkar,* our king. Perhaps that would've been more merciful.

Vodan, my *pujerak,* looked stunned by my reaction. I'd never once lost my temper, I'd never once lost control of my tightly restrained emotions.

Bury them deep, my son, so you never know the pain of them. Only then will you be powerful.

My mother's words came to me and I bit out a curse under my breath, realizing that I was being watched by all, even the *vekkiri* behind me.

The villagers all looked half-starved and exhausted themselves, save for a few.

It is true then, I realized. *The rumors that the human settlements are failing.*

The Uranian Federation were not providing for their refugees, as promised to the Dakkari when a deal had been settled on after the Old War. When had the last ration shipment dropped? It looked like it had been at least a year.

And I had just whipped a young female hunter who had only tried to feed herself and her village. Because it was just one thing among many that my *Dothikkar* required of me.

But *he* did not see what I saw right then. He did not feel what I felt rising within me, the horror of my actions. Seated in the capitol of *Dothik*, surrounded by his luxuries and his females and his feasts, how could he understand this?

But I understood it. I knew hunger. I knew desperation.

What I also knew was that if I left the female there, she would die of her wounds. Her body was weak, malnourished. If infection took root, it would kill her.

And *that* I could not allow. I would not allow her to die. Not her. Not this *kalles* who had torn me open with sad, old eyes, with *thissie* feathers clutched in her palm.

Not this *kalles* who Kakkari herself had marked for me... who'd just been whipped bloody on my orders.

"*Vok*," I cursed, belly churning, crouching in front of her. Her breaths were shallow and her eyes were closed.

Shame filled my chest, though it was an emotion I was well-acquainted with, especially growing up on the streets in *Dothik*. I'd clawed my way from the darkness and filth to become a horde king, but I'd never felt more like a fraud than at that moment.

A growl left me and I turned to the villagers, calling out in the universal tongue, my voice booming in the clearing, "Who claims this female?"

No one stepped forward. Not a single soul moved.

Was that relief I felt? That she was unclaimed? Or something else? Something darker?

I made my decision then. Careful of her wounds, I lifted her with ease, cradling her against my chest. She hissed at the jostling movement, her wounds pulling. Then she loosened in my arms, the pain finally overcoming her body. A small mercy.

I ignored the ripple of low murmurs that went through the villagers behind me, ignored my *pujerak's* furious, baffled expression, ignored all but Lokkas, my *pyroki*. I held out my hand for my loyal beast and he came to me, nudging his long, pointed snout into my outstretched, calloused hand.

Vodan approached me then, the tension between us palpable, the tension in the village thick.

"*Vorakkar*," he hissed. "This is...you cannot take her. As your *pujerak*, I *must* advise against this. The horde will not—"

"I am not the first to take a *vekkiri* female," I told him. "I will not be the last."

He sucked in a breath. "Surely you do not mean—"

"*Enough*," I growled, my patience threadbare. "You have questioned me too much as of late."

"You chose me as your *pujerak because* I question you, *Vorakkar*," he replied softly, his eyes straying to the female in my arms.

"She will die if I leave her."

"She was always supposed to die," Vodan argued. "From the moment her arrow sunk into the *rikcrun*, even before then, she was always meant to."

I stilled, drawing in deep lungfuls of air to calm the maelstrom swirling inside me.

"Ready the *pyroki* and the warriors," I bit out at last, holding his gaze, *daring* him to challenge me.

His jaw ticked. Finally, he inclined his head. "*Lysi, Vorakkar.*"

Then he turned from me, biting out orders to the *darukkar* and they began to clear from the village.

I hefted the *kalles* onto the back of Lokkas before swinging up behind her, tucking her close. Taking my *pyroki's* reins in one fist and using my other to steady her, my gaze connected with the village's leader, a male who offered his given name much too freely, though I did not care to remember it.

He only held my eyes for a moment before he looked away, a muscle in his cheek twitching.

Circling Lokkas, I urged my *pyroki* into a run through the village's open gate, kicking up dust in my wake.

"*Vir drak!*" I bellowed.

Answering cries from my horde pierced the air and I pushed Lokkas faster and faster, gaining distance from the village until it turned into a speck on the horizon.

The female in my arms didn't wake once on the journey, though her blood soaked my chest. It soaked into my skin, marking me as certainly as the golden tattoos across my flesh.

When we reached the edges of our temporary encampment, I swung off Lokkas and brought the *kalles* down gently, grim determination coursing through me as I carried her to where I slept.

Mercy. It was what Arokan of Rath Kitala's *vekkiri* queen had asked of me, with her rounded belly and shining eyes, pregnant with his child, with his heir. Had that just been yesterday, when I had visited the other *Vorakkar's* encampment? When I had told them I was journeying to an eastern human settlement to punish the hunters responsible for the *kinnu*?

We only ever needed mercy, she'd told me in her soft, human way. Arokan had given her mercy, had spared her brother's life, and her life had been forever changed.

As I laid the *kalles* down on her stomach over my bare pallet, as I looked down at her wounds, I knew this was not mercy.

Vodan appeared at my side as I peeled away the female's cut tunic, exposing the entirety of her back, the evidence of my brutality.

Monster? *Lysi*, I'd been becoming one for years. Or perhaps I'd always been one, shaped and crafted, like a blade, since my youth.

"I will bring clean water," was all Vodan said, knowing that my mind was made up, knowing that it was already done. And *that* was why I'd chosen him as my *pujerak*. For all his faults, for all *mine*, he was loyal to me, to the horde.

I stared down at the female with her cheek pressed against the hard pallet, taking in her strange features. She had dark hair, the palest skin I'd ever seen, a pointed nose, a small mouth. I hadn't encountered many *vekkiri* in my time as *Vorakkar*, though I was certain my horde warriors had when I'd sent them on patrols.

When I turned to look for Vodan, I saw my horde warriors dismounting their *pyroki*, casting speculative glances my way, though none met my eyes out of respect.

Perhaps they thought I'd gone mad, like the horde king to the north.

Perhaps I have, my mind whispered.

Still, the weight of their stares prickled my neck.

"*Ovilli, vir drak drukkia!*" I called out, my voice echoing around the encampment.

Prepare, we ride at midday.

For home.

The warriors were eager to return, as was I. In a flurry of activity, they began the process of breaking down the camp, leaving me to tend to the *kalles* without the weight of their eyes on my back.

Vodan returned with a pot of water and clean cloths. I took both from him and went to work. I was no healer, but I wore enough scars across my flesh to have ample knowledge of wound care.

"No *uudun* salve?" I asked Vodan.

"*Nik*," he replied. "We did not expect...this."

Vok, I thought but pressed my lips together. I soaked the clean cloth in water and pressed it to the *kalles'* back. She was dirty and the cloth came away a muddied red, grey with filth.

"Hold her down."

Once her arms were secured, I tipped the clean water over her back, washing the dirt and blood away. She came awake in an instant, her body tensing, a muffled cry falling from her lips.

"Be still, *kalles*," I told her in the universal tongue. "I need to dress your wounds."

"*You*," she whispered, her face turned to me. Her dark eyes were unfocused, dilated, but they were on me. "Why?"

It was unnerving, I realized. Once I became a *Vorakkar*, no one met my eyes, except for other horde kings, my *pujerak*, and my *Dothikkar*. To have this *kalles* look upon me so freely, I was reminded that once, I had been nothing more than a *duvna*, a scurrying, poor gutter rat in the streets of *Dothik*. Everyone met my gaze then.

What was most strange was that, looking into her eyes, I realized how much I'd missed it. That simple connection of looking at another being.

Yet, with her, it was something more. Something that called

to me, something I recognized, pulling me in, threatening to consume me as surely as it promised to *free* me.

"Because I must," was all I told her.

She hissed in pain when I poured more water over her back and I gritted my teeth, an uncomfortable sensation swelling in my chest with her cries.

From experience, I knew it hurt like Drukkar's fire.

"I don't think I want to die," she said, teeth clenched, looking straight at me. "I don't t-think I..."

She trailed off, the pain pulling her under again. Released of her gaze, with a grim expression, I washed as much of the wounds as possible, but without the *uudun*, I knew the risk for infection was high. We needed to reach the rest of the horde soon.

"Why are you doing this?" Vodan asked me quietly, releasing her limp arms, watching as I bound her back in clean cloth. "You are a *Vorakkar*. She is a *vekkiri*. You punished her for her crime, yet now you seem driven to save her."

I didn't answer him.

"What did she say to you?" he asked quietly. "When you ended her punishment, she spoke to you."

It wasn't about what she said. It was about what I *saw*, what I *felt*.

Again, I didn't answer him.

Instead, I told him, "*Vir drak drukkia.*"

We ride at midday.

4

Time blurred and I was in and out of consciousness in flashes and waves. Every time, I woke to pain. The searing pain of my back and then the new pain between my thighs. That pain frightened me at first, until I realized it was due to riding the Dakkari's black-scaled creatures, the hard flesh chafing my own, a new soreness taking root.

My eyes stung and my lids felt heavy as I looked over land I didn't recognize. It was dark. Endless black plains that would be frozen over soon met my gaze, though I spied the shadows of mountains and heavily shrouded forests in the distance.

Every thump from the creature's gait jostled my fresh wounds but I bit the sides of my cheeks to keep from wincing.

"You wake," came *his* voice behind me. I felt his hand tighten at my hip, where he kept me steady, and when I glanced down, the golden cuff around his wrist flashed in the low moonlight.

There was something thick on my back, covering the wounds. When I tried to reach around to investigate, he squeezed my hip in warning and I stiffened.

"*Nik*," he said. "Leave them, *kalles*."

I couldn't look over my shoulder to meet his eyes. It twisted my back when I tried, but I did crane my neck as far as I dared and in my peripheral vision, saw his golden hair in the darkness.

A wave of dizziness hit me and I clutched at the creature's neck as I steadied myself. I kept my head forward from that moment, feeling nausea rise, thick saliva coating my mouth. To distract myself from it, I stroked the creature's scales, tracing the edge of one. It was as hard as metal, yet warm like flesh. I felt its power, its unbridled strength, as palpable as its master's behind me.

My breath hitched, eyes widening, realizing what was missing.

"Blue's feathers," I rasped, looking down at my lap, as if I'd find them there. "Where are they?"

His hand moved from my hip. I didn't care about the pain from my back as I dove my fists into my pockets, searching, fearing that I'd lost them—*her*—forever.

Relief sagged my shoulders when the feathers appeared in my line of sight, held out by his clawed fingers. I snagged them quickly and clutched them to my chest, swallowing.

"You took me from my village," I whispered, another wave of dizziness hitting me from my sudden physical effort. I looked down at the feathers before placing them safely in the pocket of my torn tunic.

"*Lysi.*"

I remembered that moment, before my whipping. I'd felt like I was out of my own body, floating feet above the ground. I felt that way now, like none of this was real. My mind was fuzzy, my head felt heavy. I felt warm and chilled.

Was this real? Was he real?

The throbbing in my wounds told me it was. The nausea, the dizziness, the tiredness told me it was. Surely if I was dead, I wouldn't feel this much pain.

Reaching down with one hand, I curled my stinging palm

around the black-scaled creature's nape, right where its long neck met its back. Perhaps this was what shock felt like.

Cold wind slapped against my face, but tendrils of it slid over the heat radiating from my back. It felt nice, but also terrible.

"Where are you taking me?" I asked.

"To my horde."

"Isn't this your horde?" I asked, remembering the Dakkari warriors spilling into the walls of my village. Just thinking about them made me tired, made me want to fall back into that dark place of sleep, where I felt nothing at all.

"A part of it, *lysi*."

There were more?

My eyes slid shut, but my head swam when they did, spinning and spinning in circles. My stomach felt like it was filled with acid.

I was going to vomit. The pain made the nausea worse. Bile rose in my throat and I sucked in a lungful of air through my nostrils before my stomach heaved.

At the last moment, I turned my head and managed to miss vomiting all over the creature we rode. I heard the horde king curse and pull at the reins, slowing the beast to a halt.

I had nothing to throw up, not even water.

When I touched my forehead, I realized I was sweating, which explained the chill.

Something was wrong.

I felt him dismount and then he was standing next to his creature, looking up at me.

Fear struck me in that moment, a ridiculous reaction considering I'd just been speaking to him without it. In a flash, I remembered the bite of the whip and I flinched away when he reached for me.

The horde king frowned, a scar on the edge of his lip pulling down slightly. He ignored my flinch and pressed his clawed fingers to my cheek. I hadn't been touched in so long that I froze, staring down at him.

"*Vok*," he said under his breath. "You are burning."

"Don't touch me," I whispered, turning my face away, fingers reaching for an arrow that wasn't there. "Please."

He growled, low in his throat, but his hand retreated. Instead, he jerked something away from the harness around the creature's flank. It was a flask of animal hide. "Drink," he ordered, thrusting it into my hands.

"What is it?" I asked, suspicion tinging my tone, even as another wave of nausea rose. Black spots appeared in my vision and I swayed.

"Water."

I sniffed it before I took a sip. It was clean and fresh, possibly the cleanest water I'd ever had. I took a greedy mouthful, then another, feeling it soothe my scratchy throat.

When I realized that I had drained the whole skin, I gave it back to him and managed to meet his eyes.

Nik, nik, he'd murmured, right before the whipping had stopped. He'd looked at me like he'd seen an old spirit. I'd thought him cold and detached, but his expression then had been anything but, hungry demon that he was, bent on consuming my soul. He was *still* doing it, right then. I felt it. What would happen when there was nothing left of me?

My vision went black for a moment. I heard him curse, I felt my body slide.

Then everything went dark.

———

THE NEXT TIME I WOKE, I smelled something strange. Pungent. Earthy.

My back was on fire. Twisting, I cried out, bucking like a

frightened animal, feeling a foreign weight on me. I sensed others, wherever I was, and heard the Dakkari language, rasped in roughened tones, just above me.

"Be still, *kalles*," came *his* voice. The demon horde king.

I was lying on my front, on a bed of soft furs. My ripped tunic had been torn away, my bare breasts pressing into the bed.

When I lifted the heavy weight of my head up, I saw him kneeling by my right shoulder, grasping both my wrists in a firm hold, restraining me to the furs.

Panic and pain lit my veins. Despite the fogginess in my head, I was lucid enough to realize I was half-naked in the presence of Dakkari males, being held down by their brutal horde king. And I'd heard the rumors of the Dakkari. Barbaric, dark things that were whispered about from village to village.

I thrashed against his hold harder and felt a rush of warmth on my back, followed by a sharp pain.

Then came a female voice, urgent and firm. My brows drew together just as the demon king said, "*Cease*. You are reopening the wounds."

Not caring about the burning sensation from my back, I craned my head so I could look behind me. A female was there, kneeling next to my hips. In her hand was a needle and thread. Another male—the one that had first spoken to me in my village —stood a few feet away, his arms crossed over his chest. Other than that, no one else was there. No trace of the horde warriors that had flooded into my village.

"What...what are you doing to me?" I rasped, my throat and mouth dry. The female glanced at me. A Dakkari female. I'd never seen one before.

But she didn't reply. Her gaze dismissed me when she bent her head and lowered her needle to my back.

"She is suturing your wounds closed, *kalles*," the demon king said, his voice rough and dark. I hated his voice. It made fear saturate my belly and rise up in my chest.

"*Why?*" I asked, hissing when I felt the coolness of her needle pierce my hot flesh.

He didn't answer. I saw his jaw set, I felt his hold tighten.

Then I closed my eyes. It was easier.

I drifted back into sleep again.

LATER, it was quiet, except for the crackling of a fire.

My eyelids felt heavy and my back felt numb. When the fire popped, my breath hitched, my gaze tracking over to it. The fire was encased in a raised metal disc and I watched sparks fling out from its center.

It was warm and it was so quiet. My skin felt damp, but my mind floated in a painless haze.

A dream?

My cheek was pressed into soft, tickling furs and I worried about Blue's feathers because I no longer wore my tunic.

A hissing sound met my ears and I looked up slightly, across what looked like the inside of a domed tent. It was richly and warmly furnished. Piles of clean and plush furs, thick red rugs with golden swirling accents, heavy chests lining one area of the tent, a low table with cushions on the opposite side. A yellow glow of oil lamps and candles made the inside gleam, yet cast other places in deep shadows.

It was in one of those shadows that I saw him.

He was sitting with his back to the wall of the tent, his golden sword in his lap. I watched as he ran what looked like a black stone across the blade, creating that sharp hissing sound, before flipping the sword to run it across the other side.

As if he sensed me awakening, his gaze darted to mine. The hissing sound stopped.

His grey eyes looked frightening in the shadows, like a creature of nightmares. He was bare-chested and the markings across his chest and shoulders seemed to glow bright yellow in the darkness.

I swallowed. But just like with the men in my village, I did not want to show him my fear.

"Where am I?" I whispered, because I didn't trust my voice not to shake.

"In my horde," was what he replied.

He wasn't that far from me. In fact, I could see that he'd recently bathed, his blond hair damp, his skin scrubbed clean.

Frowning, my eyes flitted, looking for a bathing tub, and I saw one near the entrance of the tent, tendrils of steam still curling from the surface.

I didn't remember the last time I'd bathed.

My gaze flickered back to him when I sensed him set his sword aside.

"What did you do to me?" I asked, feeling something wrapped tightly around my back. Reaching around, I felt the soft cloth of bandages, wet with something sticky and thick.

"The healer cleaned and dressed your wounds."

"Why?"

His gaze narrowed. "To save you."

"You should have left me," I whispered, licking my dry lips.

"You would have died," he told me, his jaw ticking. With irritation? With regret? With impatience? I didn't know. I couldn't read him and usually I was very good at reading people.

"Wasn't that the point?" I couldn't help but ask, remembering the way I felt before I knelt on the ground of my village, thinking it was an execution.

"*Nik*," he bit out. "I told you before. I was never going to kill you, *kalles*."

I closed my eyes. I didn't know how I felt about that knowledge, but I heard the truth in his voice. If he wanted me dead, I would be. But why had he taken me from my village? Why did he bring me here?

I didn't think I wanted to know. One possibility flitted across my mind, but it was ridiculous. I'd heard of Dakkari males taking human females from villages before. But I was not the taking kind. I was small and pale and strange-looking. If anyone from our village was the taking kind, it would have been Viv. She was beautiful.

"What does *kalles* mean, demon king?" I whispered, my eyes popping open when I heard the fire spark again. The fire was beautiful too. A swirl of red and orange and gold and all the shades in between.

I almost smiled because it was so beautiful...and I liked beautiful things. Like a full moon, all round and silvery, or the shimmering pink fog that sometimes settled over the land on a cold morning.

But my eyes would not remain away from him for long. He was beautiful too.

"*Kalles* means female in my language," he told me after a brief pause.

I thought *kalles* was a pretty word, but I would certainly never tell him that.

His jaw ticked and again I couldn't read him. "Demon king?" he rasped.

It took me a moment to realize I had even *called* him 'demon king.'

"You think me a demon?" he asked.

"Yes," I said, my fingers stroking the furs underneath me. I didn't know what beast they came from, but it was the softest thing I'd ever felt. "Jana told me about demons. She told me when you look too closely, they steal your soul."

He went still. He even seemed to stop breathing. Those grey eyes burned into me.

"And I felt you taking it," I whispered, my breath quickening in fear, remembering that sensation. "I *felt* it."

So why was I still staring into his eyes?

Swallowing, my gaze dropped to his chest and I traced one edge of a tattoo until I ended my perusal at his side, where I saw a deep scar. A scar so deep it puckered his skin inwards.

I was a curious being—sometimes to a fault—but even I knew not to ask how he'd received such a scar.

"So, Kakkari has shown you as well," he said softly, that brutal voice cutting into me, making my chest tighten. He said it with an almost speculative tone.

"Shown me what?" I asked, my gaze drifting over to the bath again, wanting it. When I moved slightly, my back tugged and that icy numbness lifted for a moment, my lungs squeezing from the throbbing pain.

A noise whistled from his slitted nostrils. He didn't answer my question.

Instead, he said, "I am no demon, *thissie*. Because if I am one, then you are one too."

I frowned, surprised by the way his words dragged something fierce and angry from me.

"I want to leave," I said, glaring at him across the domed tent. "You should not have taken me from my village."

"You will not leave, *kalles*," he said, his tone harsh but firm. I tensed when he rose from his seated position. "Not until I say you can."

My breath whooshed from my lungs in disbelief, in confusion.

He turned, heading towards the entrance of the tent. I was

about to argue, about to push up from the furs. Then the words died in my throat.

My lips parted when I saw his bared back.

He'd been whipped too. Only, instead of three lashes, it looked like he'd received a hundred.

"Rest," he growled out, a sudden anger in his voice. "I will return with the healer later."

Then he left. And I was left with the quiet and the crackling fire and the shadows.

5

"Her fever grows, *Vorakkar*," the healer said. "She will burn up before the dawn."

I stared down at the wreckage of her flesh. The human female was slick with sweat and she trembled every so often in sleep. Despite the healer's attempts, infection had already taken root. It had been three days since I'd brought the *kalles* to my camp. She had not woken up on the second day.

"What will you do?" I growled. Out of the corner of my eye, I saw the healer still at my tone.

"I recommend an ice bath," she replied, her voice hesitant. "Have your warriors bring in the water from the river. They will need to break the ice to retrieve it."

"Very well," I said, rising.

"*Vorakkar*," the healer called out softly. I turned back to her, but her gaze remained averted. "I—I have never treated a *vekkiri* before. They are different from us, weaker. I do not wish for you to be angry with me if I cannot heal her. I—I cannot go back to *Dothik.*"

My brows drew together. She thought her place in the horde balanced on the *kalles'* life. Had I given her that impression?

"Your home is always here, *kerisa*," I told her, trying to soften my tone. "But do not let her die."

Vodan found me when I exited my tent. His eyes strayed to the entrance but I caught the flash of disapproval in his gaze.

Beyond him, I saw a small group of horde warriors standing around a barrel fire, laughing and eating.

"*Darukkar*," I called out. The group immediately turned and straightened when they saw me standing there.

While I relayed my orders to the horde warriors and watched as they filed out of the camp, heading west towards the river, I sensed my *pujerak* close in.

"What is it?" I asked him, breathing in the crisp air through my nostrils and looking out over my horde.

"There are already whisperings around the camp," he told me. "You will need to address her presence soon. Many wonder why a *vekkiri kalles* stays in your *voliki*."

"Tell them what you must," I said.

"That she is your war prize? That she is your whore?"

I huffed out an impatient breath, my eyes seeking the moon hanging above our camp. It was only a crescent moon, but once it was full, whether the cold season descended or not, I had to be in *Dothik*.

"Should I tell them everything but the truth?"

"And what is it?" I rasped, locking my gaze with his. "Tell me, *pujerak*, what you believe the truth is."

He said nothing, but I could see the knowledge of it in his eyes.

I shook my head, my eyes returning to the moon. Then, I said, "You are not my blood brother, Vodan, but you are my family. You always have been, since we were young."

Vodan sighed. I remembered him right then as when I'd first seen him. Dirty and small and hungry. Just like I'd been.

"We built something in *Dothik*. Together. We built this horde because I could not have done it without you," I said. "Now, I need that support. I need you to stop questioning me. Because though you are my brother, I am still your *Vorakkar* and I need you to remember that."

He held my gaze but I saw when my request permeated.

"I will not pretend to know what it is like, going through the Trials of the *Dothikkar*," my *pujerak* said after a brief pause. "I will not pretend to know what it takes, mentally and physically, to become a *Vorakkar*."

"Maybe it takes a monster," I said, meeting his eyes. "Maybe that is the only way."

Vodan huffed out a sharp exhale, dismissing my words. "You believe you are a monster? I disagree. I believe that you have to be strong in order to best lead this horde. You cannot have mercy because mercy can kill. You cannot be swayed." His eyes went to tent. "And this female? She sways you. She will."

"The horde always come first. You know this," I told him, furrowing my brow. "One female will *never* change that."

Vodan sighed. He looked out over the horde encampment at the gentle golden glow from the drum fires and oil lamps.

"I will tell them that she is yours," Vodan said simply, quietly.

Desires I'd long thought dead reawakened at his words, but I pushed them from my mind as best as I could.

Discipline. It was required of us all, I reminded myself. The *Dothikkar* had ensured that in his selection of his *Vorakkars*.

"Return to your wife, Vodan," I rasped, turning from him, my voice husky from my thoughts. "Enjoy her warmth and think no more of this tonight."

"Then return to yours, *Vorakkar*," my *pujerak* said, tilting his head towards my *voliki*. His eyes were watchful and knowing as he added, "Because that is what she will become, is it not?"

WHEN THE HORDE warriors returned with the river water, I returned to my *voliki,* following them inside, watching as they filled the bathing tub.

After I dismissed them, the healer said, "Can you lift her in, *Vorakkar*? Her back cannot get wet or the sutures will fail. Keep her bent forward."

The healer stripped the *kalles* of her pants, leaving her naked on my furs. I froze for a moment, looking at her backside, her legs, the jutting bones of her hips. I swallowed. She was much too thin. I hadn't realized how much until just then.

And she was much too light, I thought, when I picked her up, careful of her back. She was shivering in my arms.

When I placed her in the icy water, she didn't even wake and I maneuvered her body as the healer said, kneeling by the side of the bathing tub to keep her steady and in place.

Her back was red and inflamed from my lashes, little veins spearing out from the wounds.

"How long?" I asked the healer, not lifting my gaze from the *kalles'* face.

"Not long, but we will need to do this multiple times through the night."

When her trembling vibrated the water around her, I took her out. A short while later, I put her back in, once we brought in more ice to cool the water.

It was a long night, but once morning broke, the exhausted healer told me that her fever was under control, that the worst of it was over.

"I will return," the healer said, packing up her serums and vials, "in the evening. Or if she wakes before then, you can send for me, *Vorakkar*."

"*Kakkira vor, kerisa,*" I said.

My gratitude made color rise in her cheeks, but I was already looking back down at the *kalles* and I didn't notice when the healer slipped from the tent.

Lowering myself onto the furs next to her, I stretched out in my bed, knowing I needed to sleep, though dawn was just breaking. I hadn't slept for three days and exhaustion was beginning to pull at the edges of my mind.

Now that I knew the *kalles* would make it through another day, I let myself relax, if only slightly.

When I turned my head to look at her, I saw her closed eyelids twitch.

Her eyes opened a fraction and connected with mine. She didn't react when she saw me close to her, as I guessed she might. She was a peculiar thing, unpredictable in nature, and that frustrated me.

Perhaps she didn't realize she was awake, or perhaps she was still delirious from the fever. She looked at me, *deep*, and whispered, "Hello, demon."

Her eyes closed before I could react.

"Sleep, *thissie*," I said back after a quiet moment.

Then I slept too.

6

I woke to an empty, cold tent. For a moment, I couldn't place where I was or why. But slowly, awareness drifted back to me and with it came wariness.

"Hello?" I called out softly, my cheek pressed to the furs of the bed, my back exposed to the open, cool air. It was then I realized I was naked.

I felt sick but starving, my throat parched and dry. When I tried to push myself from the bed, my arms trembled and my heart thundered from the small exertion, making me feel dizzy and out of breath.

But at least I was sitting up. Shivering, I winced when the wounds on my back pulled ever so slightly, though I noticed the pain was significantly less than what it'd been before.

Blue light filtered into the tent and I gasped when I saw someone enter through the flaps. Scrambling, I took one of the furs from the bed and held it to my chest to cover my nakedness.

I relaxed slightly when I realized it was the Dakkari female I'd seen before. Though the memory of her was hazy, I still remembered her with her needle.

"You are awake," she murmured. Was that *relief* I heard in her voice?

"You...you speak my language too?" I asked.

"*Lysi*," she said, inclining her head. "I was raised in *Dothik*."

She said it as though it would clear up any confusion, but I still frowned.

"How do you feel?" she asked, coming towards me. I tightened my grip on the furs and shuffled back a little, eyeing the small case she carried at her side. She stopped when she saw the movement and said, "I have been working day and night to see you well, *vekkiri*. I will not waste all my hard work by harming you now."

Hearing the tired truth in her tone, I felt my shoulders relax and when she motioned for me to scoot forward, I did. She turned me so that she could inspect my bared back.

"Good," she said finally, quietly, almost to herself. "The *Vorakkar* will be pleased."

I frowned at the mention of him, remembering him in flashes, in pieces.

"What happened?" I asked, tugging the furs tighter to my chest when another cold draft floated around my body. "How long have I been asleep?"

"Your wounds became infected. Your body was burning with it, but we managed to bring the fever down," she said, appearing in my line of vision again. She went to a small table at the edge of my vision and picked up a metal goblet before bringing it to me. "Drink. I tried to keep you hydrated but you were not always cooperative."

I didn't remember that, but I took the heavy goblet from her hand eagerly and drained it quickly.

She went back to the table to retrieve a pitcher and poured me more water, which I drank.

46

"You have been here almost five days now," she said, going to rummage through her case.

I looked into the empty goblet and whispered, "Five days?"

How was that possible?

"I gave you a sedative," she explained. "It kept you sleeping most of the time so your body could heal."

I'd never heard of such a medicine, one that could make someone sleep for days.

When she looked back at me, she had a small green vial in her hand, a black liquid inside. When she refilled my goblet, she tipped a little of the black liquid into it and swirled it around.

"I don't think I want to sleep anymore," I told her, looking into the goblet, wondering how to refuse it politely without offending her.

A small smile touched her lips, her yellow eyes studying me. Somehow, she looked both old and young.

"This is not for sleeping," she told me. "This will help with pain."

"Oh," I said before eagerly raising the goblet to my lips.

"You are much more cooperative when you are awake," she noted, a hint of amusement in her tone. "You must be hungry. Would you like to eat?"

My breath hitched and I licked my lips when my mouth immediately began to water. "Yes, please."

Something changed in her eyes. Pity? I didn't care. When it came to food, I could handle pity. I watched as she turned to the entrance, poked her head out, and murmured something in Dakkari to someone on the other side.

When she returned, I asked, "Where are my clothes?"

"Gone," she said before retrieving a bundle from her case. "The *Vorakkar* had these made for you. They should fit."

She held up a pair of fur-lined pants, the darkened hide expertly tanned and sewn. Then she placed a pair of fur boots

47

on the ground next to me, durable, with thick soles. Next, she showed me with evident excitement an impractical tunic of shimmering silk—which I couldn't help but notice was grey, like the demon's eyes—and a much more practical black sweater made of what looked like *kinnu* fur.

My eyes lingered on the *kinnu* fur and I remembered why the Dakkari had come to my village in the first place.

I shook my head. "I need *my* clothes. There are some things of mine in a pocket and I need them back."

"What are they?" she asked, lowering the sweater.

"Feathers," I said.

Her brow furrowed, her lips turning down. "Feathers? Why do you need those?"

"I just..." I huffed out a breath. I realized right then that I had nothing. Not that I had much before, but I at least had my clothes, my bow and arrow, and Blue's feathers. Now, I had none of those things. "They are important to me."

Her lips pressed together when she saw my expression. She looked a little uncomfortable as she said, "I am sorry. Your clothes were burned. They...they smelled quite terrible."

I nodded because I didn't know what else to do. It was done. The feathers were gone.

"Alright," I whispered. I knew I should feel embarrassed about the state of my clothes. That was what a normal person would've felt. But I just felt sad that I'd lost the last things I'd ever had.

My eyes must've gone a little watery because the Dakkari female blurred.

"I am sorry," she repeated. "I did not know."

I nodded again.

"Come," she said, shifting a little. "Let me help you wash your hair while we wait for your food. Then you can get dressed in your new clothes. They are nice, are they not?"

48

"Yes, they are," I agreed, wanting to assure her since she'd seemed excited to show them to me. I felt her hand on my arm as she helped me stand on wobbly legs.

She helped me over to the bathing tub and though the water was a little cold, I climbed into it gladly, keeping forward like she told me so I didn't get my back wet.

When I bent forward, she helped me wash my hair, lathering it with a soap that made the water white and bubbly. She had to wash it twice, as dirty as it was, and then I scrubbed at my skin with the leftover soap until I grew tired from the exertion.

Even still, when I rose from the bath and dried off, I felt lighter and better than I did before. I didn't remember the last time I'd bathed in an actual tub. I usually just tried to rinse my body by the stream in the Dark Forest. No one ever went there.

"I will bandage your back and then you can dress," she told me, having me sit on the bed. It felt strange to be naked with someone, but she didn't seem bothered by it, so I told myself that I shouldn't be either. "Unless you wish to sleep again, after you eat," she added hesitantly, peering at me.

"No, I want to get dressed and get some fresh air," I said.

"I will have to ask the *Vorakkar*," she said quietly.

Her words reminded me of an exchange I'd had with him, one that was just returning to my memory.

He'd told me, "*You will not leave, kalles. Not until I say you can.*"

Was I to be a prisoner there? Was that my purpose?

My lungs squeezed just thinking about it but I remained silent, pretending I did not hear her words as she wrapped my back with a length of cloth, winding it around my front, binding my breasts before securing it.

"Does it look very terrible?" I asked softly when she appeared in front of me. "My back?"

"Your wounds look much better than they did before. It will scar, for your skin is very delicate, but it could have been worse."

I nodded and she handed me the stack of fresh clothes. New clothes. And they were nicer than any clothes I'd ever seen.

Even still, I'd trade them for my old ones in a heartbeat if I could have Blue's feathers back.

"How did you get whipped?" she asked next, surprising me as I began to tug on the pants, though I was sitting. "Was it... your village?"

"No," I said, frowning. "It was under the horde king's orders."

I heard her suck in a breath and she cocked her head at me in confusion. "*Neffar*? Our *Vorakkar*?"

I nodded, feeling my wet hair drip over the fresh bandages.

"But...*why*?"

"Because he saw me hunting in the Dark Forest, outside my village's walls," I told her, slowly pushing up from the bed to tie the pants.

They were a little big, but they were so warm and the fur tickling my legs felt luxuriously soft.

"You are a hunter?" she asked me, still blinking, trying to understand.

"I'm good with my bow," I said softly, thinking of the grounder's three eyes that night. "The job was assigned to me when I was young."

"But you are a female," she argued, frowning.

"I can assure you that females are still capable of hunting," I told her. "I did not like it, but it kept me fed."

Most of the time, at least.

The healer went quiet and watched as I slowly pulled on the silk tunic, followed by the black sweater. My back felt tight and tender, but whatever the healer had put into my water seemed to be working for the pain.

Just then, a Dakkari male's voice sounded outside the tent

and the healer went to the entrance, returning with a tray of food. Desire grew in my heart as I watched the healer set the tray on the low table and beckon me over.

"Go slowly, *vekkiri*," she warned. "Except for some broth I managed to get down you, you have not eaten much for a while."

A pale, silky broth steamed from a small bowl and she thrust that into my hands first when I came to sit at the table. But my greedy eyes were already looking at the chunks of braised meats, piled neatly in a small mound on a plate, and a steaming loaf of something that looked like bread, though it was a deep purple in color and looked slightly wet.

But I took it as slowly as I could. When I was finished with the broth, it warmed my empty stomach, and I was startled by a strange sensation of fullness.

When I plucked one piece of braised meat from the plate and popped it into my mouth, flavor burst on my tongue, delicious and warm and spiced. My eyes went wide because I'd never had anything like it.

I ate another and another before tearing off a small piece of the bread and stuffing it into my mouth. It had a strange, spongy texture, slightly sweet, nothing like the dry, brittle bread from the village, but I decided I liked it very, very much.

There was still half a loaf and a small pile of meat left when I couldn't eat anything more. My belly churned from the sudden influx of food, but I would not vomit. My body desperately needed the nutrients.

"I think I'm done," I told the healer, looking up at her. "Can I..." I trailed off, unsure if what I was asking was appropriate. Jana had always told me I asked inappropriate things when I shouldn't.

"*Lysi?*" she asked, staring at me. She'd been staring at me since I first started eating and I wondered if she thought my food manners were deplorable. I *had* been a little too eager and it had been a long time since I had eaten with anyone.

"Nevermind," I said quietly, looking down at the uneaten food. I'd wanted to ask if I could wrap it up for later, but then realized I didn't know when 'later' was or what it meant for me. I didn't know anything about why I was there, eating this rich, almost sinfully good food, dressed in new clothes that would keep me warm during the cold season, in a luxurious tent that I was very certain was the demon king's.

"I think I'll get that fresh air now," I said softly, looking up at her, my stomach tight and stretched.

She gave me a small smile and rose. "I will need to ask the *Vorakkar*. Wait here. Drink the tea while I am gone," she told me, pushing the small cup that came on the tray towards me.

When she exited the tent, my eyes went back to the food and then I looked over at the healer's case. Standing, I slowly made my way over to it, digging inside until I found a small, clean scrap of cloth. Then I returned to the table, wrapping up the last of the meat and the bread, squishing it until it was small enough to fit into my pocket.

Once it was safely tucked inside, I relaxed, feeling better that I had another meal at the ready. My eyes strayed to the tent flaps and then to the fur boots at the end of the bed. Going over to them, I slipped my bare feet in, wiggling my toes inside, and then walked to the entrance, wondering if I would be punished again for disobeying the horde king's orders.

I didn't like being cooped up inside, which was why I hated the cold season so much. My need for fresh air and my curiosity about the horde camp won out, so I ducked through the tent flaps into frigid air.

I won't go far, I told myself, knowing I shouldn't push my body too much, especially since I'd been sick and bedridden for the last five days.

When I straightened and took my first look at the horde encampment, my lips parted and my eyes widened.

"Oh," I whispered, my breath fogging in front of me, given the coolness of the early morning.

Close to sixty or seventy domed tents stretched far and wide in front of me. The encampment was tucked close to a mountain range, which jutted up directly behind the horde king's tent. There was a clear entrance to the encampment, a tall fence with a gate, much like my own village's. When I looked to the west, past the rows of tents near the entrance, I saw a river, and when I looked east, I saw a large enclosure almost equal in size to the entire camp, the Dakkari's black-scaled creatures roaming within.

As I studied the camp further, I saw training grounds. I saw what looked like a crop field beyond the walls. I saw a massive domed tent, ten times as large as the rest, with steam curling from a hole at the top. Actually, I saw that there were a handful of tents that were larger than the others, though I couldn't guess their purpose from that distance.

The horde king's tent was set apart from the rest, up on a small incline, so I was able to see the entire camp with ease. And I could see beyond the walls from that vantage point. Lonely plains met my gaze, which would soon be frozen over.

"*Vekkiri kalles, juniri ta voliki,*" came a male's gruff voice behind me. I jumped and turned around. I'd been so surprised by the sight of the camp that I hadn't noticed a Dakkari male standing guard a short distance away.

He was a horde warrior, judging by his size and the scar that ran down his cheek.

"Oh, hello," I said, a little hesitantly, eyeing his bulk and the tail that flicked behind him.

He frowned, stepping towards me, studying me as carefully as I was studying him. "*Juniri ta voliki,*" he repeated, this time more slowly. And if I had any doubts about what he was saying, he made a sweeping motion towards the tent's entrance with one of his massive arms.

"I just want to walk a little," I responded. His frown deepened and when I took a step down the short incline, he stepped towards me. "I'll come back, I promise."

He was speaking in rapid Dakkari the further I ventured from the tent, but he didn't move to grab me, simply stayed close, no doubt trying to urge me back towards the tent in a language I didn't understand. But the cold air felt good across my cheeks and it smelled fresh and crisp. I almost smiled with how good it felt.

I didn't notice the stares at first when I began to venture into the camp. Staring didn't bother me. I'd been stared at before. I just walked slowly, curiously inspecting the tents, and shamelessly attempted to look inside any open flaps I saw. I came across Dakkari along my way, females and males and children, from young to old.

It was all so *new*, so vibrant, so exciting.

An older Dakkari male was watching me closely from the entrance of his own tent, munching on the same purple bread I'd had earlier. I looked at it, perhaps too long, because I saw him hold it out to me in offering. When I looked into his eyes in surprise, I said, "Oh, no. Um, *nik*. I already ate."

"You look hungry," he replied, his voice raspy with age, his accent the deepest I'd heard. Behind him, I saw movement and a small boy appeared, looking around the older male's legs at me. The irises of his yellow eyes went rounder, widening.

"I have some already," I said, patting the pocket of my new pants, feeling the weight of the food at my thigh. Even still, a part of me was tempted to take the offered food and add it to my stash. "But thank you. That's very kind."

All he did was grunt and chewed off another chunk before handing the rest to the boy.

"Are you from *Dothik*?" I asked. Behind me, I heard the guard break into another tangent of Dakkari, but I ignored him.

The older male cocked his head to the side at me. "How do you know that?"

I swore he looked amused as I said, "I learned today that if you grow up in *Dothik*, you learn the universal language, though I don't quite understand why."

It made me wonder for the first time if the demon king was from *Dothik* too, since he spoke the universal language.

The male guffawed and I jerked a little at the sound of the deep laugh. "*Lysi, kalles*, I am from *Dothik*." The boy said something in Dakkari and the older male translated. "He says your eyes are odd."

"You can tell him I think his eyes are odd as well," I said gently, my lips quirking at the corners when I looked down at the boy. When the male translated my words, the boy's own odd eyes went wide again. For a moment, I feared I would make him cry and I bit my lip, unsure and worried. But then he too broke off in a strange little high-pitched laugh.

Something rose in me at the sound and right there, for the first time in what seemed like years, I chuckled too. Brief and short, but a laugh nonetheless.

A smile lingered on my lips but then I heard heavy footsteps approach behind me. I saw the boy's eyes dart to whoever approached and then his eyes went wide for a different reason entirely.

"*Vekkiri*," came a familiar voice, deep and harsh. His presence was unmistakable, overwhelming. I would've known it was him even if he hadn't spoken.

The smile died from my face. I looked at the boy once more and then I turned to face the demon king.

7

"Y ou should be resting," I growled out at the female, halting before her, the *kerisa* trailing behind me.

The healer had informed me the *kalles* had woken, bathed, dressed, and eaten. Hearing the news filled me with relief, but when I reached the *voliki* and found neither the guard or the female inside, I'd grown irritated...and worried.

She hadn't gotten far. I'd heard her laugh before I saw her... and that laugh, as small and quiet as it was, made my pace quicken towards her.

"I've been resting for five days, apparently," she told me when she turned to look up at me. I couldn't help but notice she took a step away, putting distance between us, but I hid my scowl as best as I could. "I needed some air."

I'd forgotten how small she was, how delicate she seemed. I hadn't stood next to her since I'd ordered her punishment.

Nostrils flaring at the memory, I looked past her and saw Arusan, an older male who'd been with my horde since the beginning. He looked after and crafted our weapons...an accomplished blacksmith. One of the masters trained in *Dothik*.

I inclined my head at him and noticed his daughter's son, Arlah, peering at me from behind his legs. How had they made the *kalles* laugh, I wondered?

"I apologize, *Vorakkar*," Neeva said, coming forward. He was the guard I'd posted outside my *voliki*. "I tried to have her return, but she—"

"I know," I said, cutting off whatever he was about to say. In Dakkari, I told him, "She has a will of her own, it seems."

I watched as her dark gaze fluttered between the guard and I, her expression unsure.

A small crowd had gathered, I noticed. Vodan had been right when he'd told me that whispers had begun through the horde. They were curious about the *vekkiri* I had brought into the camp.

"Come," I told her, gesturing her forward.

"I still intend to see that enclosure over there," she informed me, pointing towards the *pyroki* pen. "I can meet you back at your tent if you wish to discuss something."

The *kerisa* made a sound of surprise behind me. Then a growl escaped me, sudden and low. "*Kalles,* you will—"

She turned her back to me, looking at Arusan and Arlah. The older male had a speculative expression on his features, almost amused. He'd told me long ago that he enjoyed laughing, that he liked to do it whenever something pleased him. He looked on the verge of it now.

"My name is Nelle," she told him, making his eyes widen and making me clench my jaw. *Nelle.* "It was nice to speak with you." She looked down at the boy. "And you."

Vok, she knew nothing of the Dakkari, knew nothing of our ways. I looked around at the small crowd and saw some of them murmuring to each other. There were those in attendance that understood the universal language, those that now knew her given name. And it would spread among the horde until all knew.

Nelle.

She turned and continued on her way—towards the *pyroki* pen—and I stared after her, irritation and frustration and a heavy dose of disbelief pulsing hot in my veins.

To the guard, I said, "I will send for you when I need you. I will handle this."

"*Lysi, Vorakkar.*"

Gritting my jaw, I stalked after the *kalles*, leaving the crowd behind me, though I was sure some brave souls followed.

She was heading towards the pen and I stayed a short distance behind her, letting my temper cool before I spoke to her next. As I waited, I studied her. I studied the way she walked, the way she turned her head to regard any Dakkari that stared openly at her, the way she peered into an unlit drum fire she passed, as if trying to ascertain its purpose.

Vok, she even poked her head into the common bathing *voliki,* though her cheeks appeared reddened when she straightened and continued on her way.

She was a curious thing. Perhaps to a fault.

Finally, she halted at the *pyroki* pen, to the east of the encampment. The *mrikro,* the *pyroki* master charged with overseeing their care and training, was busy inside, ordering around a handful of spare horde warriors. They were still building the *pyrokis'* nests for the cold season, though only a few more needed to be crafted.

I watched as the *kalles* pressed her belly to the fence, leaning on the rails heavily. She was tired, I realized. When I drew closer, I saw a sheen of sweat on her forehead.

"You need to rest," I growled, halting just behind her.

"I would rather be out here," she said without looking at me. She sounded out of breath.

I blew out a sharp exhale, unused to my orders being ignored completely.

"Why did you do it?" she asked softly, not meeting my eyes. Instead, she looked at the *mrikro*, who paused when he saw us standing there.

She could be asking many things. Why did I punish her? Why did I take her? Why did I keep her in my *voliki*, knowing it would spark rumors among my horde? Why did I want so desperately to save her?

I decided to pretend she was asking the obvious question.

"Because under my *Dothikkar's* laws, you had to be punished," I told her, squeezing my fists at my sides. In my mind's eye, I remembered the way her body jerked when that first lash fell over her exposed, delicate skin. She hadn't cried out. She hadn't made a sound.

"No," she said, shaking her head, finally looking back at me. "Why did you stop at three?"

I stilled. The way she looked at me right then...her gaze was indifferent. I expected fear or perhaps disgust, but she gave me neither.

I lied. "Because you would not have lasted through the fifth."

"That's not true," she said. "How many did you last through?"

She'd seen my back then, my own scars. And for once, my tongue failed me. I couldn't answer her.

"Did you think my body would break first, or my mind?" she asked, tilting her head, as if she was curious how I would respond.

I was unable to read her. I couldn't understand why she was asking these things. One thing I did know was that I regretted lying to her now. Part of me wanted to see how she would react if I told her the truth...that I had stopped because of Kakkari. That I had stopped because I recognized this female as mine.

Monster, my mind whispered.

"I have a strong mind," she informed me, her voice smooth and light. "You might not think so. Many might not think so. But my mind would've withstood anything you gave me. My body would've broken long before."

"I believe that, *kalles*," I told her quietly.

Her hair was wet, I realized, curling black over her shoulders to the middle of her back. Her small eyes were dark, tilted slightly up at the corners, and her upper lip was larger than her bottom one. She was small and too thin. She didn't look like she could lift a bow, much less draw her arrow back. But I'd seen the evidence of her skill firsthand.

She seemed satisfied with my answer and when a *pyroki* ventured close to the fence, she turned her head to look at it. They were curious creatures as well, and I watched as she held her hand out to it without hesitation or fear. I watched with even more disbelief as the *pyroki* nudged the palm of her hand with its sharp snout, smelling her skin.

"Hello," she whispered to it. It towered over her, but she didn't seem afraid. I studied her again, my chest pulling tight with something I didn't want to recognize.

"Have you encountered Dakkari before?" I asked, watching her and the *pyroki* closely.

"From afar, as they rode past our village on these creatures," she responded.

"You do not seem to fear the Dakkari."

"Should I?" she asked, looking over her shoulder at me, frowning. "I've never had reason to."

"I whipped you," I rasped. "You believed you were walking to your execution and you say you never had reason to fear the Dakkari?"

"Your horde warrior whipped me," she said, her brows furrowing in a glare.

"Under my orders!" I growled, my normally tame temper rising again.

"Do you wish for me to be angry with you?" she asked. "Do you wish for me to hate you or to cower in fear whenever you are close?"

Nik, I did not wish for any of those things, though I deserved all of them.

"I want to understand you," was what I told her. "Because I do not know what to make of you."

She sighed. She looked back to the *pyroki*. "I do not respond to things as others might. People in my village...it made them uncomfortable. They like it when you respond like them because it makes you predictable. Somehow predictability means you are safer to be around."

I heard the sadness in her voice as surely as I heard the pounding of my heartbeat in my own ears.

"I neither like you nor dislike you," she told me, looking back at me, holding my gaze. "And I do not hold grudges. You had to punish me because of your king and so you did. It is not my place to question the justness of your laws. This is your planet, after all, and I knew it was forbidden. But unless I break any more of your laws, I have no reason to fear you, yes?"

"You called me a demon," I reminded her. "You seemed to fear me then."

That drew an uncomfortable expression from her and her eyes darted away. "You are one," she informed me, her voice certain and firm. "But maybe you cannot help it."

I had the strangest urge to laugh, but I feared I'd forgotten how. This otherworldly creature, who both mesmerized and maddened me, drew me to the edge of something I'd never explored, something I wasn't sure I wanted to.

But did I have a choice? She would pull me over to the other side whether I liked it or not.

Vodan's words of caution flickered through my mind.

You cannot be swayed. And this female? She sways you. She will.

Sobering, I knew I had to tread carefully. I was a *Vorakkar*. Despite Kakkari's guiding light, despite what I knew to be true, my horde would always come first. Vodan worried because he believed this female would make a home for herself in my mind, that I would forget who I was—what I'd become—because of her.

It was a ridiculous notion, but I had seen it happen before. It had happened to the *Dothikkar*. A female prostitute had whispered into his ear, asking him to grant me entrance into the Trials, though before, only those that came from ancient bloodlines were considered for the position of *Vorakkar*. I did not even carry my father's name. I had grown up in the streets of *Dothik*. No one had known me. I'd stolen to eat. I'd lied to live.

It had sparked outrage in the capitol. Because of that prostitute—my mother—I entered the Trials, breaking centuries of tradition simply due to whispered suggestions and unspoken promises in the *Dothikkar's* bed.

Females were powerful creatures. Dangerous ones. I'd learned that from my mother and I would not underestimate the *vekkiri kalles* standing in front of me, stroking the *pyroki's* snout. The *pyroki* seemed just as enthralled by her as I was and I wondered if she *did* possess a power of her own.

"When can I return to my village?" she asked.

"You wish to?" I asked, my voice nothing but a dark rasp.

She shivered and I frowned. "I don't know," she said. "But I am afraid to stay."

"Why?"

She exhaled, her breath puffing out in front of her. She took her hand away from the *pyroki*, giving it one last pat.

"Because I think I could like it here," she said. I noticed she patted the pocket in her freshly crafted pants and I saw something there. She'd done it almost unconsciously, as if reassuring herself. "And I don't like being disappointed."

Taking a step towards her, I saw the way her eyes flickered up to me in surprise when I drew close. I'd been a thief once, so she didn't feel it when I slipped my fingers into her pocket.

But her dark eyes did go wide when I pulled the small bundle out swiftly and inspected what it was that she hid.

Her cheeks went a little red again and my lips pressed together when I saw it was wrapped food, squashed into a ball, the meat sticking to the *kuveri* loaf, blending the colors and textures together.

Though her cheeks were red, I noticed she tilted her chin up, meeting my eyes directly, as if daring me to challenge her.

"It is a hard habit to break," I told her instead, "but you do not need to do this. Not here. There is always food, even in the cold season."

Even still, I rewrapped the food and held it out to her, knowing she would feel more comforted having it close.

"Eat that by nightfall so the meat does not spoil," I said. "I do not want you sick again."

Her features were expressive, so I knew my words surprised her. She plucked the bundle from my hand, her small, cold fingers brushing mine, and hastily hid her food away again.

"And you should not give your name so freely," I told her next.

She frowned. "Why not?"

"To the Dakkari, given names are important. Those who know yours have power over you."

"What is your name then?" she tried, dangerous creature that she was, looking up at me in expectation.

I was tempted to grin. I was tempted to tell her. A selfish, foolish part of me wanted to, just to see how her mind would use it against me.

But I remembered Vodan's warning and so I did not give her my name. Not then.

"You may continue calling me demon king if you wish, Nelle," I rasped. Her lips parted at the sound of her name. "I *like* it."

8

One, a drum fire sparking into the air.

Two, two Dakkari children running through a hidden maze only they could see between the tents.

Three, a guard at the entrance to the encampment, walking the line of it on patrol.

I closed my eyes, but then paused. I didn't count silently in my head but let the sounds and the smells and the wind float over me. I heard a collection of deep murmurs among horde warriors that floated up to the horde king's tent where I was sitting, perched just outside the entrance. I heard children laughing and yelling in merriment as they played. I felt the icy cold night breeze across my cheeks and swore I saw the gentle orange glow that seemed to hover over the camp behind my closed eyelids. I heard my assigned guard shift from one foot to the other behind me. I heard the Dakkari male in the enclosure I visited earlier barking orders, constructing something in the pen. I smelled the delicious scent of cooking meat combined with a crispness that told me the cold season winds were near.

When I opened my eyes, I saw that the moon, almost a half moon now, hung overhead in the night sky. Sighing, I tucked my knees closer to my chest, resting my chin on my bony kneecaps. My seated position pulled at the wounds on my back, but I tried to ignore it. I'd slept the day away on accident and I woke groggy, thirsty, and hungry to an eerily quiet tent. I'd chugged the water I'd found on the table and then taken out my saved meal, chewing it down quickly.

When I appeared outside the entrance, my guard had taken up his post again, though he didn't protest when I sat in front of him.

I didn't know how long I'd been sitting there. Long enough for my backside to grow numb from the cold ground and to watch the sky deepen from a soft lavender to a darkened indigo.

The horde camp was vibrant, even on the cusp of the season. My village was nothing like it. In the past, my village had held celebrations if there was a marriage, or if the Uranian Federation had dropped a large ration shipment. But they'd seemed like depressing events to me, where villagers where most concerned with when they would eat and who received the largest cut of the rationed meat.

There had been no children playing together—there were very few children in our village at all. Most villagers kept to their homes after dark. Laughter was rarely heard.

There was life here. And though it was cold, I didn't want to give up the sounds of the horde for the oppressive quietness of the tent, as luxurious and warm as it was.

A dark figure approached the small incline up to the tent. I studied the way he walked, how his strong legs ate up the distance quickly, and marveled that someone so large could seem so graceful. I hadn't seen him since that morning, at the enclosure, and I wondered what a horde king of Dakkar did with his day, what tasks he had to oversee.

"Why are you sitting out here, *kalles*?" he asked, frowning when he reached me.

"I don't like to be inside much," I told him. He towered above me, but I kept my eyes on the camp below.

Out of the corner of my eye, I saw him turn to the guard. He said something in Dakkari, no doubt dismissing him for the night, and I watched the guard leave down the slope, disappearing behind a tent towards the middle of the camp.

Nerves began to creep up on me now that we were alone and away from the others. It made me wary, being alone with any male, especially after what Kier attempted with me.

I looked up at him from my seated position. "I was wondering where I go."

"Go?" he murmured.

"Where I should sleep," I corrected.

He exhaled a sharp breath. "You will sleep here tonight."

"But...I'm not sick anymore," I explained to him slowly, as if he didn't understand what I was trying to tell him. When I'd slept in his bed with him—though unknowingly on my end—I'd been sick with infection and fever. That was different.

"My warriors have been busy preparing for the cold season," he told me. "You will have your own *voliki* soon, but not tonight. Unless you wish to sleep out here..."

Frowning, I looked back to the camp. "Surely, there is a spare tent."

"*Nik*," he said. "New *volikis* are only built when a warrior takes a mate or when members join the horde."

My shoulders sagged. Another figure approached the incline. It was a Dakkari female carrying a covered tray. Of food?

"Come inside, *kalles*. Come eat," he told me before entering through the flaps himself, ducking low to maneuver his large body inside.

The female reached me just as I stood, but she brushed past me. When I caught her eyes, they narrowed on me and there was a very decided chill emanating from her stare that had nothing to do with the crispness in the air.

She ducked inside after calling out in Dakkari at the tent's entrance, announcing her arrival. Though Dakkari had certainly stared at me that day, none had seemed hostile or angry...simply curious, as if they'd never seen a human before.

When I took a small breath and ducked into the tent myself, I saw the female out of the corner of my eye. She was bending low at the table, unloading the heaping plates of food and a double loaf of the purple bread I liked. Among the plates were other things, but the food didn't hold my attention for long.

The female was looking at the demon king from under her lashes, taking considerably longer to unload the tray than necessary.

When I looked at him, he was standing by the bed of furs, unbuckling the wide strap of leather attached to his sword's sheath. He'd worn a heavy pelt of fur over his shoulders that day to protect him from the growing cold, but when he shrugged it off, I saw he was bare-chested underneath, revealing his gleaming, golden skin.

I forced myself to look away, though I felt something strange at the sight of him—intense curiosity and something else I didn't want to place. When I looked back to the female, she was straightening, a small smile playing over her painted lips.

She said something in Dakkari, her voice soft and low.

"*Nik*," the demon king replied, only sparing her the smallest glance. "*Rothi kiv.*"

The female's smile dropped ever so slightly. When she saw me watching her, that coldness entered her gaze again and she stalked past, out the tent's entrance, leaving me alone with the horde king.

The silence prickled at my skin. I longed to be outside, longed to be away from him.

To fill that silence, I informed him, "She wants you."

Throughout the stages of my lifetime, I'd always observed the men and women in my village. I saw their secret smiles, I heard the unspoken meaning in their words. I'd singlehandedly discovered that Sam and Una were having an affair, despite their spouses not knowing. It seemed like a lot of work to me, the seemingly endless mating dance of humans. I wondered how Dakkari courted their chosen mates. Was it any different?

But I'd recognized the look in the Dakkari female's eyes and knew what she wanted.

My words caught the horde king's attention. He turned to face me and I was briefly distracted by how his markings shimmered in the dim lighting.

"*Neffar*?" he murmured, but I got the distinct impression that he'd heard me perfectly. He simply wanted me to repeat it.

"I said she wants you. You could be nicer to her, I suppose," I added.

"Wants me in what way, *kalles*?"

Now I got the distinct impression he was laughing at me.

I frowned. I didn't like being laughed at. I was only trying to fill the silence with something he might find useful.

Except...

My eyes narrowed on him.

"You already know," I accused.

"*Lysi, kalles*," he murmured, walking towards me. His eyes burned bright in the low lighting and for a moment, I held my breath. "I already know."

Swallowing, my brow furrowed when he slipped around me to kneel at the low table, the one I was beginning to understand was only for taking meals at.

"Come," he said.

I mirrored his actions, hiding my wince when I knelt. The

black liquid the healer had given me for the pain that morning had begun to wear off.

When I felt him studying me, I commented, "You hardly looked at her. How would you know?"

"She has been with my horde for a few years now," he informed me. "She has made her intentions clear."

"Intentions?"

"She aspires to be *Morakkari*," he told me. "As do others."

"*Morakkari*?" I asked softly, the strange word filtering over my tongue. I thought that like *kalles*, *Morakkari* was a pretty word, one I liked.

"My queen," he told me. His voice went slightly lower as he added, "My wife."

Something pierced my chest at his words and I looked down at the food on the table.

"Oh," was all I said, though I had numerous questions bubbling up inside my mind.

Thinking about it, I figured he was right. He was beautiful—handsome, masculine, and seemingly virile. He was powerful, a king in his own right. Wasn't that what females wanted in their chosen male? Beauty and power and sex?

Now that I thought about it, I wondered why half the females in the horde weren't at his tent, trying to deliver his meals every night.

"What are you thinking of, *thissie*?" he rasped and when I looked up at him, I saw him studying me, his brow furrowed. There was an expression etched into his face, one that reminded me of frustration, but why would he be frustrated?

"Nothing," I said, looking back down at the food. "Can I eat now?"

A muscle in his jaw ticked and he tilted his head down. I took that as my *yes* and I plucked a chunk of meat from the plate.

There was a lot of food, almost four times as much as that morning. In the back of my mind, I thought that this much food would last me a whole week in my village and I mentally determined how I would ration it.

It took me long moments and many stuffed mouthfuls to realize that he wasn't eating. He was watching me from across the low table and seemed very content to do so.

His gaze made me uncomfortable and I snatched my hand back when I realized it was outstretched towards the purple bread loaf.

Tucking my hands in my lap, I licked my lips and stared at the golden inlaid design on the wooden table.

"Here," he rasped a stretch of silence later. When I looked up, he was offering me a small plate of shriveled greens I'd ignored in favor of the meat. "Try."

With hesitation, I took one from the plate and he set it back on the table, taking one himself and chewing it. I watched the way his strong jaw worked and felt a little of my unease drain when he began eating too.

I ate the cold, withered green, but made a noise when the strange flavor burst on my tongue. It was tart and tangy and delicious.

The demon king's lips quirked when he saw me reach for another, but he didn't say anything more during our meal together and I didn't either.

When my belly was full to the point of bursting, I waited for him to finish, since I thought that was the polite thing to do. Jana had always told me so and she'd grown up on one of the old Earth colonies, before they'd been destroyed. Out of the corner of my eye, I studied his markings again. They were intricate and detailed and beautiful.

When I met his eyes, I jolted as I realized he'd caught me looking at them. I didn't want him to think I'd been admiring his chest, like the Dakkari female had, so I asked quickly, "Are those symbols Dakkari words?"

"*Lysi*," he murmured.

"What do they say?" I asked. Jana had been able to read, but she'd never taught me, though I had begged her many times.

He finished chewing his last bite and I saw the thick, golden column of his throat bob as he swallowed.

"They are my *Vorakkar* markings," he told me after a lengthy pause. "My oath to protect my horde above all else."

I looked at them as if I could read them. There was a looping shape with two perfect dots inside it and I wondered what that word meant. I wondered what exactly a *Vorakkar* oath would say.

"Have you always been so curious?" he asked me.

"Yes," I replied immediately, tearing my eyes away from the beautiful, foreign words and looking down into my lap. My wounds gave another sharp throb and I swallowed. "Jana hated it. She told me that it was dangerous to be so curious all the time, to want to know so many things."

"Who is Jana?" he rumbled. "Your mother?"

My breath hitched and my gaze jerked up at him. "No. *No*, I was orphaned on my way to Dakkar. Jana...just happened to be there."

I'd called Jana my mother once when I'd been young. She'd grown so angry that I'd never attempted it again.

His expression was unreadable, but I saw the way his eyes narrowed on me, pinning me in place. Those eyes held mine, ate at me, and my throat grew tight when I realized the demon was doing it again.

It was a relief when I heard a Dakkari announce his presence at the tent's entrance and I jerked my gaze away from him with a shuddering inhale.

"*Lysi*," the horde king called out and I jumped when the tent flaps slapped back.

Not just one but three Dakkari males entered, carrying in buckets of steaming hot water, pouring them into the bathing tub that still remained from that morning, though it'd been emptied sometime during my nap.

When they left, I sat, frozen on my cushion.

"Do you wish to bathe first?" came his low voice.

Swallowing, I watched a trail of steam rise from the surface of the water. I'd never taken a hot bath before. What was it like?

"No," I choked out. "Of course not. That is inappropriate."

That was what Jana would've said, right?

The corner of his lips lifted ever so slightly but he stood.

"Very well," he said, walking to the bathing tub.

"What are you doing?" I asked, my voice reminding me of the Dakkari boy's high-pitched laugh from earlier that morning.

He didn't look at me as he unlaced his hide pants and slid them down his legs, being mindful of his tail.

I blinked, frozen, as the expanse of his bare flesh came into view. For once, my thoughts momentarily went silent.

"Bathing," he told me, as if it were obvious.

9

I think I let out a small squeak of outrage. I couldn't be certain.

All I knew was that I was staring. The demon king effortlessly dropped into the large bathing tub and between his legs, I saw that his massive cock was somewhat erect, swinging with his movements.

Panic seeped into my veins, freezing me in place.

I blinked and stuttered out, "You know, I-I...I'm not like that."

When the demon king sank low into his bath, he made a grunt of pleasure, his eyes momentarily sliding shut as the hot water enveloped his body. My mind caught on that detail and I imagined being cocooned in complete, delicious, soothing heat that way. Longing grew in my heart, even though it fluttered with panicked disbelief.

"Like what, *thissie*?" he rasped, a splash of water meeting my ears as he scooped water over his broad shoulders.

I jerked my gaze away, tapping a rhythm on my wrist with my fingertip. I desperately ached for my bow. I needed that centered focus, that simple act of calm as I nocked my arrow and drew it back. As I inhaled a slow breath and then...released. I used to practice on the wall of my home.

"If this is your plan, keeping me here as a prisoner, all for the purpose of...of *sex*, your efforts will be wasted," I explained in a rush. "I think I am quite immune to such things."

When I chanced a peek over at him, I saw him regarding me, carefully analyzing my words.

"You are immune to what, exactly?" he rasped.

"Sex," I told him, frowning. "Desire. Need. I don't feel those things."

"I think you are lying," he said, ignoring what I was trying to tell him.

"And even if I did feel those things, it wouldn't be for you," I said, irritated and nervous. The tapping on my wrist grew faster.

He went still in the bath at my words. Then he rasped, "If you are immune to such things, if you are immune to me, then my bathing should not bother you, *thissie*. Certainly not this much."

I bit the insides of my cheeks hard and made a conscious effort to slow my breathing.

"I am just informing you now, since I must sleep here tonight," I told him. "The last male who tried to take from me ended up with my arrow in his shoulder."

Silence came from the bathing tub except for an odd scratching noise. When I looked up to identify it, I saw his claws were curled into the sides of the tub, gouging marks into it.

Momentarily, I forgot that I wasn't supposed to look too deep into those eyes and he snared mine quickly as punishment. Right then, he looked every bit like an enraged demon, from the scowl on his face to the scorching heat in his eyes.

"And did he?" he growled, his voice darkening. "Take from you?"

"No," I whispered. "I told you. I had my arrow and..."

The look in his eyes was making me nervous, but oddly enough, it made me stop tapping on my wrist. The look in his eyes made my body still and my mind quiet.

I had a ridiculous thought that maybe Jana was wrong. Maybe letting a demon take your soul wasn't such a terrible thing. It didn't *feel* like a terrible thing. Not right then at least. I felt almost *calm*.

"Who was it?"

"What?" I whispered.

"*What is his name*?" he said slowly, but clearly.

"I thought it was rude to ask for names," I said, wondering why he would ask, given what he'd told me that morning.

"*Vok*," he cursed under his breath before jerking his gaze away. Released of his eyes, I felt my shoulders sag and my nerves return. "You are..."

I waited, tensed and quiet.

Then my eyes shot to him when he rose from the bath, water racing off his bared flesh. Miles and miles and miles of it. I remembered that I'd thought of him as a wall when I'd first seen him. A wall of strength and power, one that took up the entirety of my vision. All I could see right then was him. Even the tent seemed to fall away.

He trailed water all over the rugs as he stalked to a metal chest. He rummaged through it, found what it was he sought, and came towards me, all naked flesh and sinewed power. The sight of him made my throat bob and my eyes wander. For once, I cursed my own curiosity as I felt my cheeks grow warm.

He halted in front of me, his cock swaying between his legs, his heavy, dusky sack just beneath.

Before I had time to react, he dropped something in my lap and then returned to his bath.

A gift? I wondered, my breath hitching when I looked down

at it. It was a dagger hilted inside a beautiful sheath of white bone, etched in gold pigment.

Pulling out the dagger, I saw it was lethally sharp. I could see my reflection in it and I peered more closely, seeing my pale face and dark eyes. I wished I was more beautiful, but figured it couldn't be helped. It was a ridiculous, vain thing to wish for anyways.

"Is...is this for me?" I asked him softly, slowly. With hesitation, I looked over at him. He'd situated himself back inside his hot bath, the steam twirling around him. He'd dunked his head under water and his blond hair dripped droplets over his shoulders.

"*Lysi*," he grunted.

"I can keep this?" I asked, looking down at the dagger, wanting to be sure. "It's a gift?"

He exhaled a rough breath. "*Lysi*. A gift."

"Oh," I said, staring at my reflection in the blade. I'd never been given a gift before. My expression was perplexed, my lips turned down. "What do you want for it?"

"*Neffar*?"

"What do you expect for it in return?"

"I just told you it is a gift," he growled, glaring at me.

"Nothing is free," I told him. "There is always a reason."

"That reason," he rasped, "is so you know you can protect yourself if the occasion arises. That is Dakkari steel, forged by blade masters in *Dothik*. It is far better and far sharper than any arrow and I give you my full permission to gut me with it if you feel unsafe in my presence."

"Are you mad?" I asked softly, disturbed that he was so trusting. "You don't know me. I could kill you in your sleep tonight if I so choose."

"*Vok, thissie*, you will *drive* me mad by the night's end," he growled. "Enough. Let me enjoy my bath in peace."

Looking back down at the blade, I touched the tip, testing its sharpness. Only using the lightest of pressure, a bead of red blood appeared on my fingertip. Satisfied, I sucked the drop away and sheathed the dagger carefully.

"Will you react this way every time I give you a gift?" he muttered, as if he couldn't help but ask the question, though he'd demanded peace.

I frowned, though a treacherous excitement wound its way up my chest. "Will there be more?"

He said something in Dakkari, a longer phrase that he knew I wouldn't be able to understand. Then he went quiet.

"You..." I trailed off, looking at the dagger, wondering if I would have need of it while I remained in the Dakkari horde's encampment. "You really don't want me in that way, right?"

He was a horde king of Dakkar. I was a human. Surely, males like him expected their bedmates to be more experienced, more beautiful, more sensual. As for me, even if I was interested in sex, I wouldn't pick the fierce demon king who'd ordered my whipping as my first lover. I would want someone tender and kind and gentle. I was quite certain he was none of those things.

"I never said that," came his deep reply and a shiver raced up my spine, "but I assure you, *thissie*, that you will be more than willing in my furs when that time comes for us."

When. Not *if*. As if it was a certain thing.

If I'd been the surprised, gaping sort, my jaw would've dropped to the ground right then.

But all I did was glare at him, tracing the inlaid gold on the dagger's sheath.

"Is that why you brought me here? Why am I to sleep in your bed tonight?"

"*Nik, thissie*," he said and I wondered why he kept calling me *thissie*. I wondered what it meant, but knew it was the wrong time to ask.

78

"Then tell me why I am here," I demanded, growing frustrated. "Tell me why you took me from my village, why you had your healer tend to me day and night though my wounds were of your doing, why you give me gifts like this dagger and these clothes, and why I will share your bed this night, though I have been here five days already, and surely that was enough time for you to make other, proper, more...more *appropriate* arrangements."

I was shivering as I spoke, perhaps a little frightened by how he might react, though I'd told him earlier I had no reason to fear him. Looking at him now, the grey rings of his irises freezing me into place, I thought that perhaps I'd been wrong. There were plenty of reasons to fear him, just not the reasons I would've believed at first.

"You call me a demon," he said quietly, "because you believe I am stealing your soul away. But I already told you, Nelle, that if I am a demon, then so are you. Because you are stealing more of mine right at this moment."

His words made goosebumps break out over my flesh, underneath the warm *kinnu* fur sweater.

"That is why I took you from your village. Why you are here."

"I—I don't understand," I whispered, frustrated. "I don't understand what you want from me."

With a growl, he tore his gaze away from mine and leaned his head back on the lip of the tub, staring up at the ceiling of the tent. He splashed his face with water and then rested his wrists on the edge, water from his claws dripping onto the rug.

"I do not understand either," was all he said in reply.

All I heard was the soft thumping of my own heart and a slight, whistling wind that picked up outside the tent.

I didn't know how long we remained in silence, but it wasn't long after that I realized my legs were numb underneath me.

When the horde king finally stood from the bathing tub, I kept my gaze averted. Out of the corner of my eye, I saw him reach for a wrap of fur to dry himself off with.

"You cannot return to your village until after the cold season," he said, his hair dripping across his shoulders, his voice hard and strange. "I will not task my warriors with making that journey now. Until then, you can make yourself useful here. There is much to be done in a horde, even after the first frost."

Biting my lip, I offered hesitantly, "I am good with my bow."

He made a sound in the back of his throat and tossed the fur aside, close to the raised fire basin, so it could dry.

"I know, *kalles*. I saw you hunt the *rikcrun* that night," he rasped and I felt shame fill my chest. "But there is no game during the cold season here and so I will find you another task."

He was still nude when he went around the tent, extinguishing the flickers of flames from the oil lamps, one by one, until the only source of light was the fire. It cast long shadows over his body, but I kept my eyes on his. The fire reflected in those dark, shining orbs made me think of Drukkar, one of the Dakkari's deities. He was said to be unyielding and merciless and fierce.

"Come sleep if you are not going to bathe," he ordered, tossing back the furs on the plush bed before climbing in. Still completely naked.

I rose from the low table, my dagger tight in my grip, and hesitantly approached. Unlike him, I kept every stitch of my clothing on, save for my boots, though I was tempted to wear them. But his furs were thick and soft and I didn't want to muddy them. They were much too nice to be ruined and I trusted, perhaps naively, that he would remain true to his word, that he wouldn't touch me if I was unwilling.

I kept my dagger within reach, however, as I lay down beside him on my stomach, on top of the furs since my back was still too tender.

The winds outside were growing in intensity and I wondered if this was the night the cold season would come.

A rikcrun? I questioned silently, thinking over his words in the stretching silence. Was that the proper term for a grounder?

Hesitantly, I turned my face towards him, pushing my hair away from my eyes. It was the softest and cleanest it had ever been, but I was learning that it seemed to possess a wild mind of its own in this new state.

When he saw me look over at him, he tilted his chin to return my stare, watched as I tucked strands of that wild hair behind my ear.

I'm no demon, I thought. *Or am I?*

"Your hair looked lighter before, but now it is black," he commented quietly. It had looked lighter because of all the dust and dirt clinging to the strands, no doubt. "Just like a Dakkari's."

"Not like yours," I pointed out. I'd seen no one else that day with blond hair in his horde, which led me to believe he was an outlier, an anomaly.

His lips pressed together and I thought I'd displeased him in some way, but didn't know why.

"I want you to know," I began softly, "that I don't like hunting."

He exhaled a long breath, but said nothing.

"I like using my bow and arrow," I continued, "but not for the purpose of killing. I hunted because I had to, because I'm good at it, though sometimes I wish I wasn't."

"I know, *thissie*."

I didn't know why it felt important to tell him. But it did. Perhaps it was my own guilt bubbling up inside me, spurred by the reminder he'd watched me kill the grounder that night. Because sometimes I thought that if Blue hadn't been injured that summer day in the Dark Forest—if she'd been perched on a branch or flying close above the canopy of the trees—would I have leveled my bow at her too? Would I have calculated how many credits Grigg would've given me for her? It made me sick thinking about it.

"What does *thissie* mean?" I asked, clearing my throat when it tightened.

He didn't tell me. Just like his name, he kept that answer close, too.

"*Veekor, kalles,*" he told me. "Sleep."

10

On my second day of exploring the horde encampment, I realized that I was being followed.

Not just by the scarred guard that the demon king had posted outside the tent, but by a small crowd of curious Dakkari, mostly females and children, though a few males were among their number.

It was strange, I thought. Except for the occasional frowning stare, I'd gone so long remaining unnoticed in my village, going about my day-to-day activities. Now, wherever I went, every Dakkari seemed to notice.

Of course they would notice, I whispered quietly to myself. I was the only human in the horde. It was hard to blend in.

I just hadn't expected an audience trailing me, murmuring quietly in Dakkari whenever I turned to inspect something new.

Just when I had made my way to the front of the encampment, I felt a tug on the back of my sweater. Two sharp tugs.

When I looked behind me, to my surprise, I saw the little Dakkari boy from yesterday, the one who thought my eyes were odd.

I was happy to see him and felt the corners of my lips tug up.

"Hello," I greeted him quietly, noticing that he clasped something in his little palm.

"Heel-loo," he repeated, sounding out the strange word, his voice loud but happy. When he grinned up at me, I saw that he was missing one of his sharp, small teeth, something I hadn't noticed yesterday.

A sensation tugged in my chest. Something warm and simple. I'd always liked children. There weren't many in my village, but of the ones there were, I thought they were honest and pure and innocent. Their words didn't hold any other meaning than what they truly meant and the happy light in their eyes hadn't yet faded from weariness and hard years.

"Hello," I whispered again, smiling, before clearing the lump in my throat. I knew he didn't speak the universal tongue so he wouldn't understand anything I said to him. Instead, I touched the silky black strands of hair on his head, patting him, wanting him to know something that couldn't be spoken in words.

Aware that a small group of Dakkari were hovering a short distance away, I belatedly hoped I didn't commit another social sin in their eyes, considering the demon king had told me yesterday that I shouldn't have given my name out.

I didn't want to offend anyone. If I was going to remain in the horde through the cold season, I wanted them to like me.

I wanted...

I bit my lip. I wanted to not be so lonely there. For a short time at least, I had a fresh start in a place that was completely different than my home. I had the rare experience to live among a Dakkari horde, something that was completely unheard of among humans. The prospect might seem daunting or intimidating...but I also found it incredibly exciting. An *adventure*. Something I'd always wanted, right?

And so, I wanted them to like me, even if I was strange.

Relief burst through me when the boy's grin only widened

after I patted his head and then he was thrusting something towards me, whatever it was he had in his palm.

It was a rock.

Taking it from his hand, I brought it closer to my face and saw that it was beautiful. It was small but held a shimmering, iridescent sheen, transitioning from blue to green to pink to silver, depending on how I tilted it in the light.

I wasn't used to smiling, but it felt natural on my face when I looked back at the boy.

"It's very beautiful," I said softly, holding it back out towards him.

A thread of worry shot through me when his face dropped, his grin sliding away. He looked crushed as he looked at the rock in my hand, outstretched towards him.

"Oh, no, I didn't..." I trailed off, at a loss, wondering what Dakkari rule I'd broken now.

"He wants you to have it," a soft, accented voice said to my right. When I turned, I saw a Dakkari female standing there, her dark hair braided down her back, in a white fur shawl and a dark yellow dress that brushed the tops of her booted feet.

"He...does?" I asked, my gratitude mixing with worry.

The female stepped forward and held her arm out for the boy, who immediately wrapped his arms around her legs. My lips parted in realization and I felt longing pulse in my breast.

"You're his mother?" I asked.

"*Lysi*," she replied, running her fingers through his dark hair. "All he has done is talk about you since yesterday. I wanted to meet you for myself."

The rock still hung in my grip and the boy hid his face against his mother's leg.

"Please tell him I'm sorry," I begged softly. "I didn't know it was a gift. I hope...I hope he's not upset with me."

The female smiled at me and despite the circumstances, I

felt myself relax. She tilted her chin down and spoke to the boy in Dakkari, a string of soothing, soft words that made him raise his head.

When he looked at me, I saw that his eyes were wet as he peered at me, as if trying to assess whether his mother's words were true.

"I'm sorry," I told him, bending at my knees so I could look at him straight on. "I didn't know." I looked down at the rock and forced a smile for his sake. "It's lovely. The best thing I've ever seen."

His mother spoke to him again and only after she translated my awkward words did the boy chance a small, hesitant smile at me.

When his smile grew, I felt relieved. Slowly, he disentangled himself from his mother's legs and looked from the rock in my palm to me. Then he seemed to grow shy, the space just underneath his eyes growing darker, and he took off before I had a chance to say anything else, weaving his way through the tents until he was out of sight.

His mother's small chuckle drew my attention. When I looked at her, I couldn't help but feel envious of the obvious love and affection in her eyes as she gazed after her son.

When she turned to me, she said, "My father told me he met you as well."

The older male who'd offered me some of his food?

"Yes," I replied, a little unsure what to say as I clutched the rock in my palm, my hand growing damp around it despite the bitter chill in the air.

Though her voice was accented, her words were sure and confident as she asked, "How are you finding your clothes? I was not sure if they would fit."

Surprise jolted through me and I looked down. "You were the one who made these for me?"

"*Lysi*," she replied. "I hope you find them suitable. There was only so much I could do in that short time. I am still working on your shawl for the cold season, but it will not be ready for another few days."

A shawl too?

"Oh," I murmured. A little overwhelmed, I realized I didn't know how to handle all these niceties, all these gifts being thrown my way. Her expression dropped a little and I said quickly, clutching the rock, "They are wonderful. Thank you. It's just...I, um, had the same clothes for years. I didn't expect all this." I gestured over the garments she'd created for me.

She frowned. "You cannot expect to wear the same clothes every day, *lirilla*. These will be sufficient until I can finish your shawl and then begin on another set."

Blinking, I protested, not wanting her to waste time on something unnecessary. "These will be more than enough for me. Truly."

"It keeps me busy," she said, her tone a little defensive. "I enjoy the work."

Sucking in a small breath, I bit the inside of my cheek, fearing that once again, I was insulting another Dakkari.

"I'm sorry," I whispered. "I'm terrible at this."

"Terrible at what, *lirilla*?"

I thought *lirilla* was a pretty word too and I told her, "I don't know your customs. I don't know what to say so I don't hurt anyone's feelings. What I meant was that I'm used to not having many things. I wouldn't want you to waste your time making garments for me when you could spend that time for others in your horde."

Understanding dawned on her face, though it was subtle. There was a calmness about her, a steadiness and a patience that I envied.

She reached out to touch my clothed forearm and I stared at her hand.

"For one, *lirilla*," she said, stepping closer when she cast a look at the growing crowd, "always accept gifts given by the Dakkari."

A terrible thought occurred to me. "Did I insult your father yesterday morning by not taking the bread?"

Her soft chuckle made me feel better. "He is an old male who does and feels what he pleases. He has earned that right with his age. He likes to laugh and he said you made him laugh. That is all you need to know."

Thinking of the dagger the demon king had given me last night, the dagger that I had tucked into the deep pockets of my pants, alongside the leftovers I'd wrapped again that morning, I asked, "Do you give something to someone who's given you a gift?"

"Only if you wish to," she assured me, "but reciprocation is not expected."

There were a thousand questions bubbling up in my head but I decided to hold my tongue. She was being kind enough to explain these things to me and I didn't want to take advantage of it.

Instead, I said, "Thank you." I opened my mouth, about to introduce myself, before I realized that I wasn't supposed to give out my name.

"*Lysi*?" she asked, tilting her head to the side.

Sheepishly, I said, "I was told not to give my name out, but among humans, it is polite to introduce yourself to someone new."

Wasn't it? I frowned, realizing I hadn't spoken my name in a long time. At least until yesterday. Before then, when was the last time I'd told someone my name?

I couldn't remember.

"*Lirilla*," she informed me.

"What?"

"It is what females call one another when they have become acquainted, but are not yet friends."

Not yet friends.

Hope and longing burst in my chest so suddenly that it surprised me.

"And there is a possibility to become friends?"

Her eyes darted between mine. "*Lysi*," she said softly. "If you wish."

I nodded, wondering if I should hide my excitement or not. Except for Blue, I'd never truly had a friend. Jana had perhaps been the closest to it, but the label seemed strange attached to her.

"I wish that," I told her softly, giving her a small smile. She didn't look to be much older than I was, though she had a young son. I wondered if that meant she had a mate. "*Lirilla*."

Her hand on my forearm squeezed and then dropped away. "*Lysi*."

"That is only for females? What do you call a male who is an acquaintance?"

I wondered if I could give the demon king yet another name, since he refused to give me his own. At the very least, I could address my guard, who stood a short distance away, among the onlookers.

"*Kairill*," she said slowly.

Ky-reel, I whispered the word in my mind, committing it to memory.

I heard a strange ringing sound echo throughout the camp, beginning suddenly and without warning.

Frowning, I looked around trying to identify it. "What is that?"

The Dakkari female said patiently, "Training begins. It

sounds as if the *Vorakkar* is among them." My confusion must have been evident because she smiled, though it seemed strained to me, and said, "Go around the *voliki* there, *lirilla*. You will see for yourself."

Her mood had changed, though it was slight. An uncomfortable tension stretched in the empty space between us, becoming more palpable as the ringing sounds grew louder.

"When I have your shawl finished, I will come visit with you, *lysi*?" she told me.

Nodding, clutching her son's gift in my hand, I said, "I would like that."

She gave me one last smile and then disappeared quickly in the direction her son had gone. Then I turned where she gestured and slowly walked towards the sounds, my curiosity stoked like an ember.

It didn't take me long to find the training grounds. They were quite hard to miss, in fact.

Inside a gated area, near the front of the encampment, were about a dozen horde warriors just beginning to spar one another. Close to the center, the demon king was among them, his golden sword ringing and hissing loudly as it connected with his opponent's. For an incredulous moment, I thought that surely the blades weren't real. The sparring looked much too real, brutal and rough. What happened if they accidentally injured one another?

Perhaps that is the point, I realized. How else would you become a better warrior if you did not know fear?

I didn't dare to venture closer, instead deciding to stick close to the nearest tent, as I watched what unfolded before me.

Pure strength radiated from the warriors. It was in the graceful lines of their bodies, the strong, powerful arcs of their swords as they brought them clashing together in teeth-chattering rings. But it was also in the rough edges—the punches, the shoves, the physicality of fighting that went beyond their talented swordsmanship.

So, this is the might and power of the Dakkari, I thought, wide-eyed. And it was as terrible as it was mesmerizing.

My eyes couldn't stay away from the demon king for long. Naturally, my gaze sought him out, trying to ignore the knowing that went through me, remembering waking in the middle of the night only to find my cheek pressed to his shoulder and my fingertips over his bare, chiseled abdomen. I'd reared away from him the moment clarity had returned, but I'd been too shaken to fall back into a deep sleep. What was worse was I knew I'd edged over to him during the night, as if, in sleep, my body knew how lonely and desperate I was for simple touch, for the warmth of another.

I remembered that right then, looking at the demon king. He'd been so, so warm.

Watching, I saw him grab his opponent's sword arm at the wrist, twisting his body forward before bringing his own blade up to the warrior's neck. A single line of blood appeared, a warning, a reprimand for the warrior's defeat, and then the horde king pushed him away, looking for another.

In his determined perusal, his eyes caught mine across the barrier of the training grounds, his chest heaving, earth coating his legs and the sides of his chest from a brief scuffle. Though other warriors, even horde members—females, males, and excited children alike—had gathered at the fence to watch, his eyes still found mine.

Like a coward—with my breath hitching and my heart jolting at whatever I saw in his eyes—I turned on my heel and fled.

11

I t was dark when I returned to my *voliki*. The biting wind
made my jaw clench and in the distance, I heard the *mrikro*
still in the *pyroki* enclosure, barking orders at the warriors I'd
assigned to him. Though the hour was late, the *pyroki* master
was driven to finish the last of the nesting dens before the first
frost came.

When I reached the entrance of my tent, I inclined my head
at the warrior standing guard.

"Any problems?" I asked him.

He shook his head. "*Nik*. She wandered around the encampment most of the day and then watched the *pyrokis* in the enclosure. The healer is in with her now changing her dressings."

Inhaling a long breath, I said, "*Kakkira vor*," and then
dismissed him from his post for the night.

When I ducked inside the *voliki*, I heard a splash of water
from the bathing tub and saw Nelle inside, obviously startled by
my appearance. The healer was kneeling by her side, carefully
washing the edges of her wounds, and my lips pressed together
when I saw they were still reddened and raw, though they had
healed considerably over the past week.

The sight of them brought a swift reaction of anger—though I did not know whom that anger was directed towards—and I jerked my head away, crossing to my cabinets to undress.

Out of the corner of my eye, I saw the *kalles* watching me. She was leaning forward in the bathing tub, aided by the healer, pressing her breasts to her knees. Humans were strange about nudity, I noted, whereas Dakkari were not.

"Up. Let me dress the wounds," the *kerisa* said in the universal tongue, finished cleansing the *thissie's* back. Her inky black hair was wet and washed, clinging to her damp shoulders. Her skin was unblemished and smooth, but so pale that it seemed almost translucent, making the wounds on her back seem all the more brutal and vicious.

A sensation rose up in me, powerful and consuming. I wanted to protect her. I wanted to shield her from beings like me.

Monster.

I didn't understand it, but my whole body tensed with the need to protect her.

I watched the *kalles'* eyes dart towards me at the sound of the *kerisa's* order. I heard her thick swallow. Her eyes went to the furs on the bed and she gestured towards them wordlessly.

The *kerisa* stood and gathered one, brought it back, and held it open as Nelle stood, small rivers of water racing down her body. My jaw clenched when I caught sight of her rounded breasts, despite her best attempt to hide them, and focused on unstrapping my sword, ignoring the pulse of awareness that went down my spine.

Once the *thissie* dried her body, the healer began dressing her wounds, covering them in a light cloth. When she was done, Nelle immediately began to dress and only when she was fully covered did her shoulders relax.

Her nerves and wariness around me were insulting, but

given what she'd told me the night before, how a male in her village had attempted to rape her—a thought that made violence and fury burn in my gut—I could understand it. I didn't like it, but I could understand it. So I didn't comment and after I dismissed the healer, once we were alone, I asked her instead, "Have you eaten yet?"

I noticed her tapping a rhythm on her wrist as she faced me, something she'd done last night as well.

"Yes," she said, nodding. "Earlier."

"Are you tired?" I asked next. She was nervous inside the *voliki* with me when we were alone, I noticed. At the hesitant shake of her head, I decided not to undress and instead brought her one of my coverings, a heavy pelt of *kinnu* fur that would keep her warm enough. When she was within reach, I placed the fur over her small shoulders and secured it. It looked like a cape on her body, falling to her knees.

I watched as she touched it hesitantly, stroking the softness of the fur, and at her bewildered look, I told her, "Do not worry, *kalles*, it is not a gift. Come with me."

She didn't ask where we were going as I led her from the *voliki*. Something told me she was just pleased to be outside. I wondered if my home felt like a cage to her. I wondered why she grew calm but focused when she was in open air, underneath the night sky, with the chill brushing her reddening cheeks.

The encampment was quiet, the hour late. I had come straight from a meeting with my council after discussing what else needed to be done before the first frost, which could come at any moment. We also discussed my impending journey to *Dothik*, when the moon was full at the request of the *Dothikkar*. I would go alone, which Vodan hadn't liked, but I would not subject any warriors to that long journey during the cold season, not when they could be with their mates and their families instead. The cold season was a time for rest and reprieve. I would not deny them of that.

"Why is it that you train as hard as you do?"

Her question was soft-spoken, but curious, and I was reminded that I'd seen her at the training grounds earlier in the day.

"Why is it that you fled the moment I caught you spying?" I asked her in return. Her legs were shorter than my own and I slowed my pace when I noticed her struggling to keep up.

She frowned up at me and when I caught her eyes, I wanted to grin. She ignored my question completely, commenting, "Humans are surely no great threat to you or your horde. You must know that. Yet you are all so skillfully trained in combat, one would think you were preparing for war."

"Are you complimenting me, *thissie*?"

Her frown deepened and I was relieved that she no longer seemed tensed and wary. Rather, she was back to her inquisitive self—the one who'd shamelessly peeked into the common bathing *voliki* as she paraded around my encampment—and frustrated I was not giving her the answers she sought.

"Especially during the cold season, I would think you would not need to train at all," she continued. She waited. When I remained silent, she tried, "*Do* you train through the cold season?"

"For someone like you, I am wondering," I said, the training grounds coming into view, "how much you need to know the answers to your questions. Is it painful not to know?"

"It is very irritating," she replied immediately.

I couldn't hide my small grin and she stared up at me, her eyes darting between my bared teeth and my eyes in surprise.

I sobered and asked, "How many questions do you have?"

"Too many."

"What do you wish to know the most?"

She opened her mouth, the question right on her tongue, but then she hesitated. When we reached the barrier to the training grounds, I halted and turned to look down at her, giving her the full weight of my attention. She blinked up at me with those dark eyes, but asked me nothing.

"You are right, *thissie*," I informed her when she chose to remain silent, frowning. "It is very irritating."

"I will tell you if you answer the question I ask," she told me.

"Bargaining now?" I asked, pressing my lips together, trying to hide my own interest. "You wish to bargain with a *Vorakkar*?"

"I do," she said, though she seemed surprised by her own answer. In fascination, I watched her next expression flicker across her features: doubt. Then her resolve hardened and she seemed determined.

I thought I knew which question she might ask, but I couldn't be certain. I could never be certain with this *kalles* and I didn't know if that frustrated or intrigued me.

"Come," I told her, stepping through the opening in the barrier to the training grounds, waiting as she followed.

"What are we doing here?" she asked finally, gazing around the darkened, empty space. A single barrel fire illuminated the large enclosure and cast most of the far end into shadow.

Walking over to the weapons rack built into the back barrier of the enclosure, I pulled a bow and a quiver of steel arrows out. They were rarely used, as most Dakkari warriors preferred swords and blades, but they were useful on longer hunts.

When I handed them to Nelle, she looked up at me with her wide eyes, her hand curling around the golden bow instinctively.

"What is this?" she asked softly. She knew exactly what they were, that wasn't what she was asking.

"You told me you like to use your bow and arrow but not for the purpose of hunting," I said, reminded of what she'd quietly murmured to me the night before, laying in my furs. "Why is that?"

"I..." she trailed off, licking her reddened lips, and stared down at the bow in her hand. "I like the focus of it. The steadiness of it. Sometimes it feels like breathing." Then she frowned and jerked her head up at me, "That is unfair. Now you owe me an answer to one of my questions."

"We have not made that bargain yet," I reminded her. I plucked a few arrows from the quiver in her hands, leaving her with three. "Three chances to hit the farthest pole on the barrier over there."

I gestured to where she could direct her remaining arrows, to a thin, narrow, wooden pole that stabilized a section of the fence in one of the darkened corners of the training enclosure.

She looked over at it and I watched as her shoulders straightened, as her mouth parted and her eyes hardened. A sizzle of awareness heated a path down to my belly and her obvious confidence made my cock twitch behind the pelt of fur, a reaction that took me off guard. My nostrils flared when she met my gaze and said simply, "I can do it. Three chances?"

"*Lysi.*"

"And since we are bargaining...what else do I get besides an answer to my question?"

Greedy kalles, I thought, my lips twitching in time with my hardening cock.

"*If* you hit the target," I said slowly, putting emphasis on the first word, "I will give you your answer and you may use the bow whenever you wish, as long as my warriors are not using the training grounds."

She wanted that. I saw it in her gaze.

"And?"

My brows rose. "What else do you want? But I warn you, *thissie*, the more that's at risk, the more I will demand if you fail."

"I want my own tent by tomorrow night," she said, raising her chin. "No later."

A memory rose from the night before and I took a step towards her. "Ah, *lysi*. I agree. If I do not build you your own *voliki* soon, then I am in danger of being suffocated in my own bed, considering how you clung to me last night."

Her cheeks flamed through her glare.

"Very well," I told her, inclining my head. "Anything else?"

She was tempted, I could see it. But the looming reminder that I had yet to state my demands if she failed made her shake her head. "What do you want, demon king?"

"I do not think you want to know."

She pressed her lips together. "If you want sex, you can forget this bargain altogether."

"Not sex," I corrected. "But I do require an *alukkiri*."

Her expression showed her suspicion. "An *alukkiri*?"

"In addition to whatever task I assign to you, you will also assist me with my oils every night."

"Your...*oils*?" she asked slowly, her expression bewildered instead of appalled.

"During the cold season, our skin becomes very dry and can crack if not properly cared for," I informed her, suppressing a grin. "As *Vorakkar*, I have the luxury of selecting an *alukkiri* to assist me with this. That will be you if you fail."

"You cannot be serious," she said slowly.

"It is entirely up to you," I told her. "You wished to bargain. This is my demand if you are unsuccessful."

"For how long?" she asked, frowning.

Amusement rose in my chest and I informed her, "Any female would jump at the chance to be my *alukkiri*, *thissie*. I am starting to feel insulted."

"*For how long?*" she repeated, her question clipped.

98

"Two weeks," I told her. "Or I suppose I can just choose to make it your task in my horde for the entire season."

Her lips pressed together. "One week. And my dagger will be very close by, demon king."

I couldn't hide my grin then.

"We are in agreement," I told her. Her eyes narrowed on me and I jerked my chin in the direction of the pole. "You may begin whenever you wish."

Her shoulders set and she turned. Setting the quiver on the ground next to her, she plucked out a single arrow and I saw the first instance of doubt on her features.

"What is it?"

"It's heavy," she murmured, almost to herself. She judged the distance again, looking towards the single pole in the darkened corner.

"It is not made of wood and feathers." Like her old bow had been.

She took in a small breath and I watched as she expertly nocked the arrow despite her observation. Her movements were smooth and familiar, as if she'd done it hundreds of times before. Which, perhaps, she had.

The bow was much too large for her. It was made for a Dakkari warrior, not a *vekkiri kalles*. But she didn't hesitate again and I admired that.

Rapt, I watched her pull back the arrow, the cord of the bow pressing into the side of her cheek as she steadied it. Though her arm trembled slightly from the weight, from the tension of the cord, I saw her inhale a slow, measured breath, her eyes focused, her shoulders relaxed.

I couldn't tear my eyes from her as she exhaled on the release, not even turning to see where the arrow landed.

By her expression, I knew she'd missed, and when I finally

managed to look, I saw it had skidded low on the ground, a short distance from the pole.

She had her second arrow nocked before I turned back towards her. Adjusting her stance, adjusting her grip, adjusting the angle of the bow, she inhaled...and then released.

A dull thud sounded but when I turned, I saw she'd hit the bottom of the fence, not the pole.

"One left," I murmured, my feet taking me a step closer to her. When her gaze flicked up at me, I saw her determination, but I didn't see a hint of worry.

It should disturb me how much I was drawn to her. Vodan's warning filtered through my mind but I shook it away as she nocked her last arrow.

Heart thudding a deep, even rhythm in my chest, I noticed she took more time assessing the distance.

However, she was growing fatigued from the strain. The tension from the bowstring was more than likely irritating the wounds on her back, though she didn't show it. And though she'd been steadily eating and regaining her strength, she'd been bedridden with fever just a couple days ago.

A part of me thought I shouldn't have brought her out here. But something told me she wanted to be there, regardless of the outcome, that she would spend the entire night in the training grounds if she could.

She inhaled and then exhaled. The arrow shot from the bow with a whistling hiss.

Thud.

When I turned to assess her final shot, my shoulders straightened.

"A deal's a deal," she murmured. Her eyes met mine, the bow hanging from her grip, her chin tilted up.

My cock was hard and pulsing underneath my fur coverings. Her hair was still wet from her bath and the bowstring had cut a vertical line across her cheek, stung from the cold. Her dark eyes gleamed, reflecting the light from the single barrel fire. I saw pride there, not the expected defeat.

Did it make me a monster to want her so much? To want her warming my furs? To want her on my cock, on my lips, to want her wherever and whenever I could have her?

"When do I have to start?" she asked quietly, the only question she would have answered that night.

Swallowing, I took the bow from her grip, noticing that a small shiver raced through her body despite my heavy pelt across her shoulders. An animalistic, primal part of me liked that my scent was on her now. A claim. *My* claim.

My voice was as dark as my need as I rasped, "Once the first frost comes, *rei alukkiri.*"

12

Three nights later, the winds came, aggressive and punishing, scouring their way across the planet's surface like crawling, seeking fingers.

A small part of me was relieved that my own tent wasn't yet finished. While I'd lived through many cold seasons in my village—and many of those alone—being out on the plains of Dakkar was a different experience altogether. Though the encampment had the mountain at its back, protecting us from the south, it made the winds from the north—and east and west—seem even more violent, whistling around the ancient stone behind us so that a constant hiss reverberated around the camp.

It set my teeth on edge and made me tap on my wrist, though that tapping had extended down to my toes as well.

The horde king noticed my nerves that night and reassured me with, "It will quiet in the morning, *thissie*."

Even the jarring sound of the wind wouldn't stop me from eating my meal. Though the normally delicious fare tasted like ash in my mouth, I still chewed and swallowed mechanically. I'd already gained much-needed weight in the past week. I could feel it in my hips, in my thighs. No longer did my bones protrude almost obscenely from my pale skin.

"The winds last year went on for three days before the frost came," I told him softly.

"Drukkar was punishing last year," he said. "He was angry because of what happened in the east."

He'd already finished eating, not seeming at all concerned about the winds. However, he was still sitting with me at the low table, his back to one of the poles that stabilized one side of the tent's domed ceiling, one leg bent, the other stretching out towards me. In his lap was his sword, which he was sharpening and cleaning with efficient precision after his training session earlier that afternoon.

We'd done this every night for the last three nights. We took our meal together and he waited for me to finish, either looking after his seemingly endless supply of weapons or simply watching me, which always made me squirm. It was as if he knew my nerves were already on edge, so he directed his intense attention elsewhere that night.

After I finished eating, he would take his bath, which was already set up in the far corner of the tent. He would undress in front of me without a care and I would try not to look at his golden, sculpted flesh as he sank into the bathing tub. I would try not to hear his pleasured groan and I would try to ignore the strange sensation deep in my belly whenever I heard it.

After he was done, he would climb out, dry off, snuff out the flames, and tell me to come to bed, since he knew I would not bathe with him in the tent. In fact, I specifically bathed in the mornings, once I was certain he was gone for the day.

Then we would sleep. I would sleep fully dressed and he would sleep fully naked. And always—*always*—I would wake sometime in the night to find myself pressed close to him.

Last night, I'd found my face against his side, my lips

brushing the hard edge of his pectoral muscle. I'd felt his heart-beat against my cheek—steady and strong and sure, everything he was—and I'd lain there longer than I would admit to myself, listening to it, imagining a life that I didn't have as I smelled his skin before I pulled away. I could understand the appeal of bed partners and that knowledge made me uncomfortable.

"What's east?" I asked, picking at a chunk of meat.

"The Dead Lands," was what he replied, his eyes on his blade.

I frowned. "I've never heard of them. What's there? What happened last year?"

He met my gaze then, his lips slightly quirked at the corners, and I knew what would come before he said, "More questions? You know our arrangement."

Pressing my lips together in annoyance, I returned, "So the Dead Lands must be important. If you don't want me to know the answers, you always bargain with me for them."

Ever since the night in the training grounds, he'd been doing it. If I asked simple questions, safe questions, about horde life or what a word meant in his language, he would answer me easily and without hesitation. But for other questions, about his scars or about whether he'd been raised in *Dothik*—which I assumed he was, considering he spoke the universal tongue—he threatened me with more time as his *alukkiri*, whatever that meant.

"And I know what you're doing," I continued. "You bait me with the Dead Lands, knowing I need to know more, and then you won't tell me anything. It's simply cruel."

"You gave me the title of demon king, yet you are surprised when I act like one, *thissie*?" he returned.

"Fine," I said. "Will you at least tell me of Drukkar?"

He set his sword to the side, giving me the full weight of his stare, and suddenly, I wished I could take the words back.

Whenever he looked at me this way, I felt pinned in place, wanting to move, but also wanting to stay completely still.

"The only thing you need to know about Drukkar is that he will punish any who threaten or harm Kakkari," he said, his voice low and soft, "in any way."

"Why?"

"Because he loves her," he replied simply. My chest jolted at the word, longing shooting through me with a sharpness that stole my breath. "He is bound to protect her at any cost and to seek vengeance on those that wrong her."

"As are you," I reminded him softly, knowing that it was his duty to punish those that harmed Kakkari, who embodied the earth, who embodied *life* itself for the Dakkari. Whispers had recently come to our village that another human settlement had set fire to their land...and that the nearest Dakkari horde had gone to execute the one responsible.

"The *Vorakkar* are extensions of him, *lysi*," he said, but his voice held something strange I couldn't place.

"And is that what you did, or one of the other *Vorakkar*? Did you punish those that wronged Kakkari in the Dead Lands last year?" I probed. "Or was Drukkar still not satisfied and that was why the winds came so strongly?"

He knew what I was doing and he stood, his hands going to the tied leather belt that held his fur pelt in place over his groin. I held his eyes, not about to be frightened into submission as his pelt dropped to the rug and he was standing nude in front of me.

I could see his cock at the bottom of my vision, though I kept my eyes glued on his. It was large and seeing how it was almost fully erect—a state I'd grown so used to the past few nights that I wondered if all Dakkari males were like this—it made it near impossible to miss.

However, unlike other nights before, my eyes dipped, seemingly on their own because surely, I would never look intentionally. My eyes widened when I saw the thin golden markings, similar to the tattoos covering his flesh, around the thick base and head of his cock, glimmering in the low light.

The astonished words were out of my mouth before I could stop them. "Surely *those* aren't your *Vorakkar* oath as well."

He made a sound in the back of his throat—low and deep and amused—even as his cock twitched. My head swam, my face heated, and I jerked my gaze away, that strange sensation of warmth prickling my skin again.

"*Nik*," he rumbled, walking around me, his bare thigh brushing my shoulder. "They are my oath to my future *Morakkari*."

I stared across the domed tent at the bed of furs, hearing the demon king enter his bath. I waited for his small groan and when I heard it, my lips parted and my breath hitched in response.

His *Morakkari*. His queen. His *wife*, he'd told me.

"Why is it that you haven't taken a *Morakkari* yet?" I asked next, itching to know exactly what the oath said, yet too cowardly to ask *that* question. Something told me he would tell me, too, if only to watch the tapping on my wrist increase in rhythm.

"Would you like to add another week, *rei alukkiri*?" he replied, his tone almost lazy, and I knew it was another answer he didn't want me to know.

When I was certain he was safely cocooned in his bathing tub, with only his broad shoulders and the top of his chest visible, I turned to regard him.

"Is it required that you take one?" I asked, squeezing my fist together when my fingers started twitching. "Perhaps there is a time limit for that sort of thing once you become *Vorakkar*."

"A time limit?" he repeated slowly, his lips quirking again into that maddening smirk.

The ends of his hair darkened into brushed gold as it pooled in the water. Disappointed, I licked my lips and asked him quietly, "Will you answer none of my questions tonight?"

Something in his face softened, but I thought that surely it was just a trick of the light.

"Come here and I will answer your question, *thissie*," he murmured, looking over at me from the edge of the bathing tub.

For a moment, I stayed completely and utterly still. His voice was deep and quiet, but somehow, both panic and calmness infused my veins at his command.

That was when I knew he was truly a paranormal entity—a demon or a god, I couldn't be certain—because right then, with that voice, with those eyes, I thought that surely he could make me do anything he wished.

Curious, though my hands trembled and a shiver raced down my spine, I drew closer. With a heavy gaze, he watched me inch over to him. Only when I was kneeling next to the bathing tub, when I was within arm's reach, did he say, "It is not a requirement to take a *Morakkari*, but no *Vorakkar* has led a successful horde without one for very long."

"Why is that?" I asked, my voice edging towards a whisper, my gaze rapt on his own. Though the winds outside the domed tent had picked up in intensity, I still felt the need to whisper.

"A horde is only as strong as its *Vorakkar*," he told me. "And a *Vorakkar* is only as strong as his *Morakkari*."

Lips parting, I heard the truth of it in the reverence of his voice. His grey eyes bore into mine and I sensed him shifting closer towards me.

"So why is it that you haven't taken one yet?" I asked. "If she would make you stronger?"

"Because there is much I wish to accomplish as *Vorakkar*. I have great plans for this horde, for myself. And when I take my wife, I want to be certain."

"Of what?"

His jaw set and I watched his throat bob as he swallowed. "That she will have the strength, the determination, and the will to stand with me, at my side, to see those plans through, no matter the cost."

He was weaving a thick spell around me, pulling me in deeper and deeper. His voice threaded down my throat, into my chest, looping around my ribs, until it tangled in my belly, filling it, warming it.

"Stop," I whispered, my brows furrowing, my voice clogged in fear. "Please."

He knew what he was doing. I saw it in his eyes, but I also saw his lips set in a firm line.

I heard the trickle of water as he lifted his hand. My eyes closed briefly when the roughened pads of his fingertips made contact with my cheek. His hand was warm from the water and his actions held no hesitation or doubt as he traced my face.

Eyes opening, I felt the tip of his claw brush my bottom lip and I sucked in a small breath, the sensation startling, goose-bumps breaking out over my flesh.

"You do not have to fear me, *thissie*," he murmured softly.

"I still think I should," I said back. Because whatever he was stirring within me, whether they had been dormant or nonexistent before, were certainly fearsome things.

He pulled his hand away and rested it on the edge of the bathing tub. I stared at it like it was a lethal weapon, even though I felt warm from his surprisingly gentle touch.

Just then a loud, violent, echoing crash sounded from somewhere in the encampment and I let out a startled squeak. My heart stuttered and the demon king cursed, jumping from the bathing tub with lightning quickness.

Worry clogged my throat when I heard cries of alarm follow

the crash and the horde king was already dressing, though he was soaking wet.

"I can help," I said, trying to calm my racing heart, already reaching for my boots at the end of the bed.

"*Nik*," he growled, hastily securing the heavy pelt of fur over his wide shoulders. "Stay here. Stay warm."

He was storming from the tent before I could get another word in and the chilling wind that blew inside after his departure made my bones freeze.

Still, I heard the echoing shouts from outside. They sounded like they were coming from the front of the encampment and I didn't want to sit around and wait if help was needed.

Mind made up, I disregarded the demon king's order and snagged his spare pelt quickly, looping it around my shoulders, though it dwarfed my small frame and my muscles grew tired under its weight.

Without a second thought, I ducked through the entrance of the tent, straight into the beginning of the cold season, straight into Drukkar's wrath.

13

"What happened?" I growled, intercepting a warrior who was racing towards my *voliki*.

"A portion of the fence failed," he shouted over the wind. "It collapsed inwards on three *volikis*."

My lips pressed together. "How many were injured?"

"Two warriors," he said, keeping up with my rapid pace as I raced my way through the camp. "But they are not fatally wounded. The healer is with them now."

Relief only made my pace quicken, but grim realization swiftly took its place once I reached the front of the camp and saw the extent of the damage.

It was chaos. Freezing rain had begun to fall and it pricked my exposed flesh before turning to ice on the ground. Through the rain, I saw five posts of the towering fence had fallen, just as the warrior had said. Three of the *voliki* were crushed in, the hides soaked from the rain, the wood splintered into fragments.

The wind was fiercer there, now that there was no protection from that portion of the fence. Funneling inside, it whipped its way through the front of the camp and I heard shouts from warriors, from families, from females and children, as they tried to keep the protective layer of hide from tearing off their homes. Without it, the wind would tear through the *volikis* like they were made of parchment.

I saw Vodan across the way as more of the horde rushed from their homes, roused by the commotion.

Over the wind, I shouted, "Keep the hides tied down! Get these posts up and brace them!"

I joined the group of warriors hefting up the heavy posts. They would need to be placed back one at a time, given their weight and the ferocity of Drukkar's winds.

I met Vodan's eyes across the clearing and I bellowed, "Get the steel braces from the reserves!"

He inclined his head and ordered a group of warriors to follow him as we lifted and fought to reposition one of the posts. By the time Vodan returned, we had it in place so the other group could hammer the heavy steel braces into the remaining post at its side and secure another brace behind the post to give it strength against the winds.

We worked methodically through the freezing rain, our muscles shaking from the cold and the strain.

After the second post was secured, I looked behind me at the horde and saw groups at the affected *volikis*, struggling to keep the hides tied down.

For a moment, my stomach dropped because I spied Nelle among them. Despite my orders for her to stay inside, she was gripping one of the ropes in her small hands, leaning back as she fought to keep it from lifting. Two warriors and another female were securing the same *voliki*, and even from that distance, I saw her strain and fight to keep the rope in her grip.

A growl rose in my chest when I saw the end of the rope whip across her cheek, her face jerking to the side...but she never let go.

"*Vorakkar*," Vodan shouted through the rain. When I looked

at him, I saw they were ready with the third brace and I forced myself to look away from Nelle, refocusing my attention on the task at hand. The sooner we repaired the fence and stabilized it, the sooner we would all be out of immediate danger.

It took us a chunk of the night to repair the damage. I ordered every last fence post to be braced so none of the others were in danger of falling, depleting our stores of spare steel. I would need more delivered from *Dothik* or from one of the outposts after the cold season.

Throughout it all, I saw Nelle a handful of times when I turned to look for her. Always, she was helping the horde, helping with the *volikis*, though I saw the strain it put on her.

When the half moon was beginning to sink in the sky, once I was satisfied that the fence would last through a dozen cold seasons, once I was certain that no more homes were in danger from the winds, I went to look for Nelle.

When I found her, she was next to a young warrior named Odrii and a barrel fire, which barely flickered with flame. The warrior wore a worried expression on his face, which made my pace quicken.

"What is it, *thissie*?" I rasped when I reached her.

In the low light of the fire, I cursed when I saw she was pale and shivering violently. When I touched her cheek, it felt colder than the rain. It was then I noticed that she was soaked through to the bone. Even my furs around her shoulders did little to keep her warm.

"*Vok*," I growled. Turning to the warrior, I bit out, "Bring hot water to my *voliki* immediately."

"*Lysi, Vorakkar*," the warrior replied and rushed off.

I scooped Nelle up, ignoring the stares of the horde members I passed, and raced to my *voliki*. Once we were inside, I drew her over to the fire, which still burned, and threw on more fuel, growing it until it roared and flickered in its gold basin. In the light, I saw her skin looked a little blue, her veins more noticeable under her translucent flesh.

She hadn't spoken and that was enough to make me worry.

"I told you to stay inside, *thissie*," I murmured, ripping my furs from her shoulders. Her clothes were dripping on the rugs and though my own were soaked through, Dakkari could withstand colder temperatures. Humans, apparently, could not.

A violent shiver racked her body just as the young warrior ducked his way inside the tent, followed by another, each carrying bucketfuls of steaming hot water from the common bathing *voliki*.

Once they filled the bath to the brim, replacing the cold water from earlier, they left, though Odrii threw a worried glance at Nelle on his way out.

Quickly, I stripped her of her clothes, throwing them near the fire, and steam curled off them.

"What is this?" I rasped down to her, still worried that she hadn't spoken. "You will not fight me when I undress you, *kalles*?"

When she was naked, I scooped her up again and she hissed when my wet clothes touched her bare flesh.

"I am sorry, *thissie*," I murmured to her, slipping her into the hot bath.

A startled cry escaped her and I gritted my teeth, knowing the hot water was probably painful against her freezing flesh.

"It will pass," I tried to soothe, kneeling next to the bath. "It will pass, *kalles.*"

Her eyes were dilated when they met mine. I dipped my hands into the water, warming them so they wouldn't startle her, and I ordered, "Dunk your head under."

She was still shivering, but did as I said. I helped her resurface as she sputtered.

I rose and went over to one of my chests, pulling fermented

wine from my stores. I brought it over to her in a goblet and had her sip it.

"This will help warm you from the inside," I told her, having her take another sip, though a rattling cough rose from her chest after the first.

Another shiver ran down her spine and finally she spoke, through pale lips, "I c-can't get w-warm."

My jaw clenched. "Just give it time, *rei thissie*."

There was a harsh mark across her right cheek and I knew it was from the rope. I remembered the way she'd fought to keep the hides tied down and my chest squeezed with a familiar sensation, the same one I'd felt when I saw Kakkari's light in her eyes.

"You were brave tonight, Nelle," I murmured, my voice low, as I skimmed the backs of my fingers over the mark. "Thank you for helping."

She blinked at my words, her pale lips parting. Outside, Drukkar's winds still raged and for a brief, startling moment, I was furious with him. For putting my horde in danger, for putting Nelle in danger. For injuring two of my warriors.

Let it go, I ordered myself, like all fierce emotion I experienced. I didn't let myself feel it for too long. I couldn't.

A drip of water ran down my arm from the furs around my shoulders, into her bath, and I was reminded that I was still soaked.

After I gave Nelle another sip of the fermented drink, I rose and went closer to the fire, undressing quickly to warm up. I stood there, nude, for a brief moment, feeling the heat flicker across my skin. But it didn't take long for my body to return to its normal state, even as my *thissie* continued to shiver in the hot bath.

When I returned to her, she had dragged her knees up to her

chest and hugged her arms around them, folding in on herself in an attempt to get warmer.

The three lashes across her back looked purple in the light. The *kerisa* had Nelle stop wearing the bandages and the salve once the skin had begun to heal over. Though they still looked tender, the flesh had mended, but it didn't stop my belly from churning at the sight of them. It didn't stop my mind from going back to that morning, from remembering the way her body jerked as the first lash fell, from remembering her soft cry after the third.

She'd told me she wasn't angry with me for the whipping, but how could she not be?

My fists clenched as I kneeled next to the bathing tub. Her face was turned towards me, her uninjured cheek pressed to the top of her knee, those dark eyes tracking my own.

"W-will the fence h-hold?" she asked.

"*Lysi*," I rasped, my voice dark with my thoughts. Underneath the water's surface, I saw her breasts, her slim waist. She had put on weight in the past week, for which I was relieved and grateful.

"Was anyone hurt?" she whispered.

"Two warriors, but the healer is with them," I said. I would check on them in the morning.

I saw her eyes flutter briefly before she reopened them and I knew she needed sleep. When I dipped my hand into the water, I realized it was beginning to cool from her body.

After another long moment, I decided that I could keep her warmer than her bath could and pulled her from the tub.

I dried her off quickly next to the fire, though I was still worried when she didn't try to fight me off. Once I was satisfied, I wrapped her in a thick fur and carried her to bed.

She didn't fight me when I dragged her close. Even when I parted the furs, even when I pressed her bare skin against my body so that she could absorb my heat, she didn't fight me. I cocooned the both of us and she pressed her still-cold cheek into my side, shivering, and shoved her hands between the furs and my back.

I felt her pebbled, tight nipples but I tried to fight off the poorly timed desire that rose. She would only retreat if she felt it, so I kept my need close, knowing that getting her warm was the most important thing that night.

But I didn't expect how good it would feel...holding her close. That primal part of me that I tried to keep locked away reared its head and thickened my cock and made that moment feel so right. Like I was always meant to hold her like this.

"*Veekor, thissie,*" I rumbled, tightening my arms around her lashed back, spreading my warm palms over her thickening scars, and tucking her legs between mine. "I will keep you warm tonight."

14

When I woke the next morning, I knew where I was the moment I opened my eyes.

I knew that I was naked, flushed and warm, my lips and fingertips tingling, wrapped in the demon king's arms. My cheek felt raw from where the rope had whipped me.

My first coherent thought was, *He is still here?*

Usually when I woke in the mornings, he had already left, gone to seek out his duties for the day. Usually, I only saw him again after nightfall, when he returned to the tent, which I now knew was called a *voliki* in Dakkari.

The night before returned to me in an instant. The winds, the fence crashing, the ensuing chaos in freezing rain, the hides ripping up from the tents as families rushed to save their homes.

And then what happened afterwards...

The icy coldness that spread through my body after hours of being exposed outside. Any ounce of warmth was immediately sucked away. I remembered the demon king taking me inside, stripping me, placing me in the bathing tub of hot, painful water as heat prickled through my limbs. I remembered his gentleness...I remembered him calling me brave.

My limbs were all around him, clinging to him. Legs between his own, one arm draped over his abdomen, my face pressed into his warm neck, my breasts pushed against the massive barrel of his chest.

It embarrassed me. But I was warm, that frightening coldness banished from the night before.

When I dared to pull my head away and braved meeting his eyes, I found that he was already awake. I found those eyes on me, half-lidded from sleep, yet somehow still alert.

The need to say something, *anything*, made my throat tighten, but a single sound would not emerge.

It was him that broke the silence between us.

"I think I wish to keep you in my bed, *thissie*," he rasped, his voice dark and rich. "I thought it was I warming you, but it was you warming me through the night."

My face went hot but when I went to pull away, his arms tightened around me, keeping me in place. One of his arms was underneath my head, cradling my neck, the other was draped over my hips. I felt his palm grip me there and my skin had never felt so hot before.

Though he held me in place, I didn't feel the fear I'd felt before. For a strange reason, I knew he would never touch me, or try to take from me, if I did not wish for it. I felt that truth deep in my gut.

I think I surprised myself with that realization because I frowned, my brow furrowing together.

His grey eyes flickered between mine and he asked, "What is it?"

"Nothing," I replied quickly, not wanting him to know the direction of my thoughts. "I'm quite warm now," I informed him, hoping he would take the hint to let me go.

"I know."

"Why are you still here?"

"Because I wanted to be certain that you were alright," he replied, his expression changing from slightly amused to serious. "You made me worry last night, *thissie*."

His words made my hands curl into his chest unexpectedly. No one had ever worried about me before and I didn't know how his admission made me feel.

"I'm alright," I assured him softly.

"And this?" he asked next, bringing his hand from its place on my hip to gently brush over the rope mark on my cheek. "It will bruise."

"I'm alright," I repeated, swallowing thickly at his touch. Because I felt an uncomfortable sensation building in my chest, I asked him, "What does *thissie* mean?"

"That reminds me," he murmured, not answering my question for the hundredth time. "I have a gift for you."

Why was it that the prospect of a gift made my breath hitch and excitement flood my belly? I was discovering that I liked gifts very much—my new clothes, my dagger, and my rock most of all—and I wondered in the back of my mind if I should be embarrassed about that. Jana would tell me I was being greedy.

His fingers moved at the nape of my neck, sliding up into my hair. My scalp tingled pleasantly as my treacherous and curious tongue asked, "What is it?"

The demon king seemed content to look at me for another long moment, his eyes tracing over my face. But then he shifted and rolled away from me, pushing up from the bed. His sculpted backside met my eyes as chilly, frigid air rushed forward to take his place.

Wrapping the furs tighter around me, I watched as he moved to the three chests lining the opposite side of the tent. I'd never seen him open them before and I'd often been tempted to snoop inside, though I'd denied that curiosity.

Still, it didn't stop me pushing up and sitting on the edge of the bed, craning my neck around him to try to catch a peek.

The horde king lifted the lid on one and took something from within it. I spied silks and sheer things, something glittering gold and blue, before he closed the chest again.

His expression was knowing when he turned back to me and saw me trying to look into the chest.

"You cannot help yourself, can you, *kalles*?" he murmured, his lips quirking.

My eyes darted to his closed fist and I said, distracted, "No."

When my gaze caught on his cock, still hard and erect and bobbing as he walked, I felt my belly tumble, though it wasn't... unpleasant. It was the opposite, in fact, and I didn't know how to feel about *that* either.

He stopped in front of me, drawing my eyes away from his cock, and I tilted my neck back to look into his eyes. He reached for me and helped me stand as I clutched the heavy furs around my body.

Whatever was in his hand, he looped it around my neck and I felt something familiar settle just above my breasts.

When I looked down at his gift, I sucked in a shocked breath, my nose tingling with tears as unexpected emotion flooded my chest.

My vision went blurry as I gently reached for the pendant of the necklace he'd given me.

They were Blue's feathers. Cleaned and soft and shining. The bases of the whitened, pointed shafts were embedded in a spherical gold clasp, keeping them secured to the chain of the necklace.

I'd thought them burned, gone forever, but he must've taken them from my old clothes when I'd been sick with fever.

"Now you will not lose them," he said.

A tear fell down my cheek and I dashed it away with the back of my hand before I looked up at him.

"I would have given them to you sooner, but they were brought back to me just yesterday. There is an older female in the horde, one who crafts jewelry and trinkets. She made it."

I smiled up at him, overwhelmed that he would give me such a precious thing. When he saw my smile, something in his expression changed.

"Thank you," I whispered, delighted and happy with the gift, reaching out to take his hand, lightly squeezing his palm. Before I pulled away, he threaded his fingers between my own and kept me close until the furs I had wrapped around me brushed his chest. "I thought they were gone."

"Why are they so important to you?" he asked softly, his eyes flickering to the feathers.

"She was my companion for a few years," I told him. "I found her in the Dark Forest with a broken wing, fluttering on the ground. I took her back to my village and fed her and cared for her for a long time. I named her Blue because of her feathers. She couldn't fly anymore, but I think she was happy and so was I." I looked down at the pendant, feeling his fingers tighten briefly. "Then I woke one morning and found her dead. I don't know why. But I took some of her feathers to remember her and then buried her in the Dark Forest because that's what we did with Jana when she died."

His hand came to my cheek and he tilted my face back so I met his grey, stormy eyes. It was then I realized I was growing used to his touch. It was then I realized I could easily grow to crave it, to *need* it.

"*Thissies* prefer the mild seasons towards the south, so it is very abnormal to find one so far east. But perhaps you were meant to find your *thissie*. Perhaps Kakkari wanted you to."

My lips parted as realization hit me. "Blue was a *thissie*?"

He inclined his head.

"But why do you call me one?"

"Because I saw you that first night in the woods outside your village. I saw the *thissie* feathers on your arrow and thought that you were very much like one. Watchful, rare, and beautiful."

I'm not beautiful, I wanted to inform him. But then I realized I didn't want to. If he thought I was beautiful, then I would allow him to continue thinking that. It made a strange thrill race down my spine at the prospect.

A strong desire to know his name entered my mind. "Does this mean that we're friends now?"

His lips quirked. "You wish to be friends with me, *thissie*?"

My bare toes curled into the rug underneath my feet when he said that word. Because now I knew what it meant and why he called me it.

"Yes."

"Very well, we can be friends."

"So that means you have to tell me your name," I informed him as his fingers began to stroke over my own. "That's how it works, right? That's what the seamstress told me."

His laugh was husky and warm, contrasting against the bitter temperature in the *voliki*.

"Relentless," he murmured gently. "*Nik, kalles*, I quite like our games. But since we are friends now, I will give you another chance with the bow once the winds die down. *Lysi*?"

I was eager for the bow again and I nodded, looking back down at Blue's feathers, admiring the pendant and the chain, only mildly disappointed I wouldn't know the demon king's given name that morning.

"I won't miss again," I told him. "I'll have your name when the winds are gone. I am quite determined."

"Then I may just have to raise the stakes to deter you," he said.

"What does that mean?"

He laughed again and I felt it all the way to my toes. He pulled away and began to dress.

"You will find out, *thissie*."

15

The winds still raged through the morning and afternoon that day. Shortly after the demon king had left, I'd attempted to venture outside. The thought of being cooped up for the entire day made me antsy, but the moment I'd stepped outside, my stomach had dropped.

The ice rains had begun, whipping through the air with the furious winds. A droplet had caught me across my exposed cheek, right over the mark the rope had left. When I'd squinted out over the camp, I'd seen with relief that the fence was still standing. However, with the exception of a few brave souls, the encampment had been empty and quiet. Briefly, I'd wondered where the horde king had gone, but soon, as another drop of frozen rain narrowly missed my eye, I'd been forced back inside.

So, instead, I'd paced the domed space, listening to the rain hammer down on the *voliki*.

Sometime in the afternoon, the rain seemed to lessen, but before I could explore outside, two Dakkari warriors were entering the tent with buckets of hot water.

One of the warriors I recognized. He'd been with me the

night before, helping me secure the hides when the wind had ripped them up.

I smiled at him as they replaced the bath water, but then noticed that a third person had entered the tent, another familiar face.

"Oh," I said. "You came!"

The seamstress, the mother of the young boy who I'd met earlier in the week, smiled and inclined her head in greeting.

"*Lirilla*," she greeted with the familiar word. "I am glad to see you are well. My brother told me what happened last night, how you'd taken ill."

My brow furrowed but when I watched the warrior from last night step closer, my lips parted in realization. "He's your brother?"

"*Lysi*," the warrior replied. "I am."

I wondered what it was like to have a sibling and as I watched them exchange a look, I couldn't help but feel a tad envious of their bond.

"Thank you," I told him. "For staying with me last night, for helping me."

My appreciation made him uncomfortable because his eyes darted to the floor of the *voliki*.

"It was nothing at all, *kalles*," he said once his sister prodded him in the side. He looked back at the other lingering warrior near the threshold of the tent and inclined his head. Gruffly, he said, "We will leave you now. I am glad that you are well."

Before I had the chance to say goodbye, he departed with the other warrior, leaving me alone with his sister, who I noticed had a heavy bundle of furs in her arms.

My pelt, I realized when she set it down on the rug and unwrapped it.

"I apologize for the delay, *lirilla*," she said, shaking it out and presenting the pelt for me. It was white and heavy and thick. It was *clean*, spotless, and I'd never seen something so luxurious. "I also have another set of clothes for you."

It took me a moment to realize she was eyeing the clothes I was presently wearing with interest.

When I looked down, I flushed, remembering that I was wearing the demon king's clothes, considering my own set was still wet from the night before and drying by the fire. He'd given me a long, heavy tunic that reached my knees and a heavy pelt to help fight against the growing chill.

Even I knew what this looked like. I was a human female staying in a Dakkari horde king's tent, sleeping in his bed, eating his food, and wearing his clothes.

Naturally, she would assume I was his whore so I said carefully, "The *Vorakkar* has been very kind letting me stay here while my own *voliki* is built."

Although now I wasn't certain I would get my own. Three *volikis* had been crushed last night during the winds and several more had been damaged. Surely my own would take last priority.

My *lirilla* gave me a small smile. It was kind, but I got the sense that it was just as careful as my tone had been.

"*Volikis* are easy to build," she told me. "If the *Vorakkar* has ordered yours, then it will be ready soon. Now, how about you try these on and I will see if any adjustments need to be made."

I did as she requested and tried on the new set. It was similar to my other one, consisting of long, fur-lined pants, a heavy tunic, and another sweater...in addition to the pelt that wrapped around my shoulders and covered my back.

The seamstress hummed and inspected everything thoroughly. "I will need to shorten the hides slightly. Perhaps you wish to bathe while I finish them."

I nodded and took off the clothes. Strangely enough, I was getting used to being naked around the Dakkari. Between the healer, who'd helped me bathe, and the demon king last night, getting undressed in front of my *lirilla* seemed easy.

When I sank into the tub, I felt the heat wash over me and in the back of my mind, I heard that groan that the *Vorakkar* made whenever *he* slid inside his bath. It prickled my skin and I reached for the washing rag as a distraction.

When I looked over at the seamstress, she was already hard at work on the bottom hem of my pants.

"These are only for the cold season, obviously," she said. "Once the frost leaves, I will make you other sets for the warmer months and for travel. Dresses and skirts. Prettier things."

I stilled. Something in my chest warmed at her words, as if it was an obvious thing that I would remain there.

"I am only to remain during the cold season," I said softly, remembering the horde king's words, that he wouldn't risk journeying back to my village during that time.

She looked up at me. "You miss your home and wish to return?"

I swallowed.

No, I thought. I had only been among the horde for a short while, but already, I felt like a weight had been lifted from me. During my time there, I hadn't killed a single creature, I ate regularly and heartily, I was properly clothed and outfitted for the coming frost, and there was a prospect for...for a life beyond just trying to survive from one day to the next.

"Life is very different here," I said softly, scrubbing at my arms, avoiding her question. I was growing used to bathing every day as well, to my hair always being clean and my skin being streak-free from dirt and grime and sweat.

"We do not know much about the *vekkiri* settlements. I have never seen one," she commented.

Pray that you do not have to see one, I thought.

ZOEY DRAVEN

"I will begin on your clothes regardless, *lirilla*, later in the season," she told me. "You never know. You may decide to stay."

I didn't think it was up to me, but I kept quiet.

"As for the frost feast," she continued, sighing, "perhaps I can alter one of my old gowns for you."

I frowned. "The frost feast?" I repeated.

"*Lysi*," she said, smiling up at me as she began to hem the pants. "There is no set night for it yet, but I suspect the *Vorakkar* will announce it soon. We celebrate the beginning of the cold season with a feast. Usually a few days after the first frost comes."

"And...I would need a special gown for this?" I questioned.

"*Lysi*," she replied, frowning. "Of course."

My lips twitched at her slightly offended expression and I nodded. "Alright then."

"There is much to do before then," she said. "But I will alter one for you. Do not worry, *lirilla*."

"Do you need help?" I questioned, watching her fingers work over the cloth. I'd crafted my own clothes before and I'd quite enjoyed it. I liked that it kept my fingers busy, that it required quiet concentration and carefulness.

"Help?" she asked.

I bit my lip. "It's only that the *Vorakkar* told me he would find a task for me to do through the cold season. To earn my keep here." The seamstress blinked. "I was thinking that perhaps I could help you, if you need it. I might not be good at first, but I learn fast."

Something in her expression softened and she let out a small chuckle.

"*Lysi*," she said. "If the *Vorakkar* says that you can, then I would welcome your help. Females and males alike have already been making orders and requesting repairs. It is always like this

128

during the cold season and there are only so many seamstresses among the horde."

"I'll ask him," I said eagerly, hopeful for something to do during the day other than wander around the encampment.

She inclined her head and we lapsed into a small stretch of silence as she finished taking off a finger's worth of material from the pants hem.

After I finished scrubbing my body with the washing rag, I glanced back over at her, only to notice she was looking around the tent in between her sewing.

When she saw me looking, her head ducked and she smiled, though it seemed sheepish. "I have never been in *Vorakkar's voliki* before."

I thought of the females that brought our meals in the evenings and remembered the demon king's words about them, how most aspired to be *Morakkari*.

"Does that mean you've never vied for his attentions?" I asked without thinking. It took me a moment to realize that the question may have come off as rude and my face heated. "I'm sorry, I didn't mean it the way it sounded."

She didn't seem offended, which made relief rush through me. I liked her and I wanted her to like me. I wanted to be friends, so the last thing I wanted was to offend her.

"*Nik*, I never sought his attentions," she murmured, looking back down at her work. "When we came to this horde, I had a mate and I was pregnant with his child. I was in love and when you feel that kind of love, of Kakkari's light, you look at no other. Not even a *Vorakkar*."

The reverence in her voice pulled at my chest and I felt longing at her words.

"I wondered if you had a mate," I commented, thinking of her son.

Even from the short distance, I saw her lips press together. "I do, but he is dead."

I sucked in a breath, stilling in the bath.

"But for me, matehood is lifelong. He is still my mate and always will be. I will not take another. I could never, knowing that he would never measure up."

Her pain was palpable, as tangible as a solid thing.

"I'm sorry, *lirilla*," I whispered. "I didn't realize."

"You could not have," she said, threading another stitch and glancing around the *voliki* again. "He was a warrior for the horde. He died in battle, earlier in the year."

I remembered the day I met her, when the warrior training had begun at the training grounds. I remembered her face when she heard the ringing metal and the hiss of blades. I'd thought at the time that I had somehow made her uncomfortable, but perhaps the sounds had been a reminder of her warrior mate.

"I'm sorry," I said again, not knowing what else to say, frowning. I knew loss, but I didn't think I could ever understand her kind of loss. Being in love was a luxury few experienced. Only three couples in my village were love matches and I remembered watching them, thinking they lived in their own world, where it was just the two of them. I remembered being envious, all while knowing I would never experience something like that. Not there.

She waved her hand and gave me a small smile before refocusing her attention. "He gave me many wonderful years and a son. I could ask for nothing else, though sometimes it is painful to be here."

"Have you ever thought of leaving the horde?" I asked softly.

"*Nik*, never," she replied. "My son is happy here, my father loves horde life, the freedom of it. My mate grew up in a horde, as my son will, and I feel closer to him here." She looked back up at me. "As for the *Vorakkar*...well, most would follow him anywhere. He is good and fair. He wants what is best for us all. So, *nik*, we would never leave."

I could believe that, that many were loyal to the demon king.

We lapsed into silence again and when my skin had begun to soften and prune, I stood and dried off with a spare fur.

When I reached for my new sweater—since the thought of putting on the demon king's tunic once more left with me a strange sensation—the seamstress said quietly, "*Lirilla,* you are bleeding."

My brow furrowed and I looked down my body, turning my arms, searching. "What? Where?"

But then I saw it. A trail of red blood leaking down my inner thigh.

I stilled, my lips parting. I hadn't bled for four or five months, so the sight surprised me at first.

"Oh," I murmured, biting my lip. I looked at the seamstress and said, "I need some..."

There were scraps of spare cloth from her bundle and she grabbed one and brought it to me.

Pressing it between my legs, I said softly, "Thank you."

16

S he was sitting at the low table, quiet and still, looking down at the half-eaten meal laid out before her.

"*Thissie*," I called, ducking low into the *voliki*, but remaining near the entrance. Startled, she looked over at me, her back straightening ever so slightly. "You have eaten?"

"Yes," she replied.

I'd been gone since morning, meeting with my *pujerak* and the elders before checking the fence, checking in on the injured warriors—who'd suffered a few broken bones, but were on the mend—checking in on the *pyrokis*, on Lokkas, whose nests had miraculously avoided destruction last night. Then I'd helped with the *volikis'* construction and repairs once the freezing rain had ceased. They would be finished by tomorrow afternoon, even Nelle's promised one, and a part of me was tempted not to tell her quite yet.

"Then come," I murmured. "The winds have stopped."

She blinked, looking around the *voliki* as if she could discern the truth of my words with her eyes and not her ears. But after a moment of quiet, she said, rising, "So they have. I didn't even realize."

She was wearing a fresh pair of clothes and I saw a new pelt of white lying across the edge of the bed. One of the seamstresses must've come that day and I was pleased that she would have something warm to wear that night.

She approached me after looping the pelt around her shoulders and toeing on her boots.

"I've offered my services to the seamstress," she informed me, slipping from the tent when I held the heavy flap open for her.

Following her, stepping back out into the icy air, I felt my lip quirk. Something had loosened in my chest at the sight of her, at the sound of her voice. I'd found myself thinking of her much too often that day. She was slowly becoming a distraction.

When I said nothing to her words, she looked back at me and raised her brow.

"What are you asking, *rei thissie*?" I murmured, amusement helping to unknot the tension I felt in my shoulders from the long day.

"Can I work for her?" she asked, falling into step beside me. "You said you would assign me a task through the cold season and I think I would like to help her with her work."

"I was going to assign you to her father," I informed her, glancing over to judge her reaction.

She blinked. "Her father?"

"He is a weapons master. Trained in *Dothik*, one of the best," I told her. "Since you are so fond of your arrows, I thought you could assist him in making more for the horde. Our hunting season begins after the thaw."

The prospect intrigued her, I could see it plainly on her expressive features.

"I can do both," she offered quickly. And with those wide eyes, I could deny her nothing. That should have made me wary, but I ignored the warning in my mind.

"If you wish to," I told her. "You can work with her father in the mornings and with her in the afternoons, *lysi*?"

She nodded eagerly. "Now, with that out of the way, are you ready to negotiate for your name?"

A surprised chuckle escaped me. "I thought you would not miss again, so is there a need for negotiation?"

"I still want my own *voliki*," she reminded me, her tone going a little low and quiet, "in addition to your name."

I sobered slightly, reminded that her new home would be ready tomorrow.

"But perhaps I can negotiate a practice shot in?" she murmured, casting me a hopeful look. "Just one?"

"Now you are being greedy, *kalles*," I rasped, the training grounds coming into view.

The encampment was mostly deserted that time of night. With the winds gone, it was the quiet before the storm. The frosts would come soon, perhaps tomorrow or even during the night—I couldn't be certain.

"But since we are friends," I murmured, that word bringing a flurry of amusement into my chest, even as a darker need and a wicked idea mingled with it, "I will give you the first shot for a price."

"What is it?" she asked, her tone tinged with suspicion.

I hopped the barrier of the training grounds and reached out to pull her over easily, if only to get my hands on her again. She sucked in a surprised breath when her feet left the ground, but I resettled her close so that her breasts brushed my chest when she breathed.

Nelle blinked up at me and my eyes settled on her lips, desire beginning to pulse through me. I remembered my reaction to her when I'd seen her skill with the bow. I remembered her easy confidence, her intense, quiet focus that felt erotic to me. I remembered my need for her, even as I remembered her professing her immunity towards sexual desire and arousal.

Vok, I cursed silently, before releasing her. A part of me wanted nothing more than to test her words and make a liar out of her. Perhaps I would.

As I walked over to the weapons rack, I tossed over my shoulder, "For your first shot, if you fail, I want a kiss."

Silence.

The request was innocent enough, yet I held my breath as I waited for a reply.

After I collected her bow and a sheath of arrows, I turned back to her. She was watching me. Unlike the bewilderment I'd expected, she looked pensive. Her watchful eyes tracked me carefully, as if I were the intended prey for the head of her arrow.

I felt my cock thicken in a dizzying rush and my hand squeezed around the bow. Sometimes I did not understand my own reactions to her, as if she controlled my body and played with it as she pleased.

"How is that for a starting negotiation, *thissie*?" I rasped down to her, my voice husky from my thoughts, before handing her the bow.

"Very well," she said.

I stilled. "*Neffar*?"

"You did not expect me to accept?" she asked. *Now* her expression veered towards bewilderment even as she plucked an arrow from the sheath in my hands. "A kiss is a very small thing, isn't it? And this is a very large bow. I would be foolish not to accept so I can practice at least once."

She explained it so matter-of-factly that I could only stare as she nocked her arrow.

"The same target as last time?" she asked, her eyes already

tracking to the post on the far end of the training grounds. She'd nearly hit it before with a bow twice the size of her old one, made of heavy Dakkari steel. I was certain that if she didn't make the first, she would surely connect with her target on her second attempt.

"*Lysi*," I said, though my voice came out more like a growl.

Her eyes flicked to me, connecting. Her lips parted even as her gaze narrowed. I could practically read her thoughts.

Demon king, her eyes said.

Demon thissie, mine said back.

She jerked her attention back to the target. Her hand was exposed to the icy air and looked pink, her veins a mixture of green and blue. I didn't want her outside for long, given what happened last night, but at least the rains and the winds had ceased...for now.

I heard her soft inhale, saw the way her lips pursed, how her features relaxed.

On her release, the arrow flew, whizzing past me, and I heard it connect with the fence.

When I turned, a sizzle of victory burned down my spine.

"When do you want it?" she asked, staring at her arrow, which had gone only a finger's width too wide.

"After," I rasped. "If you do not make this next shot, what will you give me, *rei thissie*?"

Her lips settled into a hard line. She plucked her second arrow from the sheath and had it nocked before I could blink.

"*Now* negotiation will not be necessary. I won't miss this time. I'm certain," she informed me. A second later, her arrow flew and I couldn't stop my grin from forming when I heard it *thud*.

I didn't even need to turn to know she'd finally hit her target. Her expression was pleased, her accomplishment settling over her shoulders as surely as her fur pelt.

"My *voliki*?" she asked, her breath fogging silver in front of her, her cheeks pink, and her eyes wide.

"It will be ready in the afternoon," I assured her, taking a step closer until she was within arm's reach. "This will be your last night in my bed."

Her eyes darted between my own. When I looked down, I spied the chain of the necklace I'd given her earlier underneath her pelt and the thick sweater. Reaching out, I touched the chain. It was warm from her skin. Her skin was soft underneath it.

Nelle's breath hitched, but she didn't look away.

"And your name, demon king?" she whispered.

Vok, I wanted to taste her lips.

And I can, I reminded myself, my blood pulsing and hot at the thought. *I will*.

Threading my fingers into her hair at the nape of her neck, I pulled her closer and dropped my head.

Her surprised exhale whispered across my lips, small and hot. I stopped before our lips touched.

"You are the one who owes me the kiss, *kalles*," I purred, feeling my bottom lip brush her top one, and I felt that contact all the way down to my cock.

Her solemn, wide eyes were dark. I felt her heartbeat thrumming between us. Underneath my thumb, I felt a vein in her neck throb wildly.

I saw when her mind was made up. She leaned forward and pressed a chaste, short kiss to my lips before trying to pull away.

A dark grin curled my lips but I kept her in place, dragging her forward when she tried to retreat.

"Nice try, Nelle."

Her eyes widened when I took what I wanted from her, *how* I wanted from her.

I kissed her. Hard yet gentle, slow, and consuming. My hand

tightened in her hair, my amusement dying quickly as realization and lust took its place. Just like last night, holding her in my arms, *this* felt right. Fated. A deep growl rose in my throat.

Her lips were as soft and sweet as they looked and I felt her shuddering sigh between us as a shiver racked her body. I groaned, pressing closer, pressing *her* closer. I could never be close enough. Her heart raced under my fingertips but I was certain the pace of my own matched hers.

She pulled away after another moment. Too soon, but I let her retreat. Placing a palm on my chest, she used me to steady herself. Her eyes were half-lidded and wild, her lips red.

Her expression was slightly frightened, as if she was *now* just realizing that she wasn't nearly as immune to me as she first believed.

But we'd made a deal. She'd held up her end of the negotiation. I would hold up mine.

"Seerin," I murmured softly to her. Under a dark sky and in the quietness of that cold night, I told her my name, which I had not spoken in a long time.

Her eyes were capturing my soul even then, the little demon that she was. How much of it had she taken already?

I rasped, my voice dark and low, "My name is Seerin of Rath Tuviri."

17

Throughout the quiet night, I slept restlessly beside the demon king. My dreams were filled of strange things, of warped memories, and when I woke, I was sweating and a throbbing, dull pain was radiating from below my abdomen.

The demon king was still in bed when I came awake.

Seerin, I corrected myself quietly. Seerin of Rath Tuviri, whose kiss made the whole night sky spin.

I let out a small breath when I cramped and breathed through it. I hadn't missed *this* when I'd stopped bleeding, but now I remembered the pain well.

"What is it, *thissie*?" came his husky, sleep-roughened voice.

"Nothing," I replied, not daring to meet his eyes. Something had changed last night. A line had been crossed that I couldn't come back from.

I wanted *more*. I wanted to run. Whatever happened last night, I had the strange sense that it was only a matter of time...

Before what though?

I didn't know. Yet time ticked by in my head regardless.

I sensed him shifting in the bed, moving furs. When his

hand tilted my face up, his eyes narrowed on me, his features sharpening.

"You are in pain?" he asked, his voice losing its drowsy edge. "Where? I will call the healer."

Could I hide nothing from him?

"It's nothing," I insisted, gritting my teeth. Jana had always told me to hide my bleeding time from men, though I didn't know why.

He scowled. "Tell me now, Nelle."

I let out a small, even breath as my cramping peaked again. His voice was sharp, the same tone he used with his warriors, the same tone that was both a warning and a command.

I swallowed and chanced a look at him. When my eyes strayed to his lips—remembering that now I knew the feel of them—I said quietly, "It's just my bleeding time. It will pass."

His shoulders relaxed ever so slightly, his muscles shifting under the expanse of his golden skin. I saw him daily, slept next to him during the nights, and somehow I always managed to forget how *big* he was.

"Why did you not just say?" he rumbled.

"Because..." I whispered. "I'm supposed to hide it."

"It is natural, *kalles*," he murmured. "There is no shame in it."

I didn't answer him as another wave of pain came and went. He rose from the bed, going to his cabinet on the far side of the tent. I couldn't help when my eyes perused his body, glancing over the plethora of dark scars on his back that did nothing to hide the evidence of his strength and physical power.

I watched as he mixed together something in a goblet, filling it with the pitcher of fresh water that was always present in the *voliki*, before he brought it over to me.

"The *kerisa* left it here for you, if you felt any pain," he explained, returning to me. I recognized the black liquid in the goblet and I took it from his hands, sitting up in the bed.

"Thank you," I said quietly and drank it down. My eyes met his as he took the goblet away and set it beside the bed. I cleared my throat and asked, "My *voliki* will be ready today?"

His expression didn't change. "*Lysi*."

I nodded. He stood from the bed and began to dress.

The sudden silence between us felt different, charged and thick, and I wasn't sure I liked it. To fill it, I asked, even as I began to tap on my wrist, "What is it that you do all day?"

"Today, I meet with my *pujerak* and the elders again," he told me.

"About what?" I asked, grasping onto my curiosity as more cramping clenched my abdomen.

"I ride for *Dothik* soon," he informed me, casting me a glance out of the corner of his eye as he shrugged on a fresh, thick tunic that molded to his flesh.

"What?" I asked, shocked, my fingers stilling. "But...but it's the cold season. Surely you can't travel now."

"Worried for me, *thissie*?" he rasped, giving me the full weight of his attention.

I stilled under that gaze, pinned.

I licked my dry lips then I was reminded of his own. How they were impossibly soft yet firm, how I'd felt his heat through those lips. How his growl and his groan had reverberated inside me and awakened something fierce and aching.

Clearing my throat, I asked, "Why are you going now?"

"The *Dothikkar* requests his *Vorakkars'* presence in the capitol when the moon is full," he told me.

That was in less than two weeks' time. Depending on how far away *Dothik* was, he would leave within the week.

"Are you taking the warriors with you?"

"*Nik*," he said, fastening his pelt over his shoulders. "I go alone."

I didn't know what was bubbling up inside me—all I knew was that I didn't like it. Biting my lip, I told him, "It's foolish for you to go. It's dangerous."

"I will not be gone long," he told me, studying me closely as he approached. "I will stay in *Dothik* for as long as I am required to be there and then return."

Something sharp in his voice made me look more closely at *him*.

"You do not like *Dothik*?" I asked.

His eyes narrowed on me.

"But you grew up there, didn't you?" I questioned, shamelessly trying to pry.

The corner of his lips quirked, but I sensed there was no amusement behind his smile. His expression was fierce, watchful, and dark.

"Do you like where you grew up, *kalles*?" he threw back, his voice mocking.

I sobered, but didn't let him deter me. "What's it like? The capitol?"

"Full of beings who only worship their gold, a stiff drink, and a good fucking," he replied easily.

"Careful, Seerin," I murmured, watching him, so strangely fascinated by his words that I didn't even realize I'd used his name for the first time, "or else I might think that you're bitter."

"If you live in *Dothik* long enough, *rei thissie*," he murmured, reaching out to brush my lips with his claws, making my breath hitch and my scalp tingle, "you are nothing but bitter."

"Then I am glad you left," I told him, the truth soft in my voice, "and sad you must return."

His lips quirked again, but this time, I was relieved to see a familiar softness. His fingers left my lips and he pulled away.

When he stepped towards the entrance of the tent, my shoulders sagged and my breath left me in a rush, released of his eyes.

It took me a moment to realize my heart was pounding in my chest and my pain seemed lessened.

The demon king ducked his head out, but then paused. He turned to look at me and then ordered, "Come here, *kalles*."

Curious, I rose from the bed, feeling blood soak into the cloth between my legs underneath my clothes. I clutched at Blue's feathers around my neck as I approached him.

He pulled back the flaps of the tent ever so slightly and my eyes widened.

The first frost.

A sprinkling of white shimmered over the land, not yet the blanket of heavy snow and ice that would come later. The air was dry and frigid. Even then, I felt it sting my cheeks.

Another cold season had come, but looking out over the land right then didn't fill me with as much dread or fear as it had before.

I knew why he was showing me.

A reminder. Of our first wager, the one I'd lost. That with the first frost, my duty as his *alukkiri* would begin, though I was still uncertain what that meant.

I will find out, I thought.

"I will see you tonight, *rei alukkiri*," he purred.

Then he was gone.

18

I rritation was making my temple throb as I looked around the *voliki*, at the three elders, Vodan, and my head warrior.

"The reports from the Dead Lands prove nothing," I said, keeping my tone even and calm despite the rising heat within my chest. "We all know that during the cold season, the Gher-tuns go underground. None are seen for months."

One of the elders argued, "Which is why our *Dothikkar* wants to attack soon. We strike *them*. It is why you are meeting in *Dothik*, is it not? To formulate a plan of attack?"

"We are meeting in *Dothik* because of the *Dothikkar's* whim," I replied. "Nothing more."

Vodan cut me a sharp look. I locked eyes with the elder across the high table we stood around. It had been a long day, a wasted one, because I felt we'd gotten nowhere.

"I am not eager to send my warriors to battle during a season where even the elements can kill them," I told him slowly. "The Dead Lands are two weeks' ride away, if the frosts do not slow us. It is madness to even attempt."

"The *Dothikkar*—"

I cut him off with a growl, "Is not responsible for this horde. *I am*."

Silence permeated the tent. My lead warrior, a male named Ujak, shifted on his feet to my left.

"I agree with the *Vorakkar*," Ujak said quietly. "We are unprepared for a battle during the cold season. We do not even know where the Ghertun hide underground, where to even attack. They will not resurface for months."

"And what of the rumors that they tunnel beneath the earth? That they create a network across the planet?" another elder asked. "Kakkari demands retribution for that alone."

"Those rumors came directly from *Dothik*," I said. "Speculation and nothing more. Our scouts, as far as I know, have never gotten close to their stronghold in the Dead Lands, so how would the scouts get underground? It is a rumor to strike fear in the hordes and those in the capitol and that is its sole purpose. I will not sacrifice my warriors for a mere rumor and you are a fool to believe it."

The elder pressed his lips together but remained quiet. Tension permeated the tent, thick and heavy.

"I am not saying the Ghertun are not a threat," I started quietly, looking around at my council, "because they are. A terrible threat that has grown with every passing year. But I am certain that the other *Vorakkar* will agree that the hordes will not attack now. No *Vorakkar* would agree to that. I go to *Dothik* with the sole purpose of making the position of Rath Tuviri clear."

"And if the *Dothikkar* does not see our way?" Vodan asked quietly, looking at me from across the table.

My fists clenched. Vodan knew as well as I that unrest among the *Vorakkar* had been rising, unrest directed at the *Dothikkar*. It could be considered treason, going against the king's orders.

"We will sway him," I said, my voice hard.

"As your mother did?" the first elder scoffed. His anger was palpable and I didn't miss the way every Dakkari in the *voliki* froze.

"I will ignore that you just said that, *terun*," I rasped, my eyes darkening, "because you have been on my council since the beginning. But make no mistake, I will not be disrespected in that way again or else you may join the *Dothikkar* in *Dothik* instead of here in *my* horde. Do you understand?"

The elder held my eyes. He'd always possessed less control than the others. Though we'd disagreed many times, he'd never taken his insults to such a personal level before.

The *terun* dropped his eyes in respect. "*Lysi, Vorakkar*. Forgive me."

"We are done here," I announced to the council, my jaw ticking. As the council began to file out, I leaned against the high table with both hands, staring down at the letter that had come straight from *Dothik* through a messenger just two days ago.

I stared at the words scratched out in dark ink. Words that at one time I wouldn't have been able to read. The letter had brought a report of Ghertun sightings close to *Dothik*, though I didn't believe a word of it.

Only Vodan remained once the council left.

"He is an old fool," Vodan murmured to me, knowing any mention of my mother brought me to the cusp of rage. "Angry that he cannot have his way, like a child."

"He spoke the truth," I said, "though he was a fool to say it to my face."

"The *Vorakkar* of Rath Kitala will stand with you. Certainly," Vodan continued. "He has a mate now, a child on the way. He would not welcome war during this time either."

"That is the problem," I murmured, looking up at my *pujerak*. "Would he avoid war because of his own needs? Am *I* avoiding war because I am weary of it? *Vorakkar* are always meant to place their horde first, not themselves. Am I doing that?"

"You have doubts?"

I thought of Nelle, of things I wanted and craved, yet held myself back from. "It is hard not to."

"You are right in this, Seerin," Vodan rasped. Twice I'd heard my name today. "The *Dothikkar* is mad to send warriors to the Dead Lands now. You know this. The warriors do too. Just because the elders, who have not wielded a blade in decades, cannot see that does not mean you are wrong."

I reached out with my fist and crumpled the parchment the messenger had left before tossing it into the fire burning in the basin. The words blackened and hissed as the letter caught fire.

"The cold season is a time for peace," Vodan said. "Even the Ghertun know that. Once the frost thaws, we can make plans for battle."

"*Lysi.*"

We both left the *voliki* and spoke no more of it that night. It was dark outside, the encampment was quiet. Vodan lived with his mate towards the back of the camp, where my own *voliki* was, and we wound our way through it in silence.

When we neared my *pujerak's* home, Vodan finally broke that silence with, "I saw you with the *vekkiri* last night."

I stilled and turned to look at him. Next to a barrel fire, I watched my oldest friend's face glow yellow.

"In the training grounds," Vodan added. He met my eyes. "Are we never going to talk about her?"

"I do not want to do this tonight," I rasped.

"The council has been talking. I thought you should know."

"*Vok*," I cursed, temples still throbbing.

"You assigning her a separate *voliki* has calmed them somewhat, but it is only a matter of time before they will confront you about her."

I wondered if Arokan of Rath Kitala had needed to deal with his council in this way when he chose to select a *vekkiri* as his *Morakkari*. Or had he simply done it without fear of the elders? As far as I knew, Arokan hadn't even informed the *Dothikkar* of his choice of a bride.

"I am not taking her as my *Morakkari*," I told Vodan, though the words felt heavy falling from my tongue.

The horde always comes first, I reminded myself.

Arokan could do whatever the *vok* he pleased. He'd come from a long line of *Vorakkars*. His father had been one, his mother a *Morakkari* herself. His blood line was strong, unbroken.

I, on the other hand, could not afford such luxuries. There were those in *Dothik still* waiting for me, a whore's bastard son, to fail. I could not show weakness in anything I did.

Vodan's expression revealed his skepticism at my words, yet he said, "Then choose another and be quick about it."

He clasped my arm and then disappeared into his own *voliki* a short distance away. I heard his mate greet him inside and right at that moment, I envied him fiercely.

Inhaling the piercing, icy air, I scrubbed a hand over my face. Then my eyes seemed to find *her voliki* straight away. Newly constructed, it was small...and it was the closest *voliki* to my own.

Longing built in my chest. Just the thought of seeing her, of looking into those dark, solemn eyes, eased the tension that had been building throughout the day.

Of their own accord, my feet carried me towards her *voliki*. I'd had a warrior escort her there earlier in the afternoon, as promised, but hadn't heard anything since.

I am not taking her as my Morakkari.

Vodan had said, *Then find another and be quick about it.*

When I reached her *voliki*, I knew that I should walk past it. I knew that I should go to my furs alone, that I should never kiss her or touch her again, though just the thought made me mourn the great loss. It would make letting her go so much easier, when she'd already clawed her way inside me with her demon eyes.

Leave, I told myself. *Go*.

Before I could, I saw her. Her head popped out from the *voliki's* entrance, peering at me with a frown.

"What are you doing?" she asked, her soft, strange, accented voice like a balm on the stresses and irritations from the council meeting.

That was when I knew I was weak. When it came to her, I was so damn weak. Though the council disapproved, though Vodan disapproved, though she risked everything I'd built, I didn't know if I had the strength to stay away from her.

I walked towards the *voliki* and ducked inside, forcing her back in. She was shivering, though she'd barely been outside for a moment. Within, I saw her small fire was going and it was warm. The whole *voliki* smelled like her, soft and clean.

There was a small bed of furs in the middle, where it was warmest. She had a low table for her meals, one chest, and a small cabinet. On top of the cabinet, I spied the dagger I'd given her and a shimmering rock next to it.

"It's lovely, isn't it?" she asked me, smiling with pleasure as she looked at her *voliki*, obviously very pleased with her modest home.

My chest throbbed. I wanted to give her everything. I wanted to care for her, to protect her, to shield her from this life.

Yet I couldn't.

She seemed to notice I hadn't yet spoken and she peered at me, tilting her head to the side. "What's wrong, Seerin? You look strange."

I felt my lips lift of their own accord but instead of answering her, my hands went to my pelt, sliding it off before I pulled my tunic over my head.

"What do you think you're doing?" she asked, her eyes going wide.

When I kicked off my boots and my pants shortly followed, I crouched and slid, naked, into her furs. I sighed, her bed plush and comfortable, and the warmth from the fire flickered over my skin.

"Seerin," she snapped. She was in a long tunic that reached her thighs. Her legs and feet were bare, her hair curling around her shoulders and down her back wildly.

"You can begin your duties as *rei alukkiri* tomorrow, *thissie*," I murmured. "I need sleep."

"That is what your own bed is for. This is *my voliki*, in case you've forgotten."

"I like this one just fine," I rasped. Her expression was baffled and I couldn't help but say, "As *Vorakkar*, I can sleep wherever I please within the horde."

She paused, nibbling on her bottom lip, hesitation playing over her features. "You can?"

My irritation from the meeting slid away in an instant, replaced with amusement and affection for the little *thissie,* who was slowly driving me to madness.

"*Lysi*, now come here, *kalles*," I murmured, holding out my hand for her. "I want to kiss you more."

She frowned. "More? We haven't negotiated for more."

"*Nik*, no more bargains between us," I said, my gaze burning into her. "No longer."

19

The demon king wanted to kiss me again?

My heartbeat raced in my ears as I looked down at him, sprawled on my new bed, underneath my new furs. His massive erection tented the material and I swallowed as I watched it bob slightly.

Fear took root in my belly, but not of him. Of *me*. Of this new thing that flushed my skin and made my stomach flutter.

He was watching me carefully, his golden hair spread like a halo around him, his markings flashing with the fire's flames. He was beautiful, achingly so. I'd thought so the first moment I'd seen him, even when I'd believed he would kill me for breaking the laws of the Dakkari.

I cleared my throat and pointed out, "If there are no more bargains between us, then that means you have to answer my questions when I ask them."

"*Lysi*," he murmured in solemn agreement, rubbing at the deep scar on his side.

My brow ticked up in surprise.

"Then again, so do you," he added. Something in his eyes

changed and he continued, "I'll begin. Did you like when I kissed you last night?"

My face heated, but I felt uncomfortable telling even him a lie, so I said, "Yes." I didn't wait for him to respond. "How many Dakkari have hair the color of yours?"

"That I know of? Myself and another." I opened my mouth, but he beat me to it. "Do you want to kiss me again, *rei thissie*?"

I stared at him. When I swallowed, it was loud. It sounded more like a gulp.

I'd been thinking about that very question on and off throughout the day, trying to make sense of what it would mean.

But I didn't think of myself as a coward. The possibility of kissing him again excited me—*he* excited me. He fascinated me more than anyone had before.

"Yes," I whispered, shifting on my feet, still standing in the center of my new domed tent. A growl escaped him and my eyes flitted to the low table, where the remnants of my meal remained, remnants that I'd been planning to save. Still, I asked him, "Have you eaten yet?"

"*Nik*," he rasped.

I frowned and brought the tray over to him. Those eyes pinned me when I knelt beside him on the bed and tucked my bare legs under me. I'd fashioned underwear that day to secure the fresh cloth between my legs but it still felt strange.

He sat up in my bed when I placed the tray on his lap. His eyes flicked from the food to me and he murmured, "You care for me, don't you, *thissie*?"

"What do you mean?"

"You would not give me your food otherwise," he pointed out. "Food is too precious. You know that."

"You're my friend, Seerin," I told him, avoiding his question indirectly. "Aren't you?"

His eyes flickered. He murmured something under his

breath in Dakkari. Then he reached out a hand, cupped the back of my neck, and pulled me to him.

"*Lysi*, friends," he murmured, though his voice sounded strained.

A long inhale whistled through my nostrils when he kissed me once, twice, three times.

The third time he lingered and seemed to be waiting for something. Hesitantly, I parted my lips for him. A shocked gasp escaped me when I felt the warmth of his tongue flick inside and he responded with a deep groan.

"*Vok*, Nelle," he rasped, pulling back slightly, his breathing a little ragged. I felt a little dizzy when I saw him adjust his bobbing cock underneath the furs with the side of his palm. "You do not know how much I have denied myself with you."

"You should eat," I said hurriedly, swallowing—gulping—again. My nipples were tightened in hard points and despite my bleeding time, I felt my belly sizzle with arousal. It was a sensation I'd rarely felt before.

"Eat?" he repeated slowly then looked down at the tray of food I'd placed on him, as if he'd just remembered it was there. He blew out a sharp breath, catching my eyes again. "Very well."

I watched him eat, trying not to think of his dizzying kiss. He ate methodically, efficiently, and I watched his jaw flex with fascination. A tiny part of me mourned the loss of the food, but a larger part of me liked that he was fed.

"You were hungry once, weren't you?" I asked softly. He'd made comments here and there and my mind had catalogued them all. "You made the remark about breaking the habit of saving food. And now, you told me I cared for you because I was giving you mine."

"You *do* care for me," he corrected.

"I never thought a horde king of Dakkar would know hunger. The hordes always seemed so rich in resources."

He polished off the food quickly and then took a swig of the fermented wine that came with my meal. I'd left it because it made my blood rush too fast, but he seemed to enjoy it well enough.

"Before you take me to your bed," he murmured, "you wish to know this?"

"We're not having sex, Seerin," I informed him, the thought making me nervous.

"Yet," he rasped, reminding me of when he'd arrogantly told me that when, not if, he took me, I would be more than willing. "Perhaps you should know who I was before this. It is only fair," he murmured over the goblet's rim before he drained the wine.

My brow furrowed. "What are you talking about?"

He set to tray aside.

"*Vorakkar* come from long, ancient lines. Strong blood lines that can be traced back for centuries," he said, reaching out to tuck a strand of hair behind my ear. I hadn't known that. "However, they are selected during the Trials, a series of challenges set by the *Dothikkar* to test the strength, will, and determination of those that aspire to become *Vorakkar*. Only those that come from ancient families are allowed into the Trials."

"So your line must be very old," I guessed, wondering how far he could trace his ancestors.

"*Nik, thissie*," he said with a bitter chuckle. "Not at all."

I frowned.

"They called us *duvna*," he said.

"*Duvna*?"

"Little creatures in *Dothik*, who scavenge and eat trash and hide in dark, warm corners to avoid being seen."

"I don't understand," I said, shaking my head.

"I grew up on the streets of *Dothik*," he told me, his voice dropping and darkening, and I stilled. "So, *lysi*, I know hunger very well."

"What about your parents?" I whispered. "Are they...are they still alive?"

Or was he an orphan, like me?

"I never knew my father. My mother told me he left with a horde before I was born," he said. "My mother still lives in *Dothik*."

"But you didn't live with her when you were younger?"

"I saw her often," he said, pressing his lips together, "but she lived in a brothel. She had to. The young were not allowed inside."

I froze but held his eyes.

"I formed a small group, slowly, with other *duvna* I encountered. We watched out for one another, we stole for each other, we ate together or we did not eat at all. My mother gave us gold when she could."

"Seerin," I whispered.

I thought of the young Dakkari boy, my *lirilla's* son, the one who'd made me laugh with his innocence, and I wondered if Seerin had been that young, living that way in *Dothik*.

It made my chest ache.

"So, you see, *rei thissie*, I am the bastard son of a *Dothiki* prostitute," he rasped, his eyes straying to my lips when I swayed close, "who became a *Vorakkar*."

"How?" I whispered.

"My mother."

There was a strain in his eyes, a tightening around his mouth, that made me want to stop him. Yet, selfishly, I needed to know everything about him.

"My mother is very beautiful," he informed me.

"I believe that," I said, looking into the eyes of the son she produced.

"The *Dothikkar* heard of her. A beautiful prostitute with golden hair. You know why gold is important to the Dakkari?

Why we ink it into our skin and use it for our weapons?" I shook my head. "Because gold is from Kakkari herself. She pushes it from the earth like she is giving life. So, when the *Dothikkar* heard of this female with golden hair, he had to have her. In his arrogance, he believed Kakkari had given her to him. A gift from our goddess, the highest of honors."

I looked at his hair, soft and long and yellow. I'd just asked him how many Dakkari had hair his color and he'd told me two...himself and another. Now, I knew it was his mother he'd referred to.

"I was older when he took her from the brothel and made her one of his concubines. But my mother is intelligent," he said. "She saw her opportunity, saw the lengths to which the *Dothikkar* would go to possess her, and so she struck a deal with him. She would forever bind herself to him if he over-looked her son's ancestry and allowed him entry into the next Trials."

Realization sparked in my mind.

"And so she became his madness, his obsession," he murmured, tracing over my cheek before running his fingers down my throat. "He denied her at first."

"But not for long," I guessed, my heart thrumming at his touch, at his words.

"*Nik*, not for long, *thissie*."

The fire in the small basin I'd built crackled and sparked loudly, making me jump.

"What happened next?"

"I entered the Trials with his permission. I am certain he believed I would fail in the beginning stages," he said, his jaw clenching. "But I finished one challenge after another until the *Dothikkar* himself could find no reason to deny me."

"I can almost picture that," I told him.

"*Lysi*?" he murmured, one corner of his lip curling.

"I can imagine that you were very stubborn and determined."

"I was," he said. "And there are many who wish I hadn't been so stubborn and determined."

"The *Dothikkar* included?"

"Him most of all," Seerin said, a dark grin appearing. "He faced a lot of backlash for allowing me into the Trials. Even now, he seeks any reason to strip me of my title."

"Can he do that?" I asked, frowning.

"*Nik*," he said. "Short of treason, there is nothing he can do. The hordes have their own laws, though we must adhere to the laws of the *Dothikkar* as well."

"You are all kings in your own right," I said.

His head inclined.

"What did the Trials consist of?" I questioned. Then a dark thought came to me and I asked, "The scars on your back...were they...?"

"It is the last challenge during the Trials," he confirmed. Then he warned, "But I will tell you no more about them, *thissie*."

Then they were barbaric, terrible challenges, I decided. Still, I couldn't help but wonder what he'd gone through to get to where he was.

"Do you..."

"You have never been shy with your questions before, *kalles*. Why begin now?" he asked, his eyes holding a challenge.

"You said you had great plans for the horde."

"I want it to be successful," he told me, trailing his fingers over my exposed throat before running his hand back up to cup my cheek.

"Because you have something to prove? It already seems successful to me," I told him honestly. "How would you measure your success?"

He exhaled sharply, his lips lifting. "Successful hordes last through the death of their *Vorakkar*. But I want my horde to never question that I did everything in my power to keep them safe. I never want them to know hunger, I never want them to know fear."

I thought of Seerin as a young boy, leading his pack of wandering children. I pictured him sharing his mother's gold. I pictured him going hungry so others could eat.

"And if you didn't have the horde?" I asked. "What would you want for yourself, Seerin?"

His brow furrowed at my question, as if he'd never thought to ask himself that before.

"I hardly know, *thissie*," he told me and I heard the truth in his voice. "What do you want?"

I swallowed. I said the first thing that came to mind. "It's not that I want anything specifically, like riches or food. It's just that I don't want to go through life alone." My mind flickered to Jana. "I don't want my hair to turn grey and find that I'm still alone."

It was my worst fear.

"Your hair will turn grey?" he rumbled, rubbing a few strands between his fingers.

"Yes. Eventually." I gave him a small smile. "Maybe it will be grey like your eyes."

His expression was unreadable. He was silent for a long moment. Then he was leaning into me again and his lips were on mine, nibbling at my mouth, wanting me to part for him again, to let him inside.

My head swirled and I reached forward to clutch his bare shoulders, my fingertips gripping his warm flesh. Why did this feel so good? *How* could this feel so good?

"Your hair is not yet grey, Nelle," he rasped against my lips. "And right now? You are not alone."

20

There was a designated *voliki* for the weapons master near the training grounds. Truthfully, I was a little nervous, as I'd been the previous afternoon when I'd started work for the seamstress, my *lirilla*. But I was especially nervous, yet intrigued, to work for her father.

I ducked my head inside, too antsy to feel the cold weaving its way into my boots. The ground was frosted over throughout the encampment, my hands were numb, and my breath fogged in front of me, but I didn't feel it.

"Hello?"

"*Lysi*, come, come," the weapons master said, not looking up from the bench he was hunched over on the far wall. The first thing that hit me was the heat. It was sweltering inside the tent, which was arranged very, very differently than others I'd seen.

The heat came from three large barrel fires and two basins, the smoke funneling out through an opening towards the top of the dome. Then there was a forge, molten heat glowing from the inside, directly in the middle of the *voliki*. Even the walls of the tent were covered in a different material, perhaps a more heat-resistant one, or else I was certain that over time, the whole structure would simply melt away.

It helped explain why there was a solid ring around the *voliki* that was devoid of any ice whatsoever.

Immediately, I shrugged off my pelt and laid it carefully over a nearby stool, approaching the bench the older male was working on.

"Oh," I said in surprise when I spotted a familiar little boy, whose head popped out from underneath the bench. He smiled at me, still missing a couple of his teeth. "Hello," I greeted, crouching down to ruffle his hair. "How are you?"

He repeated the words slowly, "How are you?" but his accent made 'how' sound more like 'who.'

I grinned and turned my attention to his grandfather, who still hadn't looked up from what he was working on. It was a dagger, I realized, and he was carefully etching markings—no, words—into the solid, curving handle.

"It's beautiful," I commented softly.

The weapons master grunted and said, "The *Vorakkar* tells me you have made arrows before."

The mention of Seerin made my belly flutter, but I tried to ignore it. I tried not to remember last night, of him kissing me until he tucked me into his side and told me to sleep. I wanted to make a good impression and not mess up on my first day after all.

I bit my lip. "Well, yes, but I made them from wood. And feathers." Because I'd had nothing else.

"Feathers?" he asked, finally turning his head to blink at me. "You will work with Dakkari steel. It heats like glass, but is unbreakable once it hardens. You must work quickly."

I sucked in a small breath, but told him, "I learn fast."

"Good. You will need to."

For the next couple hours, I learned my way around the

voliki, trying to remember every word the weapons master said, committing it to memory. I didn't think I spoke once during the process. Instead, I carefully observed and memorized, all while the Dakkari boy watched, perched on a stool next to his grandfather's seat at the bench, nibbling on something that looked like a blue root.

"Keeping rolling," the weapons master ordered. "Faster."

On the metal slab in front of me, dusted with a white, shimmering powder, I rolled a small ball of heated, glowing Dakkari steel, my hands covered in protective, yet thin gauntlets. A bead of sweat dripped from my face and sizzled on the steel.

"Too slow," he murmured after a moment, watching the steel lose the glow, cooling. The shaft of the arrow, instead of being cylindrical, was flattened and fat. "Try again."

It took me seven more attempts until I finally got it right and I beamed up at the weapons master in triumph as he grinned. "Good. Now do the same thing, except roll the arrowhead, carve the nock, and pinch the fletching."

I blew out a long breath and said, "Alright."

"IT TOOK me three days until I created a usable arrow," the weapons master, or *mitri* as he was called, assured me. "You did well for today."

"Thank you for teaching me," I said, rolling the hardened steel between my fingertips. It was far from usable, but the shape was right, albeit slightly curved in the middle. The fletching was a mess and the nock had folded over at the end when I'd tried to clamp it, but the tip was sharp and pointed. "I'll do better tomorrow."

His smile was kind. I'd never seen a Dakkari—other than his

grandson—who smiled as much as he did, but it made me feel comfortable around him, relaxed.

"Off you go. Take the boy to his mother, will you? I need to finish the dagger."

I nodded and stood from the work bench, peeling off the gauntlets. My hands were red underneath and my fingertips were throbbing. I felt both accomplished and defeated, a strange mixture of emotion, but I was exhilarated nonetheless.

A thought occurred to me. "Can I keep this?" I asked the weapons master.

He slanted his gaze down to the pitiful arrow and inclined his head in a nod, biting back a laugh. "*Lysi*. Whatever you wish."

At that, I tucked the arrow into the waistband of my pants.

"Thank you. I'll see you tomorrow," I said before making my way to the entrance, wiping my arm over my forehead, and securing my pelt. The Dakkari boy handed me his own small pelt, no doubt crafted by his mother, and I felt something like longing lodge in my throat as I helped him secure it. "Ready?"

"Ready?" he repeated slowly. It sounded like 'reedy.'

I smiled and nodded, and we both ducked from the tent.

"Oh," I whispered, stunned. The first thing that hit me was the cold. How much colder it felt outside than it had that morning, on account of being inside the sweltering heat of the *voliki* for the majority of the morning. The cold began to seep into my clothes, beginning from my boots, threading its fingers underneath my pelt and tunic. My sweat did nothing to deter it—it only made the cold worse.

The second thing I noticed was that the warriors were training. I hadn't heard the sounds of blades and grunts above the roaring forge and my own concentration, but now the sounds hit me square in the chest. And it answered one of my earlier questions...that they *did* train even during the cold season.

Seerin was among them. My gaze zeroed in on him, another shiver going down my spine that had nothing to do with the icy chill. He was taking on two opponents, his brow furrowed in intensity, his lips turned down with concentration and focus.

His head jerked when he spotted me with the Dakkari boy at my side. I probably looked like a wild mess, flushed and shivering, but I felt his hot gaze seep into me, banishing the tendrils of cold that crawled over my flesh.

He'd been gone that morning when I woke, but my new bed still smelled like him. Now, his scent would be all over my furs and, thus, all over my skin until I washed him away.

It only took that small moment of distraction on his part and I gasped when one of the warriors leveled his sword at his throat, nicking the strong column of his neck.

Seerin froze, a strange expression whipping across his features. His eyes left mine and went to the warrior, who lowered his sword. But even from a distance, I could see that the demon king was...disturbed.

He didn't meet my eyes again. In fact, it seemed like he did everything in his power *not* to look my way again.

Throat tight, I said to the boy, "Let's go find your mother."

21

"Come," I rasped to Nelle when I ducked my head inside her *voliki*, seeing her sitting at the low table, though it was clear she was finished eating her meal.

Her eyes turned to me and she rose. I waited outside in the night air as she dressed for the short walk to my own *voliki*.

I was irritated and on edge and conflicted about this night.

After the distraction in the training grounds that day, after another mind-numbing and frustrating meeting with the council, Vodan had once again confronted me about Nelle, telling me I'd been seen leaving her *voliki* in the early morning hours.

I'd told him to *vok* off, which I only marginally regretted and which shocked him greatly. But I was growing impatient with the constant speculation and pressure from my *pujerak*. Sometimes, he seemed to forget *I* was *Vorakkar* of the horde, not him.

Not only that, but being in Nelle's bed the night before, taking her mouth when I pleased, feeling her wrap her body around me in sleep, had left me aching and needful.

As *Vorakkar*, it was easy for me to seek out sex. There were dozens of unmated females within my horde who had made their interest clear. And I *had* fucked a few of them throughout the years when the needs of my body grew too great.

Otherwise, I'd learned to abstain. I didn't believe in using my horde as a harem, which had been the case in the ancient years of the *Vorakkars*. Sex blurred lines better not crossed...and like I'd always known, females were dangerous.

But now, with the maddening *thissie* sleeping in my arms, which was of my own doing, I was growing hungry. All I needed to do was think of her, of her wide eyes and her pink lips, and I needed her *desperately*.

Nelle emerged from the tent just then, tucking a strand of hair behind her ear. Did she sense the blackened waves of my mood? She looked at me evenly, without fear, but watchful.

I turned and made the quick stride up the incline to my *voliki*. I heard the soft crunch of her footsteps behind me, over the forming ice.

I held the entrance flap open for her and then followed her inside. One of the horde females must've delivered my meal earlier because it was perched on the low table. A bath, still warm, was in the corner and a low fire flickered in the basin.

Approaching, I threw more fuel onto it, letting it roar.

"Time is strange," she said softly behind me. "I was just here and yet it feels like it's been weeks."

"Time seems slower in the cold," I murmured, staring at the flames.

"I have something for you."

I blinked and then turned to look at her, frowning. "*Neffar?*"

She approached, a hint of a smile on her lips. Her cheeks were red even from the brief moment outside. She pulled something from her waistband and thrust it towards me.

I took the slim shaft of metal from her grip, my chest tightening when I saw a *thissie* feather tied to the end, and I realized what it was.

My eyes went to her pendant, which hung around her neck, noticing there was one less, and then back to the feather tied around the arrow with slim black cord.

"It's terrible, I know," she said, looking down at it between my fingertips. "But the weapons master said it took him three days to create one, so I figured I have time to learn."

It *was* terrible. The shaft of the arrow was bent, the metal fletching skewed. Yet it was the best thing I'd ever seen because of what it was...a gift. A precious one, judging from the feather tied to the flattened nock, because I knew how much those feathers meant to her.

"*Vok*," I cursed softly, something rising in my chest, threatening to choke me. "*Vok!*"

Her face fell. Her voice went quiet when she asked, "You don't like it?"

A memory rose in my mind, from the day I took her from her village, and I grabbed the back of her neck. Pressing my forehead to hers, I rasped, my voice bordering on anger, "How is it that no male in your village claimed you?"

"What?" she whispered, wide-eyed and bewildered.

"If I was a *vekkiri* male in your village, I would have claimed you as my own long ago, *rei thissie*."

She looked stunned by my words, words I probably should not have spoken out loud. Her lips parted but I didn't hesitate. I kissed her hard, devouring her mouth the way I'd craved all day. It was almost punishing.

I poured my rage and my need into her. Her hands clutched at my chest and her little sounds of surprise drifted across my lips.

When she flinched, I realized I had gripped her waist too hard and my claws had pricked through the thick material of her tunic.

With a curse, I pulled away, dragging deep breaths into my nostrils.

"I should not have told you to come tonight," I growled softly, avoiding her eyes, realizing that I still had her arrow pinched between my fingertips. "I am in a dark mood. You should leave."

"I won't, Seerin," she said softly.

"Why?" I snarled.

"Because you're my friend," she explained easily, "and you said so yourself...I gave you my food so I must care for you."

I closed my eyes, scrubbing a hand over my face.

"Tell me what's wrong."

I laughed. "What is wrong?" I repeated.

With *Dothik* looming—knowing I would face not only the *Dothikkar* but my mother—with the fissures within the council, and the constant disapproval of my actions by my oldest friend, there was much to choose from.

But what I was angry about the most?

It was the realization that I wanted this female as *mine*. It was the realization that I wanted her in the most primal of ways, that I wanted to plant my seed deep in her belly, and have her at my side and under my furs as my *Morakkari*, as my wife, as my *mate*...just as Kakkari had shown me.

It was the realization that I wanted Nelle as mine and I *couldn't have her*. Not without risking alienating the rest of my council, my *pujerak*, and the horde. Not without risking the wrath of the *Dothikkar*, who still thought of me as a bastard *duvna*. Despite what I'd told Nelle last night, the *Dothikkar* still held sway within the hordes and there were those that remained faithful to him even on the plains.

And the horde always come first, I repeated for the millionth time, as if I needed to remember.

My expression must've been thunderous, indeed, because

she said, "You *are* in a dark mood tonight, Seerin. But don't worry, I'm not afraid."

"You should be."

"Will you hurt me?"

My brow furrowed and I growled out, "*Nik.*"

"Then why should I be afraid?"

Belatedly, staring down at the feather on the arrow, I realized that I *would* hurt her. Before this was done. Just not in the way she referred to.

The honorable part of me should've sent her away right then. That was what a kinder male would've done.

Instead, I placed her arrow on my cabinet carefully and told her, "Very well, *thissie*. If you will not leave, then you can begin your duties as *rei alukkiri* this night."

"And what will you have me do?" she asked, curiosity warring with wariness in her gaze.

If she knew what an *alukkiri* really was, she never would've accepted the bargain I'd offered her.

"You will wash me. And then you will apply my oils afterwards," I told her, the thought of her hands gliding over my body making my voice darken.

I heard her swallow.

I couldn't help but step closer, couldn't help but run my fingers through her soft, black hair.

"A good *alukkiri* would bathe with me," I murmured.

Her eyes went wide and then accusation entered her gaze. "Your bargain was an attempt to get me in your bed, wasn't it?"

"You were already in my bed," I pointed out to her.

"You know what I mean. You wanted sex. *Alukkiri*...they are lovers, aren't they? During the cold season?"

Despite my darkened mood, despite my overwhelming need, I wanted to laugh.

"More often than not," I rasped, my hands going to my pelt. "*Lysi.*"

She made a sound in the back of her throat, a small, surprised one, and watched as I began to undress.

"How many have you had?" she asked next, her voice soft. I heard something strange in her tone and looked at her closely.

"*Alukkiri?*"

"Yes."

I finished undressing, turning towards the bath. "None."

"What?"

"Did the thought make you jealous, *rei thissie?*" I rasped, stepping into the bathing tub, the warm water wrapping around my body. I relaxed, leaning my head back.

"I don't know," she said, her tone bewildered, drawing closer to the bath. "I suppose I felt something like discomfort at the thought."

I shook my head, unable to stop the affection rising in my chest at her innocent and refreshingly honest words. "You are supposed to play coy, *kalles.* You are supposed to deny my words and make me wonder if you truly care for me at all."

"That seems like a lot of work for something you already know the answer to," she informed me, frowning. "Is that what a Dakkari female would've done?"

"*Lysi.* Undoubtedly."

She jumped into her next question. "Why have you never taken an *alukkiri* before? I thought you said it was your luxury to choose one as *Vorakkar.* And I am certain that many females would have been willing."

"You are certain?" I asked.

"Yes, don't you remember the female who delivered your meal?"

"I do."

"You could've chosen her," she pointed out before her lips pressed together, as if, belatedly, she realized the idea upset her.

"I wanted you," I rasped when she kneeled next to the bathing tub.

She blinked and went quiet. Then she said softly, "You didn't answer my question."

"You ask a lot of them, *thissie*."

"Seerin."

I liked my name on her lips too much. "Because sex can be complicated and it was easier not to take an *alukkiri*."

"But..." she trailed off, her gaze dropping. It drove me to madness when she grew shy, because it was not a word I would ever use to describe her. This was the *kalles* who'd shamelessly peeked into the common bathing *voliki*, after all. "But you want to have sex with me."

I growled. "You wish to talk about sex, *thissie*?"

My cock throbbed at the thought and I swallowed past the thick lump in my throat.

"You know I'm untried, Seerin, don't you?"

A virgin.

My nostrils flared. I hadn't known for certain, but I had my suspicions.

"You said you were immune to desire," I rasped. The corner of my lip curled slightly. "Immune to me."

Her face heated. "I said that because I didn't trust you then."

I stilled. "You trust me now?"

She blinked twice before she said softly, "Yes, I believe I do."

I didn't know if her words made me feel elated or disturbed. How could she trust me after what I'd done to her?

"I don't think any female could be completely immune to you," she added quietly.

I inhaled a long, slow breath through my nostrils.

"I don't know if I'm ready for sex yet," she said. "But I do

170

know that I like when you kiss me. I like how you make me feel and I know I want more."

I licked my bottom lip. My body reacted to her words like she'd just whispered the filthiest things in my ear.

"*Lysi*?" I growled.

"Yes," she whispered, holding my eyes.

"There is so much that I can show you, *thissie*," I told her.

Her lips parted. I could see her burning curiosity. Curiosity I would assuage *thoroughly* once she was ready. My female was curious about sex and that knowledge was almost my undoing.

"That I *will* show you," I promised.

Her eyes caught on the washing cloth draped over the edge of the bathing tub. I reached out to take it before holding it to her, raising a brow, a challenge in my gaze.

One thing I was learning about my *thissie* was that she never backed down from a challenge.

My dark grin formed when she took the cloth from my grip.

22

"Tell me about how you came to be on Dakkar," Seerin requested, as if he knew I needed a distraction as I dipped the cloth under the water and touched it to his bare skin.

I was thankful for the change in subject given the way my pulse was fluttering in my throat.

The warm water came up to the crease of my elbow. I started somewhere safe, though my body was humming with something he pulled from it. The cloth glided over his arms as I started at his shoulders, scrubbing his skin gently.

I'd never washed another, but it was surprisingly...intimate.

I swallowed, watching the cloth drag over his body, and I said, "I was a newborn when I came here."

"So young?" he asked, frowning.

"Jana said my father was a pilot. After the old Earth colonies fell during the war, he would shuttle human refugees across the universe, delivering them wherever they were agreed to be taken in."

Like on Dakkar. That was why there were human settlements, because the *Dothikkar* had accepted gold from the Uranian Federation as payment. Allegedly.

"He died on one such transport. His ship was destroyed, leaving my mother alone. She was pregnant at the time and his death left her...Jana said she wasn't in her right mind. She loved him very much, but I think it was the prospect of caring for a child, alone, after losing the only home she'd ever known, and rebuilding on a new planet was too painful."

I spoke of these things as if they were stories I'd heard, as if they weren't the events at the beginning of my life. And they were just that...*stories*. Stories Jana had told me because she'd been there. I couldn't remember these things.

I dragged the cloth down his other arm, leaning over the tub, the ends of my hair dipping into the water.

"I was born in the stars," I told him, my throat tightening.

"You are a starling?" he rumbled, his brow furrowing though I didn't know why, wrapping his finger around a strand of my hair.

I'd never heard that term before, but I nodded. "I suppose. My mother gave birth to me on our way here, to Dakkar, on a refugee vessel. And then three days later, she decided to join my father willingly, wherever he is."

He stilled.

"Jana was just a woman she met on the ship. They shared one of the rooms together and Jana had helped deliver me."

"But you didn't consider her your mother, though she took you in and raised you?" he questioned.

"She never wanted to be," I confessed, a familiar feeling of sadness and rejection washing over me. "I loved her and I think in her own way, she loved me too. But she also saw me as a burden, another mouth to feed besides her own in an already hungry village, a child she hadn't asked for. And so, a large part of her always resented me for it."

His lips pressed together, but his expression was unreadable. "How did Jana die?"

"Sickness," I said and that was all I would say. I didn't like to think about those days I'd tried to help her. I didn't like to remember.

"Then you were alone," he murmured, reaching out to stroke my face, his lips turning down into a frown.

"Yes," I whispered, a shiver racing down my spine. I moved the cloth to his chest and made little circles.

He made a rumbling sound in the back of his throat and went quiet. Water trickled and I felt the heavy weight of his eyes, but I avoided them.

Finally, he said, "The Dakkari believe that starlings are powerful beings."

My hand paused on his chest and I tilted my head, meeting his gaze.

It was an unspoken invitation, one he answered with, "In the stars, you become everything."

"What?" I whispered, not sure I understood.

"You feel the loneliness of endless space, but you also hear a million beings' prayers, their hopes, their tragedies, being lifted up to you, whispered towards the sky from their homes, towards their deities. The Dakkari believe that starlings are born hearing those prayers and that they are closer to Kakkari for it. We believe that you become a thousand different species in that moment, that you would be neither human nor Dakkari, but *everything*."

My breath hitched when he pressed a small, gentle kiss to my lips.

"I am not surprised to learn you are a starling, *rei thissie*," he murmured against me. "For I felt your power when I first felt you taking my soul."

My heart gave one powerful thud and then I looked at him as if I'd never seen him before.

I felt a little dizzy looking at him, my head throbbing, the blood in my ears rushing, and I wondered how we'd gone from him trying to send me away this evening...to me wondering if this was what falling in love was like. This dizzying, maddening, uncomfortable sensation that grew with each passing moment.

Swallowing, I looked back to the cloth, blinking, and I resumed the circles over his chest as if he hadn't spoken at all.

I washed him in silence, methodically, distracted. When I reached his lower abdomen, my breath hitched as his hardened cock brushed my forearm, almost searing me with its heat. His nostrils flared and a harsh breath expelled from his chest.

Underneath the water, I saw his cock bob, the flushed head surfacing briefly. He wasn't shy in his arousal. He never had been.

The warmth between my thighs returned in a rush and I swallowed. I found I *wanted* to touch him, explore him, but I didn't know if I should or even how I would begin.

"Nelle," he rasped.

His cock brushed against my arm again when I circled down towards his hips and I paused, my lips parting, when I felt him *pulse* against me. I didn't pull away. I kept my forearm steady.

His thick swallow reached my ears and I looked up at him. Whatever he saw in my expression made his eyes flare and he gripped my hand, pushing the cloth away. It sunk to the bottom of the bathing tub, forgotten.

A strange ringing started in my ears when he guided my hand to his cock, erasing the indecision from my mind. My sex throbbed when I heard his roughened curse, when he wrapped my hand around his impossible heat.

"You can touch me however you wish, *kalles*," he rasped. "Or you can stop."

Unconsciously, my grip tightened at his words, dragging a deep, delicious groan from his throat.

"Come into the bath, *thissie*," he rasped. "I need to touch you too."

I shook my head, though my voice sounded far away and my eyes were locked on his cock underneath the water. "I'm still bleeding."

My flow had lightened considerably since yesterday. My bleeding would most likely cease tomorrow on the fourth day, but I didn't want to dirty the bath water regardless.

"I do not care," he protested before I watched the column of his throat tighten and his chest heave, all because I'd ran my fist down to his base. My hand didn't encircle him completely, but I was still fascinated—and aroused—by the reaction it wrung from him. "*Vok!*"

"Does it feel that good?" I questioned, tilting my head to the side, excitement winding its way to my core.

A strangled laugh came from him. "I told you to come here… and I will show you how good it feels."

"No, Seerin," I said, the prospect leaving me shy.

"Very well, *rei thissie*," he rasped, his eyes hot and focused on me. "But when your bleeding stops, I will touch you as I please. *Lysi*?"

I shivered. I could only nod.

"What does *rei* mean?" I asked him softly. Sometimes he used it, other times he did not. I had a suspicion but I wanted to be certain.

His jaw ticked. I tightened my grip and stroked back up his shaft. His face twisted and his back bowed.

"Seerin," I whispered, licking my lips.

"It means 'my,'" he finally choked out, his chest heaving.

Longing burst in my chest. Longing to belong to someone and have someone belong to me. He'd been calling me *his*. Why did that word sound so sublime?

I squirmed on my knees, squeezing my thighs together.

"I think you care for me too, my demon king," I told him softly.

He froze.

His expression changed, ever so slightly, but he didn't confirm or deny my words. Suddenly, his hand was stilling my own before he unclasped my grip from around his cock, and I frowned when he stood from the bath.

His voice was cold, different, when he said, "You can do my oils now, *alukkiri*."

Kneeling, I watched him with confusion as he roughly dried off his wet skin, his cock bobbing angrily against his abdomen. His dark mood had returned, as palpable as my racing heart, but I was left reeling, wondering if I'd done or said something wrong.

I hadn't, had I?

The only thing I could think was that he was angry, or embarrassed perhaps, that he cared for me. I knew he did. But why would he not admit it unless he wished he didn't? Unless I shamed him in some way? I'd always known that he was a *Vorakkar* and I was a human, but I thought that perhaps it didn't matter to him.

But it seems like it does matter, I thought, familiar rejection tightening my chest, making it difficult to breathe.

Gone was my desire. Left in its place was an icy chill that rivaled the temperature outside. The tension in the *voliki* had changed from charged and exciting to heavy and thick.

"Seerin," I said, rising from my knees, my jaw set, wanting to give him a chance to explain, wanting to believe I was only making it all up in my head.

"*Neffar*?" he rasped, his back to me, rummaging through something in his cabinets.

"Why are you being this way?"

"I am not yours, Nelle," he growled. "Do not ever think of me as yours."

"But I can be *yours*?" I asked, furrowing my brow, not understanding. "Why are you allowed to call me yours but I cannot do the same?"

"Believe me, I will *not* make that mistake again," he rasped and I barely held back my flinch. When he turned to me, a tall, yellow bottle was in his grip. His oils.

So, this *was* a rejection.

I wouldn't lie, it *stung*. There I'd been...thinking I was falling in love with him as he talked of starlings. My inexperience with males had never been more evident than it was right at that moment.

And he'd flipped so quickly, my words obviously a trigger, something he'd been thinking about. Why else would he react so strongly?

"I see," I said softly.

Then a tiny flame of anger snuffed out a little of the hurt. Perhaps I didn't hold onto pride as much as others did. Perhaps I was a little pathetic in his eyes—I couldn't be certain anymore how he viewed me. But if he believed that I would touch him now, knowing that he was only interested in sex and repelled that I'd called him 'my demon king,' then he had no idea how brightly my pride could shine.

"You can start with my back," he rasped, stalking towards me. He seemed even larger in his anger and he held my eyes, as if daring me to challenge him.

This Seerin was cold, biting. This Seerin I didn't recognize. Perhaps this was the darker *Vorakkar* underneath, the one who'd ordered my punishment unflinchingly, but certainly not the one who'd been hell-bent on saving me from fever and infection.

Perhaps they were one in the same and I'd been blind to it.

"I think I *will* leave now," I informed him softly, lifting my chin. His eyes narrowed. "You're being unnecessarily callous when I've done nothing wrong. I won't let you treat me this way."

If caring for him and assuming he cared for me was wrong then he could very well go find another *alukkiri*, our agreement be damned. I didn't care. Not anymore.

Something in his gaze flickered, but I didn't wait for him to reply. My head had begun to throb, so I turned my back.

I left the *voliki* without another word.

23

That night, I went to the training grounds. I was too upset to return to my tent. The idea of sitting inside, with Seerin's words ringing through my mind endlessly, left me restless.

The training grounds were empty, as I suspected they'd be. The whole encampment was quiet. Only a crazy person would be out in the dead of night during the cold season, but the numbness I felt enveloping my body felt *good*.

I walked to the weapons rack and plucked off the bow and the quiver of arrows. As I walked, I inspected the Dakkari arrow of steel, memorizing the lines, the expert way the fletching tilted up, and wondered if I'd ever be able to make something so intricate. Would I be in the encampment long enough to learn how?

I frowned, feeling my chest pinch slightly at the thought. I thought of Seerin. I felt like my hand was still warm from his cock and I drew in a ragged breath, trying to ignore the hurt that burned in my belly.

One, I thought quietly, in desperate need of a distraction, *the frostbitten mountains.*

Two, the glow of the barrel fire.

Three, the blackened hide roof of the weapons rack.

I picked a different target since the post at the far corner reminded me too much of Seerin and his kisses and the bargains we'd made in the dark.

Instead, I leveled the bow at the opposite end of the enclosure, at a tall pole with a flag posted at the top. It was the image of a shield and a sword.

Holding my breath, I nocked the arrow. I adjusted my grip, though my fingers were beginning to tighten and freeze.

Exhaling, I released and the satisfying sound of the string snapping met my ears, followed by the satisfying *thud* as the arrow bit into my target.

Success.

I nocked another. It hit.

Another...it hit.

I emptied the quiver into the pole, stacking the arrows up high until I wasn't certain I'd be able to pull them down.

A voice came to my right.

"You are an archer?"

I cried out, startled, and whipped around...only to find a familiar warrior standing within the shadows of the weapons master's tent.

I relaxed when I recognized him. The brother of my *lirilla*. The warrior who'd tried to get me warm after the fence had collapsed.

My heart was racing from the sudden disruption and my exertion from the bow. I watched as he stepped closer to the fence of the training grounds until he was just on the other side.

"An archer?" I asked softly. "No, I'm not."

He frowned, looking back towards the pole, at the ten arrows lodged into it. "Yet you have the skill of one."

"I was a hunter," I explained.

Hesitant understanding dawned in his face. He was young

and handsome, I noticed, his features strong. His hair was black, trailing to his waist. His eyes were ringed in red. He looked like how I'd imagined his grandfather, the weapons master, would've looked in his youth.

"That was why the *Vorakkar* whipped you?"

"You know about that?" I asked quietly. At his words, my wounds felt tight, though the flesh had already healed over. Would I always feel them? "Were...were you there that day?"

"*Nik*," he replied, his lips pressing together at the prospect. "But the Dakkari like to talk. You will find that soon enough."

"Then yes," I said. "He saw me hunting and did what he had to do."

I didn't want to talk about Seerin, especially since I'd come out here to escape him.

"There are not many skilled archers among the Dakkari hordes," he said further. "How did you learn?"

My skill meant I ate or I did not, I thought, slightly irritated by his question, though I didn't know why. Perhaps Seerin's darkened mood had rubbed off on me.

"It was necessary to learn," I told him instead, walking over to the pole, pulling out as many arrows as I could. But the shafts were icy cold and slipped from my grip. There were three that were too high for me to reach.

"Do you mind if I watch you?" the warrior asked next, leaning his forearms against the fence, looking as if he had no intention of moving.

"If you want to," I replied. I stood a little farther back than I did last time and asked, "Why are you out here, anyway?"

"Why are you?"

A surprised laugh rose from my throat. Obviously, I wouldn't tell him of what happened with Seerin, so I said, "I just didn't want to be inside right now."

He shrugged. "It is the same for me. I enjoy the cold season.

Most Dakkari like warmer temperatures, but I always thought it was more pleasant in the cold."

"Even *this* cold?" I questioned, looking back at the pole, bringing my bow up. I tilted down slightly, trying to loosen my fingers when they curled too tightly.

He was quiet until I let the arrow fly. It hit, a little more left than I'd aimed for.

Then he said, "*Lysi*, this cold. It makes everything seem...quiet."

"Then you must be sad when the cold season comes to an end," I murmured, glancing over at him.

"*Lysi*, a part of me. But the end of the cold season also means traveling to a new home, so I look forward to it as well."

I paused. I'd always figured the hordes moved around, following their game, but that was before I saw the massive layout of the encampment...the fences, the tents, the *pyroki* enclosure.

"*Neffar*?"

"It just seems like a lot of work to move this place somewhere else," I told him, waving my hand at the encampment behind him.

"It is," he said. "But during the cold season, we protect the encampment with the fence and build larger enclosures for the *pyrokis'* nesting grounds. Once the cold season ends, it is not as much work. You will see for yourself."

"I return to my village after the cold season," I informed him, nocking another arrow.

"But the *Vorakkar* surely wishes for you to stay," he said quietly, his voice dropping. "*Lysi*?"

My breath left me but I didn't release the arrow. "Why do you say that?" I rasped, turning to him.

He shifted. "Like I said, the Dakkari like to talk."

I frowned. "And what's been said around the horde?"

"That he has taken an interest in you," he explained, with only slight embarrassment. "Why else would you be sharing his *voliki*?"

"Because my own needed to be built," I explained, feeling strangely defensive. "There were other tasks to finish first."

"A horde child could build a *voliki*," the warrior scoffed. "It would have taken a day at most."

Yet I'd stayed in Seerin's bed for much, much longer.

Well, of course, I thought after thinking about it. *He wanted sex.*

"It's not like that," I protested. "The *Vorakkar* has no interest in me."

My words didn't satisfy me, however. Just that evening, Seerin had told me if he was a human male in my village, he would have claimed me long ago. Had he meant sex or something else, something more?

"Rath Kitala's *Vorakkar* took a human *Morakkari* recently," the warrior said next. "Most are wondering if our *Vorakkar* will do the same."

Shock held me frozen as longing and disbelief created a strange mixture of bubbling emotion in my chest.

"What do you mean? Another *Vorakkar* took a *human* as his wife?"

"*Lysi*," he said, inclining his head. "You did not know?"

Of course not.

How could I have known? Seerin certainly hadn't offered up that information.

I am not yours, Nelle. Do not ever think of me as yours.

His words felt like they'd punctured through my chest.

"I assure you," I told the warrior, "that the *Vorakkar* has no interest in me for his *Morakkari*. *That* I know for certain."

"So that means you are free to choose a mate?" he questioned next, something in his tone making my brows raise.

I surprised myself with my chuckle. His small, crooked grin caused embarrassment to rise within me.

"I've never considered it," I told him. At least, not within the horde.

I'd always dreamed of having a mate, of having love, of having children. So many children. *Family*. But my yearnings always seemed so unattainable that I'd written them off as fantasies. Fantasies I visited whenever I got overwhelmed with loneliness, though they always seemed to make me feel lonelier...so I tried not to think of them at all.

Yet when Seerin had spoken of a *Morakkari*, when he'd whispered to me in the dark that I wasn't alone as he kissed me, I'd felt that similar yearning, returning to me in full force as if it had never left. Only, in addition to that yearning, there'd been *hope*.

I cleared my throat when it felt tight. I was shivering, I realized. I walked a short distance away, replacing the bow and the quiver of arrows on the weapons rack.

"I hope I can choose a mate soon too," the warrior told me with another shameless grin. For a moment, that grin made me feel better.

I chuckled again, though it felt like the last thing I wanted to do.

"Can I walk you back to your *voliki*?" he asked quietly, when he realized I was done in the training grounds.

"Yes," I said, giving him a small smile. "I would like that."

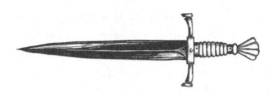

24

From the shadows, I watched Nelle and the young warrior —Odrii was his given name—walk away from the training grounds, towards her *voliki.*

A savage feeling had risen in me when I'd first heard them speaking, when I'd heard the young warrior flirt and hint at mate courtship. Though Nelle likely wouldn't understand his meaning, Odrii had essentially announced his interest in her. If other Dakkari had been present, it would have seemed like a formal declaration of courtship.

The only reason I stayed rooted in place and didn't tear off after them was that Odrii was still a young warrior. A young warrior who I had not yet given permission to take a mate. He needed to prove his place in the horde, to me, before I formally granted him the luxury.

Still, I was not used to jealousy when it came to a female. When I'd been young, I'd certainly felt envy. Envy for food, for warmth, for nice trinkets. But never for a female.

Until Nelle.

I'd always prided myself on my steel-clad control. My control had helped me through the Trials. Not letting emotion guide me was what made me a better leader to my horde.

But this ball of jealousy knotted my chest and made it hard to think. She'd declared that I had no interest in her as my wife and soon, her words would make their way around the horde. Others would approach her without a doubt. They would see the same things I saw in her...her bravery, her optimism, her strength.

I clenched my fists so tightly I felt my claws puncture my palms. Because I had not officially declared her as mine, others would be free to pursue her.

Vok.

I stared at her arrows, still sticking out from the pole she'd aimed them at. It was the flag of my shield, of my horde, of Rath Tuviri. Worried about the frost, I'd followed her out here when I realized she hadn't immediately gone to her *voliki*. But Odrii had reached her first.

I pressed my palms to my eyes, cursing quietly under my breath. My thoughts and wants were jumbled, my body still lusted for her, yet I remembered the way my words had cut her *deeply*. I'd seen it plainly on her face. She'd always been easy to read.

She'd been nervous to touch me. Nervous, yet curious. She'd *wanted* to. And the moment she had, the moment she had begun to explore that curiosity I so desperately wanted to satisfy, I'd pushed her away. Earlier she had opened up to me about her parents, about Jana, who had rejected her.

And I'd done the same.

My chest felt tight with the knowledge. But she'd frightened me in a way I hadn't been frightened before.

Because it had felt so *right*, hearing her call me her own. She'd looked at me like I was her own too, like she owned me as I owned her. It felt fated. It felt otherworldly.

And it was a warning. A reminder that if I jumped in too deeply, I would never find my way out. I would be lost in her and a part of me feared I wanted to be.

Jolted and uneasy, I'd put the necessary distance between us. I thought it was the kinder thing to do.

So why did I feel like a monster again?

EVEN VODAN AVOIDED me the next day, as word of my darkened mood floated around the encampment.

It had begun in the training grounds that morning. I'd seen Nelle's arrows embedded in the flagpole of my shield and had taken on opponent after opponent in an attempt to distract myself. Though I must've been especially ruthless that day, since no warrior would step forward after I defeated my ninth.

It didn't help that I'd seen Nelle emerge from the weapons master's *voliki*, the young Dakkari boy once again trailing her. Our eyes had connected just for a moment—I'd devoured the sight of her as if starved—before she jerked her gaze away and left the clearing without another glance.

My mood only blackened when I saw Odrii approach her from his place outside the fence where he'd been watching the training session, walking next to her and his nephew as they disappeared from sight together.

When a tenth brave warrior finally stepped forward, I defeated him with a ferocity that surprised even me.

The rest of the day passed slowly. The council meeting was cut short after it turned particularly vicious and I left towards the *pyroki* enclosure after dark.

"Ready my *pyroki*," I told the *mrikro* when I stopped.

"*Lysi, Vorakkar,*" he replied, inclining his head before hurrying towards Lokkas' nest.

My beast was displeased to be roused that late, especially during the cold season, but once he saw me, his long neck straightened and he made a chirring sound in his throat, trotting over to me without the *mrikro's* aid.

I took him from the pen, telling the *mrikro* not to wait, that I would settle him in his nest once I returned. Then I mounted his back and steered him towards the entrance of the encampment.

"You will be very displeased with me once we must return to *Dothik*, my old friend," I murmured down to him once we passed through the fence, once the land was open to us. I pressed my hand to the back of his neck, feeling his heart beat strongly against my palm.

Affection helped banish some of my darker thoughts. Lokkas had been with me since the beginning. I'd chosen him from the *Dothikkar's* breeding grounds once I'd completed the Trials. He'd been small then, smaller than the rest, but I'd looked into his eyes and known that he would be mine. I'd felt Kakkari's influence then too. We were bonded and always would be.

What affection could not distract me from, the open plains of Dakkar could. Lokkas needed no instruction. He knew what I needed and he began to race against the winds. It whipped in my ears until it was deafening.

A light snow had begun to fall, stinging my flesh, but I paid it no mind. My eyes drank in the lightened landscape, the moon-light reflecting off the ice and the snow that was beginning to blanket Dakkar. It was eerily beautiful. Haunting. Lethal.

The towering mountain range of *Hitri* in the distance met my gaze. Once the cold season was over, I would be leading my horde through it to the forests and valleys of the south.

Nelle would like to see it, I couldn't help but think. My starling had lived on Dakkar for the majority of her life, yet had seen only a fraction of it. I wanted to show her the beauty of it, the vastness of it.

My growl was whipped away by the wind. Lokkas continued to sprint, stretching his legs, his claws digging deep into the ice as he went.

I didn't know how long we were gone from the encampment. But once my mind felt quieter, once my flesh was tingling from the cold and I longed for a hot meal and a hot bath, I had Lokkas return us.

Once back at the enclosure, I guided Lokkas to his nest, pressing my hand to his heartbeat and murmuring soft words to him as he lay down.

"We leave for *Dothik* soon," I told him. "But for now, rest deeply, my friend."

I locked up the *pyroki* enclosure and made my way to my *voliki*, my heavy boots crunching into the ice as I went, my ears ringing from the winds across the plains.

I had no intention of going to her. At least that was what I told myself when Nelle's *voliki* came into view, a soft yellow light from inside making the domed tent glow like a lantern.

When I paused in front of it, I told myself that I had pushed her away for a reason. That she was dangerous. That there was no reason to go to her now.

But I was weak. So *vokking* weak. And last night, that day had left an uneasy, restless sensation in my chest. The need to see her, to look at her, outweighed every logical argument I could make *not* to go to her.

With a curse, my heartbeat ticking up in speed, I ducked through the entrance of her *voliki*.

She was standing at her cabinet, brushing through her hair. Hair I knew was soft, that ran through my fingers like silk. She was dressed in a long shift night dress. A new one from her seamstress friend? It was slightly transparent, given the fire in her basin was behind her, outlining the softening lines of her body and the dip of her waist.

My swallow was loud and hard. For once, words escaped me. I felt the ice crystals in my hair begin to thaw and drip down the side of my face.

Her eyes locked onto me, but she never stopped her brushing.

"Have you come to apologize?" she questioned softly.

I blinked. For once, her expression was unreadable. Or perhaps it was wary? I couldn't tell and that frustrated me.

"Because if that's not why you've come, you can leave right now, horde king," she informed me.

My eyes narrowed. Very rarely had she called me 'horde king.' And I didn't like it. It felt cold, impersonal.

Which was how my words last night had made her feel, I was reminded.

My chest squeezed, making me growl.

"No?" she asked quietly, her lips settling into a firm line. "Then *go*."

Morakkari.

The word was echoing through my mind before I could stop it.

This was what a *Morakkari* would do if her *Vorakkar* displeased her. She would have a spine of Dakkari steel and wouldn't break.

Nik. If I wanted this fixed between us, I would have to crawl back on my hands and knees because she would demand nothing less.

But a *Vorakkar* didn't kneel before anyone.

She'd told me once that she didn't hold grudges. That she didn't react to things as others might. I knew all she wanted was an apology and an explanation. I knew all she wanted me to say was that I *did* care for her.

"*Rei thissie—*"

Belatedly, I knew it was the wrong thing to say.

"*Don't* call me that," she said quietly, laying her brush down on the cabinet, furrowing her brow. "Because I'm not yours. Last night, you made that very clear to me."

My jaw clenched. It was a mistake to come here. I saw that now.

But how much longer could I stay away from her? I was drawn to her like a bonded *pyroki* and each passing moment away from her felt like it was taking its toll.

What I feared had already happened, I realized. I craved her. I needed her.

"Go," she said softly. There was a crack in her expression, one that tugged at my gut. It was her hurt and it ate at me, knowing I had caused it. "Please."

With one last, lingering look, I did as she requested. I ducked back through the entrance, away from her, though everything in me wanted to stay.

25

"The *Vorakkar* announced the frost feast," my *lirilla* told me, glancing up at me from the piles of cloth in her lap.

She was creating a tunic for a female I'd seen briefly, while she'd tasked me with easy repairs, tears and holes.

"Finally," she added. "I expected it to happen already. The *bikku* are already in a frenzy."

"*Bikku*?" I questioned, threading my needle through a pair of hide pants. My hands felt blistered from my morning in the weapons tent, but I'd gotten close to pinching the fletching just right and I'd been on a high ever since.

"The females who prepare our meals," she said. "Who do you think makes all the food?"

Just another one of my curiosities satisfied. "I'd always wondered. Where do they make it?"

"They have a tent towards the *pyroki* enclosure."

"The one next to the baths?"

"*Lysi*."

I'd been there over two weeks now and I learned something new about the encampment constantly.

"But only *bikku* are allowed inside," she added, "or else the warriors would be too much of a distraction."

I smiled. "They try to steal food?"

"Constantly," she said. "So do the children."

"When will the feast happen?" I asked, taking a break from my work to look up at her. I rolled my neck, hearing it crack.

"In two days."

And then Seerin will leave for Dothik, I thought. For how long, I didn't know.

It had been three days since he'd come to my tent. Three days since I'd sent him away and, except for the barest of glimpses around the encampment, I hadn't seen him or spoken to him since.

The distance between us made me feel dejected. I'd been closest to Seerin. Despite my stronger feelings for him, I thought of him as a friend. I always felt he was honest with me. He intrigued me, somehow managing to assuage my curiosity about him while making me want to know so much more.

Yet in a single moment, our friendship—or whatever the hell it had been—had seemed to crumble. And I was still uncertain *why* he'd chosen to do that. Because it had been a calculated choice.

"I always love the frost feast," the seamstress said. "Even though it means that we have to go to our dried meats and soups for the rest of the cold season."

My gaze refocused on her since it had begun to drift with my thoughts. "Rations?" I asked, my chest squeezing, an old feeling of panic returning.

She looked at me carefully and said, "*Nik*. There is still plenty of food. Our fresher meat is usually used up during the frost feast. But I assure you, *lirilla*, the *bikku* dry the most delicious smoked *kinnu* and throw together rich, flavorful, nutritious broths. You might not even miss the fresh meat again until the thaw comes."

I relaxed slightly and nodded, a little embarrassed that she'd had to reassure me so much.

Hesitantly, she asked, "You were very hungry before coming here, were you not, *lirilla*?"

My brow furrowed and I looked back at the hide pants in my lap, at the needle still in my grip.

"Like I said before, my village was very different than here," I said softly. Though I'd grown up in that village, it seemed like months had passed since I'd been there.

What had Seerin said? That time moved slower in the cold season? It certainly seemed that way.

Another pang went through my chest, thinking about him, but I shook it away and resumed my work.

"I am sorry," she murmured, "that you suffered. I feel strange now, knowing that I have not given much thought to *vekkiri* settlements before. Now I wonder constantly. You have given me another perspective and I am grateful for it."

Her words surprised me. In return, I said softly, "And your horde has given me another perspective as well. I am grateful too."

We went back to our work, talking idly of the frost feast. She told me that there would be dancing and music and plenty of fermented wine.

"Perhaps you will dance with my brother," she teased.

A startled laugh escaped me. "Your brother? Why? I don't even know how to dance."

"You have been spending time with him," she noted.

"Yes," I said. The last couple nights, I'd been in the training grounds with him, teaching him how to shoot the bow. He'd been interested in learning and I found I liked teaching my favorite hobby. "He is kind. I consider him a friend."

I'd never thought of him otherwise, though I'd grown used to his flirting. It was harmless, but I was careful not to encourage it. Not when Seerin was still constantly in my thoughts.

"Hmm," her lips quirked. "Do you consider me a friend?"

"Of course," I told her. "You've also been very kind and patient, as I've bombarded you with questions."

"If that is the case," she said, "then you may call me by my given name of Avuli."

My hand stilled, the needle hovering. "Avuli," I repeated softly. I knew what it meant for her to give me her name. "Then you must call me Nelle. Although, I am sure your father already told you my name after my mix-up that day."

Her laugh was lyrical and light. "*Lysi*, he may have. But I wanted your permission to use it."

"Well, you certainly have it."

She smiled at me. I was suddenly struck with a fierce emotion, one of grief. Because when I left this place once the thaw came, I wouldn't only be leaving Seerin behind, but her, and her father's teachings, and her son following me around repeating my words, and nights in the training grounds with her brother.

"What is wrong, Nelle?" she asked, frowning when she saw my expression.

"Nothing," I said, shaking my head, forcing a small smile. "I'm just...happy."

With the exception of what had happened with Seerin, I realized I *was* happy. Happier than I could ever remember being, even when Jana had been alive. I felt useful here in the horde. I felt like I was slowly carving a place for myself here. I felt *free*. I felt *safe*.

But it wouldn't last.

Nothing did, I was reminded.

However, instead of dwelling on it, I pushed it from my

mind. I would spend my months in the horde embracing that happiness, that contentedness, as long as it lasted. And once I had to return to my village, I would remember my time here, I would remember Seerin and my friends fondly, and those memories would sustain me. Wouldn't they?

It was no use to think about anything else. Because I was quite determined to make the best of it.

That thought was still at the forefront of my mind when, later that night, Seerin finally came to me.

Some of my anger had drained over the course of the last few days, but I was still hurt. I was still confused. I still wanted him. I still *missed* him.

So, when I saw him duck inside my *voliki* without warning that night, I drank him in. Somehow, he'd grown even more handsome over the last few days, despite the strained look in his eyes that I knew didn't belong there.

We stood staring at one another as my heartbeat tried to thud its way from my chest.

"I cannot do this any longer, Nelle," he rasped.

"Do what?" I asked softly.

"Stay away from you," he rasped, raking a hand through his golden hair, his gaze flickering. I'd never seen him so...undone. So uncertain.

Though my breath hitched, I didn't want to get my hopes up. I'd heard whisperings the past few days in camp that the *Vorakkar* was in a terrible mood, along with warnings not to cross paths with him.

I could see why unsuspecting members of the horde wouldn't want to get in his way.

"Will you come with me?" he asked after a silent moment.

"Where?"

"Out on the plains," he replied.

My brow furrowed. I still wanted to hear an apology for that night—I still wanted an explanation. Did this mean he wanted to talk?

Still...anywhere that wasn't his *voliki* was a much safer bet. And I'd always itched to go beyond the fence, hadn't I?

Take advantage of your time here, I remembered.

"Alright," I said hesitantly, but I couldn't hide my frown. "I'll come."

He nodded, though I thought I spied relief in his gaze. "Dress warmly," he said before ducking out, giving me privacy, which seemed so unlike him.

Inhaling a long breath, I found I was nervous as I pulled back on my fur-lined pants, a thick tunic, an even thicker fur sweater, and my pelt. My hair was still slightly wet from when I'd bathed in the common *voliki* earlier that evening and I stood over the fire, drying it as best as I could, before I pulled it back into a braid.

I was still securing it with a piece of black cloth when I emerged from the tent and saw Seerin standing next to a *pyroki*. *His pyroki*, I realized.

For a moment, I froze, remembering the last clear memory I had of the beast. Of Seerin astride him, looking down at me with a cold gaze as I wondered if he would kill me.

It seemed like so long ago, but I was still jarred by the memory.

"Lokkas," he murmured, running his palm down the creature's wide snout. Its hot breath came in heavy pants, silvering the air around it.

Lokkas. It was his *pyroki's* name. I wondered, briefly, if *pyrokis'* given names were just as secretive as their masters'. Somehow, I thought it might be the case, and I wondered why Seerin would share it with me so easily.

"Hello, Lokkas," I said softly to him, reaching out hesitantly to stroke the side of his neck. Right then, I remembered that I'd been on his back before. I'd awoken on our way here from my village, bandaged and aching, and I'd felt the beast's strength underneath me.

I was all too aware that Seerin was close to me. How strange it seemed now that I'd slept beside him for over a week, yet just being within arm's reach of him now sent a shiver down my spine.

Perhaps that was why I couldn't quite meet his eyes. And when I did, it wasn't for long.

"I will help you up," he rasped. Before I could protest, his hands were around my waist, strong and sure, and he lifted me easily, settling me feet above the ground on the back of his *pyroki,* as if I weighed nothing more than a feather.

A moment later, he swung up behind me and my face heated when his thighs clasped around my own. Though I'd touched his cock, bathed him, and seen him naked more times than I could count, just being cradled between his clothed, thick thighs was enough to make me question whether this had been a good idea or not.

He took Lokkas' reins in one fist, his hand coming around my waist to steady me as he urged his *pyroki* into a gentle trot.

The entrance to the encampment came up quickly.

Without hesitation, we went through the gate...and out onto the open plains of Dakkar.

26

We rode on Lokkas' back in silence beyond the gates of the encampment. An easy, gentle pace so the wind didn't chill Nelle too much.

We rode until the encampment was nothing more than a glowing speck, until the *Hitri* mountains grew sharper through the thick clouds.

"Why did you want to come out here?" she asked.

I'd felt starved for her voice and the way it wound through me, pulling away the tension that had been building over the course of the last four days and nights.

"Because I feel less like a *Vorakkar* out here," I rasped. "I am simply a Dakkari male on the back of my *pyroki*, as it should be."

"I don't think you could ever simply be a Dakkari male, Seerin," she said quietly. "You will always be a *Vorakkar*."

And therein lay the problem.

"I knew who you were the moment I saw you in my village," she added. "You were dressed no differently than the others. But I knew that you were one of *them,* a horde king we'd only heard about in legends and stories, because I felt it. You could be nothing else."

"Would you wish that I weren't a *Vorakkar*?" I asked, my fist tightening on the reins.

"It doesn't matter," she told me and I could hear the confusion in her tone, her confusion as to why I would ask such a question. "This is who you are. This is who you'll always be."

I dropped my head, pressing my forehead to the back of her warm neck. My breath fanned out over her flesh and I felt a responding shiver rack her body.

"Seerin," she said quietly as I inhaled her soft scent, letting it fill my lungs. "You shouldn't—"

"I *am* yours, Nelle," I rasped.

She froze as a gust of wind whistled past us, rustling her braid.

Then she turned in her seat until she met my eyes.

"And you are mine," I said. "You know this."

"Yet you denied it," she answered.

"I am sorry for that," I murmured, reaching out to cup her face. "I am sorry for pulling away and for hurting you, *thissie*. You do not know how much. I have thought about it every moment of the day, every moment of the night."

It was what she wanted. It was exactly what she wanted to hear, I could see that in her expressive face.

But still, she demanded more. "Then why did you do it?"

"Because you frightened me," I told her honestly. Her lips parted. "I have lived my life a certain way for a long time. Even when I was young in *Dothik*, I had a certain freedom. I did not have to answer to anyone, not even my mother. As *Vorakkar*, one would think I would have more freedom, but there are certain things to be considered and sometimes it leaves me shackled, not free."

"You..." she trailed off, her eyes flickering between my own. "These things you have to consider...is one of them your choice of *Morakkari*?"

My lips pressed together. It was here I had to tread carefully.

"*Lysi*," I rasped, running a hand through my already disheveled hair. "I...I will not lie to you, Nelle. I cannot make you promises, not the promises I wish I could make to you, but I will try. For us."

"You're still frightened," she observed softly, frowning.

"Aren't you?" I returned.

Her gaze dropped to my chest as she pondered my question.

"You're offering me not a 'yes' or a 'no,' but a 'maybe.'"

I inclined my head, my nostrils flaring, my heartbeat ringing in my ears. Because truthfully, I didn't know what I would do if she rejected me—if she rejected *this*.

The past few days had proven that she'd found her way into every part of me. I'd barely eaten, I hadn't slept, and when I'd tried, I'd found myself reaching for her throughout the long nights.

"I'll need to think about it," she said softly, meeting my gaze.

It wasn't the answer I wanted to hear, but it was better than a refusal.

I swallowed, nodding. "*Lysi*. I understand."

"You'll be leaving for *Dothik* soon," she said next.

"I leave the morning after the frost feast. I have lingered too long here and the moon is almost full."

Its light shone over her even then, growing with each passing night.

She let out a small breath and nodded. "You're still my friend, Seerin. No matter what. I'll still worry for you. I'll still miss you."

I brushed her cheek once, but then my hand retreated.

"And I will miss you, *rei thissie*."

27

The night of the frost feast came quickly yet slowly. During the days, time seemed to speed up because I spent my time between the weapons tent and in Avuli's *voliki*, helping her with the seemingly endless amount of repairs that had flooded in over the past two days.

At the end of the day, I was exhausted, my hands cramping and aching. Truthfully, I was thankful for it, because it meant I was distracted.

But even that distraction didn't last long and lying in my bed of furs at night, time slowed because all I could think about was Seerin. After the night out on the plains, I'd seen and spoken to him briefly around camp, but nothing more. As if he was giving me space and time to decide what I wanted to do, he hadn't attempted to come to my *voliki* after dark.

Truthfully, I'd already had my answer for him that night. I'd felt it deep in my chest. However, I hadn't wanted to be too impulsive. I deserved the time to think, to weigh the possibilities and risks, but when the night of the frost feast came, my answer remained unchanged.

And I was all too aware that he was leaving for *Dothik* in the morning.

I'll tell him tonight, I thought, a fluttering sensation of anticipation and excitement flowing through me as Avuli helped me lace up the back of my dress.

Only a slight hesitation remained within me, a warning, but I ignored it. If I was going to do this, I decided, I would give it my all. I didn't want to regret anything. I remembered my vow to take advantage of my time here and if that meant having Seerin as mine, I would do it.

"All done," Avuli said, turning me so she could inspect the front of the dress. I'd never worn one before, unless my night shift counted, but it was the most beautiful thing I'd ever donned.

It was fur-lined on the bottom half of the dress, yet the material swayed and pleated as if it was made of the lightest silk. The color was an inky blue, as dark as the night sky. Despite the chill, the neckline was low-cut, but Avuli assured me that I wouldn't be cold that night.

"Between the wine and the barrel fires," she said, smiling, "you will hardly feel the chill."

I wrapped my white pelt around my shoulders, a little uncomfortable that my breasts were so...on display. Regardless, I was grateful that my friend had taken the time to alter one of her gowns for me, though she was already so busy.

"Thank you, Avuli," I told her, smiling. "It's beautiful."

I watched as she helped her son, whose name I now knew was Arlah, pull on his best tunic. I would go with them to the feast, which I was thankful for. Despite my excitement and my curiosity for the night, I was still incredibly nervous.

Once Arlah was finished dressing, Avuli said, "Shall we go? My father and brother are already there. They do love their wine."

In the distance, coming from the open space next to the training grounds, I heard what sounded like drums reverberating around the camp. I nodded and we set out from the *voliki*.

Even the energy of the horde was different. Dakkari were pouring in from all directions of the encampment, laughter and excited voices following in their wake. When the frost feast came into view, I was surprised to see most of the horde was already there and I was stunned by the beauty of it, the picture it made in my mind.

The Dakkari were a race of physically beautiful, physically overwhelming beings. The females had their hair long, black and silky down their backs. Their dresses were in different colors, ranging from the palest of blues to almost darkened blacks. Some were even in dresses of silver and white, showing off their generous, voluptuous curves. They were all in silks, which were so different from the garments of fur and hide they usually wore around camp.

As for the males, I was surprised to see most were *bare-chested*. *Bare-chested*, only wearing thick-soled boots and fur-lined hide pants.

Almost all the barrel fires from around the camp, along with familiar golden basins, were placed through the feast. Roaring and hot, they made the space glow, reflecting off golden skin and golden markings.

When we drew near, I understood why the males could go bare-chested and why Avuli had told me the cold wouldn't be a problem. The plethora of fires heated the entire space, even thawing the ice on the ground below. Once we entered the feast, I could feel the flames licking against my skin and I knew I'd have to remove my pelt before the night's end.

Next to the tall, broad Dakkari females, I felt small and out of place as we wound our way through the growing crowd.

"I see my father," Avuli said. "Let's go join him."

I nodded, but she didn't see. Arlah grabbed my hand, his small palm enveloped in mine, as we followed his mother and stopped in front of a small table where the weapons master sat, happily chatting with another older male to his right, a goblet of wine in his hand.

He saw his daughter and greeted her jovially in Dakkari, as if he hadn't seen her in weeks. When his eyes turned to me, he grinned and said in the universal tongue, "And here is my favorite apprentice."

"I am your only apprentice, *mitri*."

"She crafted a near-perfect arrow today," he told the older male before taking a healthy swallow from his goblet.

The older male, one I recognized from around camp, one of the elders, narrowed his gaze on me. I felt a decided chill from him and the smile died from my face.

He stood, saying something to my *mitri* in Dakkari, inclining his head at Avuli, ignoring me completely, before he departed the table.

I looked after him, swallowing, but Avuli ushered me to sit and my *mitri* was pressing a goblet into my hand before I had time to think about the elder's abrupt and cold departure.

The table was circular and high. I was so used to the low tables and sitting on my cushions to take meals that it seemed strange now, though the height and design were very similar to my table back at my village.

Now that I was sitting, I felt less uncomfortable, less out of place, and observed the feast at my leisure as Avuli and her father talked in the universal tongue for my benefit. I half-listened, taking a small sip of the wine, feeling it burn down my throat.

There were fifteen tables I counted, including a smaller table on a raised dais at the front of the feast. Each table was packed with Dakkari, with warriors and families and unmated females and children.

At the far corner, a group of older males and one female played four sets of drums, beating out a primal rhythm I felt deep in my chest. Groups stood next to the barrel fires, packing in all available space. I spied a group of females next to one, a few I recognized because they'd delivered Seerin's meals once or twice. Females who vied for his attentions, females who'd made their distaste of me known.

I swallowed and looked away, searching the crowd for Seerin, though I knew he had yet to arrive. I didn't feel that prickle of awareness whenever he was near.

However, it was only a short while later when he appeared. The crowd hushed and the drums died down when he entered the gathering and my heart picked up at the sight of him. I imagined every female's heartbeat did the same because how could they not?

His golden hair was half tied back, revealing the hardened lines and edges of his jaw and nose and cheekbones. He wore his black pelt that night, but once he ascended the dais, he took it from his shoulders and draped it on the back of his chair, leaving him as bare-chested as the rest of the males.

He wore his golden cuffs on his thick wrists, his scars and markings on full display, reminding all present that he had *earned* his right to be *Vorakkar*, that he had earned his right to sit on that throne.

Seerin dropped into his seat as his horde watched him. I wondered if he felt every single pair of eyes on him—if he felt *mine*.

He looked into the crowd, searching. When his eyes connected with mine, they held, and I heard his voice clearly, as if he spoke directly into my ear, as he rumbled out, "*Delni unru drikkan kussun bak.*"

Cheers rang up into the night sky and in a flurry of motion, females suddenly appeared with heaping, massive plates of food. They deposited them on every table. When one of the females came to ours, the platter thudded down and it was the most meat I'd ever seen in my entire life.

I caught Seerin's gaze again, noticing that an older *bikku* had brought him a specially prepared platter.

"Eat, Nelle," Avuli said to my left. When I looked over at her, I saw that Arlah was already eating, plucking chunks of meat from the platter happily and stuffing them into his wide mouth.

My friend had a knowing expression on her face and I knew I'd been caught looking at Seerin. I nodded and began taking some meat, though my stomach was now fluttering.

After a while, I noticed that the tables began passing platters and our mound of meat disappeared, only to be replaced by one of my favorites: precisely cut squares of the purple bread I now knew was called *kuveri*.

Avuli's brother, Odrii, who'd shared his given name with me during our last shooting lesson, appeared, sauntering over to our table from a group of warriors he'd joined. In his hand was a goblet and he wore a wide grin when he saw me.

He collapsed with a deep sigh into the chair across from me and reached out to take my hand, leaning towards me.

"How pretty you look tonight," he murmured, his eyes glittering.

I shook my head at him, chuckling slightly because it was obvious that Odrii was slightly drunk off the fermented wine, which spilled from his goblet. His hand was heavy and warm.

"Will you dance with me later?" he asked next, his gaze intent on me.

His father replied, "Leave her alone, you fool. You will only embarrass yourself if you force her to dance with you."

Avuli's hand covered her brother's and peeled it away from

my palm. "If you wish to keep this hand, brother, you would be wise to keep it to yourself."

Shock at her words made me regard her, but her lips were pressed tightly together. I wondered why she would say that, but it only took another moment to realize why.

Seerin looked thunderous from his place on the dais. His eyes were on Odrii and I could *feel* his displeasure on the opposite side of the feast. It rolled off him in waves.

He was *jealous*.

Intensely so. But his jealousy seemed deeper, as if what Odrii had done was an insult.

Odrii didn't seem to comprehend his sister's words. Instead, he grabbed some *kuveri*, placing it into his mouth, chewing happily, gazing around at the females that swayed past.

I, on the other hand, turned to look at Avuli. She met my eyes and held them.

She'd never asked me directly about my relationship with her *Vorakkar*. But I knew she was no fool. Even Odrii had heard the rumors around the encampment, so of course Avuli would've too.

I didn't know what to say so I ate another *kuveri* square, half-listening as my *mitri* drew his son into conversation about learning to shoot the bow and arrow.

"She is a good instructor," Odrii said, grinning over at me. I forced a smile, all too aware of Seerin's gaze. "I did well last time, did I not?"

"You did," I agreed, before looking at his father. "He finally hit the target at least."

His father laughed and the platters switched again. Another pile of meat came to us, though this was a marinated meat and thinly sliced.

I took another healthy sip of my wine, feeling a little looser and more relaxed because of it. More platters rotated and my table talked and laughed, though I only felt half present. The other half of me felt elsewhere, on the dais, held by piercing grey eyes.

Once most of the eating was finished and I was stuffed full, I noticed a beautiful, tall female in an icy blue dress approach Seerin, a goblet of wine in her grip.

Conversation from my table seemed to fall away as I straightened and watched the female climb the stairs towards him.

His attention turned to her as she bent low and placed the goblet on his table. Then they spoke, her smile brightening at whatever he said.

Something knotted in my stomach watching them. I couldn't help but notice how beautiful they looked together. She was exactly the kind of female I'd always envisioned Seerin would prefer.

They only spoke for a few moments, but it seemed like it lasted a lifetime before she inclined her head and rejoined the feast.

As if her exit was a cue, another female approached the dais, one I recognized because she'd glared at me once when she'd delivered our evening meal. She placed her goblet of wine on the table.

I didn't understand what was happening, but my belly tightened once more with something I didn't like, especially when I saw this female reach out to *touch* Seerin's bare shoulder.

"It is a custom," Avuli said quietly to my left and I looked at her. She must've seen the distress on my face because her smile softened. "An old tradition for unmated *Vorakkars*."

"What is it exactly?" I asked, not wanting to know, but *needing* to.

"Celebrations like this are not only for the horde, but also an opportunity for unmated females to put forward their interest to the *Vorakkar*."

My gut sank even lower and I took another sip of wine as it did.

"If he had already taken a *Morakkari*, then the females would not dare approach," Avuli said. "They bring him wine and if he takes a drink from their goblet, then it means he shares their interest. It could mean he has interest just for the night. Or for longer."

It was even worse than I thought. I knew that Seerin could have his pick of the unmated females in the horde. I knew a male like him had most likely enjoyed the company of some of the females present. It didn't make it any easier to stomach.

I stared at the goblets of wine that began to litter his table and watched one female after another approach him, speak with him, *touch* him.

He is mine, I thought suddenly, fierce and wanting.

He'd told me so himself.

With that thought, some of my jealousy sizzled away as I realized the truth of his words. Did it matter if other females wanted him after he'd told me he was mine? I relaxed slightly. After another female left his table, his eyes came to me again and I saw what was in them.

A challenge. An invitation.

Dancing had begun, the drums providing a heavy beat for swaying and gyrating bodies. My heart throbbed with the instruments and before I knew what I was doing, I was standing from my seat at the table, clasping my goblet.

I caught Avuli's smile but I was already walking towards the dais, threading through warm bodies, weaving around barrel fires until he was in perfect view once more.

His expression was unreadable as he watched me emerge from the crowd. Behind me, I heard the noise had quieted, though the drums still beat. Out of the corner of my eye, I saw a group of unmated females, females who had already presented their goblets to him, looking at me, *glaring*.

A part of me felt like a fraud, carrying my goblet to a powerful horde king of Dakkar. Though I was dressed in a beautiful gown, I was nothing like those around me. A part of me knew I didn't belong there.

Then I saw Seerin. And even if I didn't belong there, at the very least I knew I belonged to him. He was my demon king, who already owned half my soul. That was all that mattered to me.

I climbed the steps of the dais, my heart thundering in my throat, knowing that whatever happened next would change me in a way I would never come back from.

28

My goblet never even reached his table.

When I was within arm's reach, Seerin wrapped his hand around mine, clasping the goblet and guiding it to his lips, taking a healthy swallow.

The frost feast fell away behind me as my heart thudded in my chest and it was just the two of us. Like we were on Lokkas out on the plains. Those grey eyes regarded me as he drained the wine.

When he pulled the goblet away, my mouth was dry and my belly was fluttering.

"I'll take your 'maybe,' demon king," I said softly to him. "Because maybe you'll realize you can't let me go. And maybe I'll realize that I don't want you to."

His eyes flared and then his hand was tugging me forward until I was standing between his thighs.

Even sitting down, his head was level with my breasts and his gaze burned up into mine. I hadn't expected him to touch me like this, not in front of his entire horde, but the fact that he was filled me with pleasure.

"I already know I do not want to let you go, *rei thissie*," he rasped.

"I'm not frightened, Seerin," I whispered, remembering his question to me when we'd been out on the plains. "Not of this. But it's alright if you are."

His eyes sharpened on me.

I smiled, my body warm and tingling from the wine, as I teased, "I have courage enough for the both of us."

He exhaled a sharp breath. I was relieved to see the corner of his lips quirk up because it had been so long since I'd seen his smile.

His hands tightened on my waist. They were so warm I could feel them through my dress.

Out of the corner of my eye, I noticed he'd barely touched his food and I frowned. "Why haven't you eaten?"

"Because I have been waiting for you," he murmured and my breath hitched. "And trying not to challenge that warrior who dared to touch you."

Jealous, indeed, I thought.

"He is my friend," I told Seerin, "so you'll do no such thing."

His lips pressed together in discontent.

"Besides, considering your table is covered in goblets of wine, perhaps it is *I* that should be the jealous one here," I informed him.

He frowned. "I drank from yours so the rest do not matter, *thissie*."

"Then it would seem there is no reason for either of us to be jealous," I pointed out, raising my brow.

He quieted at my words. Realization flashed through his gaze and I was relieved at his short nod.

"Will you eat now?" I asked. He looked tired and I knew he would start a long journey tomorrow. He needed the sustenance.

"Only if you feed me, *kalles*," he rasped.

I sucked in a breath, that voice curling lower in my body.

"People are watching, Seerin," I told him. And they were. I could feel their eyes on my turned back, though I heard laughter and chatter and cheers during the dancing.

He took mercy on me and reached out to grab some food, popping it into his mouth and chewing. I'd seen him eat so many times, yet I was still fascinated by his strong jaw and the corded column of his throat as he swallowed.

It didn't take him long to polish off the tray. Then he stood. I sucked in a breath, looking up at him, and he murmured, "Come, Nelle."

The frost feast was still lively behind us.

"Won't they care if you leave now?" I asked.

"*Nik*. They will be here until the early hours," he informed me. "I would not be surprised if they are still here in the morning."

His gaze was fierce and knowing. I knew what would happen once we left. I knew what would happen once we returned to his *voliki*.

And I *wanted* it.

He knew it and I knew it.

At my nod, his eyes flared and a growl tore from his chest. He pulled me from the dais, leading us through the throng of dancing Dakkari at its base. I tried to look for Avuli and when I spotted her, she was watching me. She smiled and I inclined my head to her. No doubt she would ask me about what happened when I saw her tomorrow.

I tried to ignore the other stares, however. No one met Seerin's gaze directly, I noticed, but they certainly met mine.

When we were away from the crowd, I felt like I could breathe again. Seerin's pace was quick and I noticed that he'd forgotten his pelt.

"Won't you be cold?" I frowned, looking at his bared flesh.

"*Nik, thissie,* I am certainly not cold right now," he rasped. That voice reached me in places I didn't know existed.

My swallow was loud and audible, given the quietness of the rest of the camp. It was deserted, since everyone was at the feast. I was suddenly very happy I'd had the wine because it helped ease my nerves.

When we reached his *voliki*, he wasted no time in pulling me inside.

Not a second later, he had his hand around the nape of my neck and his lips were on mine. He kissed like he was starved for me and I could only clutch his broad, warm shoulders and surrender as he took what he needed with a ferocity that made me whimper.

"*Vok,*" he cursed, pulling away, nibbling his way down my jaw. I gasped when he suckled on the sensitive place just below my ear and growled, "You do not know how much I need you, *rei thissie.*"

"I-I have some idea," I whispered, my fingers sinking into his shoulders as my eyes closed. A shiver raced down my spine and my scalp tingled from his kiss.

He dragged the pelt away from my shoulders, tossing it down onto the rugs, and I gasped when he pressed his lips down my neck, over the tops of my breasts.

His fingers tugged at the straps of the dress, pushing them down until my breasts sprung free of the silky material.

I hardly comprehended his roughened growl before I felt his lips on one pebbled, aching nipple.

"*Ohh,*" I breathed, eyes widening, my fingers digging deeper into his shoulders, shamelessly anchoring him to me. Because I never wanted him to stop kissing me there.

A small moan escaped me when he switched to my other breast, drawing it deep into his mouth and suckling *hard.*

Warmth flooded between my thighs and the *voliki* spun as pleasure washed over me.

"*Seerin*," I cried out softly between ragged breaths.

He released my breast, tugging me forward forcefully by the material of the dress and capturing my mouth once more. I met his tongue when it slipped between my lips, acting purely on instinct, and he groaned deep in his chest.

"*Want you*," he growled into my mouth. "Need you, *rei thissie*."

His grip tightened but I wasn't afraid. Instead, I found I was eager and excited and curious...because I wanted to explore this potent, heady desire with him. It was desire I'd never felt before him and it made me feel...*powerful*.

Surprisingly so.

His fingers tugged at the laces of my dress, but they were tightened in a complicated pattern and my demon king was impatient with his need.

I gasped when his claws raked through them in one smooth, quick motion. The next moment, he pushed the dress from my body until it pooled at my feet—until I stood completely naked in front of him, looking up at him wide-eyed.

"That wasn't mine," I whispered.

He growled, "I am certain the seamstress will not mind."

His eyes were rapt on my body, trailing over my bared breasts, my waist, my hips.

When his gaze reached my sex, his eyes sharpened and focused...as if *that* was exactly where he wanted to be.

He'd seen me naked before, but this felt different. This felt like how it should be...primal. He looked at me like a predator looked at its prey and I found that sensation erotic, not frightening.

I was up in his arms, my legs wrapped around his hips,

before I took my next breath and he carried me over to the furs, lowering me onto them.

"I have dreamt of this," he rasped against me. "Dreamt of you like this. I'd wake *aching* for you."

He shifted his body until his head was hovering just between my thighs. His nostrils flared, his gaze still intensely focused on me, and then he was lowering his head.

My lips parted in realization when he pushed my legs wide open for him.

A strangled cry tore from my throat, my mouth dropping open as I watched his warm, wet, dark tongue lap at my clitoris.

Wicked demon, I thought in disbelief, my toes curling of their own accord as foreign sensations rushed through my body.

A rough groan rumbled from his throat. "*Need more of you, kalles*," he growled.

Why did we wait so long to do this? I thought in awe. Everything was so new to me and so *sublime*.

His tongue returned with vigor. With the tip, he flicked my aching bud mercilessly, transitioning from quick, vibrating movements to slow and languid and soft.

It drove me *insane*.

My back arched from the furs, sweat beginning to bead on my forehead and chest. Outside, as though through a thick haze, I heard the steady beats of the drums from the frost feast and felt the intense throbbing between my legs match their frantic rhythm.

It was building within me, that unfamiliar pleasure I'd felt only a handful of times in my life. It seemed strange to me now, but I'd only ever orgasmed in sleep. I would wake to piercing pleasure, my limbs thrashing, and afterwards, I would be desperate and frightened to feel it again—that overwhelming, overpowering sensation. I'd only learned exactly what I'd experienced in sleep when I'd overheard a group of women talking in my village years later.

"Are you going to come for me, *rei thissie*?" Seerin rasped, looking up me, rubbing his lips lightly over the top of my clitoris.

I'd never heard that word before, but I didn't need to. I knew what he wanted with that word, as delicious and wicked as it was. How could it mean anything else?

"Yes," I croaked. "I will."

"*Vok*," he whispered. He pressed a long kiss to my clit, making my breath hitch and a surprised moan tumble from me. "So sensitive, *lysi*?"

"Yes," I breathed, feeling Blue's feathers flutter over my nipples. I hadn't taken off the pendant since he'd given it to me. "*Please*, Seerin."

"I need to get you ready for me."

I watched as he brought his hand up and from his third finger, he tore the end of his sharp claw off with his teeth, blunting it. So he wouldn't hurt me?

That finger circled my opening and Seerin wet it with the arousal that dripped from me.

When he pushed inside me slowly, I gasped, my core muscles tensing. Then his tongue and lips returned to my clit, distracting me from the sudden sensation, and I whimpered, my hips rolling of their own accord against him.

My hips shot up when he gave my sensitive bud a soft suckle and it was enough. To my disbelief, that familiar feeling zipped up my spine and I hung, balanced, just on the edge of mindless pleasure...

That thick finger curled inside me. He suckled my clit again. A single, strangled cry was wrenched from my throat and then I was orgasming. *Coming.*

His groan vibrated my flesh and his finger slid inside and out as I came apart completely—until I was writhing on his tongue and fisting the furs underneath me and crying out his name.

My breathing was ragged and deep when my muscles finally relaxed. Between my thighs, Seerin stood, looking down at me with a possessive and dark gaze.

Even though I'd just orgasmed, I felt my clit tingle at the look in his eyes.

As if reading my thoughts, he rasped as he unlaced his pants, "We are only beginning, *rei thissie*."

I may have whimpered at his words. I couldn't recall. Because just then, his cock sprang forward as he kicked his pants away, leaving him as naked as I, save for the thick gold cuffs around his wrists.

His cock seemed even larger than it had before, bobbing with his desire against his hard abdomen. The broad head was swollen and glistening, his shaft engorged. The markings I'd asked him about before were flickering with the fire's light.

Magnificent demon, I thought, my own possessive streak rearing its head.

I'd never felt sensual or desired in my lifetime. I'd never felt this sexual, consuming awareness and pull to another being before Seerin. The way he looked down at me was enough to have me aching again.

He murmured something under his breath in Dakkari as he brushed his palm over the head of his cock. His eyes ran from my swollen sex up to my eyes and I heard the awe, the roughened reverence in his words, though I didn't know their exact meaning.

"I cannot wait any longer, *kalles*," he growled, his hands coming around my waist, pushing me higher on the bed of furs until he could kneel between my splayed thighs. "*Too long already*."

"I want to feel everything, demon king," I said, though my

voice didn't sound like my own. This female's voice, whoever she was, was throaty and lush and wanting.

"My *thissie* is still so curious," he rumbled, his calloused, warm palm sliding up my thigh.

In answer, I let my legs fall even wider, baring everything to him, not entirely sure what to expect...but I felt like my body knew this. My body knew what to do. It was instinct. It was Seerin.

He hissed, grabbing the base of his shaft and squeezing hard. "*Vok*, the sight of you will make me *come*, Nelle."

I wanted to see that. Something in my expression must've told him so because he squeezed his cock harder, his abdomen clenching, as he tried to gain control.

"Not like this," he growled, and I gasped when he tugged me forward by my hips, until his thick cock was poised just at the entrance of my sex. It was so hot I could feel it, mere inches from my flesh. His voice was rich and deep and sinful as he said, "When I release my seed, it will be deep inside your cunt, *rei thissie*. I will demand nothing less."

I gasped at his words, the *voliki* swirling slightly.

"You want me deep inside you?" he growled, pressing the broad head of his cock to my entrance, and the contact made me shiver. "Do you want to feel that?"

"Yes," I breathed, feeling my sex tighten and squeeze in response, as if it knew what it was missing.

But he was so large. In the back of my mind, I wondered if we would fit that way.

We must, I thought. Because if I didn't have him, I would regret it forever.

"Then take me, Nelle," he ordered as his cock began to *press* and press deep.

I bit my lip, my muscles tensing again at the unfamiliar invasion.

"*Nik*," he rasped. "*Relax, thissie.* Let me in."

At his urgings, I purposefully focused on unclenching my inner muscles and gasped when he slid inside more.

Pain began to make itself known. I was stretched to the brim and so full.

Seerin pulled back slightly before he thrust back in, a choked groan falling from his throat, and a hiss of pain fell from mine as I felt something pinch *hard*.

My demon king stilled, deep inside my body, and he leaned over me, his forearms dropping on both sides of my head, his chest flattening against my own.

Lips parting, I looked up at him because I felt him *everywhere*. Our flesh touched, our skin slid together, and he was embedded so deep inside me that I felt him at my core.

His lips found mine, distracting me momentarily from the pain.

"*Vok*, you feel so good, *thissie*," he murmured against me, his voice ragged and torn.

"Yeah?" I whispered, tilting my hips slightly, testing the pain. It was lessening bit by bit.

"*Lysi*," he growled, trailing his mouth down my throat. He hunched over me, lifting slightly, and a startled moan emerged from my throat when he began to tongue my nipples.

He kissed and rolled and nibbled at them until I was squirming. He read me well and by the time he finally pulled out of my body, only to thrust in even deeper, only a lingering ache from the pain remained and something much more pleasurable had begun to take its place.

I gasped when he thrust again, my fingernails digging into the rippling muscles of his strong back.

"More?" he purred.

"*Yes!*"

I sensed energy building within him and my belly quivered when I realized what it was.

It was the full extent of his need, his intensity. It was something I always sensed just simmering underneath the surface, ready to boil over.

Anticipation grew in my breast and I braced myself.

I'd wanted to feel everything he had to give me?

Well, I was about to.

29

D*eeper.*
    I needed to be deeper inside my female.

Gripping her hips, I drew out from her sex before thrusting back inside *hard*, until I was seated entirely in her tight cunt. Through a mindless haze, I saw her eyes widen. I knew, wedged as deeply as I could be, she felt my *dakke* against her swollen bud.

Her dark, half-lidded eyes went between us, saw the small swelling of my *dakke* that protruded just above the base of my cock. It pulsed with my arousal, with blood, with my heartbeat, with my crazed need for her.

"*Seerin*," she moaned, and I knew she felt that vibrating heat against her clit. "*Ahh!*"

I didn't give her time to catch her breath. I ground my cock into her, forcing her to take me even *more*, working my hips between her thighs.

Then I pulled back, her cries of pleasure meeting my ears, and drove in.

And then I didn't stop.

Too long had I needed her this way. Too many nights had I

woken fucking the furs, needing her even in sleep, trying to release the dizzying tension inside me.

My fucking was frenzied once I was certain the worst of her pain was over. I knew she'd been untried before this night. I knew she was unaccustomed to the demands that my body made on hers, but my *thissie* took me deep and she took me *well*.

Her blunt little claws raked over my back and the thought that she marked me in her own way only heightened my need. It was a primal, animalistic sensation, and it drove me to mark her as well.

I leaned over her, pulsing my hips in quick, fast, thorough thrusts, and bit at her neck before sucking on her sensitive flesh. I growled in satisfaction when her helpless moan reached my ears.

I would be leaving for *Dothik* once the sun rose. But I would leave knowing that I'd marked my female's flesh as *mine* and all males who dared to look at her would see the evidence of my claim.

It only marginally satisfied this beastly urge growing in me, an urge I'd never experienced before, but it would be enough until I returned.

"Your cunt takes me so well, *rei thissie*," I rumbled, my voice nothing more than a guttural rasp.

"*More,*" she whimpered, her brow furrowing. "Please, Seerin, I need *more*."

Vok, she pleased me.

My gaze narrowed on her, on the mark on the side of her neck, and I pinned her hips, keeping her still when she'd begun to squirm.

"Ahh!" she cried out when I began to fuck her even harder, unleashing upon her the full extent of my strength. "*Oh*, I'm—"

I felt her inner walls flutter around my unyielding cock, hot and tight.

Then her back arched off the furs, her nipples straining and budding hard, and she began to orgasm with an intensity and violence that made her scream.

"*Vok*," I grated, my breath wrenched from my lungs. "*Vok!*"

Disbelief shot through me as her cunt clamped down on me. Nothing had ever felt so good, so *right*.

A harsh snarl escaped me before I bellowed my release into her neck. My body jerked and my seed shot forward, sizzling up my shaft, emptying inside my female. Euphoria seared me, punishing wave after punishing wave.

"*Lysi, kassikari*," I rasped, shuddering over her still. "*Bnuru tei lilji rini, rei kalles.*"

Turning my face, I caught her mouth and kissed her deep. I felt her heart thundering against my own and she whimpered when she felt my *dakke* pulse in time with it, matching her rhythm.

It took me a good, solid moment afterwards to realize what I'd called her. *Kassikari*. My mate. My *destined* mate.

I growled, ignoring how right that word felt, assigned to her. I didn't have that luxury, so I pushed it from my mind. I distracted myself in another way.

Her sharp inhale reached my ears when I rocked my hips into her, grinding into her sensitive, heated flesh. I was still hard inside her, the extent of my need barely assuaged.

"A-again?" she rasped, her eyes half-lidded and glazed with her pleasure.

"*Again.*"

"Seerin," Nelle whispered. "I can't...anymore. *Please.*"

It was the early hours of morning. Even the drums from the frost feast had finally died down, leaving my horde wrapped in the quietness of the night. Unless, of course, they'd heard my female's pleasured screams.

Her chest was heaving, her body sweating despite the chill. She was spent and was begging for mercy. The smallest of touches set her off, flying up to new heights. Her flesh was sensitive, sore, and tender, no doubt.

I groaned out a harsh breath, my throat raw and scratchy from my bellows. I'd been...relentless. Even I recognized that.

I didn't trust my voice. So, after our last orgasms, the last of many we'd shared throughout the long night, I tucked her close, though I never left the tight sheath of her sex.

Her hot breath came in pants against my chest. Between us, I felt our thighs slick with my seed and her arousal. I'd pumped endless amounts into her tonight and the knowledge made that beast inside me immensely satisfied.

"*Veekor*, my starling," I rumbled. "I will have you again before dawn. So rest now."

Her eyes were closed before the last words fell from my lips. And even though she slumbered deeply, her little blunt claws still clutched tightly to my chest, as if afraid to let me go.

I'd never known such peace as I did at that moment. I felt it settle around my shoulders, loosening decades of old tension. I felt it cocoon the both of us, the rest of the universe floating away, until all I saw was her face.

I knew what this feeling was. I'd never experienced it before, but I knew what she pulled from me, from the dark depths of my mind and my heart.

Brushing my lips against the top of her head, I inhaled her scent deep, memorizing it.

Then I followed her in sleep.

PERCHED on the edge of the bed, clutching the furs around her naked shoulders, she looked at me with a solemnness that tugged at my chest.

It was too soon to leave after the night we'd shared, but I no longer had a choice. The moon would be full in four days' time. If I rode Lokkas hard, I would reach the capitol in time.

My female watched me dress in my warmest clothes, watched as I sheathed my sword and pulled on my boots. The *voliki* was utterly silent, save for the fire crackling in the basin.

Outside, the horde was quiet, still slumbering away after the night of celebration. Dawn had just broken and stale blue light filtered through at the entrance. Life would be slow in my horde that day and time would move even slower still, the further from my *thissie* I was.

"It is already difficult to leave, *kalles*," I murmured softly, eyeing her. "Do not make it harder."

She sighed and pushed up from the bed. I watched her expression pull and I knew she was sore from our matings. It was the only thing I regretted...that she was hurting from it.

"Come," I rasped, holding my hand out for her. She came into my arms as if she belonged there, as if she'd been in them her entire life. "I will send for a hot bath once I leave, to help with the pain."

"I'll go to the commons," she told me. "Don't worry. No one will be there at this time of morning and I would hate for you to wake the warriors. Let them sleep."

I frowned, but knew that even if I roused a few warriors to bring her hot water, she would still go to the common bathing *voliki* regardless.

"Very well," I rumbled, running my fingers through her dark hair.

"Will you see your mother in *Dothik*?" she whispered.

My jaw clenched. "*Lysi*. I will see her as soon as I can."

She nodded against my chest and then her eyes met mine. "Be safe on your way and on your return, alright?"

I was reminded of her words when I'd taken her out onto the plains. That, regardless of what happened, she was still my friend. That she would still worry for me, that she would still miss me.

Pressing my lips to hers, I kissed her deep and slow, unlike the frenzied, overwhelming way of last night. Even still, when I felt her respond, my body heated, banishing the chill and dread. Her breath hitched and I felt her eyelashes flutter against my face as her hands clutched my shoulders.

With a groan and a soft curse, I pulled away, knowing that if we continued, we would end up right back in the furs. I needed to leave. It was my duty and I could not disregard that, no matter how much I ached to.

She licked her lips and met my gaze. She'd always been so expressive, but through her desire, I saw her sadness.

"I will return to you, *rei thissie*," I promised her, cupping her cheeks. I pressed one last kiss to her forehead, lingering.

Then I growled, turning away from her. I picked up my travel sack, filled with rations and furs for my journey.

Briefly, I hesitated, stilling on the threshold of my *voliki*, but then I pushed through the flaps with a rough exhale. I didn't look back at her because I knew if I did, I would never leave.

The icy morning air met me, embraced me. Not a single Dakkari was in sight. I collected Lokkas from the *pyroki* enclosure, saddling my travel sack, and then I swung up onto his back.

"*Vir drak*," I murmured down to him once we reached the protective fence of my horde.

At my command, he raced through the gates.

At the last moment, I turned, searching for my *voliki* on the incline of my encampment. And I saw her. Standing just outside the entrance, in nothing but her boots and the fur blanket wrapped around her shoulders, watching me leave despite the cold. Even from there, I saw her shiver—yet her eyes never left me.

Longing rose in my chest, but I forced myself to turn forward in my seat, my eyes roaming the whitened landscape of my home planet. As harsh and unforgiving as it was during the cold season, I found it beautiful.

To Lokkas, I growled, "*Vir drak ji Dothik.*"

We ride for Dothik.

30

Thud.
   Thud.
Thud.

The arrows connected, one right after another, into the makeshift target that my *mitri* crafted for me. I'd found it out on the training grounds one evening. He'd told me it was so I wouldn't utterly destroy the flagpole.

It had been four days since Seerin left. My body had recovered and healed from the night before his departure, but I still ached for him. Everywhere. I thought about him too much, missed him too much, needed him too much.

I sighed, breathing hard as I stared at the arrows covering the target. I was growing used to the Dakkari bow, though it was much too large for my frame.

Odrii would usually be practicing with me, but he seemed to be avoiding me. I knew it was because of what had happened at the frost feast. I'd presented my goblet to Seerin and the horde king had accepted it.

Avuli had assured me that Odrii would get over it—that he was young and embarrassed. I felt partly responsible. I'd told the warrior that there was nothing between Seerin and I—which, at that point, had seemed like the truth to me—but I'd never revealed the extent of my feelings for the *Vorakkar* to my friend. Perhaps Odrii had mistaken my friendship for something more and I should've made that distinction clearer.

Odrii wasn't the only one wary of me, however. After Seerin had left for *Dothik*, there was a strange atmosphere in the encampment whenever I walked around. No one seemed to meet my gaze anymore, except for Avuli, Arlah, and my *mitri*. Even the *bikku* that delivered my meals didn't speak with me anymore. She simply inclined her head, dropped off the tray of food, and departed as quickly as she'd come.

I hadn't voiced my worries to Avuli, who usually helped me understand the perplexing intricacies of Dakkari culture. Instead, I simply minded myself whenever I walked through the camp, hoping that by publicly conveying my interest in Seerin at the frost feast, I hadn't inadvertently made myself an outcast.

The only place I found the quiet peace I craved was out on the training grounds at night. Though the cold froze my hands and cheeks, I *needed* to be out there. A part of me knew it was also to look for Seerin.

I was just nocking my next arrow when my neck prickled and I realized that I was no longer alone. Footsteps approached the fence behind me and when I turned to look—hoping it was perhaps Odrii—I saw, to my surprise and hesitation, that it was Seerin's second-in-command. His *pujerak*, I believed he was called.

I'd seen him enough times with Seerin around the encampment to know that the two males were close. Not only was this male his *pujerak*, but he was also Seerin's friend.

The only time I'd ever spoken to the *pujerak* directly was back at my village, so I was surprised when he emerged from the shadows of the darkened, quiet camp to approach me on the training grounds.

I angled my bow down, but kept it gripped in my palm as the Dakkari male studied me, though he seemed in no rush to speak first.

Growing uncomfortable with his silence, I thumbed the bowstring back and forth as I waited.

"Did you know, *vekkiri*, that the way hordes are classified, how they are recognized, are by their *Vorakkar's* family name?" he asked softly, forgoing any kind of greeting.

My brow furrowed, but I didn't look away from him.

"This horde is Rath Tuviri," the *pujerak* said.

Seerin of Rath Tuviri, I remembered him telling me.

"'Rath' in our language is directly translated to 'the end' in yours. 'The end of Tuviri.' I have always thought that strange. That family names mean 'the end of,' even when they are ancient lines."

I didn't know why he was telling me these things and my confusion must've shown on my face.

"What is your family name, *vekkiri*?" he asked, unmoving. "Do you know it?"

I shook my head, but I watched him closely. "No. I am only called Nelle."

Or *thissie*, but only Seerin called me that and I wanted to keep it that way.

Something in his expression changed, just a slight down-turning of his lips. He didn't look any older than Seerin, but the grave expression on his face reminded me of one of the elders I'd seen in the encampment.

"You will be his end, *vekkiri*," the *pujerak* rasped, "in the literal sense of the word."

My hand tightened on the bow and I realized now why he'd sought me out.

"I have known him longer than any Dakkari in this horde," the *pujerak* said next, confirming my suspicions that the two males had a long history. "I know his strengths and his weaknesses. And I see clearly that *you* are a weakness. One that must be ended before it threatens everything we have built."

He was warning me. That was his intention in coming here.

"You knew him in *Dothik*," I guessed. "You were one of the ones he watched over."

The *pujerak* didn't seem surprised that I knew Seerin's history.

"And *I* watched over him," the male returned. "As I have always done. As I continue to do, even now."

"You love him as a brother," I guessed next. Why else would the *pujerak* threaten me like this, unless he thought he was protecting Seerin?

His eyes narrowed. A silent wind ruffled the furs draped over his shoulders as he said, "You understand nothing of what we have gone through, *vekkiri*. But our reward was this life, this horde. I will not watch it fall because of one female, who comes from nowhere, who comes from no family."

Something occurred to me just then and I asked, "Rath Tuviri…it's his mother's line, is it not?"

Seerin had never known his father. He wouldn't have taken his name.

The *pujerak* didn't need to answer for me to know I was right.

"So, perhaps you are wrong," I said, clutching my bow tighter, lifting my chin. I wouldn't be cowed by his threats. "One female's will helped create this horde. A female who was not of an ancient line, who may not have seemed important to anyone. But she only needed to be important to one." The *Dothikkar*. "You believe that *I* will destroy this horde? I'm almost flattered you think I have so much power."

His laugh was bitter. "Make no mistake, *vekkiri*, his mother is as calculating and as ruthless as they come. She knew exactly what she was doing." His head tilted. "Perhaps you are more like her than I first realized."

My lips pressed together at the barb. Calculating and ruthless?

"Even still, you are not strong enough to be what he needs," the *pujerak* said next, twisting the knife deep.

Doubt crept into my mind even as I turned away from him, looking back to the target riddled with my arrows.

"If you care for him," his voice came from behind me, "then you will end it."

"I will do no such thing," I said softly, nocking my arrow. But I was rattled, my hand shaking, and when I released, the arrow flew wide, nowhere near its intended mark. My first miss of the night.

"You will leave this horde if you want what is best for him."

"Are you finished threatening me now?" I asked, whipping around to meet his gaze. A small ball of anger burned in my belly. I wasn't used to anger. I steered clear from it, but it pinched hard right then.

He was obviously pleased to see he'd struck a nerve and I hated that I'd given him that satisfaction.

"You will see for yourself, *vekkiri*," he said, turning, already walking away. "You are a mistake. He will realize that soon enough."

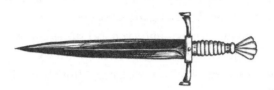

31

The *Vorakkar* of Rath Drokka was spinning a blade, the pointed end wedged into the *Dothikkar's* wooden banquet table. Round and round, he twisted the handle until it made a deep notch into the wood, the blade flashing with each smooth rotation.

I watched him across the table and he watched me. He was called the Mad Horde King for a reason, but I liked him better for daring to deface the *Dothikkar's* property in his presence, no less.

He had ink-black hair, which hung long over his shoulders and shielded half his face. His eyes were red and glowing. A deep scar ran down his cheek. It looked old, as if he'd received it when he was a child.

Even the *Dothikkar* at the head of the table, who'd grown fatter since I'd last seen him, seemed wary of Rath Drokka. He pressed his lips together, staring at the blade for a brief moment, before he turned his attention back to the *Vorakkar* of Rath Dulia.

Rath Dulia, on the other hand, I had never liked. He was an

older male, one who'd been *Vorakkar* for more seasons than I'd been alive. His time was ending, but even still, he would do anything to please the *Dothikkar*, to extend that time on the plains a little longer.

My lips pressed together in distaste when Rath Dulia said, "I have brought warriors with me here, *Dothikkar*. Three dozen of my best. I will send them to aid your fine soldiers in search of the Ghertun that were spotted close to the capitol."

"Very good, Rath Dulia," the *Dothikkar* replied, before looking out at the rest of us seated at the table. "You see? He will do whatever it takes to eliminate this threat to *Dothik*, at a great personal cost to himself. Why is it that you will not do the same?"

The *Vorakkar* of Rath Rowin, who sat to my right, spoke. "Because unlike Rath Dulia, we do not need three dozen of our best warriors to guide us to the capitol, *Dothikkar*. Nor would we take the best warriors away from our hordes in our absence."

My eyes connected with Rath Kitala, who sat next to the Mad Horde King. All the horde kings had come alone, with the exception of Rath Dulia.

"Because I knew my warriors would be of service to the *Dothikkar*," Rath Dulia growled in response.

My patience was wearing thin. I had been traveling day and night to reach *Dothik* in time, battling the icy frost winds and running on next to no sleep. For what? To argue endlessly for hours in the *Dothikkar's* hall? If I'd wanted that, I would've stayed in my horde and argued with my council. At least then, I could go to my female afterwards.

"We have accomplished nothing here," I growled. "We have been at this table for hours and what have we decided about the Ghertun? Nothing. Why? Because there is *nothing* to be done until after the cold season."

The *Vorakkar* of Rath Loppar, another older horde king, one I deeply respected, said, "*Lysi*. My encampment is situated closer to the Dead Lands than the others. I have sent out multiple scouts to monitor their movements and they have all reported the Ghertun have moved underground." His eyes came to me. "I agree with Rath Tuviri. This meeting will lead nowhere, given the time of the season. We should reconvene after the thaw, after they slither out from their hibernation."

The *Dothikkar* leveled his cold gaze on me. I'd felt it multiple times throughout the long meeting. His yellow eyes narrowed as he asked me, "And what of the Ghertun sightings? You think seeking them out is pointless too, Rath Tuviri?"

"I believe they are untrue reports."

"You call your *Dothikkar* a liar then?" the *Dothikkar* asked next, which was what he was *always* going to ask.

I knew what he was doing but I wouldn't play into it.

My lips quirked as I responded, "Of course not, *Dothikkar*. I simply question the validity of the reports, since we all know Ghertun cannot *survive* above ground during the harsher season. Or perhaps you do not know, considering you stay within the comfort and warmth of your halls and have not traveled out to the plains as your father had done before you."

His father had been a true *Dothikkar*. He'd brought about a prosperous age on Dakkar during his rule and had incited deep loyalty among the outposts, among the *Vorakkar* roaming his plains.

The outrage on the *Dothikkar's* expression brought just enough satisfaction to make my words worth it.

Rath Drokka began to laugh, deep and booming, still spinning his dagger.

It was Rath Kitala that spoke up to try to diffuse the sudden tension. "*Dothikkar*, I suggest that we break for the night. We can resume in the morning, once all of us are rested. We have traveled a long way."

The *Dothikkar* didn't even look at Rath Kitala. After he'd learned that he'd taken a human *Morakkari*, he'd hardly spoken two words to him.

Rath Okkili, the last *Vorakkar* present, said, "*Lysi*. I need sleep, a good wine, and perhaps a female or two to warm my furs."

It was the perfect thing to say to the *Dothikkar* to ease the rising tension. I both appreciated and hated Rath Okkili for saying it, however.

"*Lysi*. You will be shown your rooms," the *Dothikkar* said. Though he knew three of the *Vorakkars* present—Rath Kitala, Dulia, and Loppar—had taken *Morakkaris*, he still said, "Then you can all have your pick of my concubines for the night." His gaze came to me. "Except for my favorites, of course."

My lips pressed together. Rath Drokka's gaze came to me, watching as my claws raked across the surface of the table. They all knew my mother was one of his favorites, naturally. They all knew the barb was meant for me and me alone.

Rath Kitala scraped his chair away from the table, loud and echoing in the great hall built from stone, just one room in the *Dothikkar's* stronghold. Rath Drokka did the same, but he immediately strode from the room, followed shortly by Rath Okkili and Rath Rowin.

I stood, never taking my eyes from the *Dothikkar*. Rath Kitala rounded the table, clapped me on my shoulder and urged, "Come."

With a soft growl, I tore my eyes from the *Dothikkar* and walked from the hall, Rath Kitala at my back. I trusted him the most out of all of the *Vorakkar*. He had my given name, after all, and I had his.

We ascended the stairs of the stronghold, following one of

the *Dothikkar's* servants to our rooms. I'd never liked being so high up. I thought the *Dothikkar's* ancestral home was unnatural. The heartbeat of Dakkar could best be felt through the earth, on solid, fragrant, rich ground. It felt confining to be away from it.

After the servant showed us our rooms and assured us a bathing tub was already prepared for us inside, the *Vorakkar* of Rath Kitala stopped me in the long corridor.

When we were alone, he said, "You seem different, Seerin. What has happened?"

"I do not know what you speak of," I rasped.

"You have always been controlled," Arokan said, studying me. "Unnaturally so."

Because I'd had to be.

"Yet you openly challenge the *Dothikkar* and show your emotions to all," he continued. "I saw you only a month ago and you were not like this."

Because I had not known my *thissie* a month ago. When I'd last seen Arokan, it had been to congratulate him on his human bride and I'd been on my way to Nelle's village, to punish the hunters responsible for the *kinnu* herd.

It had seemed so long ago now.

"I am simply tired," I told him instead of the truth. "I need rest. And you know I always hate coming to *Dothik*. It sets my teeth on edge."

Arokan nodded. "Then rest, my friend. Let us try to persuade the *Dothikkar* quickly tomorrow, so that we may all return to our hordes."

Nothing sounded better to me. The *Vorakkar* of Rath Kitala no doubt itched to return to his pregnant mate. And I could feel Nelle's absence like it was a tangible thing.

I nodded and then we went into our separate rooms. Mine

was richly appointed, with a high bed, plush carpets that covered the entirety of the floor, and tall windows.

I went to them. Looking out, I saw the glimmer of the capitol below. Of winding, stone roads, square, tall buildings, and alleyways that connected the city like veins in a body. There were no domed *voliki* here. There was no sense of community. There was only loyalty to gold and riches.

I knew every inch of the capitol. I knew every hidden, ugly secret. I knew timetables and routines. I knew which elders and council members liked to visit the brothels and which liked their brew strong. I knew that from afar, the capitol seemed like a glittering possibility of hope, but up close, it was covered in grime.

Then I looked beyond the capitol, towards the plains. I could see the mountains of the *Hitri* and from there, I knew which direction my horde lay. I knew where my female was and I wondered if she slept right then, or if she was awake, thinking about me as I thought about her.

Turning from the window, I went to my steaming bath, undressed, and stepped in. My body ached from the long journey and I tilted my head back, closing my eyes as the heat helped soothe my muscles.

A small sound came at the door and I watched as it opened.

My mother didn't say anything as she stepped inside the room and closed the door behind her.

I hadn't seen her in over a year, since I'd last been summoned to *Dothik*. She looked older, deep creases beginning to form around the sides of her mouth and through her forehead.

But her golden hair still shimmered in a soft wave down her back and her light grey eyes met mine and held them.

She was dressed in a rich gown of maroon velvet and a heavy, gold necklace spanned wide across her throat like a collar. It was the only thing I was grateful for...that as one of the *Dothikkar's* favorites, she was treated well. She had her own room in the stronghold, she ate the best foods, she dressed in luxurious things she'd only ever coveted as a brothel prostitute. She never had to worry about poverty, or earning enough gold, or forgoing another meal so I could eat instead.

My gaze went to the necklace she wore and I mused that it had more gold in it than she'd ever made during her time at the brothel.

She came to kneel next to my bathing tub and she reached out to cup my face.

"How I've missed you," she whispered to me, looking into my eyes. For all my mother's faults, I'd never once doubted her love. Not ever.

I pressed my damp forehead to her own. When I'd been younger, this was how she'd always greeted me. Sometimes, I wouldn't see her for weeks on end, other times just a few days, but regardless, she always acted like she hadn't seen me in decades.

She pulled away, her eyes running over my face, studying every change in me as only a mother could. I wondered if she sensed something different in me, as Arokan of Rath Kitala had.

"How far did you come?" she asked softly, still keeping my face in her hands.

"From the east," I told her. "Four days' travel on Lokkas."

She nodded. "Tell me everything that's happened since I saw you last."

I did my best. She sat beside the bath as I told her the events of the last year. How, shortly after the thaw, as we tracked a pack of *ungira* to our new encampment, we were ambushed by Ghertun. We'd lost two warriors and three *pyrokis* in the attack but managed to eliminate every last Ghertun. One of the warriors who fell had been the seamstresses' mate and I'd always carried guilt that I could have foreseen the events of that day, that I could've stopped them.

I told her of the waterfalls of the *Trikki*, a place we'd made our second encampment for the year, during the warm season, towards the south. I told her that the *wrissan* herds there were so plentiful that we'd managed to dry enough of their meat for two cold seasons.

I told her of the journey east, as we sought a new encampment to base at for the approaching cold season.

My bath was growing cold when I finally told her about the human settlement to the east, that I'd gone there on patrol with my warriors shortly after making camp and had to punish a female for hunting. Recounting the memory left a sour taste in my mouth and churned my gut. I remembered Nelle, kneeling on the earth because I'd ordered her to. I remembered seeing the flash of the whip.

With a growl, I rose from the bath water, drying off quickly and dressing. My mother was looking at me, still kneeling next to the bath, and I helped her up, pressing her palms into mine.

Her gaze was always knowing. "You feel guilt for this? For doing your duty as *Vorakkar*?"

"*Lysi.*"

"Why? The *vekkiri* know our laws."

"You did not see what I saw, *lomma*," I told her. "They are *duvna* in their own way, only there is no wealth in the settlements to take. They are all hungry. They are all just trying to survive."

Her gaze narrowed. It was then she seemed unfamiliar to me. It was then I realized she'd long forgotten our own struggles. Had she forgotten the piercing ache of hunger? Had she forgotten the chilling fear?

Looking at her now, one would think she'd grown up in this stronghold, in the wealthiest place in all of Dakkar.

"What happened to the female, Seerin?" she asked slowly.

"I took her," I told her, setting my jaw, knowing that she already saw the truth in my eyes. I'd never been able to hide anything from her.

"What do you mean you took her?"

"She is of my horde now," I said softly.

Her expression didn't change, but her voice was firm when she said, "*Nik*."

"*Lysi*."

Her nostrils flared. Her claws curled into my palm where I still held her hand.

"I did not make you *Vorakkar* so that you could pollute our line, Seerin."

My mother had aspired to greatness all her life, though she'd been lowborn. I knew that my status of *Vorakkar* brought her more pride than being the *Dothikkar's* favorite concubine. She'd worn that pride like a badge ever since the Trials.

"Look at how far Rath Kitala has fallen already," she hissed quietly. "I hear his *vekkiri* mate is pregnant. Can you imagine a hybrid leading a horde? *Nik*. No Dakkari would follow, no matter how ancient Rath Kitala's line is. The *Dothikkar* would never allow a *hybrid* to enter the Trials."

No one would have followed a prostitute's bastard son either, I thought.

"Yet he allowed me in," I pointed out, disturbed by the hatred I heard in her voice.

"Because of *me*," she said, her eyes narrowing. "*Nik*. Take the *vekkiri* as your whore if you must, but nothing more, Seerin. I forbid it. Your *Morakkari* will be pure, from a noble line. It will solidify your place as *Vorakkar*. It will allow your heirs to enter the Trials. *That* is what we have worked towards."

My jaw ticked.

"You try so hard to erase your past, *lomma*," I said softly. "You try so hard to erase who you were, to build the life you want through me. Does it even matter what I want?"

She exhaled a sharp breath. "Do you think your council and your *pujerak* will stand behind you if you take a *vekkiri* as your queen? *Nik*, of course not."

Rath Kitala's did, I thought to myself. And Vodan was my oldest friend. He would always remain loyal to me. With him at my side, the horde would remain strong.

"If they leave you, your horde will fall. Everything will be for nothing."

"*I* am *Vorakkar* of Rath Tuviri," I said. "It is not you who controls my horde, *lomma*. And I will always do what is best for *my* horde."

Relief entered her gaze at my words. "And what is best for your horde, Seerin, is a strong *Morakkari*. One who understands our ways, one who the horde will accept and follow without hesitation."

What she didn't know was that Nelle had the will of a *Vorakkar*. I had known that since taking her from her village.

When I didn't reply, she must've assumed that the matter was settled, that she'd gotten her way, just as she had with the *Dothikkar*.

She touched my jaw. "Come, Seerin, I do not want to argue over this. Not now. I very rarely see you. We will put this behind us, *lysi*?"

Her words left me in a darkened mood. I detested the way she spoke of Nelle, as if she was soiled, when in reality, she was the purest being I'd ever encountered.

A part of me felt guilty, knowing that if given the choice, I would rather be with Nelle right then rather than in *Dothik* at all, though it was the only time I got to see my mother.

She has sacrificed much for me, I reminded myself, looking into her grey eyes, almost identical to my own. And I would always love her, though sometimes she seemed like a stranger to me.

Let it go. Bury the emotions deep, I thought to myself. Just as she'd taught me.

"*Lysi, lomma,*" I responded, brushing my lips across her cheek. "Let us not argue this night."

32

It was eleven days before Seerin returned.

Eleven long days and even longer nights.

I was in Avuli's *voliki*, though our work had slowly dried up after the frost feast. Still, I liked to spend time with her and she seemed happy for the company.

Right then, she was playing a game involving rocks with Arlah, rolling them across the rugs from the farthest distance the *voliki* allowed, trying to hit a smaller pebble, which had landed just next to the roaring fire basin.

The past eleven days had brought the snow and throughout most of the days, the horde remained in the safe and warm shelter of their homes. Even at night, it was too cold for me to brave the training grounds. It was the kind of cold that froze one's bones, the kind of cold that *hurt*. Besides, being at the training grounds only reminded me of the *pujerak's* threats and the memory still made anger ignite in my belly.

I watched from my cushion, a fur wrapped tightly around my shoulders, as Arlah tossed his rock, which landed close to my foot. Laughing, I watched as he then tried to distract his mother as she took her aim.

Odrii ducked into the tent just then. Slowly, over the course of the last week, he'd warmed to me. He'd even apologized one morning when I'd gone into the weapons tent and saw him waiting there beside my *mitri*, saying that he'd been acting like a sulking fool.

There'd been nothing to forgive. I'd just been happy that most of the uncomfortable tension between us had lifted.

Odrii looked at me then, pausing at the threshold of the entrance.

"In, in!" Avuli said, frowning at her brother. "You are letting all the heat out."

"Yes!" Arlah cried, one of the only universal language words he spoke with complete confidence. The young boy used it often.

Arlah giggled as Odrii stomped in, shaking out his boots, which were covered in white, powdery snow.

"I thought you would want to know," he began, looking at me. "The *Vorakkar* returned just now."

For a moment, I simply stared at him. Then my heart skipped about four beats as excitement and profound relief burst in my chest.

"And he's alright?" I asked, pushing up quickly to stand, already reaching for my boots.

Odrii took my shoulders and stilled my hurried movements.

"*Lysi*," he affirmed. "However, he just went in with his council. You cannot see him just yet."

Disappointment made my shoulders sag, but I nodded. Of course, he would need to meet with his council first, after his meeting with the *Dothikkar*.

"That is good news, brother," Avuli chimed in. "At least he made it home safe. We were all worried about the terrible turn in weather."

It was something I'd realized over the last couple weeks...

that the members of Rath Tuviri truly cared for their *Vorakkar*. Avuli had told me she'd caught snippets of conversation all over the encampment about when he would return and that they wished it was soon. That the *bikku* worried they did not pack him enough rations for his trip and worried how his *pyroki* would fare in the snow. Another seamstress in the horde had apparently fretted that she should have made him another pelt for his long journey.

Seerin was a good male. A good leader to his horde. They all saw what I saw in him.

Now that I knew he had returned, however, the afternoon and early evening of that day passed even more slowly than usual. My heart felt like it hadn't slowed down once and even Arlah's made-up games couldn't keep me distracted for very long.

Finally, Avuli said, "Go, Nelle. Go wait for him. I am sure he will finish with the council soon. It's dark already."

I nodded, already pulling on my boots and my pelt. Avuli had made me a shawl, which covered the lower part of my face, keeping my cheeks from stinging.

"I'll see you tomorrow," I told her and Odrii before rustling Arlah's lengthening hair. He squeezed my hand, holding it for as long as possible, not wanting me to go. He never liked it when I left for the day. Finally, Avuli drew him away and I left with one last wave.

I hurried to Seerin's *voliki*, past my own and up the short incline. The cold seemed to suck all the air from my lungs and I hated that Seerin had to travel through it.

When I stepped inside his tent, I saw that someone had already started his fire and delivered a heaping assortment of dried meats, dried fruits, rich, fatty broth, and a large loaf of *kuveri*, along with a generous goblet of wine. His bath was ready in its usual corner.

My skin tingled as I unwrapped my shawl and then shrugged out of my pelt. Toeing off my boots, I went to stand near the fire, warming my fingers as I waited. I'd snuck into Seerin's *voliki* on numerous occasions during his absence, late at night as the horde slept. A few times, I'd even slept in his furs because they still smelled like him and it helped comfort me.

Though, lying in his furs held its own array of problems. Whenever I had, I'd been plagued with memories of the last time we'd been in his bed together, of possessive kisses and lingering touches, of heat and sex and the wicked words he'd growled into my flesh as he'd made me his.

The heavy flaps to his *voliki* pushed inward, a whistling wind sneaking inside, making the fire flicker.

My breath hitched as my demon king came inside. And I felt as though my heart would beat its way from my chest as his eyes connected with mine.

He dropped a fur-wrapped bundle by the entrance and then he was striding towards me.

His black pelt was icy cold but I didn't care. I reached for him as he reached for me. Then his lips were on mine and he ate at my mouth hungrily, consuming me as his arms wrapped tight around my body and mine pressed against his chest.

Somehow, I'd forgotten how big he was, how massive. When I'd first seen him, I'd thought of him as a wall. A wall of solid strength. Back then, that power had frightened me.

But now, I'd never felt safer or more protected than in his arms. Now I knew why the symbol of his horde was a shield.

"*Need you now, rei thissie,*" he rasped against me, his hands already going to my thick tunic.

I sucked in a sharp breath at his dark voice, my toes curling into the rugs beneath us.

I'd missed him. So incredibly much. Everything about him.

"Yes," I whispered, lifting my arms so he could rip my tunic from my body. Desire and need heated my blood as my breasts sprang free.

I moaned when he ducked his head and his hot tongue immediately sought my pebbled nipples.

But I didn't want to waste time. As he sucked and teased my sensitive breasts, I untied his pelt and pushed it from his wide shoulders, smoothing my hands over the cords of muscles lining his arms.

Between us, my fingers unlaced his pants before immediately delving inside.

A rough groan tore from his throat when I wrapped my hand around his cock, remembering how much he'd liked it when I'd stroked him in the bath.

"*Vok*," he whispered, pulsing hard and hot in my hand. His hands came to my pants, unlaced the knots, and when I kicked them off, I was completely naked under his gaze except for the feathers that hung between my breasts.

He looked over me with a half-lidded gaze, his hands tracing the curves of my body. I'd gained even more weight since he'd last seen me, since his hands had last been on me. My hips were softened, my breasts and thighs fuller. Considering how thin I'd been when he'd first brought me to his horde, I felt like a completely different woman. I *looked* like a completely different woman.

I ran my thumb over the slick, slippery head of his cock, making him jolt.

"Does that feel good?" I murmured to him, barely concealing my small, teasing smile. A part of me still couldn't believe he was here, that he'd finally returned.

His eyes narrowed and he finished undressing quickly, until he was as naked as I was.

He licked his lips, taking my hands from his cock as he promised, "I will show you how good it feels."

Our words were so similar to the night when he'd pushed me away—the night I'd bathed him. He knew it and I knew it. It was like we were rewriting the events of that night.

I gasped as he pushed me down onto the rugs, though we weren't far from the bed. I looked up at him with wide eyes as he kneeled, as he reached out and flipped me over until I was on all fours in front of him, on my hands and knees.

Looking over my shoulder, I licked my suddenly dry lips. He'd never taken me like this before but I found the position curiously erotic. My legs squeezed together, more than ready for him.

Then his eyes shifted over me. His gaze caught on my back and his expression changed as he brushed my long hair to the side.

His jaw ticked as he looked at the three scars across my back. From the whip. He traced one, his touch starting at the top of my shoulder, going diagonally across my spine, ending at my hip.

I looked at him, wondering what he was thinking. I knew he hated seeing them. He'd never said so, but I could feel his sudden tension.

My brow furrowed, tears welling surprisingly quickly in my eyes, when he leaned over and kissed the scars, brushing his lips over my flesh. Softly, gently, he kissed every last inch of the old wounds I'd received on his order. And I knew what his kiss meant. What it was.

It was an apology. It was his regret, his guilt.

I'd already told him that I didn't hold these scars against him. I'd let that go, even when I'd still been healing. He'd been bound in his duty as I'd been bound by his race's laws.

But my demon king had obviously still carried this with him and it was pouring from him now, all over my scarred flesh.

"Seerin," I choked out.

I thought that I loved him. I thought that was what this was, what it was *always* going to be, from the first moment I felt him taking my soul. Me...a human who didn't know the first thing about love, who found herself in love with a powerful, beautiful horde king of Dakkar. It was almost laughable, but I didn't care how strange it seemed.

"Come here," I whispered, not trusting my voice. I felt exposed and vulnerable. Yet I felt completely safe. It was such an odd combination of emotions.

He leaned over me and I craned my neck.

Capturing his lips in a slow, soft kiss, I whispered, "Enough. Enough now."

When he pulled away, his eyes flickered between my own. He knew what I was telling him. That the past was behind us. That how we'd come to find one another was behind us. I'd forgiven him a long time ago.

His nod was slight, but I knew he understood. He captured my lips one last time and then drew back.

"*Oh*," I breathed when I felt his hand brush underneath me, when I felt it brush against my swollen clitoris. Desire returned to me, even stronger than it'd been before, *fueled*, not extinguished, by what just happened.

He stroked between my thighs until I was rocking against his hand, my breasts swaying under me, Blue's feathers drifting across the rug.

"*Seerin*," I whispered, looking over my shoulder at him. "Please!"

With a growl at my begging, he positioned his throbbing cock at my entrance.

"*Lysi*?" he rumbled.

Frantically, I rocked my hips back and he slid inside a couple inches. His hiss filled the *voliki*.

Then his hands were anchoring my hips, gripping them until I couldn't move.

With one powerful thrust, he slid all the way inside and held there. My head lolled, my mouth dropping, and my eyes fluttering shut. There was only a brief pinch of pain this time, which quickly faded.

"I cannot wait any longer," he growled. "*Need you now.*"

At his words, he pulled out from my body before slamming his hips into me again.

"*Ahhh,*" I cried out. "Oh yes, Seerin!"

He didn't stop. He continued to pound and thrust and grind into my sex until the wicked sounds of mating filled the *voliki*. Until everything fell away. Until it was just him, me. Until it was just *us*.

Rough grunts and purring groans reached my ears and my fingernails curled into the plush rugs underneath me, my breasts bobbing forcefully with every teeth-chattering thrust.

Just when I thought I was hanging on the edge of orgasm, Seerin's hand wrapped around my throat.

I gasped in surprise as he pulled me up until we were both kneeling, as he continued to pound into me from behind. Impossibly, his cock seemed to slide even deeper. My back met the hardened plane of his chest as he kept his grip around my neck. His other hand went between my legs, pressing against my aching clitoris, rolling it maddeningly slowly, a juxtaposition to his almost frenzied, desperate thrusts from behind.

His hand around my throat was possessive. It wasn't frightening. It was...

It was a *claim*, I realized. The claim of my demon king.

Seerin turned my neck until he could kiss me and I met his kiss with a claim that was all my own. His dark growl threaded down my throat, sizzling straight for where we were joined, and I gasped.

The orgasm that hit me was almost violent. It arched my spine and made my whole body freeze.

Seerin felt me squeezing around his cock. He snarled at the sensation, breaking our kiss.

"Look at me while you come, *rei thissie*," he ordered, his voice nothing more than a guttural purr.

I couldn't look away from him even if I tried. His grey eyes latched onto mine. As unfathomable pleasure racked my body, as I felt his pace quicken, I never looked away.

It was then that I felt him take the very last part of me. The last lingering bit of my soul that I'd perhaps tried to keep, in fear that letting it go would change me forever.

And it did. It *would*. I knew that as certainly as I knew that I loved this demon. *My* demon.

Seerin's brow furrowed at whatever he saw in my gaze and then I felt his cock jerk and grow inside me.

I drew in a ragged breath as I felt his seed burst from him, as it lashed against my fluttering walls and pumped deep into me, hot and *so right*.

With a groan, he shuddered against me, his hand loosening on my throat. We both slid forward, tumbling together on the rugs of his *voliki*.

"I do not think I will ever get enough of you, Nelle," he groaned, his breathing ragged and rough.

He sounded almost fearful of that.

But like I'd told him on the night of the frost feast...I wasn't afraid.

33

"Your skin is dry here," I observed, looking at the ball of Seerin's shoulder. "And here," I murmured, running my palm down his side, underneath the water of the bath.

Water trickled as I shifted and he groaned when his cock rubbed between my legs. We were in the bathing tub and I was straddling his hips, leaning against his chest. We'd already washed one another and I discovered that Seerin washing my hair, those long fingers scraping at my scalp, felt like heaven. And right then, I'd never felt warmer or happier or more protected in my entire life.

"Because my *alukkiri* left me," he murmured, tilting my face up, his eyes studying my features.

"Because you were being stubborn," I replied, remembering that night well, quirking a brow.

He grunted, hard-headed male that he was.

I hid my smile when I said, "But we *did* have an agreement and I didn't hold up my end of it."

"*Nik,*" he murmured gravely, as if this was the most serious matter we'd ever discussed. "You did not, *thissie.*"

"I suppose, to make up for it," I began, "I can be your *alukkiri* for the rest of the season?"

His purr told me just how much he liked that idea. "*Lysi*?"

"Yes."

"And I can be yours, *thissie*," he growled, his hands running up from my hips, cupping my breasts, his thumbs rubbing over my nipples.

My laugh sounded slightly breathless and died completely when he leaned in to nibble at the column of my throat. "Seerin."

"Mmm?"

"You still haven't told me about *Dothik*," I reminded him before he decided to distract me. *Again*. We'd taken a break from our lovemaking to wash, but it had been hours since Seerin arrived back at the tent and he'd managed to avoid every single one of my questions about his journey.

He sighed and leaned back. "I am happy and relieved to be back at my horde, Nelle. That is all."

"It went that poorly?" I chanced.

His lips pressed together. "There were many meetings with the *Dothikkar* and the other *Vorakkars*. None of them ended well. We will reconvene after the thaw comes."

"You have to go back so soon?" I asked, frowning. The thaw wouldn't happen for another couple months, but it *still* seemed too soon.

"*Lysi*."

"And what of your mother?" I asked after a brief pause. "Did you see her?"

He inclined his head, but his eyes flickered slightly. His hands roamed down my body again and I knew what he was doing...he was trying to distract me. I caught his wrists below the water when he reached between my thighs.

Seerin made a sharp exhale. I remembered what his *pujerak*

257

had told me…that Seerin's mother was calculating and ruthless. I wondered if his words painted her accurately, but asking him would have revealed that his *pujerak* had spoken to me. And, for some reason, I didn't want Seerin to know about that night. I had a feeling it would only anger him.

"*Lysi*, I saw her the first night and again the second night," he said.

"How is she?" I asked softly.

"She is how she always is," he answered, but his words didn't satisfy me. They told me nothing.

"And how's that?"

His eyes came to mine. "She is the *Dothikkar's* favored concubine. Apart from when he needs her, she is free to do what she wishes. She is dressed in the finest clothes, adorned with the finest jewels, and is satisfied with her position in his court. To my mother, status is important. Hers is as high as it could be."

"And her son is a *Vorakkar*," I said softly. Hesitating, I added, "The *Vorakkar* of Rath Tuviri. You took her name."

His gaze sharpened, though he ran a gentle hand down my bare back, settling his palm over the swell of my buttocks.

"It is the only name I have," he said. "It is my name too, not only hers."

Because he'd never known his father.

"Do you ever wonder about him? About your father?" I whispered, tracing a path down his chest, following the golden markings inked into his flesh. "About who he is or where he is?"

"*Nik*," he said. "I have not thought about him for a long time."

I nodded, though I frowned.

"Do you ever wonder about your parents?" he murmured.

My brow furrowed. "More so when I was younger. I used to wonder what my life would be like with them. I used to think we would be happy together if they were on Dakkar and not...gone."

"And now?"

I sighed. "Now I think it was better that they never reached Dakkar."

"Why?"

"It would've been difficult to feed three," I said simply.

My father would've needed to spend long hours hunting. I thought of Grigg and how he offered extra credits for sexual favors from the females. I wondered if my mother would've given in to feed her family. I wondered if *I* would've eventually given in if I'd stayed.

No. Even then, I would have rather starved.

I'd always been so relieved, so happy to know that my parents had been a love match. I was glad to know that the hard years in our village wouldn't have diminished that love.

Seerin was frowning when I focused my attention back on him. For a moment, I wondered if this was how my parents had felt about one another. I thought that my mother's grief would've been justified after my father had been killed. Because thinking about Seerin simply *gone* from this world? It didn't make sense to me. It was unfathomable.

"But I'm here now," I said softly. Looking to lighten the mood, I said, "And I think it's time I finally make good on my promise to be your *alukkiri*."

He allowed the change in subject, though his eyes told me he knew what I was doing. He jerked his chin up and I climbed off him, stepping out of the bathing tub. Seerin stood after me, helping me dry off as I shivered slightly before drying his own skin.

"Leave it off," he rumbled when I reached for my tunic. I paused at the command and then released the material. "I will keep you warm enough tonight, *rei thissie*."

Wicked demon, I thought, watching as he went to his cabinets and returned with the familiar bottle of oil. He handed it to me and I uncapped it, pouring a small amount in my hands, noticing that it smelled earthy and pleasant. A droplet of water from my damp hair landed on my chest and ran over my breast. Seerin's gaze followed it and it felt like his tongue—not his eyes—was tracing its path.

Reaching up, I smoothed the oil over the tops of his shoulders, where I'd first seen the dryness of his skin, before running my palms down his arms. Despite the fluttering I felt between my legs, I was all business at first, working the oil into his flesh methodically and thoroughly.

He made a sound in his throat when I ran my fingertips over his dusky nipples and I quickly ran my hands over his ridged abdomen, biting back a smile. After I finished his front, I went around his back, my smile dying a little when I saw his *Vorakkar* scars up close for the first time. His back was nothing more than scar tissue and I wondered how he'd managed to survive it.

Gently, I smoothed my hands over his flesh. His skin felt tight underneath my fingertips, but I made sure to reach every inch and when I was done, I couldn't resist leaning forward. I pressed a soft kiss to the middle of his back and let my lips linger.

He stilled. A harsh sound emerged from his throat.

"Nelle," he rasped.

My hands trailed down to his firm buttocks and I spread the oil there too. They were muscled and tight and I kneaded the flesh as a choked laugh came from him.

"You will be the end of me, starling."

For a moment, I froze. His words were so similar to his *pujer-ak's*, yet I knew Seerin had meant it only in teasing.

"Nelle?" he asked, sensing me still. "What is it?"

"Nothing," I replied, my voice coming out husky. I came

around his front and reached for more oil. "I'm already halfway done," I murmured, smiling.

His cock was throbbing and swollen. It twitched at my words and twitched again when I kneeled in front of him.

I ignored his cock and spread the oils over his legs, his calves, the back and front of his thighs. That same possessive streak hit me as I rubbed, suddenly grateful and relieved that he'd never taken an *alukkiri*, that another female had never done this to him, as far as I knew.

Because it felt intimate. I could feel every rippling muscle, every shift in his body. I could feel his heat and power and the way he tensed and relaxed whenever I hit a sensitive place.

When I was done with his legs, I set my eyes on his cock before craning my head back to meet his gaze.

His grey eyes were hooded and intense, looking down at me on my knees in front of him. I was kneeling before a *Vorakkar* but I didn't feel powerless. I felt strong.

"Here too?" I whispered.

His exhale was sharp and his hand reached down to drift across my lips. "Kiss it first, *rei thissie*."

With my thighs squeezing together, I asked, "Is that part of an *alukkiri's* duty?"

"*Nik*," he rasped. "But you are mine and as my female, you will learn every part of me. As I will learn every part of you."

Thud, thud, thud. My heartbeat beat out a quick, excited rhythm in my chest at his words. I liked him calling me *his* entirely too much.

Grasping the base of his cock, I pulled it down, away from where it pressed tight against his abdomen. Leaning forward, I felt a little shy as I kissed the glistening head, letting my lips linger on his heat even as I met his eyes.

A rough growl echoed around the *voliki*, followed by his loud, audible swallow.

"*Again*," he rasped.

Between my thighs, my clitoris was throbbing. I remembered him *there*, licking and kissing and suckling softly. I wanted to reciprocate that pleasure because I wanted him to feel as good as he'd made me feel.

Holding his gaze, I kissed him again before running my lips down to the middle of his shaft. I kissed him there too.

His hand came to the back of my head. His voice came out even rougher. "*Again*."

I kissed the tip. Then my tongue darted out to slowly lick the underside of the swollen head, testing, gauging his reaction.

His hips jerked, seemingly of their own accord, and Seerin hissed, "*Vok, rei thissie.*"

"Again?" I whispered.

His eyes pinned me into place. I felt his hand tighten in my hair, as if afraid I would move away.

"*Lysi.*"

That time, I licked up the whole length of his thick shaft, feeling his cock throb against my tongue. Seerin's breath came out harsh and he murmured something in Dakkari, though I couldn't make out a single word.

"What now?" I asked him, wanting to please him. But I was inexperienced in these things. I didn't know the first thing about pleasuring a male like this.

He choked out an almost pained laugh at my eager question. "With the exception of biting, *rei thissie*, anything you do to me feels good."

"Tell me."

His swallow was audible.

"Open," he rasped, brushing his fingers against my lips. I parted them at his words and he gently eased the head of his cock inside. His voice was roughened as he said, "This is where I am most sensitive. Suck me here, *kalles.*"

A harsh growl burst from his throat when I immediately did as he instructed. His shaft was thick and engorged, but I widened my jaw as best as I could while still suckling on the tip. The beginnings of his seed pushed from the head, wetting my tongue, and I lapped at the slit for more, finding I liked the earthy, musky taste.

"*Vok*, Nelle," he groaned harshly, his hand tightening on the back of my head.

The muscles in his thighs trembled slightly as I lapped and sucked. As I moved from the head, over to the side of his cock, I saw his bump, just over the base of his shaft. I remembered, when he'd been so deep inside me, how it had lined up perfectly with my clitoris, how it had throbbed and heated and pulsed against me.

I reached out to touch it, my fingertips still oiled after running them over his body. His hips jerked when I brushed my hand over it. It was hot and hard, just like his cock.

"What is this called?"

"*Dakke*," he growled, those eyes piercing into me. Oh yes, my demon king liked me exploring him very, very much.

Leaning forward, I kissed him there too, causing a harsh breath to exhale sharply from his chest. When I dragged my tongue over it, his body rippled. When I sucked it, just like I had the head of his cock, he froze completely.

Before I knew it, I was off the floor of the *voliki*, in his arms, and then my back was on his bed, the furs tickling my tingling skin.

It seemed I'd pushed him too close to the edge, judging by the darkened, focused look on Seerin's face. I opened my mouth to ask him how sensitive his *dakke* was, but the words died completely in my throat when he immediately pushed my thighs wide...and drove deep, deep inside with one claiming thrust.

Seerin fucked me wildly, his oiled skin slapping against my own. And all I could do was grip his shoulders and receive him. I was already incredibly aroused from exploring his body, from watching his reactions as I sucked and licked his cock, from his *dakke* grinding into me, that when my orgasm began to crest, I wasn't even surprised.

"*Lysi*," he growled in my ear. Gently, he bit the column of my neck again and then rasped, "Come on my cock, *rei thissie*. *Vok*, I can feel you!"

The intense pleasure made me cry out, made my hips buck against him and my spine arch. In the midst of my orgasm, I perceived his thrusts quickening.

"*Too close already. Kassikari*, you would have made me come all over your sweet little tongue."

Seerin threw his head back and he bellowed to the domed ceiling of the *voliki* as his seed burst from his tip. His hips continued to rock into me as his heat coated me *deeply*. His head dropped into my neck, his hair falling over my heavy breasts, and I wrapped my arms around him as he spent the last of his seed into my body.

We laid there in quiet for a moment as we both recovered. When Seerin rolled us until we lay on our sides and pulled the furs over us, I pressed a kiss to his strong, marked chest.

I tilted my face back to meet his eyes. His fingertips caressed my bare shoulder and his other hand clasped the swell of my hip.

"Is it always like this?" I whispered.

I didn't know what I was asking. I didn't know whether I'd meant the sex...or something deeper. Or both.

Seerin seemed to know, however.

"*Nik*," he said back. "This is you and me, Nelle."

34

My breathing was ragged and my voice was hoarse when I groaned, "I have created a monster, *rei thissie*. An insatiable monster."

Her laugh trickled in my ears even though she was straddling my hips and my seed spilled from her cunt. Even though she'd just come so hard she'd left the imprints of her dull little claws in my flesh.

"You always say that," she murmured, leaning down to brush her lips across my own.

"Because it is true," I growled, keeping her hips anchored on me when she moved to slide away.

It had been a month since I returned from my journey to *Dothik*. A month of bitter cold, of ice and snow, of fierce windstorms that sometimes made it impossible to venture outside. A month of my female in my furs, of her laugh and kisses across my flesh, of lying in quiet at night as the fire crackled in the *voliki*, memorizing her soft eyes as though I needed to imprint them onto my very soul. As if they weren't already.

A month of a deep-rooted, consuming happiness for perhaps the first time in my life.

Her contented sigh drifted across my lips and she pulled back.

"I miss you already," she whispered, which was something she'd often expressed before we had to leave one another for our daily duties.

My *thissie* had always been open to me. She never hid her emotions and I read what she so easily expressed without difficulty.

What I had begun to see over a month ago in her eyes had blossomed and grown. A combination of desire, friendship, respect, curiosity, confidence, and complete acceptance, as though she knew her love changed everything.

She'd never verbally said it to me. She hadn't needed to.

It was I that held back, however, despite everything that had transpired between us.

"My council meeting may run into the night," I told her. "We begin planning for our journey south, once the thaw comes."

She nodded. She got quiet whenever we referenced the end of the cold season, as if she didn't want to think about it. Because she believed I would have her returned to her village, as I'd once told her. After all, I had still made her no promises, though the knowledge settled like acid in my belly.

"You will like the *Hitri* mountains," I told her softly, after a lengthy pause.

Her eyes flickered to me.

"And the forests beyond them," I added. My eyes went to Blue's feathers, still around her neck, and said, "You may even see the *thissies* you are so fond of. They make their home in the southlands."

Nelle swallowed and I felt a stinging pinch of guilt. My words were what she'd needed to hear after so long, but I thought, perhaps naively, that she would realize she would be staying with the horde. That I would not—*nik*, could not—send her away. Not now. Not ever.

"I think I will like them, Seerin," she said softly before a small, hesitant smile touched her lips.

It is settled then, I thought.

I gave her one last kiss and then pulled her off me. I rose from our furs, where she'd spent every night with me. My eyes couldn't help but go to the *deviri*, to the three closed chests that lined the wall of the *voliki*.

Inside them were gifts for my chosen *Morakkari*, to present to her after the *tassimara*, the joining celebration. Gold, jewelry, fine silks, hair adornments, and precious gems were within. Items that I had collected for her during my time as *Vorakkar*, from *Dothik*, from the Dakkari outposts or other hordes we'd passed along our journeys.

My *thissie* didn't care about gold or riches. One of her favorite gifts was the rock that Arlah, the seamstresses' young boy, had given her. It sat on my cabinet, next to the dagger I'd given her, as if she couldn't stand to be parted from it. The Dakkari steel bow I'd brought back for her from *Dothik*—a more appropriate size for her—was leaning against the wall next to the cabinet.

My Nelle liked her gifts. She didn't care what they were, just that they were given freely.

Crouching in front of one of the *deviri* chests, I pulled open the lid and took a jeweled pendant from within, one whose color matched the shimmering *thissie* feathers hanging between her breasts. Its delicate chain was gold and the gem was small, but brilliant in its beauty. It would suit Nelle perfectly.

When I returned to her, she was sitting up in bed, watching me. She stilled when she saw the necklace, her eyes flickering in surprise as I clasped the chain around her neck.

It was shorter than Blue's pendant and settled just between

her delicate collarbones. I touched the gem, feeling it already begin to warm from her skin.

"It's beautiful, Seerin," she said softly, looking down at it before meeting my eyes.

"Then it is perfect for you, *rei thissie*."

She flushed, pleased with my words and my gift, touching the necklace.

I began to dress, aware that her eyes were on me the entire time. When I was done, I leaned down and pressed another kiss to her warm lips, lingering long enough to make me question my decision to leave that cold morning.

"Thank you," she whispered between us.

With a growl, I pulled away.

"I will return to you later, starling."

And with one last look, I forced myself to leave.

LATER THAT EVENING, long after the sun had begun to sink behind the *Hitri* mountains, I finally made my way to the council's *voliki* towards the front of the encampment.

When I ducked inside, I found the elders, my *pujerak*, and my head warriors were already within.

Angled looks turned to me and one of the elders, who'd been speaking in a low tone, ceased abruptly when I appeared. I straightened to my full height and shrugged the pelt from my shoulders, hanging it near the entrance before studying my council.

A strange tension permeated the air, but one I'd grown more familiar with in the last month. This wasn't the first time I'd caught them speaking in hushed tones prior to my arrival. And I knew that it couldn't go on.

When I stepped up to the high table, I said quietly to all of them, "You must think I am a fool if you believe that I will tolerate whispered words behind my back. You must think me a fool, indeed."

My head warrior, Ujak, shifted on his feet. Only Vodan met my eyes.

"Look me in my eyes and tell me," I said, cutting my gaze to the elders, to the three that stood across the table. "I will not allow this to continue so we may as well discuss it now."

No one spoke. When I looked to Vodan, his jaw ticked, but his eyes were knowing. They said, *I already warned you this would happen.*

The back of my neck tingled. I rasped, "Tell me what you were speaking of. *Now.*"

It was one of the elders who finally spoke.

"You intend to take the *vekkiri* as your *Morakkari*, do you not?"

My gaze narrowed on him, not liking the way he twisted the word *vekkiri* on his tongue, as though it was distasteful. My mother had done the same.

"The entire horde suspects that you will," he continued. "You will make her your *Morakkari* before the thaw, before we travel to the southlands. Is that not true?"

Claws digging into my palms, I met his gaze steadily, though I did not deny his words.

"We cannot forbid you from doing this, *Vorakkar*," the elder next to him said. Slowly, he added, "However, we can *strongly* suggest against it."

I bristled at the tone in his voice.

"*Neffar*?" I asked quietly, drawing out the word slowly, meeting his eyes.

It was...a threat. A subtle one, but a threat nonetheless.

The third elder spoke, "Already, three families are planning to leave the horde once the thaw comes. Four unmated females

269

and one of the *bikku* have also announced to the *pujerak* that they intend to return to *Dothik*, to await the next horde launch once the *Dothikkar* selects his newest *Vorakkar*."

My gaze turned to Vodan and he at least had the decency to look away.

My head warrior spoke next, "Seven warriors have told me they will also detach from Rath Tuviri once the thaw comes. Unless..."

He trailed off but I knew what he would say.

Looking down at the table, at the map of Dakkar, I mentally traced the route I was planning to take to lead my horde through the *Hitri*. Over two dozen of my horde would not be a part of that journey. A significant number of my horde. Losing seven warriors didn't seem like much, given over forty would remain, but my horde would feel their loss once the Ghertun attacks started again. Losing four unmated females could potentially decrease that warrior count even further, compromising the safety of the horde.

"She would weaken us. She is *already* weakening us since there are those that will not tolerate a *vekkiri* queen. They would rather return to *Dothik* than have her rule this horde beside you," the first elder said. His jaw set, sure in his decision, as he continued, "We have decided that if you take the *vekkiri* as your *Morakkari*, then we can no longer serve Rath Tuviri either."

"We?" I rasped, feeling his words like they were a punch in my gut. My eyes turned to my head warrior, whose lips pressed together in hesitation, before they went to Vodan.

My oldest friend swallowed as he met my gaze.

"Even you, *pujerak*?" I asked slowly, a knot forming in my chest. "You agree with the council? You would leave Rath Tuviri and return to *Dothik* if I took her as my *Morakkari*?"

You would leave me, what we've built? I asked him silently. It went unspoken between us. Vodan hated *Dothik* as much as I did and he'd told me long ago that he would follow me always.

Vodan straightened, drawing in a deep breath, as he nodded. He didn't say anything. It was only a brief incline of his head but it was a physical and emotional blow that hit *hard*. It stunned me in place.

His answer was a betrayal, one that took me by surprise because I'd never suspected that he would ever betray me like this, with whispers among my council. I'd trusted Vodan more than I'd trusted anyone in my entire life. He was a brother to me, a loyal friend, an advisor. We'd been together since we were boys in the streets of *Dothik* and we'd *always* looked out for one another.

He loved me like a brother and I loved him. But in one single moment, the trust that I'd placed in him chipped and fractured and I mourned the loss of it.

Silence weighed heavy in the *voliki* as they waited for me to speak.

I thought of Nelle. I thought of her love, written plainly in her eyes, and the *thissie* feathers around her neck. I thought of when I'd first seen her in that darkened forest with a wooden bow clutched in her grip. I remembered thinking she seemed sad, but I didn't realize at the time that I'd felt that same emotion in myself. That over time, she had erased that sadness in me, as I'd erased it in her.

But it was I who would give it back to her in full.

My mother's words returned to me then, words she'd said to me in *Dothik*.

"Do you think your council and your pujerak *will stand behind you if you take a* vekkiri *as your queen? Nik, of course not. If they leave you, your horde will fall. Everything will be for nothing."*

I remembered thinking then that Vodan would stand with

me, and with him by my side, the horde would always be strong. Because, unlike the other hordes, ours was a partnership.

Now, he was threatening to leave.

"Then I see that it has already been decided for me," I said slowly, meeting the eyes of my council.

They had backed me into a corner. The horde could survive a couple dozen members leaving, but it would fall if my council and my *pujerak* left, just as my mother said. They knew that and I knew that. Even a *Vorakkar* had limits on his power.

Dread and grief lodged in my chest, making it hard to breathe.

"The horde always comes first," I murmured, though bitterness tinged my words now. I met Vodan's eyes, saw the relief in them. "Isn't that right, *pujerak*?"

Whatever he saw made his gaze shutter, made shame creep into his expression. He knew this would change us. It already had.

"We are done this night," I rasped, needing to leave the *voliki*. "We will meet tomorrow to make plans for after the thaw."

"Very good, *Vorakkar*," one of the elders said, a small smile on his lips. A smile that made my belly churn and nausea rise.

I turned my back on them and left, already struggling to breathe when I was hit with the reality of what I had to do next.

Outside, the cold bit at my skin painfully. I was already halfway back to my own *voliki*, where Nelle waited for me, when I realized I'd forgotten my pelt.

"Seerin," Vodan called from behind me. I'd heard his footsteps crunch after me immediately after I left the council. "Please. Let me explain."

"There is no need, *pujerak*," I said, my voice strangely detached. I was numbing myself, something I'd done often growing up, to keep the emotional pain at bay. It was something my mother taught me.

Bury them deep, my son. So you never know the pain of them.

"Seerin," he said, "I tried to tell you. I tried to stop this from—"

"Enough," I rasped, turning my gaze onto him. "I do not want to hear your excuses. You got what you wanted. So did the council."

"I took no pleasure in it," he assured me, as if it would make me feel better.

"I do not believe that," I told him softly. His expression tightened at my words, his brows drawing together. "Return to your mate, *pujerak*. I have no more use for you as my advisor tonight."

"I am still your friend, Seerin," he said to my turned back when I resumed my journey to the *voliki* I shared with my *thissie*. "I hope you remember that."

There were a million cutting things I could have said, but I bit my tongue. Instead, I said nothing and continued on my way, leaving him far behind me.

When I reached the entrance of my *voliki*, I closed my eyes, drawing in a deep breath before I pushed inside.

Warmth immediately infused my veins, a shocking contrast to the bitter cold outside. Nelle smiled when she saw me, sitting cross-legged in the middle of our bed, weaving a scarf for Arlah. She'd been working on it all week.

It only took her a moment to realize that my mood was off because her smile slowly died and her hand stilled on the half-finished scarf.

"What's wrong, Seerin?" she asked, frowning, concerned.

Vok, I can't do this, I thought. How was I ever going to do this?

I went to her, undressing as I went, shivering. She put the scarf aside and I caught her in my arms, pulling her under the furs.

"What's wrong?" she whispered, her hands resting on my chest. "What's happened?"

I shook my head. I lied to her. "Nothing. I just need sleep. I just want to hold you, *lysi*?"

My answer didn't satisfy her but she hesitantly settled down against me. "Alright," she whispered, her breath drifting across my flesh, laying her head in the crook of my arm.

We would talk in the morning, I knew. I couldn't bring myself to right then, though I knew that I should.

Nik, tonight, I would hold my *thissie* close because it could very well be the last time.

35

Biting my lip, I eyed Seerin, who was sitting on the edge of the bed. I could see tendrils of blue morning light filtering in through the sliver at the *voliki's* entrance. He'd already dressed, as had I, but he'd barely said a word to me this morning. Or last night, for that matter.

"Seerin," I called, sitting next to him, pulling his hands into mine. He stared down at our entwined fingers before meeting my eyes. I felt like there was a stone lodged in my throat, like my body already knew there was something terribly wrong before he even spoke the words. "Tell me. Did something happen at the council meeting last night?"

He'd been quiet and distant since then. It made the hairs on the back of my neck prickle.

His nostrils flared.

"Nelle," he said quietly. My brow furrowed because his voice was almost...*pleading*. He bit out a quiet Dakkari curse and pressed his forehead into mine, his eyes closing.

Fear infused my very bones. "Tell me what's happened right now, Seerin. You're scaring me."

He pulled away. He pulled his hands from mine, his forehead from mine, and stood from the edge of the bed. I stood too, hesitantly.

"Please," I whispered, furrowing my brow. "Just tell me. Whatever it is, I can handle it."

"Nelle," he said, his voice holding a hardened edge. "I have decided...I have decided that this cannot continue."

I frowned. "What can't continue?"

His eyes met mine. "Us."

My breath squeezed from my lungs.

"What?" I whispered.

"We cannot continue *this*," he said.

He said '*this*' as though it was a simple thing. But '*this*' was *us*. It was anything but simple.

"What are you talking about, Seerin?" I said, shaking my head, *laughing*, not wanting to believe it, even though my heart beat wildly in my chest, though nausea had begun to churn in my belly, acid rising in my throat. "You can't mean that."

"I told you even before I left for *Dothik* that I could not make you any promises, Nelle," he said, looking at me steadily, his jaw set. "For this reason alone, that was why I did not want to make you a promise that I could not keep."

Looking away, I saw nothing. Not the wall of the *voliki*, not the cabinet, nor the bathing tub or the bed, where we'd spent our long nights together. My mind simply couldn't comprehend anything beyond his words.

He was *serious*.

He was serious.

"Last night, it became apparent to me that any future for us would be an impossibility," he added quietly. "It was a fantasy, Nelle, and nothing more."

"Why just last night?" I asked, though my voice sounded far away. "Just yesterday morning, you were talking of the *Hitri* mountains and giving me another gift. Was that...was that because you already knew? You were trying to make yourself feel better?"

I saw his fists squeeze, though the rest of his body was completely still. "The council confronted me about taking a *Morakkari* and it became obvious to me that...it cannot be you."

It was then that hurt—hurt so painful and acute that my knees shook and my throat stung—penetrated my shock. Tears pricked my eyes as I stood there, staring at him because I couldn't look away, no matter how much I wanted to. No matter how much I *needed* to.

It felt like he was ripping me in half. *How* could words hurt this *much*? How was it even possible?

"I see," I whispered. Though I didn't. I didn't 'see' at all.

"Nelle," he said softly, his eyes flickering. For a moment, I thought he felt the same amount of pain he was inflicting on me. Then he clenched his jaw, the look gone, and continued, "We cannot allow this to go on any longer. It is better this way, to end it now, before..."

Before what?

Before it was too late?

"I love you," I whispered, tears spilling down my cheeks. "*I love you,* Seerin. It's already too late. Please don't do this. *Please.*"

That crack in his expression appeared again. He already *knew* I loved him—how could he not?

"Stop," he growled. "Do not make this harder than it already is, *kalles*."

"Is it?" I cried. "Is this hard for you, Seerin? Because it doesn't seem that way. How can you be so cold about this? What are you even saying right now?"

His jaw clenched and those familiar grey eyes didn't seem like Seerin's at all. They seemed more like the horde king I'd first seen in my village, hardened and detached from everything around him.

"You will always have a place here, Nelle," he told me, ignoring my questions. "You may remain in the horde for the rest of your life if you wish."

Air was pulled from my lungs, whooshing out of me in a gasp of disbelief.

"You will never have to worry about a home, about food, about your safety again," he continued, as if that softened the blow he was delivering. "You will be protected here."

He blurred in front of me as tears filled my vision and poured down my cheeks.

"And when you inevitably take a *Morakkari*?" I whispered, unfathomable hurt spearing into my chest over and over again... until I couldn't breathe. "You think I can just stand by and watch? You think I will be able to stomach you taking her to your bed? You think I will be able to withstand seeing you with her every single day for the rest of my life?"

"You must," he growled. "It is my *duty* to take a *Morakkari*, *thissie*. For the sake of my horde, I will have to, and *you* will have to accept that."

Disbelief made me stumble back, away from him. He'd said it so easily, so coldly that I wondered if I truly knew him at all.

"You're cruel, Seerin. I never realized how much," I said softly, glaring at him across the spacious distance between us. His expression contorted, ever so slightly. "You're cruel if you ask that of me."

He looked away, down to the rugs on the floor, where he'd made love to me numerous times over the last month. It hurt to think that another female would soon think of this *voliki* as hers, that another female would soon think of *Seerin* as hers. Would they share meals and baths together? Would he call her *rei thissie* too? Would he tease her and laugh with her and kiss her until the world spun?

278

Oh, this hurts, I thought, trying to breathe. Struggling to breathe. It hurt so much.

I'd been rejected all my life. By my mother, by Jana, by my village. Even by Seerin before. I should've known. I should've known he wouldn't have wanted me. No one else had before, so why would he?

He'd made me believe differently, however—if only for a little while. I hated him for it...because now I knew what it felt like to be *wanted*.

What was *wrong* with me that made others discard me so easily?

"Nelle," he rasped, approaching me.

"Don't," I pleaded, holding my hand out so he wouldn't touch me. Because if he touched me, I would crumble completely. "D-don't."

He didn't need to say anything else. His mind was already made up, I could see that. And it didn't matter what I wanted. It never mattered.

"Did you ever love me?" I asked, voice trembling, though I kept it strong. A tactic I'd used with Grigg often, so he wouldn't sense my fear. "At all?"

He said nothing. He met my eyes and said nothing.

And I felt like the universe's most naive fool. A heartbroken fool.

I looked at him right in his eyes and I looked *deep*. Once, I'd been frightened to look too deeply because he'd been stealing my soul at the time.

I laughed, but it sounded too strange, even for me.

"Now it would seem we're just two demons who possess one another's souls, Seerin." Finally, pain registered in his gaze, but it didn't make me feel any better. It made me feel worse. Because even now, I didn't want to hurt him. Not the way he was hurting me. "And believe me, I would give yours back to you if I knew how because I don't want it. Not anymore."

Turning, I walked towards the entrance of the *voliki*, numbness cascading over me.

"*Thissie*," he rumbled, twisting the knife with that word. "I am sorry."

I closed my eyes before wiping away the tears on my cheeks.

He didn't want me. It wouldn't be the first time someone felt that way. But I vowed to myself that he would be the last.

"I hope you find everything you're looking for, Seerin," I whispered, so quietly I wasn't sure he heard me. "I truly wish that for you."

Then I left without looking back. And I knew, right at that moment, as cold wind slapped against my still-wet cheeks, that I couldn't stay. I couldn't stay in the horde that I'd grown to think of as my home.

After all this time, I would need to return to my village. Because the pain that I would feel remaining close to Seerin, knowing that he would choose another that was not me, knowing he'd never truly loved me, was nothing compared to the struggle I would face returning to the only other home I'd known.

I needed to leave. Though it was the height of the cold season, I needed to leave.

If I stayed, it would destroy whatever was left of me.

36

"You cannot be serious," Odrii said, staring at me like I'd lost my mind. And perhaps I had, but all I could feel hours after Seerin had torn my heart from my chest was *numb*. "Nelle. *Nik*. I will not take you back. Your home is here."

Avuli sat at the low table in her *voliki*, Arlah at her side, looking between us. Though the young boy had learned a few words in the universal tongue, he looked confused by the exchange and his mother would not translate the conversation for him. She was looking at me, her expression knowing. As if she recognized heartbreak in me because she'd experienced it keenly herself when her mate had died in battle.

Her mate didn't choose to leave her. He was taken.

Seerin, on the other hand, had willingly chosen this.

I hadn't cried since I left his *voliki* earlier that morning. It was nearing evening and I simply felt...as detached as Seerin had seemed.

"I will return to my village with or without your help, Odrii," I said softly, looking down at my hands. They were smooth and soft now, even during the cold season, probably because I'd been Seerin's *alukkiri*, spreading on his oils every night.

A sharp pinch in my chest made me squeeze my fists hard and I looked up at Odrii. The warrior male was looking at me with a thunderous expression, as if angry with me.

"You do not know the way," he growled.

"I know," I said. "But I will still leave."

He cursed under his breath, looking to his sister, who'd still said nothing.

"You just need rest, Nelle," he argued. "Your perspective will change in the morning."

"And if it doesn't," I started, "will you be my guide back?"

"She will not change her mind, Odrii," Avuli finally called out softly. "You will take her back, brother, if she does not wish to stay. You would rather her leave by herself? *Nik.* It is safer this way."

Odrii cursed again, looking away from us both.

Silence permeated the *voliki.* I'd never questioned whether this was the right decision because in my eyes, it was the *only* decision. I simply could not stay.

"I'm sorry to ask this of you," I whispered, looking at all of them. It was then that grief slithered its way up my chest, tightening my throat. "You know how much I care for you. All of you. And it breaks me even more that I have to leave you. But if I stay...I'm worried that—that it will take everything that's left of me, everything that he hasn't taken already. I would be a shell. Nothing more."

I'd begun to envision my life in the horde with Seerin. I'd thought we had a future together because how could we not?

Had he known all along that this would be the outcome? Every single night, as I lay in his arms, had he known that he would have to break me apart like this?

I thought he'd loved me. But now, I could see that I was a fool for believing that in the first place.

He *was* cruel, if he'd known all along.

"Please," I whispered, looking at Odrii. "I-I need your help. I *have* to leave."

I would never see Seerin again. I would never touch him, or see his smile, or taste his lips, or look deep into those consuming eyes again. I craved him as much as I hated him. My heart wanted two very different things at once, so it was easier to not feel anything at all.

Once, I'd been afraid of this happening. When I'd been back at my village, I'd feared becoming so emotionally distant from everything around me that I would simply float away. I thought that I would simply cease to exist if that happened.

But right then, it felt like a blessing.

Odrii finally nodded, but he looked at me as if I were hurting him. "We will leave in the morning. At dawn."

Relief pierced that numbness with startling sharpness. Relief and grief.

"Thank you," I whispered, tears finally falling again.

ODRII MET me at the entrance to the encampment a little before dawn. Avuli was with him, but Arlah wasn't.

I'd taken only what I needed for the journey home, which consisted of my warmest clothes. After some internal debate, I'd decided to keep Blue's pendant, but had taken off the blue jewel necklace Seerin had gifted me a couple mornings before and left it on my bed. The only thing I regretted not being able to bring with me was the rock that Arlah had given me, which sat in Seerin's *voliki*. And I wouldn't dare go there now to retrieve it.

Everything else I didn't need. I'd survived for years on much, much less.

I didn't feel the chill as I approached Odrii on his *pyroki*. Avuli embraced me when I reached her and I squeezed my eyes shut as I wrapped my arms around her, letting her warmth seep into me one last time.

"Please tell your father 'thank you,'" I told her softly. She pulled back and looked at me. "I regret that I didn't say goodbye."

She nodded.

"Arlah?" I asked hesitantly.

She shook her head and I felt a prick of sadness and guilt. When I'd left their *voliki* the night before, Arlah had finally understood that I was leaving permanently and he'd barely looked at me, turning his face into his mother's dress when I'd tried to embrace him.

"I am sorry," she whispered. "He did not want to come."

I nodded, swallowing the thick lump in my throat. Avuli reached out and patted a heavy-looking sack attached to the seat of Odrii's *pyroki*.

"Dried *kinnu* and *kuveri*," she explained. "I went to the *bikku's voliki* last night and took as much as I could fit. It should last you through the cold season."

My throat tightened at her foresight. "Thank you."

"I packed an extra fur," she said. "And a blade. Just in case."

I nodded, thinking of the dagger Seerin had given me, which was in his *voliki* next to Arlah's rock. Back in my village, I'd always slept with an arrow close by, especially after Kier's attack.

Odrii made a sound on his *pyroki*, a growl. He didn't like this. He couldn't understand why I needed to do this, but Avuli seemed to understand.

"Nelle," he said softly. "Please reconsider. *Stay*. This is madness."

His *pyroki* stomped its claws into the earth, as if agreeing with his master's words.

Pressing my lips together, I reached out to squeeze Avuli's hand.

"Thank you," I whispered, pressing a kiss to her cheek. "For everything."

She gave me a watery smile, her eyes shimmering in the low light of the morning. "*Lik Kakkari srimea tei kirtja.*"

May Kakkari watch over you.

I reached my hand up towards Odrii and he sighed, his shoulders sagging, taking it as my final answer, my final decision. He pulled me up easily, settling me in front of him, his thighs encasing my own.

Out of the corner of my eye, I sensed movement between two *volikis*. When I turned my head to look, praying to Kakkari that it wasn't Seerin, I saw his *pujerak* instead. I'd barely seen him since that night, over a month ago, when he'd confronted me in the training grounds. Now, the Dakkari male stood, watching us with narrowed eyes and a frown.

When his gaze turned to me, I looked at him for one brief moment.

You got what you wanted, I thought quietly. *I'm leaving.*

His lips pressed together in answer, but instead of smug victory on his face, there was only...relief.

I looked away, giving him no more of my time or my thoughts, looking down at Avuli one last time before setting my gaze out towards the plains that I saw beyond the gate of the encampment. I didn't look back as Odrii's *pyroki* led us away. I didn't look back at the training grounds where I'd spent many nights with my bow, or my *mitri's* weapons tent, where I'd finally perfected my arrows, or the maze of *volikis* that I could navigate in my sleep. And I most certainly didn't look up the small incline at the back of the camp at the *voliki* where I'd spent some of the happiest moments of my life.

I would never see him again.

I would never see him again.

The sudden realization almost broke me completely. It was *that* crushing.

"Ready?" Odrii asked me. We were just outside the gates now, a blanket of snow and ice in front of us, stretching as far as I could see over the plains of Dakkar.

Never. I would never be ready.

"Yes," I said, as tears drenched my cheeks. "I am."

37

"*Vorakkar.*"

I blinked and focused my attention on my head warrior. When I looked at him, I couldn't help but notice that the rest of the elders' eyes and Vodan's eyes were on me as well. I wondered how long he'd been trying to get my attention.

"*Neffar?*" I rasped.

"The *Hitri* pass," the warrior said slowly. "The northern pass, specifically."

"What about it?" I asked, straightening.

Ujak looked across the table at Vodan. My *pujerak* said, "It will be the most dangerous to navigate on our journey. We need to formulate a plan on how best to cross it. The wagons may be too large."

He said it in a way that told me they'd already been speaking of this. Possibly for some time. And I hadn't noticed. Not at all.

"With all due respect, *Vorakkar*," one of the elders said, "we have been in discussions about our journey for almost two weeks now. And we are nowhere near as prepared as we should be."

"You have been distracted as of late, *Vorakkar*," another elder said quietly. "For the sake of the horde, we need your full attention if we want to be ahead of the thaw."

When I said nothing, it was Vodan that spoke.

"Let us call the meeting for tonight. The hour is late," Vodan said to the council. "We will reconvene tomorrow morning."

The fire burning in the basin crackled loudly at my *pujerak's* words. I felt a twisting bitterness in my chest for only a moment before I pushed it down. Deeper and deeper down, as I had done for the last two weeks.

"*Lysi*," I murmured. "Enough for tonight."

I didn't miss the look the elders exchanged among one another. Nor did I acknowledge Ujak when he inclined his head and said his goodbye for the evening. The elders shuffled out after him, after pulling on their pelts, but I remained standing at the high table, staring down at the map of Dakkar, left alone with Vodan.

"Seerin."

Turning away from the table, I pulled on my pelt. I didn't want to return to my *voliki*, where I still smelled her on my furs, but I certainly didn't want to be alone with my *pujerak* either.

"Seerin, I have never seen you like this," Vodan said quietly, rooted in his place. "When will it end?"

It will not end, I thought, knowing it was the truth. I believed this was permanent. It certainly felt permanent...this numbness. Except for brief flashes of emotion, I was simply existing.

"Seerin!" Vodan growled.

Piercing and sharp, I felt another flash and turned around to face him.

"What do you want from me, Vodan?" I rasped.

"I want you to act like the *Vorakkar* you are! This cannot go on."

"I have done everything you wanted," I told him. "If you are unhappy with the outcome—"

"I did not ask for you to act like *this*," he growled. With my fists clenching at my sides, I struggled to push my anger down now. Already, the emotions were packed too tightly, one on top of the other. Another would make me burst wide open, like a festering, unhealed wound. "It has been two weeks, Seerin. I thought that perhaps this obsession with the *vekkiri* would pass already."

"Obsession?" I repeated softly.

He knew it was the wrong word to pick. Anger bled from me, thickening the air in the tent until it was almost suffocating. In the last two weeks, *this* was the first time I'd felt such raw, aching, fierce emotion. I could suppress it no longer.

"I love her," I growled, though it was something he already knew. How could he not know? He knew me better than anyone. He knew I would not be this swayed by an 'obsession.'

"Seerin—"

I took a step closer to him. "After I took her from her village, you asked me something. You asked me what she'd said to me. You asked me what she'd said to make me take her away."

Vodan remembered that moment well. Nelle had been passed out from the pain, bleeding. He'd helped me clean her wounds.

"It wasn't what she said," I told him, holding his gaze. "It was what I *saw*. It was what Kakkari showed me *through* her. In her eyes."

Vodan's lips pressed together.

"I've felt Kakkari in me for a long time. I felt her when I first saw you. I know why she led me to you...because we created this. We built this horde together, as we were always meant to. She knew you would be a good and loyal friend to me," I said, though my lips twisted as I said the words. "And I to you."

He looked to the ground as I felt everything I'd dampened for the past two weeks emerge in one startling rush. All the grief and anger and loss and betrayal and longing. All the *guilt* for hurting her. All the self-hatred for betraying her trust.

At night, all I saw was the realization in her eyes the moment she knew I was pushing her away. And it haunted me to the point where I'd barely slept. It gutted me, watching her confusion, her disbelief, her heartbreak. She'd always been so expressive. I could read her so easily...and I'd seen everything. Every painful, disturbing detail.

"But Kakkari guided me to *you*. Back at the village, Kakkari guided her to *me*, as if Kakkari knew I would need her, as if I only needed help finding her. And what I found was a pure being, one who still believed in hope, though every last person in her life had failed her."

Including myself, I thought, my chest squeezing so tight I could barely breathe.

"I found strength with her. I found happiness with her," I said, swallowing. "And I pushed her away. I hurt her. For the horde, for you. Because I thought it was the right thing to do. Because if you were threatening to leave the horde, to leave me after everything we have been through, then surely I was blind to something you could see. I have always trusted you before."

"Seerin, it *was* the right decision for the horde," he said, shaking his head.

"Why do you look so hesitant then?" I rasped. "Why do I feel that it was the biggest mistake of my life?"

He went quiet.

"This will not simply pass, *pujerak*," I told him, my shoulders slumping, hearing the truth in my words. I felt the emptiness of them, the stretching emptiness that would only grow as the days passed. Because my soul had left me and all I had left was *hers*. I was tired. So damned tired. "I do not know how long I can do this."

Two weeks. Two weeks of staying away from her *voliki*,

though every time I passed it, it was a new challenge to my already-crumbling will. Two weeks of avoiding the training grounds because I knew she worked with the *mitri* in the mornings. Two weeks of looking for her everywhere, of hoping to simply catch a glimpse of her, only to be denied. Two weeks of not seeing her, not touching her, not speaking with her...and it felt like an eternity.

She had not sought me out either. She had avoided me like a plague around the encampment and every day that passed made my need to see her grow and grow.

I had chosen my horde over my *thissie*. It was a hard thought to stomach, but it was the truth. She would likely never forgive me for it. I knew I would never forgive myself for it, but I'd seen no other way.

Arokan of Rath Kitala had, my mind whispered. *He took his chosen* Morakkari *with no regard to his council or* pujerak. *He did it because he is the* Vorakkar *of his horde. He answers to no one but himself.*

I was *Vorakkar* of Rath Tuviri, so why did it feel like I was not? Why was I allowing myself to be controlled by my council, by the elders, by my own *pujerak*?

I growled, looking away from Vodan. They'd threatened to leave me. If they left, it was very likely the horde would fall. But did it matter? Without my female, did anything matter? I thought it was the right decision, but now, seeing a future without her in it, all I saw was emptiness. Bleakness.

I need to see her, I thought, my chest *burning* with the need. Now that the numbness had lifted, letting harsh, biting, sharp emotions rise in its absence, I could not stop them. They consumed me, eating at me, *punishing me.*

Was my own failing that I didn't believe I could run this horde on my own? Was my own failing that I didn't believe I was worthy to? Because I wasn't from an ancient family, because I wasn't raised a certain way, because I believed I was only a *Vorakkar* because of my mother?

Nik, I thought, my fists squeezing at my sides.

I was a *Vorakkar* because I had survived the Trials. I was a *Vorakkar* because I'd taken a hundred lashes over my flesh, more than any other *Vorakkar* in history. I was a *Vorakkar* because I was the right leader for this horde, because I kept them safe, because I defended them when they were in danger, because I had the determination and the will and the strength to do so.

My heart was pounding out a fierce rhythm in my chest as I stared at Vodan.

"I should never have let her go," I rasped, feeling weakened by the words. It was something I already knew. And I could blame it on the council, on Vodan, but in truth, it was *I* that had ended it. It had been my choice.

Just as it was my choice to risk the horde falling, in favor of my *thissie*. Because it was nothing less than she deserved.

"I have to see her," I said. "I have to…"

Fix this? She wouldn't want to see me. Not after what I'd done.

It didn't matter. I had to try.

I turned to leave the *voliki*, turning my back on my *pujerak*, my heart pumping strong in my chest—

"She's gone," Vodan said, so quietly that I almost didn't hear him.

My brows furrowed and I whipped around. "*Neffar*?"

"She left," he said, his voice strengthening.

I froze, disbelief spreading through me.

"What are you saying?" I asked slowly. "That she's not among the horde?"

"I thought you sent her away," he rasped. "I thought…"

Dread and panic made the *voliki* sway. "*Nik*. When? *Where did she go*?"

"Two weeks ago. She left at dawn with a warrior. The seamstress was—"

I was already striding through the entrance of the *voliki*, my heart pounding in my throat, before running towards the back of the encampment, towards Nelle's *voliki*.

Nik, nik, nik, I thought. Vodan was mistaken. He had to be.

When I reached her *voliki*, I pushed inside, praying to Kakkari that she within.

But the moment the cold touched my skin, the moment my eyes adjusted to the darkness inside, I knew Vodan spoke the truth. There was no fire, no warmth, no light.

She was gone. She'd left.

On her bed, something glinted in the blue, stale light and I snatched it up. Turning it over in my palm, I saw it was the necklace I'd given her from the *deviri*. It was icy cold. The sight of it gutted me because I knew what it meant. She'd thought it a gift of pity and had left it, left me, behind. And my *thissie's* pride burned bright when she was wronged, rightfully so.

Vodan said a warrior had taken her. Odrii, I knew. I'd seen him a few days ago, however, so he must've guided her back to her village and then returned himself. Just now, I remembered the darkened looks he'd speared my way, but I'd been so mentally detached that I hadn't given them a second thought.

Worry and fear washed over me, but I was already pushing out of the *voliki*, making my way towards the *pyroki* enclosure. Vodan had followed and caught up with me just as I reached it.

"What are you doing, Seerin?" Vodan hissed under his breath. It was dark, the encampment quiet. "You cannot leave."

I clenched my fist around the necklace. All I could think was that my *thissie* had willingly returned to her village, where she'd been half-starved for most of her life and almost raped. A place where no one had claimed her, protected her, *loved* her, as she deserved.

The thought that she would rather return there than stay in the horde was cutting enough.

And why would she stay? I thought bitterly. *I told her I would have to take another as my* Morakkari*, that she would have to accept that.*

If our positions were reversed, would I be able to stand aside and watch as she took another? Would I be able to withstand knowing that she took him into her arms, into her bed?

Nik, it would've killed me.

I growled, pushing past Vodan, jumping over the fence enclosure.

I'd been callous and cold to suggest such a thing to her. Like the monster I'd always known I was. The same monster that had ordered her whipping, that had pushed her away when she'd only ever wanted to be mine, that had knowingly hurt her with my words. She deserved better than me. Much better.

"Lokkas," I called, heading towards my beast's nest. I didn't care if it was the dead of night. I needed to go to her. It had been two weeks already. What if something had happened to her? What if she'd been hurt—what if her village had turned her away? "Lokkas!"

Her village was a two-day ride away. I could make the journey even quicker if I didn't stop.

"Seerin," Vodan said, following me into the enclosure. Lokkas emerged from his nest. "You are not thinking clearly."

"I am," I growled, jumping up on Lokkas' back. "For the first time in two weeks, I *am* thinking clearly."

Vok, all the wasted time!

Fool, fool, fool!

"You already made your decision," Vodan argued, holding Lokkas in place when I tried to steer him from the enclosure. "Do not make this mistake."

"It was a mistake to let her go," I told him. "It was a mistake to allow the council to steer my decisions as *Vorakkar*. Now stand away, *pujerak*."

"Seerin—"

"I will bring her back," I promised, staring down at him. We had known one another so long that he heard the fierce determination in my words. "Inform the council. Leave the horde if you must. Lead the others who do not wish to stay back to *Dothik*." His lips parted in disbelief. "From now on, I make my own decisions. She *is* what is best for the horde. I only regret it has taken me this long to realize that."

Without waiting, I pulled Lokkas away before kicking him up into a sprint.

A horde was only as strong as its *Vorakkar*. And a *Vorakkar* was only as strong as his *Morakkari*.

She is the strongest of us all, I thought, regret and grief mingling with my need for her.

I didn't care if I had to beg. I would go to her on my hands and knees, though a *Vorakkar* kneeled for no one.

This Vorakkar *will kneel for his* Morakkari, I thought, determined.

I would win my *thissie* back. I had to.

38

The smell of my own vomit made nausea rise again and I dry-heaved over the wooden basin. There was nothing left for me to throw up. I only ate my carefully rationed food in the early evening, once I was certain the sickness had passed.

When my stomach felt settled, I wiped my mouth on the nearby cloth and sank back on my heels, staring at the wooden wall of the home I'd lived in for countless years of my life. Upon my return to my village, I'd found no one had taken it over, probably because it was in serious disrepair and let in much of the cold. My table and chest had been looted, however, leaving only a broken chair behind. The hole-ridden old furs from my makeshift bed had disappeared. Even my bow was gone.

It was smaller and colder than I remembered, but over the last two and a half weeks, I'd tried to fix it up as best as I was able to. I took snow from outside, melted it, and scrubbed the floors and walls, erasing years of grime and dirt. I ripped some of my pelt away and used the pieces to patch some of the holes in the wood that let in the worst of the draft. I could do nothing about a fire, however. Since the Dark Forest was frozen over, I had no fuel to use and no starter, not to mention a proper basin.

Still, it kept me busy, at least for the first few days after returning to my village, which had already created quite a stir.

I ignored the questions, the stares, the whispers. I'd been stared at my whole life, so it was nothing new. I'd kept my head down, spoke to no one, and went about my life, as I had always done before.

After living among the Dakkari horde, where I'd had friends, companionship, purpose, and a true home, I felt even more isolated, even more lonely than I'd ever remembered being. Because now, I knew what I was missing. Because now, I knew what true happiness felt like and losing it was debilitating.

Staring into the dirtied basin—feeling some of the numbness that had shrouded me for two and half weeks slip away in favor of fear—I knew that soon, everything would change.

The morning sickness had come even before I'd left the encampment, though at that time, I hadn't even remotely suspected what I knew to be true now. It had only happened twice and I'd forgotten about it completely until I arrived back at my village. Two days in, I'd had nausea since waking. Thinking it was just heartache, that it was just missing *him*, I wrote it off. Until the next morning, it returned with a vengeance. And the next morning...and the next morning...and the next morning after that.

Two weeks in, it hadn't let up. Though I emptied my stomach in the mornings and ate very little in the evenings to extend my rations as long as possible, my belly was growing rounder, my breasts fuller. It was almost alarming how quickly my body was changing, until I realized that the Dakkari might have a quicker gestation period than humans.

I was pregnant.

And the father of my child had broken my heart. The father of my child would claim another female as his wife...and I would likely never see him again. He would never know he even had a son or a daughter.

I was too numb to truly feel anything about the pregnancy other than dread. Dread and fear because I didn't want to raise a child in this village. I didn't want my child to know hunger and cold. It was the last thing I wanted.

But it was done. I was already pregnant. I had to accept it.

And sitting there, staring into the dirty basin full of my vomit, feeling the chilly draft weaving through my poorly patched holes, I knew that I could not subject my child to this life. I thought of Grigg, who controlled the credits, who controlled our food. I thought of Kier, who'd sneered when he'd seen me walk through the village gates. I thought of the whispers and wondered how the village would treat a half-human, half-Dakkari child.

Not well.

Many blamed the Dakkari for our way of life. Would they take out their anger and frustration and fear on my child?

I couldn't allow that to happen.

Something sparked in me right then, the first flicker of strong emotion I'd allowed myself to feel. It was determination. Determination to provide my unborn child with a better life than I'd had. It was the need to *protect*.

But how?

Another horde, I thought, the answer coming easily.

Odrii had told me that another *Vorakkar* had taken a human as his *Morakkari*. The horde king of Rath Kitala. Until now, I hadn't realized that Dakkari and humans could create offspring together, but if I was pregnant...it was very likely the human *Morakkari* was pregnant as well, or had even delivered a child already.

Would she help me? Our children would be different from

all the rest, but it was likely they would find comfort in one another. A Dakkari horde with a human queen would be more accepting of a half-Dakkari child, certainly more than my village would be. *Safer.*

I could be useful to them too. I knew how to craft arrows of Dakkari steel. Before I'd left, my *mitri* had just begun teaching me the technique for crafting swords. If the horde had a weapons master, I could assist them. If not, I would learn whatever skill was required of me to be of use.

There was only one problem, however. Finding them. The realization made my shoulders slump.

It was almost impossible for me to know where a specific horde would be. All I knew was that Seerin was leading his horde south after the thaw. I knew nothing of Rath Kitala's whereabouts.

Then I will search for them after the thaw, I thought. I knew there were Dakkari outposts spread out among Dakkar. Perhaps they would help me locate the horde, or perhaps I would come across another on my way. No longer was I wary of the Dakkari. Humans feared them like they were monsters who would attack on sight. But I knew better. Approaching them didn't frighten me.

Until I found them, I could survive on my own as I searched. I was a hunter who could kill more than grounders, or *rikcrun* as I now knew they were called. I had seen enough *volikis* to know I could create a suitable makeshift shelter once I collected enough hides and dried them. I knew where to search for water.

I had time to plan. I had time to create another bow. The thaw was over a month away. I didn't know when the child would come, but I knew that I wanted to be in a safe place before the birth.

It was a risk, leaving my village, but it was a risk I was willing to take for the sake of my child. For the sake of our *future*. A *happy* future.

I settled my hands over my already growing belly, feeling a hesitant hope well in my chest.

"We can do this," I whispered softly to an empty, darkened, cold room. "I will protect you. I promise."

39

"Where is she?" I rasped to the *vekkiri* male I recognized as the village's leader, who'd approached the moment I swung off Lokkas' back. Ice clung to the black pelt around my shoulders and my face felt chaffed and raw from the wind.

The journey had been short, yet impossibly long, stretching from one moment to the next as I raced to reach Nelle. I had only stopped once to allow Lokkas rest, and to hunt a couple *rikcrun* for us to eat, which was the easiest meat to catch during the cold season in that part of Dakkar. Beyond that, we had ridden through the night, through the morning, and the afternoon. Now, darkness had long settled over the land. It was the early hours of morning.

The leader looked shocked and wary that I was there, holding up a flickering lantern between us. His eyes squinted behind me, no doubt looking for my warriors in the dark.

"Where is she?" I repeated in the universal tongue. I had not spoken the language in over two weeks and it felt both achingly familiar and strange on my tongue.

The prospect that my horde could be waiting out in the dark, beyond his line of sight, was leaving him shaken. His hand trembled as he pointed towards the back of the small village, towards a row of wooden, short homes. "I'll show you."

The village was quiet and sparse. Their homes were made of *wood*, some with small, smudged windows and chipped doors. The stench of waste permeated the village, as if they hadn't properly disposed of it. Faces appeared in the dirtied windows we passed—males, females, even children peering out. Gaunt, mistrustful, wary faces.

This was where my *thissie* had grown up, where she had lived, where she had willingly returned to.

My fists clenched at my sides. I was not indifferent to their suffering. It was similar suffering to what I'd seen in *Dothik* as a child.

The leader pointed to the end of a row of four houses. "That is hers," he said in a hushed voice.

Faint yellow light spilled from several cracks I saw in the walls, in the doors. I didn't wait another moment and stalked to it, needing to ensure she was safe. I'd thought of nothing else as I'd ridden to her village.

When I pushed open her door, something within crashed. I heard a sharp intake of breath and the unmistakable sound of Dakkari steel whistling from a sheath. I stepped inside, carefully not to let the cold in, and closed the brittle door behind me.

Nelle was within, kneeling on the floor among furs. It was her *bed*, I realized with another sharp ache in my chest. She slept on the floor with only a single fur for warmth. She'd been asleep, a small lantern burning next to her...in addition to a Dakkari dagger. It wasn't the one I'd given her, but I recognized the weapons master's work.

The sight of her released something in me, something tight and painful.

"Nelle," I said softly, drinking her in. My palm trembled as I ran it down my face, wiping away some of the ice melting from my hair.

Her eyes were on me. However, her expression was unreadable for possibly the first time since I'd encountered her. She didn't even look shocked to see me barge into her village home.

"What are you doing here?" she asked quietly, lowering the dagger. Had she needed to use it already? The thought made me want to bellow in frustration, especially when I realized the object that had crashed when I pushed inside was a broken chair. She'd wedged it up against the door as she slept. For added security and protection? *I* should be protecting her.

"You should not be here, *thissie*," I said, my words stilted. I'd been on Lokkas for over a full day and a full night. I'd had time to think what to say to her once I found her, so why were the words sticking in my throat? "You belong with the horde."

"I left," she said, as if it weren't obvious. Still, I could not read my normally expressive *kalles*. Her eyes were dark in the low light and they gave away nothing. Not even the normal glimmer of curiosity that almost constantly shone there. It worried me.

"Without telling me," I rasped, raking a hand through my tangled hair. "Without..."

"I did not realize I needed your permission to leave," she said, pushing up from the floor, standing. She was dressed in her pelt and the clothes that the seamstress had made for her. "I was not a prisoner there."

"*Nik*, I meant—"

"*You* should not be here," she said, levelling her gaze at me. I was so used to seeing her eyes filled with warmth and amusement and *life* that seeing them so empty brought me physical pain. Because *I'd* done that to her. "You should be with your horde."

"The moment I found out you were gone, I came straight here," I said, approaching her, bridging the short distance

ZOEY DRAVEN

between us. "I did not even realize you were *gone* until last night. And when I found out…"

I didn't want to relive that freezing fear, though I would remember it always. It would forever mark me, like the scars on my back.

Even then, that fear had only *begun* to thaw now that she was within my line of sight.

"It was a mistake, Nelle," I murmured, reaching out to cup her face. Her skin felt cold for the brief moment I touched her, before she stepped away. "It was a mistake choosing the horde over you."

Her expression didn't change. "No, you knew what you were doing. I think you always knew."

My fists clenched and I barely suppressed a wince before I pleaded, "Come back with me. We will work on this, *thissie*. I promise."

"I left for a reason, Seerin," she said. "Knowing what I know now, going back with you will not change anything."

"And what is it that you know?" I rasped.

There was a crack in her expression. Just a small one, but it showed me the pain I'd caused her, the pain I wished I could take from her a thousand times over. I would rather go through the *Dothikkar*'s Trials again, if only to take a sliver of it away.

"That is *was* just a fantasy," she whispered. I flinched when my words were flung back into my face. "A dream. It wasn't real."

"Nelle," I said, my brows furrowing. "It was real. It *is*. I need you to believe that."

How could she when I'd given her no reason to?

Determination coursed through me. I needed to give her a reason. I needed to give her thousands of reasons.

"I love you," I rasped, threading my hands in her hair, forcing her to meet my eyes so she would see the truth in them. "*Lo kassiri tei*. I love you, *rei thissie*. You know this, Nelle."

304

She'd asked me that morning if I'd ever loved her. And it gutted me to know that I hadn't said a single word in reply. I let her believe I didn't. I thought it would be kinder if she hated me. It would make it easier...

Vok.

"I don't," she whispered, looking deep into my eyes, though she still kept herself locked away. "I don't believe you, Seerin. Not anymore."

Stunned, I released her. Had I damaged us beyond saving?

"Please, just go," she said, wrapping her arms around her waist, turning slightly away from me.

Nik, I thought.

I swallowed, though determination coursed through me. She might hate me for it later, but I knew that I would not allow her to stay there.

"I am not returning without you, Nelle," I said. Her eyes flickered to me, a slight frown on her lips. "If I have to drag you back, I will."

Disbelief shone in her eyes, but at least it was better than indifference, than *emptiness*.

"Why are you doing this?" she asked, her brow furrowing. "You ended this, remember? *You* did. And I don't have the mental energy or the will to be your plaything anymore, Seerin. I don't trust your words and I certainly don't trust why you're here."

Her words gutted me even as I growled, "Then at the very least, believe that I do not want you *here*. In this place. There are those in the horde that care for you deeply. You think they want you to suffer? To be hungry, cold, unprotected? *Nik*."

"This was *my* decision to make, not yours, not anyone's," she replied. "Being in the horde with you..."

"*Neffar*?" I asked when she trailed off.

305

"It would destroy me," she whispered after a lengthy pause. "This is the only way, Seerin."

My chest ached—my whole body ached at her words.

And it will destroy me if you are not there, rei thissie, I thought to myself.

"I want you as my *Morakkari*, Nelle," I told her softly. "You were always meant to be my *Morakkari*."

She stilled.

"You told me once that all you wanted was to not be alone," I said, my voice coming out roughened and dark from the cutting emotions swirling within me. Her eyes flickered with recognition as mine flickered to her dark hair. "You told me you didn't want your hair to turn grey and find that you were alone."

That crack in her expression showed again.

"The horde is your true home, *thissie*. You will never be alone there. You were happy there," I rasped. "Then I hurt you. *I* knowingly hurt the one person in my life who I only ever wanted to protect and cherish. And I will spend the rest of my life making it up to you. I will spend the rest of my life showing that I love you. Until you never have to question it. Until you would never think of questioning it."

She shook her head. She was wary, I could see that, but I didn't care how long it would take to erase the doubt in her mind.

"I will not give you up," I told her. "I will not fail you or disappoint you again. *I promise you that.*"

"I'm tired, Seerin," she whispered.

I was getting nowhere with her that night.

Blowing out a long breath, I switched tactics. I asked softly, "Have you been eating, *thissie*?"

There were dark circles under her eyes and the hollow of her cheeks seemed more pronounced. Her eyes flickered to a travel sack of hide wedged into the corner of her small home. I went to it, peeled back the flap, and saw there were dried meats and *kuveri* loaves inside. It was a small relief to know she'd had *something* to sustain herself. But by the looks of it, it was already half gone and would barely get her through the cold season.

It wasn't enough. Not nearly. Knowing her, she'd been eating as little as possible to stretch out the rations.

When I straightened, I simply looked at her. After two and half weeks of not seeing her, of not speaking with her, all I wanted to do was go to her and wrap her in my arms. But even I knew she would not welcome my touch. Not anymore.

She was so beautiful to me that it made my chest physically ache.

"Nothing I say," I said quietly, "will change what I did. But it doesn't change how I feel about you either. I saw Kakkari's guiding light in your eyes the last time we were in this village together." Her brow furrowed slightly. "I saw strength and hope and connection in you. I knew that you were going to change my life from that very moment...and you have. You will continue to change it. You were always meant to be mine, Nelle. I was always meant to be yours. Kakkari knew that. I know that. I'm just sorry —so terribly sorry—that it took me this long to realize that."

Hesitation flickered in her eyes. Only for a brief moment... but it told me that she *heard* me. At the very least, she heard me.

"I will hunt and bring you *rikcrun* in the morning so you can have fresh meat," I murmured, deciding it was best to give her time to her thoughts. My eyes went to the dagger in her hand and the broken chair on the floor. "And do not fear, *rei thissie*, no one will dare to come near you. I will make sure of that."

She looked down to the floor of her home, her fingers beginning to tap on her thigh. A familiar habit of hers. One that told me she hadn't completely locked herself away.

"*Veekor, kalles*," I murmured.

Sleep, female.

They were words I'd often whispered in her ear after we had exhausted ourselves with mating, with my seed leaking down her inner thighs. Words I'd said to her when I curled her in my arms and she pressed her cheek against my chest. She'd told me she liked to listen to my heart, that counting the beats brought comfort to her as she dozed off into sleep.

In those moments, I'd known true peace. As if my singular purpose in the universe was simply to hold her, protect her, *love* her. As if I'd finally found my calling in life.

She remembered those words well and the memories that surrounded them. Her expression changed, her brows lifting ever so slightly, her nostrils flaring.

Longing. Finally, there was something recognizable in her features. It gave me hope that the love she had for me wasn't completely lost after all, that some part of her still wanted me.

I promised, "I will return in the morning."

40

Three days later, Seerin still hadn't left and my hardened determination had already begun to waver. Every morning, he came to my door, bringing with him skewers of cooked *rikcrun* and a fresh skin of water. The smell made my stomach heave in protest, though I'd always managed to hold down my nausea in his presence, but I could only eat very little.

At first, I told myself it didn't matter if Seerin was in the village. It didn't matter that I spent some moments with him. I had a plan to leave, my time in the village was only temporary, and I was numb enough to his words and his actions that it didn't matter if he was near.

At least that was what I'd told myself. But I'd somehow forgotten that Seerin had always had a way of finding his way inside.

During the day, he stayed away, as if he knew I needed space. He told me he was sleeping in the Dark Forest with Lokkas, so I assumed that was where he went. The forest had a good view of the village, even a good view of my dwelling. I refused to acknowledge the wiggling ache of guilt, knowing he slept in the icy cold and snow when there was a relatively clean floor in my home. The forest might protect him from the wind during the night, but it certainly didn't keep the wet sludge and chill away.

It's his decision, I reminded myself. *I told him to go and he will not.*

Still, a treacherous part of me had a difficult time falling asleep at night, knowing he slept out there, unprotected, with Lokkas. He had barely come with any provisions at all, giving further proof to his story that he'd journeyed straight here after learning I had left. He had no furs, no food or water—though he hunted easily.

But he gives most of his food to you, a voice whispered in my mind.

At night, he would return again with more skewers of *rikcrun*. I wondered how the villagers felt about him coming and going with fresh, cooked food to my door. He'd mentioned on the second day that he'd given my uneaten morning portions to 'the older male next to you.' I assumed he'd meant Bard, my neighbor, and a part of my chilled heart warmed slightly at the prospect.

What worried me, however, was that at night, Seerin talked. He would watch me eat while he spoke of things that made me hate him and remember why I'd fallen in love with him in the first place. He spoke of things that made me remember my life back at the horde. It was only three weeks that I'd been gone, but it felt like much, much longer.

That night, he told me what had transpired in the last few weeks. That it was the *pyrokis'* mating time, that a few of the nests in the enclosure had been accidentally destroyed and rebuilt because of it. That the *mitri* was receiving more requests for Dakkari steel bows from the warriors, even from a couple children. That a child had been born, that the mother was one of the *bikkus* and the father was a warrior.

"It is good to hear a baby's cry in the horde again," he

murmured, sitting on the floor across from me, his back to one of the creaking walls. I'd said nothing to him since he'd appeared at my door that night, though I was ravenous and had eaten the *rikcrun* he'd brought me. All of it. "Most are born after the thaw."

Because during the cold season, locked in close quarters, naturally keeping one another warm, what else was there to do but mate? I thought, pressing my lips together. It only served to remind me that I hadn't told Seerin about the pregnancy. Not yet. Everything seemed like a constant reminder. We'd never spoken about children. Did he even want them?

"And once the thaws come, there will be a celebration. Much like the frost feast, though there will be no fresh meat. Just mostly fermented wine." His eyes were steady, his voice even as he said, "For that reason alone, we will wait to celebrate our *tassimara* until we journey to the southlands."

My brow furrowed. *Tassimara*?

"Our joining ceremony," he murmured, seeing my confusion, and I swallowed loudly at his words. "We will track a *hebrikki* herd and make our new home close by. We will have the first of the fresh meat at our *tassimara*, in our new encampment, in a place that will grow warm and lush after the thaw. I know you will like it there."

"Stop," I whispered, closing my heart off to his words when it pumped too strongly with longing and desire. "There will be no *tassimara*."

Though it was the first time I'd spoken to him all day, he didn't hesitate as he said, "Then we will wait. Perhaps by the blue solstice, you will feel differently."

Later that night, after he left to return to the Dark Forest, I lay underneath my fur and stared up at the dark ceiling, my hand on my belly. My back ached from sleeping on the hard floor and I marveled at how I'd slept in this very place for almost my entire life. When Jana had been alive, there had been a bed stuffed with cloth, but Grigg had offered to pay me twenty credits for it shortly after she died. I'd been in no position to refuse and in the back of my mind, I wondered if he still slept on that very bed. I wondered if he knew that was where Jana had drawn her last breath.

My fingers traced the growing curve of my stomach underneath my belly button. I wondered why I had not told Seerin yet. It was not something that I could keep to myself now that he was here. Before, I'd never expected to see him again. Now, he was insisting on bringing me back to the horde and talking of things like *tassimaras*.

A small breath escaped me in the darkness. I knew how determined and stubborn he could be. He truly meant it when he said he wouldn't return without me. He would sleep in the Dark Forest until he turned to ice. Only the thaw would save him then.

I didn't dare believe in his perfect, pretty words. I didn't dare believe that he loved me after all, that he wanted to make me his *Morakkari*, his wife, his queen, especially after he'd told me it could never be me. If I believed in him again and then he pushed me away...I wouldn't come back from it. I wondered if this was how my mother felt after my father died. This heartache, this seemingly never-ending sadness.

But I was not like my mother. I was having a child and I would never abandon my baby like she'd abandoned me. I had to be strong. I had to do anything and everything in my power to protect him or her, to keep them safe.

I could find another horde, but even if I found one, there was always a possibility they would turn me away. Finding another horde was an uncertainty, yet Rath Tuviri was a certain thing. Seerin was here *right now*. He was demanding that I return with him. It would be so easy to give in...and yet, it would be the most difficult choice I would have to make.

This isn't about me, I realized. It wasn't even about us, about Seerin and I. It was about our child.

The baby deserved to know their father. They deserved to know their Dakkari blood, their culture, their people. They deserved to grow up in an environment that was safe, protected, and caring.

I know what I have to do, but I'm afraid to do it, I confessed to myself. Tears welled up in my eyes and leaked down my temples as I stared up at the ceiling. Wind whistled through the holes in the wood, as if in answer to my thoughts.

I couldn't stay. The safest, smartest decision would be to return to the horde of Rath Tuviri with Seerin. It might even be the *only* decision at this point.

If my guess was correct, I was almost two months into the pregnancy. It was very likely Seerin had gotten me pregnant the night he'd returned from *Dothik*. I knew nothing about delivering and caring for a baby. I didn't even know how long I would be pregnant for. I was scared and heartbroken and alone.

Except I didn't have to be alone. I had friends in Rath Tuviri. They could help me if I needed it.

THE NEXT MORNING, before the sun even rose, I packed up the travel sack Avuli had given me. I rolled up the fur, deposited the dagger within, and carried it over my shoulder. It was significantly lighter than it'd been before, considering I'd eaten almost three weeks of rations from it.

I didn't look back at my home as I closed the door behind me. At Bard's door, I left the sack, knowing I wouldn't need it, and then I turned and left.

It was still dark, the sky *just* beginning to lighten in the distance, and the village road that led to the gates was empty and quiet. My footsteps crunched into the snow, the sound loud against the hush. I marveled at how much had changed in the last three months as I walked from the village for the last time.

Once I was past the gates, I turned towards the Dark Forest. I knew it like the back of my hand and had explored every inch in my lifetime. I knew where Seerin would make his base because it had the best view of the village and of my little house. My instinct told me he would be there.

And he was. After I climbed the short incline of the ridge and weaved through the first layer of trees that stood like ancient guardians at the forest's edge, I spied him propped up against a blackened trunk, Lokkas curled close beside him.

He was sleeping. Both of them were. In sleep, with those intense grey eyes closed to the world, Seerin looked less intimidating and almost peaceful.

Agony burst in me and stayed for a long moment as I looked at him. I held still and silent as tears blurred my vision.

Why did I have to fall in love with you? I asked silently. Why couldn't it have been anyone else? Perhaps it would've been easier if it had been no one at all and then this aching sadness would disappear. I wished that three weeks could've erased the love that he'd built in my heart, but something told me it wasn't as simple as that.

I hated that he slept out here. I hated that I couldn't bring myself to offer my home, hated that being in his presence for too long brought worry and fear and longing into my heart. It was not long ago when I'd craved being with him. It wasn't too long ago when I'd missed him even when he was still near.

My morning sickness rose, but the icy chill on my face helped distract me from the nausea. I walked towards Seerin and my movements roused Lokkas, who turned his eyes towards me. Seerin had always been a light sleeper. He woke at the smallest sound, so when I approached and he didn't stir, it made me realize how exhausted he must truly be.

Guilt ate at me. He'd been sleeping out here for four nights now. He hadn't eaten nearly as much food as his body needed. And he had no shelter, no protection out here from the elements.

When I neared Lokkas, I reached my hand out to stroke his snout. He pushed his scaled nose into my palm and made a chirring sound. It was that sound that woke Seerin, whose eyes flashed open. When he sensed someone near, he stilled, his hand going to his sheathed sword at his side.

When he saw it was me, standing there in the Dark Forest at dawn, he murmured, still drowsy from sleep, "*Kassikari*, what are you doing out here?"

I wondered what *kassikari* meant. He'd called me it before, many times. Another name he had for me that made my chest pull with memory.

Seerin had always woken easily, yet slowly. How many times had I watched him wake, how many times had his bleary eyes come to me immediately as he rasped something out in Dakkari, his words husky and warm? How many times had I teased him about his love for long mornings in our bed? How many times had he silenced me with his drugging, mind-spinning kisses?

"Nelle," he murmured, trying to catch my attention.

"I'm pregnant, Seerin," I said, my voice soft but tormented from wonderful memory and my thoughts.

Air whistled through his nostrils as he inhaled a sharp breath. His eyes flared and he pushed up from the blackened trunk until he was standing within arm's reach of me. Lokkas stood with his master until I was small again beside them both.

"I will return with you for the sake of the child," I said, craning my head to look up at him. "I was not planning to stay here regardless but now that you're here...I know it's the right choice."

"Were you ever going to tell me?" he rasped, his eyes like flint. "I have been here four days and you tell me this now?"

His anger stemmed from his own past, I knew. He'd never known his father and I knew from our past conversations, though he'd never said it outright, that he'd *wanted* to. The knowledge that I was pregnant, that I had kept it to myself until now, resurfaced old wounds within him. I knew that, but I was not afraid of his anger.

"I never thought I would see you again," I told him truthfully, "and certainly not *here*."

"Did you know you were pregnant when you left?" he asked.

"No," I said. Even as hurt as I'd been, I wouldn't have left if I'd known I was pregnant then.

He went quiet, looking past me towards the village, trying to process what I'd just revealed to him. When he brought a hand up to rake through his tangled, damp hair, I saw that it shook. A sharp pang went through me at the sight.

"It is why you would not eat in the mornings," he said. "Because you were sick."

He cursed under his breath and Lokkas shifted beside me, sensing his master's emotions.

"What do you mean you were not planning to stay here?" he growled out next. "What were you planning to do exactly?"

I inhaled a long breath, knowing that what I would say would incite more of his anger. I refused to feel guilty about it, however, as I told him, "I know that the *Vorakkar* of Rath Kitala took a human *Morakkari*." He'd never told me himself. I'd learned it from Odrii. Looking back, I realized Seerin never *wanted* me to know. Because he thought it would give me hope for a future with him? "I thought it was very possible she was also pregnant or had already given birth to a child. I was planning to seek them out after the thaw."

His nostrils flared. "You were planning to brave the wild lands pregnant with no knowledge of where his horde was?"

"Yes," I said, lifting my chin.

"Do you know how foolish that is?" he growled.

"Yes," I said again. "Believe me, I know. But I felt I had no other choice. I would not raise my child in this village. I would not subject him or her to hunger and cold and contempt." His lips pressed together and I watched his throat bob with his heavy swallow.

"*Our* child, Nelle," he corrected.

"Oh, yes," I said, my hurt finally making an appearance. "You would rather have me raise *our* child in your horde. You would rather have me watch you take another as your *Morakkari*, to endure as she bore you your heirs while I raised *our* child. I believe you told me I would have to accept it because it was your duty."

My bitter words hit him but his small flinch didn't make me feel any better.

"I was wrong to say that to you, *thissie*," he murmured. "You will never know how sorry I am. But the wild lands are punishing and dangerous. To think that after the thaw, you were going to..."

He shuddered, his jaw clenching, and he looked away. A sharp wind whistled through the trees and I shivered, waiting.

"What about us?" he finally asked, his voice guttural and husky.

Carefully, I told him, "This doesn't change anything between us, Seerin. I didn't understand it at the time, but now, I can see why you did what you did. The choice you had to make."

"*Thissie*—"

"But right now, my only priority is the child," I finished, cutting him off, straightening. "Nothing more."

His jaw ticked again. He wanted to argue, I could see it just as I saw his decision to leave it for another time. He'd gotten what he wanted. I would return to the horde with him willingly.

"Very well, *rei thissie*," he murmured. "I will accept that."

For now. It went unspoken, hovering in the air between us.

He knew that and I knew that.

"We will return to the horde."

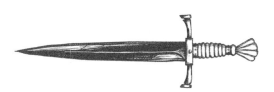

41

The council stared at me as if I'd lost my mind.

"*Vorakkar*—" one of the elders began, but I cut him off before he had a chance to speak.

"*Nik*, I will hear no more," I growled. "I am disbanding the council. Hordes have existed for generations without them. This one will too."

I would make sure of it. My horde would not fail because of it.

It was the first gathering I'd called since returning with Nelle over a week ago. The thaw was coming, there was much to accomplish within the horde, much to organize for our impending journey south, and yet, I'd made my decision to let the members of my council go.

"If this is because of the *vekkiri*, I must—"

"I said *enough*."

The second elder closed his mouth, biting his tongue.

"That *vekkiri*," I rasped, my tone sharp, "will become my *Morakkari*." I was as determined about that as anything else. Even if it took me years of convincing her, of rebuilding the trust she'd lost in me, I would do it.

The three elders shifted on their feet. My head warrior said nothing. My *pujerak* simply looked at me.

"She is carrying my child," I told them, my voice roughening with too many emotions to place. Vodan's breath whistled out of him in a deep sigh while the others froze. "Do not disrespect her in front of me again. A slight against her is a slight against me."

The council was silent in response.

"I will not turn you away from the horde after the thaw," I rasped. "You made it clear that if I took her as my *Morakkari*, you would leave. That decision is yours, but no longer will I look to you as my advisors. I will make the decisions when it comes to *my* horde from now on. If it fails, it fails. That is the risk I am willing to take."

I had nothing more to say.

To lead a horde without the support of a council would be more difficult, more stressful. And perhaps, in time, a new council would emerge, one better suited and more supportive of Rath Tuviri's future.

I didn't wait for them to respond. I didn't expect a response, not even from Vodan. Instead, I left the *voliki*, my purpose in meeting with them complete. My only regret was the distance between Vodan and I. We'd barely spoken since my return from the village. His threat to leave the horde had forever changed our friendship.

It was early evening, though the sky was dark. Nelle would still be with Avuli, but I'd requested the healer's presence that night at my *voliki*.

When I reached the seamstresses' home, I heard Nelle's muffled laugh within and it made my entire body feel heavy, weighed down. I hadn't heard her laugh in over a month, or seen her smile. The past week of being back in the horde had been a series of quiet, stilted conversations with her. She insisted on staying in her own *voliki*. She'd resumed her daily schedule, spending the mornings with the *mitri* and her afternoons and early evenings with Avuli, Arlah, and sometimes Odrii.

I looked for her always and on the rare occasion she was alone, walking through the camp, we spoke. But her guard was up, her expression closed. The conversations had mostly consisted of me asking if she was eating, how her sickness was in the mornings, whether she'd slept well the night before.

There was a barrier between us, one I'd laid the foundation for and that she'd constructed, and I didn't know how to break through it.

Time, I thought. It would take time.

I ducked my head into the seamstresses' *voliki* and saw Nelle watching Avuli chase Arlah around the domed tent. Avuli pulled up short when she saw me and inclined her head, startled.

"*Vorakkar*," she murmured in greeting.

"I do not mean to interrupt," I told her, my eyes going to Nelle, "but the *kerisa* awaits us."

Nelle nodded, the small smile on her face fading slightly at my sudden appearance. She pushed up to a stand and grabbed her pelt from where it lay by the fire basin, fastening it over her shoulders.

"*Srikkisan?*" Arlah asked Nelle in Dakkari.

It meant *tomorrow* in the universal tongue.

"*Lysi*," Nelle said softly, pressing her hand to his cheek. "*Lo terri tei srikkisan.*"

I will see you tomorrow, she said, her Dakkari slightly accented but clear. Her knowledge of our language grew with every passing day, it seemed.

Arlah nodded and Nelle said goodbye to Avuli, squeezing the seamstresses' hand as she passed. I held the entrance of the *voliki* open for her as she stepped out.

Nelle met my eyes briefly before she looked straight ahead. I hadn't seen her since that morning. And maybe it was hearing her laugh, maybe it was knowing that she opened herself to others, maybe it was missing her so damned much, but at that moment, I couldn't stomach the distance that only seemed to grow between us. I feared that if I let it grow too much, it would be impossible to close.

"I miss you, *rei thissie*," I rasped, pressing my forehead to hers. I heard her breath hitch, felt her body still under my touch. But I met her eyes, so close that all I saw was their dark, rich color. "If I knew how to make this right between us, I would."

She held my gaze. For a moment, I saw her empathy, saw it gleam in her eyes, saw her want that as much as I did.

"Seerin," she whispered, shaking her head.

"I know." My shoulders sagged and I blew out a breath, releasing her. "Come, *thissie*. The healer is waiting."

She hesitated for a brief moment but then followed me as I led her up the short incline to my *voliki*. The *kerisa* was waiting at the entrance and she nodded at the both of us before following us inside.

The healer's visit was short and something that would happen every week until Nelle delivered the child. The *kerisa* inspected the growth of her belly first. Even since last week, I saw that the baby had grown and I watched from a short distance away, my chest filling with pride and relief. Since Nelle was a *vekkiri*, it made the timing of her delivery unpredictable, which was why the healer wanted to monitor her every week.

After the healer was done with her inspection, she rose to make Nelle her tonic and said, "It seems you are almost halfway through the gestation already. Dakkari females carry for five months, and if the conception happened a little over two months ago, as you believe," Nelle's cheeks pinkened slightly, "then it is likely you will also carry for that long."

Nelle had told the healer last week, when we'd arrived back

in the horde, that she believed the conception happened the night I'd returned from *Dothik*. A night I remembered well and was very likely when we conceived the child, considering how insatiable we'd *both* been.

Longing went through me. It was just one more thing I missed with my *kalles*, our matings.

The healer gave Nelle her tonic to drink. Judging by the pungent smell and the look on Nelle's face, it wasn't pleasant, but she drank it down without a single complaint as the healer packed up her herbs and supplies.

"I will return next week," the *kerisa* informed Nelle before inclining her head at me. "*Vorakkar.*"

Then she took her leave, slipping out the entrance of the *voliki*, leaving us alone. Nelle adjusted her tunic so that it covered her growing stomach once more and I watched her from my place against my cabinet, where I stood with my arms crossed.

She looked at me out of the corner of her eye, sitting on the edge of the bed where we had spent a great deal of time together during the height of the cold season.

"We should talk about how we are going to do this," she said softly. "Don't you think?"

"Do what?" I asked.

She clasped her hands in her lap and said, "Care for the child. I do not know what to expect. Avuli told me Dakkari fathers are very involved with the rearing, but since we are not..."

"*Neffar?*"

Her lips pressed together and then she said, "Since we are not mated, since we keep two different *volikis*, we should discuss—"

"By the time the child comes," I said, "I fully expect that you will be my *Morakkari, rei thissie.*"

Stunned silence spread between us.

"You...*expect*?" she repeated slowly, disbelief tinging her tone.

"*Lysi.*"

I missed many things about my *thissie*. I missed her curious questions, the way her eyes lit up as she talked about crafting arrows, how she always waited for me so we could eat our evening meal together even if I returned late, how her breath hitched ever so slightly whenever we kissed.

I missed our whispered conversations into the early hours of morning and seeing her eyes spark with heated desire when I slipped between her thighs.

I missed feeling the press of her *thissie* feather necklace against my skin during the night, that soft feeling in my chest whenever I spied her around the encampment, seeing her secretive smile whenever she met my gaze from afar.

I even missed her temper. While she was not as quick to it as I was, it burned bright when lit.

She'd been so impassive towards me, the complete opposite of the starling who'd shyly admitted she liked when I kissed her and who'd informed me with a beguiling arrogance that she wouldn't miss with her bow again before I'd given her my name.

But right then, she was not impassive. She was not indifferent. She was *angry* and I felt relief whistle through me, clear and pure.

"You are unbelievable," she hissed, her voice soft, standing from the edge of the bed. "You have no right to expect anything from me!"

"Besides my child, you mean," I rasped, stoking those flames hotter because it felt so damn right.

Her lips parted, her eyes flashing. Then she clenched her jaw and grabbed her pelt from off the bed. She fastened it around her shoulders as she strode past me.

Catching her arm, I forced her to stop. "*Nik*, you will not retreat from this."

"I'm not running away," she countered, trying to pull her arm from my grip.

"Then what are you doing?" I growled. "All you have done is run from me!"

"With good reason," she said with a growl all her own, frustration joining her anger when I would not let her go.

"Tell me," I ordered, pulling her closer. "Tell me how much you *hate* me, *rei thissie*." She stilled, her breaths coming heavy, shock flashing in her eyes. "Tell me how much you wish our paths had never crossed. Tell me how much I hurt you. Tell me how much of a monster I am, but at least *tell me something*, Nelle!"

"Stop," she breathed, her gaze locking with mine, surprise mingled with something else in her eyes.

"Tell me!"

"Seerin, I..." she trailed off.

I let her go and took a step away.

"I do not know what to do, Nelle," I said softly. "I am sorry. I am so sorry for what I did. This past month has been the worst I can ever remember."

Her lips parted. She heard the truth of it in my words. And she knew that I'd had many terrible months, especially in *Dothik*.

I was tired. Mentally exhausted. I hadn't been eating enough. This month had taken its toll on my body, on my mind. It had taken its toll on Nelle. And it was all my fault.

"Losing you, pushing you away," I rasped, "was the biggest mistake of my life. And even though you are here now, you are still so very far away. I cannot reach you anymore, *thissie*."

"Seerin," she whispered, her brows furrowing.

"What do you want?" I rasped. "Do you want me to...do you

want me to leave you be? Do you truly want this to be over between us?"

It was unfathomable, letting her go for a second time, *willingly*. But this wasn't just about me.

"I...I don't know," she said softly.

Her words both filled me with hope and filled me with despair, a strange mixture that made me want to bellow to the domed ceiling of my *voliki*.

"I would give up the horde for you," I rasped. Her breath hitched, a stricken, stunned look on her face. "If that is what it takes, I will, Nelle. You would not be my *Morakkari*, but you would be my mate, my *kassikari*."

"*Kassikari*," she whispered, her eyes widening slightly.

"We could travel to one of the outposts and live there. We could raise our child there," I said, my heart heavy in my chest. I loved being a *Vorakkar*. I loved the horde life...but not if it meant giving up Nelle.

"Seerin, stop," she said, her voice rising, her eyes wet. "You're being foolish. I would never ask that of you!"

"Then what would you ask of me?"

Her mouth opened but no sound came out. My shoulders sagged.

It occurred to me, just then, that it was possible we *couldn't* be fixed. And that realization hurt more than her silence.

Nelle looked down to the floor of the *voliki*. I sensed our conversation was over. I knew she would leave soon.

Before she did, however, I said softly, "You asked me once if I did not have the horde, what would I want for myself?"

Her fingers began to tap on her thigh.

"Well, I finally have an answer and it is you. I want *you*, *thissie*," I told her. My lips twisted as dread settled in my belly. "Only, I'm just now wondering if I'll ever truly have you again as mine."

42

There were two things I knew for certain.

The first was that I still loved Seerin. I'd never stopped, even when I'd wanted to hate him. I'd tried to numb my feelings for him, to push them deep down until they were completely buried, but they'd always had a way of floating back up to the surface when my guard was down.

The second was that it disturbed me he would give up the horde to save our relationship and our future together. It disturbed me greatly because I knew he spoke the truth. Seerin loved his horde. He loved being *Vorakkar*. It was what he was meant to do. He'd told me long ago that he had great plans for the horde and was determined to see them through.

Which was why it made everything in me rebel at the thought of him leaving...for me.

It was the afternoon, two days after Seerin had offered to give up the horde. I'd seen him briefly yesterday in the training grounds as I left the *mitri's* workshop. Now that the thaw was coming and the temperatures weren't nearly as frigid, training had resumed for the warriors. Our eyes had connected briefly.

He hadn't been fighting, but rather watching along the far fence of the enclosure, but I had captured his attention entirely.

Seeing him among his warriors reminded me of the first time I'd seen him in my village. He'd drawn eyes. He drew attention because he was simply a commanding presence. And it wasn't his size, his broadness, his strength—though those certainly added to it—it was the way he held himself apart from his horde. He was a leader—one that had been born *and* made. He couldn't be on the same level as the members of Rath Tuviri. In order to best serve them, he *had* to detach.

It made me realize that he'd done the same to me. He'd detached from me because he thought it would best serve his horde...because he was a leader. He had to be. He didn't have the luxury of being selfish because he had to think of families, of warriors, of elders, of children.

He was a *Vorakkar*. It was marked into his skin, though I thought it was etched into his very bones, deep and permanent and lasting.

I didn't envy him his power, his responsibility. But he didn't need my envy. He only sought my support.

That afternoon, I roamed the encampment after working with the *mitri*. My hands throbbed from hammering Dakkari steel over the anvil for most of the morning. He was teaching me the proper techniques for working with blades and I was cooling off from the heat of the *voliki* before I made my way to Avuli's.

I saw him as I walked towards the *pyroki* pen—Seerin's *pujerak*. He was speaking with a female, who I knew to be his mate. She worked in the common bathing *voliki* and though she didn't speak the universal language, she'd always been pleasant towards me and greeted me every day, despite how much her mate detested me.

They seemed to be arguing about something just outside

their *voliki*. His brows were drawn together, the bright cold season sun shining across his face, and her cheeks were flushed in anger. She said something and then stormed into their home, leaving him to stand outside.

There were others roaming about, shooting him curious looks, but it was *me* that his eyes found after a moment.

There was something I'd often wondered about in the past month and I knew he had the answer. I didn't know if he would give it to me, but I didn't have a lot to lose in trying.

I went to him and asked, "Can I speak with you a moment?"

His ever-present frown was in place. I thought that he was a handsome male. Not nearly as handsome as Seerin, but I thought if he didn't scowl so much, he would be very appealing. His mate obviously thought so, though perhaps not quite at that moment since they'd been arguing.

He didn't reply, but I still turned regardless, walking towards the *pyroki* enclosure. I liked to watch them in their nests, though my regular presence often irritated the *mrikro*, the *pyroki* master. Then again, he was a cranky older male, who seemed irritated at most members of the horde, not just me. He loved the *pyroki* most of all.

I heard the *pujerak's* footsteps after a moment of hesitation and when I reached the fence of the enclosure, I saw he was only a few paces behind me.

"*Neffar*?" he growled, his mood already soured from his argument with his female.

Pressing my lips tight, I looked at him carefully. He'd never liked me, even back at the village. It was him I'd spoken to first, not Seerin, that day the horde had come for me.

"What did you talk about at the council meeting that night?" I asked.

His eyes flared. He knew which council meeting I spoke of.

The one where everything had changed. Seerin's mood that night when he'd returned to the *voliki*, and in the morning before he'd ended us, had been so...*strange*. I often thought about that and I wondered what had been said that would make him so *changed*. The change in him had been like night and day.

"The council's business is private and—"

"I need to know," I said, looking up into his eyes, unflinchingly. Determination pulsed in my veins. "Please."

His nostrils flared with a sharp breath and his features squeezed in an expression that I thought looked like...*shame*? But why?

After a long, tense pause, he finally murmured, "That night, we threatened to leave the horde."

I inhaled a quick breath, stunned.

"Who?" I asked. "*All* of you?"

"The three elders on the council, the head warrior...and myself."

"*You* threatened to leave?" I rasped, disbelief spinning in my mind. I reached out a hand to steady myself on the *pyroki* enclosure. "But your Seerin's...you're his closest friend. He loves you."

I was in such shock that I didn't even realize I'd used Seerin's given name until the *pujerak's* lips pressed together.

"I am his friend," he said. "Or at least I was. I betrayed his trust with my bluff."

So, he'd never meant to leave. It was only a manipulative ruse to get Seerin to end his relationship with me. It had worked too...until it backfired.

"He's barely spoken to me since," he said softly, his eyes shifting from me to the *pyrokis*.

It was a soft admission, one he probably hadn't meant to reveal to me of all people, but it tore from him as if he couldn't stop it.

He seemed to realize that because he straightened ever so slightly, swallowing, embarrassed.

"There were other factors, though," he said gruffly, "that we brought to his attention. Other members of the horde had also announced they would leave after the thaw. Almost two dozen, many of them warriors."

Discomfort made me shift. "Because of me."

He didn't confirm or deny it, which only added to my guilt. It started to make sense, why Seerin had changed so drastically that night. He'd been betrayed by a male he thought of as a brother, who had been at his side since *Dothik*. He'd been blind-sided by his *entire* council, who'd threatened to leave. And not only that but he also risked losing a significant number of his horde.

Briefly, I squeezed my eyes shut, gripping the fence until my knuckles turned white.

"He didn't tell me any of those things," I whispered. All he'd said was that it had become clear to him that I couldn't be his *Morakkari*.

Because he'd been backed into a corner by the advisors he trusted.

So what had changed? Even knowing that his council and horde threatened him, he'd still decided to come after me, to bring me back, to want me as his *Morakkari* regardless.

Seerin loved his horde but...

Is it possible that he loves me even more? I asked myself.

A sharp exhale squeezed my lungs. I'd told him I hadn't believed him when he said he loved me and I remembered, in crisp detail, the distraught expression on his face because of it.

Movement inside my belly made me gasp and my hand came up to rest there despite the layers of clothing I had on.

"*Neffar?*"

"I think the baby moved," I whispered, tears filling my eyes. It was such a beautiful feeling, that fluttering inside me. And my first instinct was to want to share it with Seerin, despite everything we had gone through in the past month.

The *pujerak* was silent and I blinked back the tears, hoping he wouldn't see my raw, surprised emotion. When I looked up at him, he was staring at me, his brow furrowed, his jaw clenched.

"He needs you," the Dakkari male told me.

My lips parted at his words.

"Before he realized you had left the horde," he continued, "he was not himself. He wasn't sleeping, wasn't eating. He was...spiritless."

My chest pulled in agony at the Seerin he was describing. Because I couldn't imagine him that way...although I'd seen a hint of it two nights ago. He'd seemed *defeated*.

"You are not the *Morakkari* that I would want for this horde. I have not made that a secret, even to you," he murmured, reminding me of that night he'd approached me on the training grounds. "However, I realize that you are the *kassikari* he wants and needs. If he were any other male, if he was not a *Vorakkar*, he would have joined you to him long ago. I have no doubt in my mind about that."

My throat tightened at his words. They meant a lot coming from him.

"As his *pujerak*, I thought I was doing the right thing, trying to steer him from you. But as his friend," he said, his voice growing deeper, gruffer, "I feel ashamed of what I have done. As his friend, I knew that you were always going to be his choice."

My hand shook when I pushed a strand of hair behind my ear. "I don't like this side of you," I informed him. "You're almost being *nice*."

He didn't hesitate as he replied, "Once I walk away, I will forget it ever happened, *kalles*."

A sudden, wobbly smile appeared on my face and I looked away from his eyes, staring over the *pyroki* enclosure. A short distance away, the *mrikro* frowned at us both, but minded his own business, mucking out the nests.

"My mate is upset with me because I told her what I have done," he admitted. "She thinks the honorable thing to do is give up my position as *pujerak*. She thinks the honorable thing to do is stand by my word and leave the horde."

"Seerin wouldn't want that," I told him. "It would hurt him if you truly left. You know that."

"I do not want to leave," he said, his gaze sliding over to me. "And I realize that if I am to stay, then I must make amends with you first before he would ever consider forgiving me for my dishonorable actions."

My lips twitched ever so slightly. "You want to use me to get back in Seerin's good graces?

"*Lysi*," he said, unashamed about *that*. I appreciated his honesty. It made me *like* him even.

"I'm alright with that," I told him.

His shoulders loosened.

"Thank you for telling me," I said after a brief moment of silence. "Even though the council's matters are private, I appreciate it."

"He disbanded the council two nights ago," he told me softly. "It does not matter anymore."

After my initial shock had passed, I asked, "Why would he do that?"

"Because, *kalles,* he can," he rasped, turning towards me. "I have always known that he would be one of the great *Vorakkars* of our race. He will be remembered long after his time. And now, it seems, he is finally realizing that himself. He does not need us."

I shivered slightly, though it had nothing to do with the cold afternoon wind.

"And you will be at his side," he added. "Will you not?"

I didn't answer him as we stood there together, watching the *pyrokis*.

I did, however, feel the answer echo deep in my chest.

43

Pushing away the list of names of those that would leave after the thaw, I rolled my stiff neck and groaned at the ache that throbbed in my back. I'd been hunched over the table for most of the day and my body was finally rebelling against me.

Twelve was the official number my horde would lose. Not as many as had previously threatened to leave, but I was relieved to see two of the council elders' names among that list. The head warrior, the third elder, and Vodan chose to remain.

Before, seeing such a loss to the horde would've been devastating news. Now, I saw it as an opportunity. I would lead the horde through the *Hitri* mountains and settle us in the southlands. If the *hebrikki* herds were as plentiful as I suspected they'd be and if we chose to base beside a river, I could journey to *Dothik* or the outposts and open my horde to twice as many as we would lose. Growth was the key—growth was the goal. The most successful hordes on our planet had grown into permanent outposts settled around Dakkar like markers of history and prosperity. *That* was the mark I wanted to leave. An outpost of

Rath Tuviri. It was where I wanted to rest, once my time as *Vorakkar* was over.

Behind me, the entrance to the council's *voliki*—though there was no more council, so I supposed it was simply mine now—pushed open.

As I turned, I stilled when I saw it was Nelle who'd ducked inside.

"Your *pujerak* said you'd be in here," she said, her eyes flickering between me and my surroundings. The *voliki* itself was nothing exceptional, so there wasn't much to see.

"You have been speaking with my *pujerak*?" I asked, still surprised that she'd come to seek me out. We hadn't spoken for two days.

"Yes," she said. "He's actually quite pleasant once you get past the scowl."

The sound I made wasn't quite a laugh, but rather an acknowledgement of the truth of her words. And those words were so inherently *Nelle* that I felt my heartbeat triple in speed, wondering if she was finally loosening her guard around me.

Then she bit her lip, her eyes dropping to the floor for a brief moment, to the thin rugs that were maroon and gold in color.

"Is there something you need, *kalles*?" I asked, keeping my voice soft in the quiet of the *voliki*. It was late and dark outside. I'd been inside longer than I'd anticipated, but I found the work kept my mind off the female standing in front of me.

"Yes," she said. "I was wondering if you have time to come to the training grounds with me. I...I have a proposition for you."

My heart thudded until I thought it would beat from my chest. Swallowing thickly, not wanting to raise my hopes, I rasped, "A proposition?"

"A bargain," she amended. "We like bargains, you and me. Isn't that right?"

My breath left my lungs in a rush and I said, "*Lysi*, we do."

When she turned to leave, I could only follow helplessly. All she had to do was look at me and I'd do anything she wanted. The power she held over me was humbling and frightening.

The training grounds were a short distance away. We didn't speak as we entered. In the far corner of the enclosure, the target that the *mitri* had made her was still standing. Many warriors even used it now, not just her.

We stood only an arm's length away. The setting was so familiar to me that it squeezed at my chest, yet everything had changed since the last time we'd been here together, making bargains.

Nelle looked up at me. We hadn't spoken since two nights ago. The emotions from that night still felt raw inside me.

"You did hurt me, Seerin," she said softly. "You hurt me and I was blindsided by it."

I found myself holding my breath, not daring to breathe as I absorbed her words and the way they cut me all over again.

"You hurt me and a part of me wanted to hate you. I *needed* to if I was ever going to survive it and even knowing that, I couldn't," she said.

"Nelle—"

"And I don't think that you're a monster," she said. I realized what she was doing. She was finally responding to me, when I'd begged her two nights ago to *tell me something*, anything about her state of mind. "And I think that if our paths had never crossed, I would have simply drifted away by now. I was on the verge of becoming completely numb to life before you came. It was a big fear I had. And I think your goddess sent you to me. I think you were always meant to *wake* me to this life, to the beauty of it. Though perhaps I needed to remember the pain of it first before I could rebuild myself."

Stunned, I could only listen, her words wrapping around me like a vice.

"Your *pujerak* told me what the council threatened you with that night," she said after a brief pause.

My jaw ticked in response.

"It wasn't just a choice between your horde and me, Seerin, like I thought," she said. "It was a choice of your oldest friend and the loyalties you had to him, of the dreams you've always had for this horde from the beginning, of the expectations placed upon you as *Vorakkar*, of the pressures you faced because of that. It was a choice between *all* of that and me."

I couldn't deny her words.

"And in the end," she murmured, "you still chose me. Why?"

Brow furrowing, I rasped quietly, "You know why, *thissie*. You have always known why."

"Because you care for me?"

"'Care?'" I repeated. "'Care' does not even begin to describe what I feel for you, Nelle."

She hesitated, drawing in a small breath. "Because you love me then?" she amended, her expression vulnerable and *open*.

"*Lysi*," I affirmed. "I do. I love you. And even those words feel as though they are not enough. Simple words cannot describe this feeling, *thissie*. They never will."

"I know," she whispered and my breath hitched.

Suddenly, she walked the short distance to the weapons rack and plucked off the same bow and the same sheath of arrows she'd used for our previous bargains.

When she returned to me, I asked, "Do...do you feel that you can love me again? Can we heal from this?"

"Maybe that's where the bargain comes in," she said after a moment. My lungs squeezed, my eyes darting to the bow and arrow. "What do you want if I miss, demon king?"

I was filled with longing and memory at the familiar title, but also with dread knowing her skill with the bow.

"You will connect with your target, *thissie*," I said. "You always do."

"What do you want if I miss, Seerin?" she repeated, setting the sheath of arrows at her feet.

"If you miss," I started, "I want you to promise that you will never love me again. I want you to swear that you can never see a future for us, that you will never be my *Morakkari* in this life."

All the possibilities were almost too painful to say, but only served to highlight that I knew she would not miss.

"I could miss on purpose if I wanted those things," she pointed out softly.

Fear squeezed my heart. I realized that too, but at the very least, I would have my answer. I was so wrapped up in my fear that I only watched as she nocked her arrow, steadying the bow not at the *mitri's* target, but at the far post that had served as our original target, in the darkened corner of the training grounds.

I was so wrapped up in that fear that I didn't realize she didn't specify what *she* wanted if she hit her target. Until it was too late.

Her arrow whizzed from the bow, perfectly formed Dakkar steel cutting through cold air. I watched it travel, briefly, and in another moment, its short journey was over. It embedded itself into the far post, right in the middle, a perfect shot.

My relief was short-lived.

At the very least, she didn't miss on purpose, but her success meant she could ask for anything she wanted...even my promise to stay away from her, to forbid me from pursuing her further, to make me swear that the only thing we would ever share in this life was our child. Not a future, not our love, ever again.

A part of me expected it after what I had done, after the hurt and grief I'd put her through.

The words stuck in my throat, but I forced myself to ask them.

"What is it that you want from me, Nelle?" I asked quietly.

I didn't think I moved a single inch. My body felt frozen, suspended in time at that very moment because I knew that whatever she said, it would change us. It would change everything. But time was merciless and it moved us forward, regardless of if we were ready.

Her bow hung from her grip. Her eyes consumed me but I had nothing left to give. She had everything.

"I want a kiss, Seerin."

The words floated between us, calm and simple and beautiful. They poured into me and wrung the breath from my lungs. They sped my heartbeat and sparked disbelief and blinding hope in my chest. They made my fingers curl into my palms and then I was stepping forward, closing the distance between us.

"Is that all you want?" I rasped, sliding both of my hands into her soft, dark hair.

"For now," she whispered. Then, though it started small, a shy smile spread across her features and I saw her eyes shimmer in the darkness with tears. That smile was one of the most beautiful things I'd ever seen. "We can talk about what else I want afterwards."

I didn't hesitate.

Bringing my head down, I caught her lips and kissed her the way I yearned to. Deep and passionate and thorough. It was frenzied and full of need. Her bow dropped to the ground and then I felt her arms wind around me. Our teeth clattered together, but I tasted her tears and felt her smile and I thought it was absolute perfection.

I broke the kiss to embrace her, to bury my face into her neck, feeling the fur of her pelt brush my cheek.

"I love you," I rasped into her skin. "I love you so much it hurts, *rei thissie*."

"And I never stopped loving you, Seerin," she whispered in

my ear. I was bent over, she was on the tips of her toes, but somehow we fit together perfectly. "I'm sorry I ever made you doubt that."

I groaned, hardly able to believe that this moment was real. It was all I'd dreamed about for the last month. *She* was all I'd dreamed about since I first felt her taking my soul.

"*Enough*," she whispered to me. "Enough now."

They were the same words she'd said to me the night I returned from *Dothik*, very possibly the night we'd conceived our child together.

I knew what she was telling me, in a way that only Nelle could.

We would move forward. We would put this behind us. She'd once told me, long ago, that she didn't hold grudges. When she forgave someone, she *forgave* them.

What she was offering me was complete forgiveness, a fresh start. For us both.

"You are certain?" I asked, pulling back to look into her eyes, cradling her cheeks in my palm. "Certain of me? Of this?"

I saw her answer in her gaze before she even replied. "Yes, demon king. I am. Are you certain?"

Vok, I loved her. And though she offered me a clean slate, I would still spend the rest of our lives together thanking her, worshipping her, loving her for it.

What had I ever done to deserve someone like her? This beautiful, pure, hopeful being who constantly humbled and surprised and amazed me?

"*Lysi*," I said, capturing her lips in a soft kiss. "I have never been more certain of anything in my life, *rei thissie*."

EPILOGUE

"I want to show you something, *rei Morakkari*," Seerin murmured in my ear.

I was sitting with Avuli and Nukri, who was the mate of Vodan, Seerin's *pujerak*. We were helping the *bikku* cook up a flank of *hebrikki*. A handful of warriors had gone out hunting just that morning and returned with plenty of fresh meat, the first the horde had eaten since the frost feast. It would be a night of celebration, though we were still searching for our new encampment.

Dusk had just fallen over the beautiful valleys of the south-lands. Though it was after the thaw, the air was still chilled at night and Seerin wrapped another thin shawl of furs around my shoulders as he helped me stand.

"I'll be right back," I assured Avuli and Nukri, who both gave me secretive, knowing smiles. I flushed. They thought my demon king was whisking me away for a private romp, considering we had been traveling for almost two weeks and there was little privacy among a traveling Dakkari horde. Seerin and I had to be creative in order to indulge in our sex life, though my husband had often growled into my ear that he couldn't wait to have our own *voliki* once more.

But our home had not made itself known yet. We had come across multiple herds of *hebrikki* since yesterday, so we were close. And once we found a river, an accesible water source, we would begin resettling in that beautiful place. Seerin knew what he was looking for and the horde trusted in their *Vorakkar* to find a suitable base.

And Seerin had been right. I loved the southlands. From what I'd already seen, they held a foreign beauty that I had never experienced before in my lifetime. There were lush valleys and towering, thick forests filled with color and life. I'd even seen a *waterfall* as we passed through the *Hitri* mountains, which had been equally impressive, if slightly frightening. A part of me could hardly believe that we were still on Dakkar because it was so different from the endless, stretching plains and blackened forests I'd known all my life.

The horde was resting for the night, settling down for a calm yet joyous evening of fresh meat and fermented wine. There was a hushed anticipation in the air, as if everyone else sensed we were close to a new encampment as well. While traveling with a horde had its excitements, I was more than ready to set up a more permanent base soon, if only to enjoy more privacy with Seerin.

My demon king led me over to the thick forest we'd decided to settle next to for the night, keeping his hand on my lower back the entire way.

I sucked in a breath when the baby kicked hard. "*Oh*, he is restless tonight."

Seerin grinned and the sight of it made my heart stutter in my chest, as it always did. The healer thought it would only be a little over a month before he arrived, given his advanced growth. And I was *more* than ready for him to come. Besides constantly feeling like I needed to relieve myself, the swollen ankles, the aching back, the heaviness in my breasts, Seerin and I were both eager for our child to begin in this world with us.

One night in bed, after the thaw had come and right before we'd left our encampment, Seerin had run his hands over my naked belly and pressed his cheek to my navel, feeling the baby kick and move. "It is a male," he'd decided right then. "And he will be a great warrior for all the fighting he is doing within you."

"Our little warrior is impatient," Seerin told me now, through his grin, leading me into the darkened forest until I could barely make out the laughter and voices and the delicious smell of cooking meat that we'd left behind.

"As is his father," I pointed out with a quirked brow and flushed cheeks. "All the horde will know what we are doing in here now."

"I did not bring you in here for quick mating, *rei Morakkari*," he rasped, his tone light and teasing. "Though now that you suggest it, I am certainly not opposed to the idea."

"Then what did you bring me in here for?"

"Listen," he murmured, pulling us both to a stop. "You will hear them."

Them? I wondered.

Going quiet, I met his grey eyes and did as he said. It took a moment. But then I heard a familiar sound, one that made me still with wonder and memory.

"I heard them as we rode, through the trees," he whispered to me, pressing a kiss to my temple. "I wanted you to see them."

Thissies.

My heart felt full as I listened to their calls and their songs in the trees that lit up one after another once we quieted and stopped walking. So much like Blue's calls that I felt that she was up there.

I spied one, just overhead, its beautiful wings whispering as they flapped. Another echoing *thissie* call came from somewhere to my left, and another to my right. Out of the corner of my eye, I saw one flit across one branch to the next, only a few feet away.

My breath hitched and I turned to look at it. And it looked so much like Blue that I thought I was seeing her spirit. Long, shimmering blue feathers, black shining eyes, and a brown beak. The *thissie* was watching me as I was watching it.

Before I could blink, it took flight, expertly dodging the branches of the forest, going higher and higher, until it rose out of sight.

It was only after the *thissie* disappeared that I realized I was holding my breath.

When I turned to look at Seerin, I found he wasn't watching the *thissie* at all. In fact, he was watching *me* and the look in his eyes made me melt, made my stomach flutter pleasantly.

Shortly after that night in the training grounds, after the last bargain we had ever made to one another, we'd decided not to wait for our *tassimara*. Before the thaw had even come, Seerin and I had our joining ceremony before all the horde, where I officially became *Morakkari*, where I officially became his wife and him my husband.

Those that didn't support our joining left the horde shortly after, even before the thaw. Seerin hadn't even watched them go. And while I felt discomforted by the thought that my presence left others uncomfortable, that feeling didn't last long. I was Seerin's and he was mine. That was all that mattered, and the majority of the horde celebrated our *tassimara* with joy and understanding and celebration. It was *that* spirit of the horde that would make us better, that would make us *stronger*.

I remembered that spirit whenever I looked down at the golden markings around my wrist. My *Morakkari* markings. The markings of Rath Tuviri. Markings of my own and of my mate.

It was times like these, standing in that *thissie* forest with his arms wrapped around me, when I remembered why I hadn't wanted to wait to join myself to him. It was times like these when I remembered why I'd fallen in love with him in the first place.

And though our journey to this point had not been easy, it had only strengthened our bond and reinforced the love we shared that I felt every single moment of every single day.

"*Thissies* for *rei thissie*," he teased gently, brushing a lock of hair away from my cheek. He'd promised he would show them to me one day...and he was making good on that promise, as he always did.

The smile I gave him in response made his breath hitch in his throat and a deep growl rise from his chest. That growl was full of need and I ran my palms down the muscled wall of his chest in reply. Down, down, down, until they brushed the laces of his hide pants.

He groaned when I began untying them and pulled me closer until he could lower his head for a kiss.

"Let's spend a little time in here after all, my demon king," I murmured, breathless, desire heating and pulsing through my body.

Seerin gave me a wicked grin.

"As you wish, *rei Morakkari*."

Want to read an **exclusive bonus epilogue** about Seerin and Nelle?

Sign up for **Zoey Draven's Mailing List** and get the chapter sent right to your inbox!

Sign up at www.ZoeyDraven.com.

You'll also hear about new releases, exclusive giveaways, and other exciting bonus content!

ABOUT THE AUTHOR

Zoey Draven has been writing stories for as long as she can remember. Her love affair with the romance genre started with her grandmother's old Harlequin paperbacks and has continued ever since. As a Top 100 Amazon bestselling author, now she gets to write the happily-ever-afters—with a cosmic, other-worldly twist, of course! She is the author of steamy Science Fiction Romance books, such as the *Warriors of Luxiria* and the *Horde Kings of Dakkar* series.

When she's not writing about alpha alien warriors and the strong human women that bring them to their knees, she's probably drinking one too many cups of coffee, hiking in the redwoods, or spending time with her family.

Visit her at www.ZoeyDraven.com.

Made in the USA
Las Vegas, NV
28 December 2023

83660484R00208